BURNING TIME

BURNING TIME

Leslie Glass

A PERFECT CRIME BOOK
Doubleday
New York London Toronto Sydney Auckland

A PERFECT CRIME BOOK
PUBLISHED BY DOUBLEDAY
a division of Bantam Doubleday Dell Publishing Group, Inc.
1540 Broadway, New York, New York 10036

DOUBLEDAY is a trademark of Doubleday,
a division of Bantam Doubleday Dell
Publishing Group, Inc.

All of the characters in this book are fictitious,
and any resemblance to actual persons, living or dead,
is purely coincidental.

Grateful acknowledgment is made for permission to reprint an excerpt from "If You
Could Read My Mind" by Gordon Lightfoot, © 1969 Early Morning Music.
Used by permission.

Book design by Tasha Hall

Library of Congress Cataloging-in-Publication Data
Glass, Leslie.
  Burning time / Leslie Glass. — 1st ed.
    p.   cm.
  "A Perfect crime book."
  1. Serial murders—Fiction. 2. Policewomen—Fiction. I. Title.
PS3557.L34B87 1993
813'.54—dc20   93-627
                                                                  CIP

ISBN 0-385-46933-0

For Rick

Acknowledgment

For technical assistance and inspiration, very special thanks to Dr. Richard C. Friedman, my psychology professor and consultant of many years. Thanks also to all the good people at the NYPD, particularly Lieutenant Bob Davis and Detective-Sergeant John Ranieri, who head the Missing Persons Squad; Sergeant Nancy Mclaughlin; and Detective Margie Y. Yee. In the area of forensic science, thanks to Dr. Mark Taff, forensic pathologist, President and Founder of the New York Society of Forensic Sciences at Lehman College, and Dr. Lawrence Kobilinsky, Professor of Forensic Science, Director DNA Fingerprinting Laboratory at John Jay College of Criminal Justice. For help with motorcycles, and the Navy, thanks to Dr. Jay David Glass; Kent Brown; and Dorothy Fier.

Gratitude and blessings are much deserved by my editor Kate Miciak, whose passion for books in general, and mysteries in particular, should be deemed a National Treasure; Jamie Warren Youll for a whole lot more than her beautiful book covers; my agent, Sarah Jane Freymann, friend and weatherperson for all seasons; and Alex, Lindsey, and Edmund Glass, for absolutely everything else.

*"But profound as psychology is,
it's a knife that cuts both ways."*
—DOSTOYEVSKI,
The Brothers Karamazov

BURNING TIME

Prologue

On her last day in San Diego Ellen Roane lay on the beach and reached out her arms to the dazzling sun as if it were a lover she could catch and hold tight forever. Out here you could see the sun setting and the moon rising at the same time. The moon was impressive in its cold, far-off brilliance, but the sun was right there complete in the way passion was, providing everything needed for a lifetime in a single moment.

Ellen soaked it in, trying to make all her anxieties about college and her parents' separation melt into the sand around her. Even this far away it wasn't easy to do. There was so much aggravation all the time, so much yelling. Just hearing either one of them say her name these days was enough to give her a headache.

The sea was calm, too calm for surfers, but they paddled their boards out there anyway, waiting for a wave. Ellen watched them and wondered how many times her mother had tried to call her. By now she would have her father in a state, too.

Ellen smiled to herself at how clever she was. She had crossed the country by herself to have an adventure and think things through. It amazed her how easy it had been. All she had to do was flash the credit cards her father had given her when she moved out in the fall. And suddenly she knew what it was like to be a grown-up. She could go anywhere, do anything she wanted, buy anything. It was extraordinary. All she had to do was fly away, and for the first time in her life her parents couldn't pick up the phone and reach into her brain.

The relief was extreme. She turned over to toast on the other side, thinking the thing over. She was getting ready to pick someone up. After two days of eating meals on her own, sleeping in The Coral Reef Bed & Breakfast, and going to the beach, that was all that was left to do.

At noon she had lunch at a tiny health food place across the street from the beach. She took a long walk, then settled back down on the sand and closed her eyes. She couldn't help thinking the deep warmth of the California sun was almost mystical in its healing power. New York was soul-destroying in every way. Mean and gray and cold. Now that she knew that, she knew she should have come to college here, escaped all the way instead of just moving a few blocks uptown. She checked her watch, wondering when the guy would come back.

She didn't mind that he didn't make his move the first time he saw her two days ago. She was tired of people crowding her. This guy hung back. She knew she was gorgeous. Maybe he was shy. She kind of liked that. He watched her from the parking lot, leaning against his motorcycle. He always wore shades, but she could feel his eyes on her, feel him centered on her absolutely. It was a pleasant feeling, like something out of the movies.

Her mother liked to say a beautiful girl like Ellen could pick and choose among men. Why look down when it was just as easy to look up. If she were here she'd tell Ellen to look for intellectual ability, maybe head for the mountain where the Palomar Observatory was and make some celestial discovery in the way of a balding astronomer from the California Institute of Technology. Ellen snorted at the thought of her mother turned on by intellectuals whose only hair sprouted from their ears and noses. It was a proven fact that brilliant men were arrogant, self-involved, and ugly. And none of them could see well enough to admire her.

Ellen liked the one who took her in whole, the one who didn't come down on the beach with a lot of little-boy toys and pass her by with sliding glances. This guy was blond and older than a kid, definitely a movie-star type. He wore a black shirt and black jeans and

had the most amazing motorcycle she had ever seen, a huge, glisten-
ing chrome-and-maroon thing. She began to worry that he wouldn't
come back.

But at four-thirty, just as she was getting tired of lying around,
he was there, up by the parking area staring at her. She waited for a
few more minutes before getting up to leave. Slowly she pulled on
her jeans and shirt. Then she walked up to the retaining wall where
she sat for a minute to brush off the sand and put on her shoes. He
approached her there.

"Want to go for a ride?" He indicated the machine parked
behind him with a wave of his hand.

She tossed her blond hair and looked him over as if she might
really be considering it. Finally she said, "Sure, why not?" and
followed him to the motorcycle.

She didn't become uneasy even when the ride took her way east
into the dry mountainous area of the North Country. She wasn't
frightened when he stopped far off the road, miles from the last
passing car. It wasn't until he grabbed her unexpectedly from behind
and wrestled her to the ground, pulling at her clothes, that the sharp
jolt of adrenaline shot through her. And even then she wasn't terrified. Boys had jumped on her before, lost control and bullied their
way into her. Sometimes a girl gambled and lost. It was an old story.

When he started mumbling and hitting her and shoving himself
into places in her body nothing had ever been before, it got to be
different. Suddenly he was not like a person anymore. She couldn't
talk to him, or fight back in any way. His face was frozen in rage and
every part of him was a weapon. He moved her around, twisting her
body one way and then another on the rocky ground, trying new
things to make her scream louder, beg him to stop. They were little
things at first. Then he broke her arm at the elbow, cracked her ribs,
and crushed her cheekbone. He kept at it for a long time.

Finally he staked her to the darkening desert ground, her legs
together and her arms out straight like a flattened Christ. Until then
she thought she would survive. He had a knife, but he didn't stab
her. All the time he was hitting her he had it with him, sometimes in

his hand. He made motions with it, but he didn't stab her. Now she thought he would do it, make all the cuts he threatened to make. She was so afraid of the knife she could hardly breathe.

Then suddenly he seemed to forget the knife. He started doing something else, getting things, muttering to himself. He lit some kind of torch, and a blast of light shot up into the sky. The explosion of heat and light lasted only seconds. Then the flame was extinguished.

He said something that she didn't hear because she was screaming so loud. He put his foot on her stomach to stop her bucking, and lowered the glowing brand exactly in the middle of her heaving chest. It made a hissing sound as it seared her skin off, eating the soft tissue of her breasts in some places all the way to the bone. Her screams and the smell of burning flesh rose all around.

After she lost consciousness, he untied her and left Ellen Roane nude in the gully, as the desert temperature dropped steadily, and her wounds began to weep.

1

Jason Frank, MD, psychoanalyst, writer, and teacher, stood at the podium for several seconds before speaking. An inch shy of six feet, he looked like a member of the Kennedy clan in his gray pin-striped suit. He had a determined jaw and mouth, straight nose, light brown hair cut short, and wryly humorous brown eyes. He was thirty-eight, and had a forceful intensity that made both the crazy and the sane pay attention to him.

The hundred or so members, trainees, residents, and hangers-on of the Toronto Psychoanalytic Center who had come to hear him speak paid attention to him now.

"Can anybody remember the music in *Death of a Salesman?*" he asked to begin his lecture on Listening. "What instrument is played?"

The attractive Ph.D. who had offered him her apartment and her body within the first five minutes of meeting him the previous night crossed her legs the other way and tapped her pencil on her knee.

"An oboe?" she asked.

Even though there was a smile on her face, the *rat tat tat* with the sharp point on her expensive pantyhose indicated to Jason she was still annoyed by his rebuff.

He shook his head, as he had last night. He waited for a few other wrong answers before giving the right one.

"The flute. If it had been an accordion you might well remember it. Why the flute?"

Jason allowed the audience to speculate for a few minutes before he made his point. "It's vital to see and hear everything because everything has meaning," he told them. "The background details, both visual and aural, of a projected self are like a symphony orchestra playing in a very special concert. As analysts, we have to be able to identify the individual instruments to understand the nature of the harmony, or cacophony, that's being played out in each personality." He smiled.

For example, the young Ph.D. courted rejection from a visiting speaker to fuel her paranoia and deep hostility to men. Someone else might only have seen a pretty woman looking for love. But Jason wouldn't have been tempted anyway. He was more than happy with his beautiful wife.

He sneaked a look at his watch, suddenly eager to get home to her. He became distracted for a moment as a wave of guilt washed over him, then recovered his concentration. He had three hours before he could get out of there and head for the airport.

"Ah, I'm going to present three segments of taped interviews to show how the interviewing technique is informed by what I've noticed about each subject. These are consultations. I've never met any of the subjects before."

Jason hit the button and the first interview began. He was seated opposite a youngish heavy woman. The woman fluffed up her hair for the camera and began to tell about her eating problem. She said she wanted to be a size eight and had tried to lose weight for ten years. Then she gave a list of all the things she ate from eleven at night until one.

"And then what do you do?" Jason asked.

"And then I go into the bathroom and I force myself to vomit."

In the tape there was a frozen moment as the two looked at each other, and suddenly the woman started to sob.

Jason shut off the tape and went to the blackboard that had been set up for him. He picked up a piece of chalk.

"What are the important things revealed in this interview so far?" Jason asked.

No one volunteered.

"Come on, I absolutely insist. This isn't school. Get in there and tell me what the important thing is because everyone has patients like this."

There was a minor shuffling before a hand was raised. Jason nodded.

"She overeats," a young man said.

"She has bulemia," a woman added.

Jason wrote, *Overeats, Bulemia,* and turned back. "What sorts of things does she eat? Let's make a list of what she eats. What does her refrigerator look like?" He made the list.

"All right. What's another important thing? I want you not only to tell me your observations about the things she mentioned, but also tell me things she hasn't mentioned that are directly related to the things she has mentioned. That is, your inferences about what her life is like. So what's the next important thing because we're going to have to follow up on her."

"Well, she's crying," offered a bearded man in the back.

Jason wrote *Crying* on the board. "Okay, what's your hypothesis about her crying? Why is she crying?"

Now the answers came more quickly.

"Okay," Jason said finally. "Let's put the things together that we know." He made the hypothesis. The subject was thirty years old, living alone, and desperately lonely. Something happened to her ten years ago that was connected with her eating. She was trying to fill herself up with food. Size eight had a special meaning to her. Other people were important to her because she cried when she made eye contact with him after her confession.

"All right, what should I say to her next?" Jason asked.

Everybody had a different answer. Ask about food, ask about loneliness. Ask about refrigerator.

He turned on the tape. "You're crying," he had said to the woman. He opted for feelings. And then her story came out. She was a good candidate for psychotherapy.

Next Jason presented the case of a somewhat untidy and disor-

ganized sixty-five-year-old man who began his interview saying he
hated the therapist he was seeing. He felt he wasn't making any
progress. Jason turned off the tape and pointed out that the patient
identified his frustration as connected with his therapy, but they
should not assume that was really what was bothering him.

"What did he reveal? What should I ask?" He wrote their answers on the board.

Then he turned on the tape. Jason asked the man to tell a little
more about his therapy, and the man revealed that the therapist was
focusing on what an angry person he was. As the interview pro-
gressed, Jason began honing in on the man's memory. It was soon
revealed that his subject was suffering from dementia. He was becoming senile, and that was the reason for his anger. Jason did not
blame the therapist for not catching the illness behind his anger, but
concluded that this patient could not benefit from psychotherapy.

He had left the third segment for last because it was his favorite. He pushed the button. A male in-patient in his fifties was
brought in by an attendant. He was a small man with a lot of graying
hair slicked back. He smiled broadly, gesturing frequently with his
hands.

"Look at me. I'm in so much fucking trouble, when I go out
these days, I have to go with my keeper." He sat down with a flour-
ish.

"So, what happened to you?" Jason asked him.

"Hallucinations. Hallucinations happened to me."

"That's a pretty technical term. What do you mean? Do you
hear things?"

"No. It was like I was feeling things, spiders running up and
down my body just like in the movies. I had D.T.'s. I don't have to
tell you what that is. Every fucking person knows what D.T.'s are. It
was the worst thing. Have you ever been drunk?"

Jason turned off the tape. "Here I have a choice. I can play
psychiatrist, but what do you think the guy will think of me if I play
psychiatrist? What should I say?"

The audience offered suggestions.

Jason pushed the button and watched himself say: "On occasion I've been known to get drunk."

The audience laughed.

"But you've never had D.T.'s. I can tell. One look at you, I sized you up. I can tell from what you're dressed like. You're a guy who drinks an occasional social drink. A middle-class guy. You're a teacher, a shrink. You're interviewing me here on TV. You must have some clout. I wonder who this film is being shown to anyway—but what difference does it make? I'm so fucked up, I'm in so much trouble I couldn't give a shit. I had a seizure. The ambulance came."
The man smiled genially, mugging for the camera.

"So that's your reason for being in the hospital?" Jason said.

"Well, between you and me, Doc, there's a little more to it. They happened to find a little cocaine on me." He dismissed it with a wave of his hand. "Recreational. Nothing heavy. Nothing like crack. Nothing like that. Recreational." There was a silence before he went on.

"And—they busted some of the people I was with at the establishment I was frequenting." Long silence.

"By establishment I was frequenting I bet you want to know what that is. Well, it was a whorehouse. I was in a fucking whorehouse and I had a seizure and the cops came and they busted me and they busted some of the—So now I'm here in a mental hospital. And I'm not responsible for any of this. I'm crazy and I'm not going to get in trouble with the law because—"

The audience erupted into little pockets of laughter. Jason stopped the tape.

". . . Well, now we have some interesting questions. The guy's talking about drugs. He's talking about prostitution. He says he's not responsible for his actions. At what point is someone responsible for his actions? Is he crazy?"

He didn't wait for an answer. The tape came on. The guy was still talking.

"Well, and there was an organization that put money into my business and somehow there were some questions in the minds of the cops about the legality of it all. I myself don't remember all the details. My memory has been fuzzy ever since I've been on the sauce. But the cops. I can tell you what the cops are interested in. They're interested in the whole concept of crime. Crime. What is crime? If you want my opinion. The Exxon *Valdez* is crime. George Bush is crime."

"You think George Bush is a criminal?" Jason asked.

"He's a criminal because he sells dope. He's got an organization that sells dope for politics, starts wars for oil. These are the criminals. They steal money from the American people, big money. My organization isn't involved with crimes like that. Nothing like that. A little prostitution maybe. Victimless crimes where people are not hurt personally. A little question of the law." He spread his hands wide.

"And let me tell you about the law. Ever try and get a cop to help you when you got hurt, when someone broke a law in your neighborhood? You can't talk to these people. They can't speak English. They can't even *type*. I'm not a criminal. The people I'm associated with aren't criminals. They're good family men. They care about their wives. They love their kids. And they're involved with making this country great." He paused for air.

"I bet you never think about who the real criminals are. Is it the ones who start the wars, steal our money, and ruin the ecology or is it somebody who helps horny men find a way out of their sexual tensions, huh? What's good anyway? What's evil?"

Jason switched off the tape for the last time and turned to his audience.

"Okay, what do we have here? This guy is getting us to think about what's moral, what's immoral. What's legal and should be legal. Victimless crimes—what's psychopathology? He says he's crazy, but he doesn't act crazy. He's a ham. He loves being on the show, being entertaining. He's uneducated but bright. He liked turning the tables on me, interviewing me. So what's the story here? Is he immoral? Is he crazy?"

Forty-five minutes later Jason gathered up his things, and pushed out to the icy cold wind of Bloor Street.

It had gone very well. His audience loved it. He had reason to feel elated and up. But instead he was exhausted and uneasy. For some reason this time when he watched the tape he was struck by the remark about the cops not being there when you needed them. And not helping when they were there, because they were too busy worrying about what the crime was.

Jason had been beaten up pretty badly once when he was fifteen. In the Bronx where he came from, the cops had been less than sympathetic. They saw him as just another bellicose street kid in a fistfight. They searched him, found the knife he'd never had a chance to take out of his pocket, and threatened to take him in for possession of a concealed weapon.

Jason considered himself fully analyzed. He knew being middle-class was very important to him. He had liked the last patient's analysis of him. But now, for a reason he couldn't pinpoint, the tape upset him. The more he thought about the questions that were raised on it, the less sure he was about where he stood on them.

Suddenly he felt anxious again about his wife, as if he had left her too long, or overlooked something he should have noticed. It began to snow as he looked for a taxi.

2

Detective April Woo neatened up her desk for the night shift and covered a small yawn, even though the squad room was empty except for Ginora, the glorified secretary who answered the phone and took the messages, and Sergeant Sanchez. Both were at their desks hunched over their phones talking rapidly in Spanish. Neither looked her way.

Detective Bell was at the range in the Bronx. Detective Davis was at the range at the Academy, and Sergeant Aspiranti was in the field. It was three-thirty. If nothing new came up, April was due to go home in half an hour.

Her eyes slid over to the couple who had been sitting for almost an hour on the bench just inside the door. The Squad Supervisor, Sergeant Joyce, was out on a call. No one else could make an assignment. They'd have to sit there until Joyce got back, or the duty changed and Sergeant Rinaldi took over at four.

April studied them, wondering what the complaint might be. These were the kind of people who always made her a little nervous. Clearly educated, affluent, Caucasian. Her mother was old-style Chinese. Even now she sometimes called whites round-eyes, or ghosts. That made April nervous, too.

One of the first things she was taught at the Police Academy was, "We're only one color here. Blue. Whatever prejudices you have, leave them at the door." April didn't forget it.

After six years of being one of New York's Finest, which was in fact one-third African-American, one-third Hispanic, and one-third white—with Asians at maybe three percent, a few hundred in thirty-five or so thousand officers—April Woo thought of herself as pretty much color-blind.

Even without the professor's warning to keep an open mind about people, it wouldn't have taken April many months to see that underneath the skin colors and cultural differences everybody wanted pretty much the same things. But the combination of education and class and money in people like this couple still intimidated April. When they were white and educated and rich all at the same time, she couldn't help feeling inferior. She might have a chance for one, but she'd never have all three. April went two nights a week to John Jay College of Criminal Justice where she was getting her degree so slowly she was afraid her hair would turn gray before it happened.

"Bastard!" the woman said fiercely.

April looked her over without opening her eyes all the way. The woman had a lot of dark brown, possibly dyed hair—a huge mane of it, elaborately styled—and was wearing a short fur coat. Very short. Her skinny legs in their sheer black stockings stuck out a long way. Must be cold walking around in that all winter, April thought.

The woman's face had been painstakingly made up earlier in the day, but now the eyeliner was mostly gone, there were traces of mascara under her eyes, and her blush-on was all cried off. The man beside her looked like a lawyer or a doctor. He wore a dark business suit and had a camel hair coat and a silk paisley scarf over his arm. They argued quietly on and off as they waited for someone to take their case. Must be a robbery.

The squad room had a little jog in it, a short hallway which widened out into a good-sized room with six small metal desks equipped with not much more than phones and manual typewriters. The desks were all in a row by the windows that faced Eighty-second Street. The only place for people waiting for a detective was on that one bench in the narrow hall. Across from the desks was a single holding cell with thick iron bars. Suspects brought in for questioning were kept there. But none today. It had been a pretty quiet day, but a successful one for April.

For the first time in a long time, she had a case that made her feel good. Well, not her first call. Her first call that day was a DOA on Amsterdam. Old guy hadn't been heard from by anybody for several days, and finally someone called the police. April and San- chez went in and found him on the toilet, where he had died strain- ing for his last poop. Lot of old people in the neighborhood. They died in front of the TV. They died in their beds. Occasionally, one fell down in the bathtub, broke something, and couldn't get help. But a surprising number of them died on the pot. This time it must have happened sometime in the night. The lights were on. His teeth were in a glass. His hearing aid was on the night table. He was a tiny guy with a dapper mustache, sitting there perfectly balanced, his red- and-white striped pajama bottoms around his ankles and his eyes wide open in shock as if he had been caught in the act.

About midday, when April was still looking around the apart- ment for numbers of relatives to notify, and waiting for the ambu- lance to take the old man away, a request came in just for her. Up here on the Upper West Side, on Columbus Avenue only one block from Central Park West, where there was a lot of money around and very little need for a Chinatown expert, it didn't happen a lot.

It was a case in the Westminster, one of the famous buildings on Central Park West. They sent her out to interview a Chinese maid, and she relished every second of it. Turned out the woman, Ling Ling Jee, had been assaulted when she discovered two robbers in the apartment busy pocketing her mistress's jewelry. Ling Ling was a broad-faced woman of middle age and stoical peasant stock who couldn't speak English. She was terrified by the two men, and even more frightened of being blamed for their entry into the apartment. Worse, her employers were out of town on a skiing trip. Ling Ling didn't know where they were, nor was she absolutely sure what ski- ing was.

The Haitian maid across the hall had called the police for her.

Two police officers arrived on the scene, but couldn't get enough of a story to fill out a report. Eventually April got there and sorted everything out. She calmed the woman down, got her story, tried to ascertain what was missing, explained to her what skiing was, and found the Barstollers up in Vermont. Tomorrow Ling Ling was coming in to look at mug shots.

Sorting things out for confused and terrified newcomers was what April felt she had been born to do. And for five years she had been a happy detective down in Chinatown. She knew all too well the terrors of people who didn't know what to do or who to believe about what the rules really were.

Almost nobody in Chinatown had come into the country legally. So when they got there, they lived in constant anxiety about being discovered and sent back. This and the fact that they couldn't speak the language made them perfect victims—for each other, for the authorities, and for the people who employed them.

Sometimes the people who sold them fake papers for thousands of dollars then sold their arrival dates to associates in New York, who kidnapped them at the airport and ransomed them to the desperate relatives who were waiting for them. In her years in the 5th, April had had many cases that made her happy. Not so many up here, where she felt like a fish out of water.

Sergeant Joyce came in and brusquely motioned for April to come into her office. It was three-forty. April knew by the Irish set of her supervisor's jaw that she wasn't getting out of there in twenty minutes. Something had come up.

Two minutes later she came out of the office with the Missing Persons form that had only been partially filled out at the desk downstairs. She approached the anxious couple on the bench.

"Mr. and Mrs. Roane," April said. "Come with me."

3

Three blocks from home Jason looked out the taxi window and was startled by a movie marquee that hadn't been there when he left town. *Serpent's Teeth*. What in the—?

"Stop," he said suddenly.

The taxi skidded to a halt at Broadway and Eighty-third Street. Jason paid the fare and dragged his things out into the cold. It was a foggy March afternoon, still dead of winter in New York. His flight from Canada had taken less than two hours. He hesitated outside the theater, studying the poster. There were just two faces on it, with all the names at the bottom too small to read. One face he knew well. He shivered as the cold mist turned to rain, intensified, and began pelting down. Jesus. Jason bought a ticket to get out of the deluge and ducked into the moldy old theater.

Inside it was dark and smelled powerfully of popcorn. Jason chose a row in the back and put his suitcases on the seat beside him. The film had already started. The camera pulled in tight on a girl sitting on a couch with her legs crossed. She was tracing patterns on her bare thigh with her index finger. A man sat behind her watching on an angle, so that he could see what she was doing but she could not see him. Jason frowned. He didn't want to see a story about a psychiatrist. No one ever got them right.

He drummed his fingers on the grubby armrests.

For some long moments there was no sound on the screen and nothing else happened. There was some shuffling and coughing as the movie audience became impatient. Then, just as the stagnation on the screen reached the point of being unbearable, the woman stretched out her legs and leaned back, arching her back slightly. She had been an attractive woman, but suddenly she was dazzling. Her presence in the film took ordinariness, a simple story of corruption, and gave it a dark little twist that sent it spinning into a kinky sexual corner that was scary, erotic, and disturbing.

The story was of a pretty, vulnerable woman slowly drifting into a relationship with a vaguely sinister young man with a hard empty face and very little in the way of a life. They were shown taking a number of aimless walks in various New York parks, and sitting in restaurants. The only relief from walking and restaurants came when the woman was with her therapist.

He was a paunchy, unattractive man who managed to be both passive and sexually menacing at the same time. The audience couldn't hear what they said to each other. The patient's lips moved, but only the sound of flushing toilets, of cars in the streets, a radio from next door, could be heard. The scenes looked like they had been shot through a keyhole, as if someone could imagine how therapy looked, but not how it sounded. And it looked like an unsavory seduction.

The woman sat up or lay down, turned on her side, used various kinds of body language that became more and more provocative. The psychiatrist responded in kind. Without words there was no way of knowing what the content of the scene between the two really was. Jason became tense and anxious at the thought of having to watch the code he lived by violated.

Then suddenly the scene changed and she was naked with the other man. The young hoodlum was wearing jeans and a leather jacket with a zip front. It hung open. He leaned over the woman and rubbed the zipper back and forth across her flawless neck and breasts. Then he sank to his knees on the floor in front of her.

Jason did not want to see what he was going to do, or what she was going to do. He wanted to be magically out on the street and miss the rest. He didn't like a second of this, didn't like it at all. But the woman was mysterious and unusual, mesmerizing. He couldn't leave.

She leaned over the arm of the chair, arching her back as she had earlier in the psychiatrist's office. Her rich wheaty hair hung down, and her head was bent back in that way that never looked right in films because most people couldn't do it in life. Her legs were very long. The man buried his face in her lap. She clasped him with one bare leg around his back, then the other.

Jason swallowed and looked furtively around. He could see that the men in the audience were aroused, as he was himself. Every man wanted to be that character, that aimless hoodlum making love in his black leather jacket. The shirt that had been under it was suddenly gone. Jason's unease reached the stage of extreme discomfort. He crossed his legs the other way.

Then the scene changed. They were back in the psychiatrist's office. The woman was talking with no sound. Jason's heart beat faster still. He didn't want to see her naked now with the shrink. Perspiration broke out on his forehead as the screen went white and a hum filled the soundtrack. It was unbearable. What was happening now?

Slowly the picture cleared. The woman and the hoodlum were in a room with little colorful picture transfers all over the wall. It was a tattoo parlor. Jason's heart raced. What was this about? They were looking at each other intensely. The hoodlum had his shirt off. He was on a stool with his hairless chest filling the screen. The woman caressed his shoulder as another man appeared on the screen, fiddling with some sort of instrument.

A whine that sounded like a swarm of bees filled the theater. The man took the instrument and began to tattoo the shoulder of the hoodlum. The woman watched with intense excitement as the tattoo grew. The lovers looked at each other. Their feet touched. Their fingers entwined.

Finally, the mean Chinese-looking symbol in blue and black

was finished, and the young man got up. Jason looked at his watch, thanking God it was over.

But it wasn't over. Now the woman took his place on the stool. Slowly she unbuttoned her blouse and lowered it over her shoulders until her whole back was bared. The man began caressing her neck and arms, encouraging her as she had him. Her expression changed to one of sly satisfaction as the whine began again, and the tattoo needle moved toward her naked shoulder. Freeze frame.

Jesus Christ. Jason shook his head as the credits began to roll. Emma Chapman's name came first. She was the actress Jason had come to see on the screen for the first time. He felt dizzy at the sight of his wife's name, as if he had the kind of food poisoning that shot toxins straight to the brain. Somehow, in all the months of preparation for the film and the shooting of it, she had neglected to tell him what she did in this film and what it was about. He sat there in shock for a long time.

4

The expensively dressed woman in the short fur coat examined the seat of the metal chair dragged over for her from the desk next door. There were some crumbs on it. She brushed at them, but the surface was sticky, and they didn't all come off. She sat down looking even more unhappy than before.

Another fish out of water, April thought.

The man took the chair that was already there and sat without looking at it.

"You're Chinese," the woman said. It came out halfway between a question and a statement.

"Yes, ma'am," April agreed. She was Chinese yesterday, she was Chinese today, and would undoubtedly remain Chinese for the rest of her days.

Now that she worked here on the upper West Side, however, sometimes April looked in the mirror and was surprised to discover it all over again. She didn't feel Chinese unless she was with one. And she didn't think about it unless someone reminded her. It was the hard part of working Uptown. Whenever she wasn't thinking about being Chinese, someone reminded her.

"Were you born in this country?" the woman asked. She stared at April belligerently.

"Jennifer!" The husband shook his head. Not relevant.

"Yes, ma'am, were you?" April replied, unabashed.

The woman flushed slightly. "I'm sorry. I've just never seen a Chinese cop before." She looked at April's well-cut navy blazer and slacks and the red, white, and blue silk blouse with a big soft bow tied at the neck, and blushed again.

April had a beautiful, round, delicate face, neither too fleshy nor too pointy in the jaw, and an extremely good haircut, short, expertly layered. She was wearing a little eye makeup and lipstick. She knew the woman was thinking maybe she wasn't even a cop. Maybe she was another secretary like the surly black girl at the desk downstairs who took the complaint.

Then the woman's eyes filled with tears. She blew her nose. "You *are* a police—woman."

Bang on the button. April could read people's minds. She nodded solemnly. "Yes, ma'am." A police rule was always be courteous.

"Jesus." Stephen Roane put his hand on his wife's arm.

She pulled her arm away. "Don't try to censor me," she snapped. "I needed to know."

"What would be the point?" he muttered.

April made a note of the man's hostility. She decided to reassure Mrs. Roane that Detective April Woo could do the job. She leaned back slightly in her desk chair and unbuttoned her jacket so that the Smith and Wesson .38 strapped on her waist could be seen clearly.

"Yes, ma'am," she said for the third time. "I am a cop and a detective." She took the gold shield out of her pocket. The promotion to detective had come after only two years on the force. That was how good they thought she was. Down there, anyway, in the 5th.

"You don't look like a cop," Jennifer Roane said.

"For God's sake, stop embarrassing the officer and let's move on . . ."

"Detective," April corrected. "It's all right. People say it all the time."

She never knew if she didn't look like a cop because she was a woman, or because she didn't wear a uniform except in parades, or because she was Asian.

"Our daughter disappeared," the man said. "What do we do?" He wasn't going to yell because this young Chinese person had kept him waiting for an hour when she clearly didn't have anything to do. He just wanted to get it over with.

"When did you see her last?" April asked gently.

"Four or five days ago. Saturday, I think," the man said.

The woman nodded. "Yeah, Saturday."

April made a note. She always more or less ignored the forms and started over. The forms didn't tell much of a story. And often what people said downstairs were not the same things that they said upstairs.

"You haven't seen your daughter in more than a week?"

"Well, she doesn't live with us," the father said defensively. He looked at the woman. "Either of us."

"Oh." So none of them lived together. April made a note and starred it.

"So, um, Ellen disappeared from where she lives on the twenty-first. Where is that?"

"Well, she didn't disappear the twenty-first. She disappeared the twenty-fifth," the woman said, tearing up again.

"And today is the twenty-seventh," April murmured.

"We thought you had to wait forty-eight hours," she said quickly. She dabbed at her eyes.

"We thought we'd hear from her," the husband corrected.

"Well, there is no rule about that. How old is she and where does she live?" April asked.

Maybe this Ellen Roane didn't fit into any of the categories they could investigate. People didn't understand not everyone who disappeared was missing. Over eighteen, people could go where they wanted, without fear of being looked for, harassed, picked up somewhere by the FBI. Married people who had just had enough took off all the time. They couldn't go looking for every missing spouse.

There had to be some mitigating evidence: The person was over sixty-five or had a handicap of some sort, or had a history of mental illness; or else some indication the person was endangered.

The mother chewed on her upper lip to control herself. April felt her panic and sympathized. This didn't look like too happy a scene. The daughter might just have run away. It was bad luck for the parents, but it happened.

"Seventeen," the mother said after a second of hesitation.

April nodded. Okay, anybody missing under eighteen had to be investigated, punched into the system. "Okay, where does she live?"

"She goes to Columbia. She lives in a dorm there."

"That's not in this precinct. She has to be a resident of this precinct," April said slowly.

"*We're* residents of this precinct," the man said angrily. "We can't start this all over again. We've already been here two hours."

April thought it over. Could she send them Uptown and wiggle out of this? Probably not. Sergeant Joyce had told her to handle it, and not just because she was the only one available.

"You're sensitive," Joyce had said with a smile that made it sound like sensitive was not such a good thing to be.

"Your daughter is under eighteen. That means we can put her in the system. I can do that for you. But do you have any reason to believe Ellen's in danger?" April asked.

"Oh, God. What does that mean?" the woman cried.

The man turned to her angrily. "It means the FBI and every police headquarters in the country will be looking out for her. Is that what you want?"

"She wouldn't go anywhere without telling me," the woman insisted. "We're very close. Very, very close. Yes, I know she's in danger."

"What makes you think so?" April asked gently. "Does she have a boyfriend who threatened her? Was anyone bothering her? Girls sometimes go off with a friend for a few days. Most people turn up."

It was Saturday. College girls went away for the weekend. Tough life.

"She might have gone away for the weekend," April said.

Jennifer Roane shook her head. "I feel it. I just know. I know her. She wouldn't do this to me."

"Is she having any problems at school, any reason to want to get away?"

Both parents shook their heads.

"She is an excellent student. A sweet, beautiful girl, never been in any trouble," the father said firmly. "She's never caused us a moment's worry."

He shrugged as if to say they were probably making too much of it.

April darted a look at him. "What about family problems?" she asked.

"We're separated, if that's what you mean." He looked at one of his highly polished loafers. "But I don't think that has anything to do with it. Ellen's taking it very well."

The woman started to cry again. "I don't believe for a minute Ellen is taking it well. I hardly got a word out of her the last time we spoke. How can she take it well when everything she was told her whole childhood turned out to be a *lie*?"

"Shut up," the man said coldly.

"I'll need a picture of her," April said, "and the phone numbers of her friends." She looked at her watch. She wasn't impressed by the case, didn't for a minute think this girl was in trouble. But she couldn't take a chance. They couldn't ever, ever take a chance and let it go. She told the Roanes she'd start working on it right away.

She had three days to file a report, and seven days to keep the case. If they hadn't located the girl by then, Joyce could get rid of the case, send it Downtown where it would be filed against the day something came up that fit the description.

All this went through April's head automatically as the Roanes left the squad room. At the start of every case she always made lists of what she had to do. Sometimes at night she went over and over them, terrified that she might have left something out that would cost somebody their life.

First stop Columbia, a hell of a way to get to college.

Before April took off, she called the nephew of the DOA she

and Sanchez found that morning. The Medical Examiner's office were always impatient to get rid of them. If she didn't find someone to claim the old guy soon, they'd bury him in Potter's Field. No answer at the nephew's. She packed up for the night, certain she'd have a lead on the girl to tell the parents by morning.

5

"Jesus!" A wave of dizziness surged over Jason. He reached for the wall to stop himself from staggering at the second shock from his wife in less than two hours.

Emma was in the laundry room of their apartment when he got home. She was wearing a black tank top and bicycle shorts, and she was running on an expensive treadmill that hadn't been there when he left.

Drops of sweat glistened on her neck and chest. The skin of her midriff was winter pale. He turned toward the kitchen, then looked at her again, stunned. If anything, she was more beautiful in real life, and seemed farther away from him than if she were a stranger he had never seen before.

"Hi." She turned to him, surprised to see him, smiled her dazzling, thousand-watt smile, and slowed the machine to a walk before getting off.

"I didn't expect you for hours in all this fog. How did it go?" She reached out to him.

He shook his head, speechless. The only thing he could remember about Toronto was the anxiety, the premonition he had that something was not right with *her*. Too bad it had taken him so long to have it. He felt like an idiot, seemed to have missed an awful lot.

In patients and friends with marital problems he always looked for what was missing in the relationship, not for what was there. If passion was missing, if humor was missing, if warmth and life were missing, then he worried. Bickering and nagging were often signs of life, useful outlets for the unwelcome, and sometimes frightening, ambivalence that was part of every love relationship. Jason had always felt it was fine that he and Emma didn't bicker. She didn't like confrontation. It was a cultural thing.

"Sorry. I'm sweaty." Emma backed off at his apparent rebuff.

Emma didn't nag, either. She didn't tear out her hair in violent rages, or throw the plates around. When she was troubled or in pain, a Protestant coolness settled over her and she went to another place in herself to think it out. He had always thought hers was not a bad way to deal with the vicissitudes of life. Cooling out was certainly easier than temper tantrums to live with. Pretty stupid of him to take it easy because it was easier.

Jason had no illusions about the common failing of his sex to mistake outward calm in a woman (or anyone else for that matter) for inner peace. But in his case there was more to it than insensitivity. Managing intimacy was a tricky job, and he deeply believed both partners needed space and privacy. He would never have intruded on Emma, probing for trouble when none was expressed, but clearly he should have.

He colored slightly. "No, no. It's not the sweat. It's the—" He shook his head, still unable to believe what he had seen her do on the screen.

"Oh, the treadmill," she said. "Don't be mad at me, sweetheart. I paid for it myself." She dabbed at her face and chest. Tendrils of damp blond hair curled around her face. There was the trace of a smile on her lips.

"Jesus," he muttered. She had broken his heart, and her eyes were clear. She felt no guilt.

"Why?" He coughed, trying to choke back the wrong start.

"Hey, if I'm scared of being attacked on the street, you shouldn't have to pay for my terrors, Jason." She slung the towel around her neck and changed the subject. "How did the trip go?"

He was incredulous. He couldn't believe this, and couldn't seem to get to the real subject. The antique mantel clock on the hall table chimed the hour. It was seven o'clock.

"Oh, God, Emmie. I know how you love to run. I would have paid for the treadmill. Why didn't you tell me you wanted one?" His voice was agonized.

He wasn't talking about the treadmill, and she clearly knew it. He looked at her, waiting for an answer to questions he hadn't asked. And when none came, he turned and left the laundry room. He passed through the kitchen.

Most of the books and clocks he collected were in the living room ahead of him, on the other side of the entry gallery. He paused in the gallery. Everything felt different, altered in some fundamental way. The lights were off in the living room, but the sound of several clocks ticking in different rhythms animated the darkness. He turned left and headed down the hall to their bedroom.

For more than a dozen years he'd had extensive training in handling all situations. He could deal with paranoia, schizophrenia, psychosis, violence, hysteria, furies of every description. Once he disarmed an enraged adolescent wielding a knife. Another time he persuaded a drunk GI not to shoot the rifle he had pointed at Jason's head. But seeing his lovely, reserved, ladylike wife nude, and having sex on the screen, was something Jason had no preparation for. For the first time in his life, he didn't have the slightest idea what to do.

A set of richly colored prints of the bridges and aquaducts of Rome lined the hall to their bedroom. The walls were painted a pale green above the chair rail, and white below. The bedroom was cream. Emma's clothes were strewn around, and the bed looked like it hadn't been made since he left three days ago. Of the three old clocks in the room, only the eight-day regulator was still ticking. Emma didn't like to wind the clocks. She let them run down and stop when he was away, then said they only worked for him.

Jason went into the closet, still feeling dizzy. He breathed deeply, inhaling the smell of leather and running shoes, swallowing the saliva in his mouth.

Emma followed him into the room.

"I'm sorry I missed your screening," he said. "How did it go?"

"Fine." She started undressing.

Inadvertently, he thought of Daisy, one of his favorite patients. At every session she shed several layers before speaking, her coat, her jacket, a sweater, a scarf, her backpack. A whole bunch of stuff. Only when all her things were arranged around her, on the floor, on a chair, would she sit down and stare at him contentiously.

"So?" she would demand, as if everything that had gone wrong in her life was all his fault.

He loved it. He loved her. Another patient always left something of his behind in the office. Jason was waiting for the right moment to make him start taking charge of his life. Jason loved him, too. The young man had battled cancer, and now had to face the unexpected prize of a future he had no idea how to handle.

On the table the regulator chimed its deep gong. Reflexively, Jason checked his watch. The regulator was a full five minutes slow.

"It wasn't a screening, was it?" he said suddenly.

"What?" Emma said. "Why do you ask?"

"Well, my love, it's already opened. I saw it."

"When?" She reached for a towel to cover herself.

"Just now. It's at the Eighty-third Street theater."

"I thought your flight came in at seven." She frowned, glancing quickly at her own clock, a functional, battery-operated alarm that was never wrong or quirky. "When did you get back?" she asked, confused by the discrepancy in timing.

"About four. I didn't stay for the lunch."

"Oh." She stared at him. "You didn't call."

"No, I thought I'd surprise you."

"You never surprise me." There was a long pause. "Did you like it?" she asked when nothing more was forthcoming.

"What do you think?" he replied, as calmly as he could.

She smiled almost shyly. "The *Times* said it was good. So did the *Voice.*" She warmed to the praise. "Isn't it wonderful?"

No, it wasn't. Her appearing nude in a film that made psychiatrists seem evil was very far from wonderful. Jason dumped some clothes and books off the chair by the bed and sat heavily. Why did she tell him it was a screening when it was an opening? She must have wanted him to go to Toronto and miss it. He simply couldn't believe her first film was in the theaters, had already been reviewed, and she had neglected to tell him a thing about it. He was utterly crushed.

She, on the other hand, was smiling with wonder and excitement, obviously thrilled with herself. Where was her brain? She never asked him if the film would hurt him, never consulted with him. And it was a terrible embarrassment. His patients might not know that Emma Chapman was his wife, but his colleagues did. She had just opened a big window on their life that could not fail to humiliate him deeply.

He watched her pull on another pair of stretch pants and sit cross-legged on the bed, holding the towel up to her neck to hide the breasts that were already property of the world.

"Ronnie had three calls today," she went on.

Jesus Christ, there was more. He looked at her legs. "What did she call you about?" he asked.

"About other scripts. Isn't it amazing? After all the years when I couldn't even get a commercial." Emma talked as if she hadn't done anything unusual, as if this sudden interest in her, these calls to her agent, were totally unexpected.

"No, it's not amazing," Jason said. Of course she would get other offers to fuck on the screen. The camera loved her.

"So, you liked it," she said eagerly. "It's kinky, isn't it?"

It was kinky all right. He paused for a long minute. If this were a session it would seem like an hour of empty space. Some of his patients squirmed in such spaces, felt they were falling into the abyss. He shook his head, sure of one thing. He wasn't kinky. He couldn't stand sadistic movies. Hated horror. He experienced enough terror in his work. He didn't want to see it in his free time, didn't want a wife who would do something like this—mock his work, destroy his dignity, his privacy, everything he believed in. Still, he was a professional. He kept his voice calm.

"Why didn't you mention the nudity and the sex to me?" he said softly.

She twisted the towel in her hand. "I don't know, it was a private thing."

"A private thing?"

"Yeah, kind of like therapy. You don't talk about therapy with anyone, do you? It's your private life, your work." She looked at him challengingly. "This is my work."

"Emma, there's a difference. Therapy *really is* private. No one else can know what happens in it. It has to be confidential."

Emma shrugged. "Well, I thought it would help me be more secure, because up there it isn't really me."

"Oh? Who is it?" He didn't try to control the coldness of his tone.

"It's the character. I do what the character would do."

Jason shook his head. "Baby, it's still you up there, and you have something to do with me. You're not alone in the world. You're married to me. Don't my feelings count?"

She lifted a shoulder with a provocative smile. "Well, did it turn you on?"

"Jesus, is that what you wanted to do?"

"Oh, come on, Jason, acting is what I do. You knew that when you married me. Don't you ever secretly want to sleep with a star?" she asked slyly.

"No," he said sharply. "No, I don't. And we agreed you'd never do that kind of thing."

Her lip trembled. "I thought you'd like it. Your whole world is mystery and secrets. You love your patients. You live in a secret world with them. I have nothing to do with your life."

"*That* part of my life. Only *that* part," he protested. "You're in this part. You're *everything* in this part."

But even as he said it, he knew it wasn't true. They came home with him. They lived with him in his heart. They wounded him, and touched him, and often made him want to cry. Nobody could compete with the drama of their lives.

"I can't live in anybody's shadow," she was saying.

Emma had a life of her own. She didn't live in his shadow. Jason couldn't bear this. He got up to wind one of his beautiful, silenced clocks. He heard her now, as if from a long way away, telling him she had done it to have something of her own.

6

They had seen the buzzards. That's what Jimmy said made them go off the dirt track the bikers had worn years ago into the rough landscape of the lower hills. The girl was so hysterical Darlene had to take her into the storage room that doubled as a lounge and give her some herbal tea. She'd already vomited a couple of times, but still looked pretty green.

"Horrible, horrible, horrible. I'll never get it out of my head." The little girl with bright red hair didn't look old enough to be riding around the hills behind a boy on a powerful motorcycle. She couldn't stop crying.

"Just drink a little of this," Darlene suggested. "It really works."

The girl sipped, making a face as if she'd rather be having a beer.

"What's your name?" Darlene let go of the hand she had been holding and took her pad out.

"Scarlett, don't laugh," the girl said.

"I won't laugh."

Nobody was old enough to find a dead girl being eaten by birds. "Scarlett what? I'd like to call your mother."

She shook her head. "I'll wait for Jimmy."

"You'll be here a while then."

Jimmy had insisted on taking Sheriff Regis back there to show just where it was, even though they might be able to find it on their own, the teenager said, because of the birds.

"I didn't have anything to cover it." Jimmy seemed apologetic about that.

Sheriff Newt Regis, whose hair had gone gray by the time he was thirty, and who was now forty-three, churned into action. He was not as lean as he had been and already had a grandbaby, but he was fast when he had reason to move. He roused the coroner from a nap to come out and have a look—and bring an ambulance. He called Raymond and Jesse in from the field and told them to bring the equipment. If it was a crime scene, they wouldn't have a second chance to go over it. He called Rosie and said he wouldn't be having her Monday night pot roast.

Then he sighed deeply because this could very well mark the beginning of spring, and got into his car to follow the kid.

For Newt Regis, spring was not a welcome time in north San Diego County. Spring was when bikers from all over the world started drifting in to camp in the hills and hang around raising hell. They came for the motorcycle races at Carlsbad, and some of them could do some pretty terrible things. Stealing people, or killing them, was just one. Newt didn't know which was worse. He'd heard gypsies used to take girls. Well, now the Hell's Angels roaring through a town sometimes grabbed a pretty girl off the street just like that and drugged her so bad she didn't know who she was or where she came from. Then they'd take her to another state and sell her. The fear that one of them would go berserk in his town made Newt pretty nervous and jerky from about March fifteenth to the beginning of June. Then when the races were over and it started getting really hot, they took off.

The rest of the year was pretty quiet in his small town of Potoway Village, a retreat of modest houses and stores tucked almost two thousand feet up in the hills of San Diego County, east of Carlsbad. It was a wild place, typical of California, where within the space of a few miles, there was glittering ocean and beaches; mountains that climbed as high as five thousand feet; and desert, as barren and dry as any in the world.

Newt wanted to keep his people safe, but he also liked quiet

because there were only six of them in the Sheriff's Office in
Potoway: two grumbling rookies too green to know when to wipe their
asses, two experienced deputies close to retirement, and Darlene,
who typed, manned the phone, took care of women and children, and
made awful coffee. Only six, and if there was more going on than a
bad wreck on the road, a robbery at the Quick Stop, a rattlesnake in
someone's living room, and a drunk or an OD, they just couldn't
handle it without help from outside.

Usually, though, they only had one or two of these things happening at a time. Camp Pendleton, the Marine base that covered
over twenty miles on the north-south highway that everybody called
the Five, had their own policing; and Oceanside—affectionately
called Marine City U.S.A.—and the bigger towns to the west netted
most of the drug scene and homicides.

In addition, in this part of the world so close to the Mexican
border, the Feds known as IMNAT constantly prowled the hills and
deserts looking for illegal aliens. There was a lot of Federal and
State money in law enforcement in San Diego County. But there
weren't many signs of it in Potoway, so Newt made it a special
concern of his to keep up-to-date. He went to conferences and took
some courses. Once he went all the way to Atlanta for one. And he
still worried about what the Sheriff's Office of Potoway would do if
they ever had a really big case to solve. Collecting material from
crime scenes was a complicated science these days. They could tell
a lot of things from fibers and soil and the patterns blood made when
it spattered, a lot more things than they used to. The last course he
took emphasized how it was vital for labs and crime scene people to
work together closely. Out here, close was a long way away. The
nearest lab was thirty-five miles from here, and that kind of mattered
because things like body fluids had to be handled just right, or they
spoiled.

Newt gunned the accelerator and turned on his siren. Already
the kid was way ahead of him, charging his Harley along the mountain road, clearly delighted to have a cop chasing him with no
chance of being arrested.

It took nearly twenty minutes to get to the spot on the edge of the desert where the land started chunking up into hills and ridges. It was late afternoon, nearly evening. When Newt got out of the car, the boy had already been standing there motionless beside his bike for some time, riveted to the sight of two buzzards tearing at the nose and lips and cheeks of a dead girl, whose naked red and black body had already begun to dry and split in the sun.

7

It didn't look so terrific, this college dormitory. More like a run-down apartment building. April parked the car quite far from the curb, kind of on an angle, and left it there. One thing was good about being a cop. You could leave your car anywhere and never get a ticket. She always locked it, though. April adjusted the gun at her waist. Never go into a situation alone was the rule. But this wasn't a situation. It was an investigation. You could do that alone.

Abandoned buildings were April's personal terror. When she was on the beat in Bedford-Stuyvesant for a few months, she got adjusted to a lot of things. Addicts. They used to call them junkies. Heroin was the thing, and free-basing. The addicts cooked the stuff and sometimes caught on fire when they were too high to be careful. Lot of abandoned buildings there.

"Mei Mei's daughter is an accountant," April's mother told her. "Why don't you do something up like that?" She thought a cop was a low thing to be. Not as high as Mei Mei's daughter. Another friend of hers had a son who was a doctor. She was always trying to get them to meet. Neither one wanted to.

It wasn't only that the job was not as high as maybe working at Merrill Lynch in computer programming. It was the fact that cops got infected through the eyes. They saw too many things.

Well, you got used to it. Seeing people shot up pretty bad. Stomach wounds, head wounds. April was first on the scene once when a Korean was shot in the neck in the middle of a robbery. The guy with him was already dead, and this guy was lying there in a lake of blood. It was pumping out of a hole in his neck with every heartbeat. Five months in the Academy didn't exactly train anybody to deal with neck wounds of this severity, but April didn't panic. She tried to plug up the hole, applied as much pressure as she could, and stayed with him until they got him out.

He was one of the lucky ones. Somehow the bullet missed the carotid artery. He lost his voice box, and was six months in the hospital, but he didn't die. She did the follow-up on him, so she knew how he had to learn to talk by holding the hole closed with a flap of skin.

Being a cop wasn't as high maybe as being a doctor, but April knew the Korean wouldn't have lived if she hadn't been there to get help and keep his blood from escaping out the hole in his neck while they waited for the ambulance.

She wasn't afraid of getting hit like that. She'd pulled her gun, but she'd never used it except at the range every month, and no one had ever shot at her. What scared her was the empty, falling-down buildings, with the windows boarded up, and what happened in them. There were ghosts in the buildings, living and dead. Sometimes the windows weren't boarded up. They were just holes. She could see the pigeons flying in and out.

What scared April was getting a call about a dead body in one of those buildings and having to go in and find it. Down an elevator shaft, or just lying on the floor in a room upstairs. She used to dream about it every night. Getting that call and having to climb the stairs looking for it, having no idea which room it was in. Or what else she might find. On the night shift when she was a rookie she confessed this to one person, and then everybody knew.

Long-ago advice from her mother: Never tell your weak place. People can break you from there. After she told about her weak place, April worried that they would get her there when that body turned up.

They didn't, though. When she finally got the call she had known would come because she dreamed it too many times for it not to happen, her supervisor told her she didn't have to go in. He didn't break her in her weak place after all. He told her to wait for backup. It was on the third floor of a walk-up. Boarded up except for the front door.

April stood downstairs that day, thinking they would make her go in when they got there because you weren't supposed to have any weak places in NYPD. If she didn't go in when they asked her to, she wouldn't get promoted. She'd have to stay on foot patrol in Bed-Stuy all her life. That was another scary prospect.

April knew whenever she was really frightened from deep inside it always came from something her mother told her, something Chinese that didn't make sense in America. Her mother talked constantly, and couldn't seem to stop. Her father hardly spoke at all. Sai Woo said she had to fill the silences her husband made or else ghosts would come in and fill them with wickedness. April said there weren't any ghosts in America, and her father might have something to say if Sai Woo gave him a place to let his thoughts out.

This was when her mother looked at her with the greatest scorn and dropped another one of her priceless pearls that had nothing to do with anything.

"Sun rises in the East, goes down in the West," like April was supposed to know what that meant.

Still, April did know what it meant. It meant there *were* ghosts in America, and you were supposed to eat the ones that plagued you just like in China. If you devoured them, they healed you. In China they would devour anything at all. If it was hairy or bony or truly awful, they ground it up into powder, put it in boiling water, and drank it.

As April stood outside the Bed-Stuy building waiting for backup that day, she felt old China crowding all around her. If she were a true American cop, she'd have no trouble climbing those stairs and looking at the body. So what? How bad could it be? But if she were truly Chinese under everything, she'd have to consume some little something, a hair or a piece of dust, something from the scene. If she didn't do that, the weak place would always be there inside of her.

But something magical happened when her supervisor showed up and said, "All right, April, you stay down here and secure the area."

"No, it's okay. I can do it," she had assured him.

She climbed up the three flights of stairs, not first maybe. But she was there when they found it. It had been there for months. There wasn't even any smell anymore, nothing like a dead animal decaying behind a wall. There was just a pile of rags and hair and bone with some dried skin that looked like leather covering it. Was this what I was afraid of, she asked herself. She decided she was all American and didn't have to consume it.

So this was what I wanted, she thought now, going up the stairs into the dorm where Ellen Roane lived. The place was gloomy and looked almost deserted. The girl would have been better off living at home. Better address downtown. But not the freedom to do as she pleased. April went inside. There was a fat guard sitting at a small table that didn't look like it was always there.

"I'm looking for Ellen Roane," she said.

"Well, you won't find her here," the guard said. He was Hispanic, not very friendly.

"How about Connie Shagan?" April said. Connie Shagan, the Roanes had told her, was Ellen's roommate.

"Won't find her either. Or any of them."

"Is there a teacher, uh, a professor, who lives here I could talk to?" She hadn't wanted to, but now she flashed her shield.

The guard looked at it and shrugged. "There's still nobody here. It's spring break."

April Woo cursed herself five hundred times as she walked back to where she left the car. See what happens when you leave out one tiny question. One detail that changes the whole story. The parents didn't bother to tell her everybody disappeared. All the students, and even the professors disappeared. And she didn't think to ask. It wasn't very smart.

She would talk to the parents in the morning when they came in with the girl's picture and ask them if they really wanted to put their daughter in the system when she was probably skiing in Vermont. With the Barstollers, who had a Chinese maid. She smiled at the thought, as she took the car back.

8

Troland Grebs was up all night with bad dreams again. Monkeys were beating each other. A bull in the garden was goring somebody. He was in a cold sweat, only half drunk from a long evening of drinking. He couldn't stop thinking about that girl in the movie. First time he saw it, he had to walk out.

At three he gave up trying to sleep and went outside for a walk. The smells of the ocean off Pacific Beach, the palm and orange trees, the smooth green grass of front lawns soothed him. He walked around, circling his neighborhood many times. Just as the light was graying and before the sun rose, he was back in his one bedroom apartment, sitting on the tiny terrace on the third floor waiting for the jogger to come by.

For months he had been waking up early to sit up there and watch her. She lived on the third floor, too, on the other side of the garden. He had heard people call her Jane, but he had never spoken to her. She kept her shades drawn. He never saw her undressed except this way, in the bicycle shorts and two tops. One stretchy thing made of a few straps over a similar thing with more straps in different places. Crisscrossed and so tight Troland wondered every day how she got them off. He knew how he would get them off. From the terrace he watched her dispassionately.

She came out of the door and stretched. He could see her raise her arms and breathe. She started jogging in place, looking up at the sky. She plugged her Walkman into her ears. She never saw him, never looked in his direction. She took off at a moderate pace and disappeared into the street. After she was gone, he went in to shower, then dressed carefully and went to work at the plant just north of Lindbergh Field.

He wasn't talking much any more. He sat at his drafting table for hours every day, working on the intricate details of jet engine modifications, sunk deep in his own thoughts. Ever since the Persian Gulf War he'd been moving closer and closer to the insides of the cruise missiles he'd worked on all the years they hadn't been needed, and no one believed would work. Now everybody knew that they could seek out and destroy. He felt his mark was on every hit in Iraq. It made him feel powerful. He had started seeking out and destroying, had gone back to where his own power used to be.

What the soldiers did in Kuwait got him thinking about things he hadn't wanted to do for years. But they just raped. He liked adding his mark afterwards. Long ago he got in trouble doing it to whores in Mexico, and had to stop. He had put the urge away in a drawer, along with the colored pencils and the old drawings. He had been good a long time, and then the war came. His very own missiles started killing people, started talking to him like they knew him. And he found out he could get away with it now. But right now he felt bad, and was pretty sure the movie had put a curse on him. But he wasn't sure exactly why.

At work he started thinking about it again. It was so boring. At first it was just people talking about sex and their "feelings." It was so bad he almost walked out. But then the girl suddenly was naked, and he decided to stay.

All at once he felt a flicker of something unpleasant about her. Then that was quickly overridden by the excitement he had thinking that the other actor resembled, and might in fact be, him. He was aroused. He folded his leather jacket across his lap.

The guy in the film was fucking the girl with his leather jacket on and nothing else. This was also like him and turned him on. He looked quickly around, then burrowed his hand under his jacket. The bulge was enormous, too large for his pants. He rubbed back and forth with the palm of his hand. Except for the woman's nudity and the man in the leather jacket, this was not very exciting sex. He switched his thoughts to the jogger who never had a name when he imagined fucking her.

He called her the jogger and thought about grabbing her before she got to the street. Just taking her by the arm. He unzipped his pants and untangled his dick. The softness of his skin around the hard core always surprised him. It was a tool, a defier of gravity like the cruise missile. It could seek and destroy. He thought of shoving it into the jogger and watching that stuck-up, satisfied face fill with fear. He liked the idea of scaring her—no, filling her with fear so big there was nothing left of her but cunt and pure terror.

The fuss they made in the paper all the time made him mad. Don't make such a big deal of it! Real men always did it, always would. Rape wasn't so bad. It was a natural thing, happened every day. Soldiers did it. He touched himself, thinking of the Iraqi soldiers in Kuwait. Things they did to the girls with their fathers watching. Shot the brothers in the street. No mercy. In the ass and everything. Probably did it with their clothes on, too. Grabbed women in their own houses and slammed them against the wall. Even made the children watch. Well, he'd seen his father do it.

He stared at the screen, but didn't see it. It was natural to conquer. He thought of pushing the jogger to the ground, getting on top of her and shoving his dick into her, of making her kneel in front of him and suck him off. Put her lips around him hard, and move her tongue just right.

You could kill someone that way. Shove too hard and just keep going down their throat. It was good to force his way into places he wasn't wanted. They were just cunts. Places to put sperm. They had no right to get their noses out of joint. Drops of semen oozed out onto his hand, lubricating his dick. It felt good.

The Kama-sutra advised murdering the husband, father, brothers—anybody attached to a woman who resisted a man she didn't want. That's what the famous book *said:* When every attempt to get her failed, they had the *right* to kill her protectors and then rape her.

Take her off and do whatever they wanted with her. The pressure intensified.

He didn't know why he thought of the Kama-sutra now. It was a book he read years ago. He used to masturbate while studying the chapters on the special marks you could make biting and scratching and slapping. Scraping the skin and biting so hard the skin broke or went black and blue. In India, no one was ashamed of walking around with bite or scratch marks. They were considered signs of mastery. It was only the West that was behind.

The scene changed. Troland's eyes flickered. They had their clothes on again, were talking. There was something familiar about the girl on the screen. Now she was walking down the street with her back to the camera. It was a familiar walk. It irritated him that the actress seemed to be someone he knew. He couldn't be interested if he thought he knew her. His dick became soft in his hand. Who was it?

It was impossible that he knew her. He couldn't know her. The film was somewhere else, in a city. Looked like New York. He'd been there once. It wasn't here. Was it a bimbo he knew from the beach? No, he didn't know anybody who looked like that. Her skin was really white. He tried to relax. There was no way he could know her. But he couldn't get excited again. He began feeling bad. What was the matter with this stupid movie? It wasn't even right. He felt angry.

It *was* somebody he knew. Couldn't be. He looked around. The few people who were here were now looking bored. People who came to movies like this didn't want to see talking and walking. His hand was sticky. He had gotten dirty and was no longer excited. He began to feel irritated and angry. Something was making him feel powerfully uneasy. But what?

Somebody got up and left. That was the right idea. He shook his head, unnerved. That girl. That hair. The voice, now that he listened to it. How could it be? Under the leather jacket he put his limp dick back in his pants. Small and pitiful as a sparrow. Zipped up and went out into the California night. He couldn't forget it.

He left the plant at five-thirty. It was still blisteringly hot in San Diego, even though the sun had begun its descent into the ocean. He rode over to the beach to watch the simmering red disc go down. He often went there after work. It cooled the panic. He liked to stand there for an hour or so, leaning against his Harley, with his leather jacket strapped over a six-pack of beer on the back. He knew from the way the girls studied him from the sides of their eyes that he still looked good having a couple of beers and watching them on the sand in their thong bathing suits. He hated them all.

He couldn't believe it was her. Emma wouldn't do that. She just wouldn't. She was good. She wouldn't do that. He thought he was wrong and just saw a resemblance. He wandered around thinking about it, how much he liked her, more than liked her. He hadn't ever really liked anybody that way since. He remembered how perfect she was, really smart and nice. He had watched her carefully that whole year and knew she wasn't just empty nice. She was really nice. Like all the way through. He knew she didn't do anything bad like the rest of them. Wasn't a liar. He loved her and saved her so she could go away to college. How could she betray him and turn out to be a whore?

"You've been by here twenty times. You want to buy a ticket?"

Troland turned around abruptly. "What?" He was back at the theater, didn't know how he had gotten there, and was pacing back and forth in front of it without realizing what he was doing.

"You all right?" The kid behind the window frowned.

"What're you looking at?" Troland snapped. He had a motorcycle chain over his shoulder.

The boy behind the window held up his hands in a conciliatory gesture. "Hey, what are you so ticked off about? Film doesn't start for a half an hour, but it's not full. You can go in any time."

Troland looked through him. "I'll wait for the beginning," he said furiously. The guy was crazy. He wasn't ticked off.

"Suit yourself." He tried again when Troland didn't move away. "You want to buy your ticket now?"

"You deaf or something? I said I'd wait for the beginning."

Troland looked at the teenager. His hair was combed straight back. He was wearing a white polo shirt and looked puzzled. Troland shot him between his puzzled eyes and watched him slump forward in his chair. No, better to stab him in the chest. Yes, that was better. The heart kept going for a while pumping the blood out so it drenched the white shirt and splattered the walls and counter. He walked away. He wasn't mad.

He thought about it as the movie started. Maybe he was mad. Yeah, he felt a cold rage. Really cold. He sat by himself way at the back. It was in his stomach like a big rock he couldn't digest. Cold and then hot.

Fuck you. How could anyone act in a movie like this? How could she? He watched it more intensely this time. It was her. Now it was more her. And more shocking, the guy was *him.* How could he do that to her?

He was appalled by the look on her face. She *liked* it. He hated her. Why was she letting him do that? This was no movie. She was really letting him do that. Him, Troland Grebs. That was him. He was confused. But they were in New York, and he was here in San Diego. He was aroused again, just as he had been the day before. No, he wouldn't give in to it.

He looked at the people in front of him. No one could see him. He was in the back, the leather jacket on his lap. He was fascinated. He couldn't look away from the screen. His dick was in his hand, both hands now. It disgusted him that she was doing that. How could she do that? The guy was sucking her off. It was gross. It was tremendous. Maybe he was biting her. But he couldn't be hurting her. She wasn't screaming. Too bad. She deserved it. He rubbed up and down on his soft moist skin. It wouldn't be bad to shove it in there. The screen went blank.

Shit. What was going on now? What was that sound? It was a sound he knew. What was it? The screen was white for a long time. The tension grew and then he saw it was a silvery tattoo needle. When it touched the guy who looked like him, he came in his pants.

As soon as it was over, the thrill was instantly replaced by a

feeling of intense shame. He had befouled himself. His pants were
sticky and wet. What a horrible thing he did. For some minutes he
scolded himself for losing control. Then he pulled his shirt out of his
pants to hide the stain, and thought again. Wait a minute. This
wasn't his fault. He had nothing to do with this. He didn't turn an
angel into a whore. He didn't make the movie. He didn't have anything to feel bad about. She did it. She was the one who did this to
him. She should be punished. She would be punished.

He sat there for a long time waiting for his heart to slow down.
When the lights came on, he got up. His rage was enormous. Why
did she do this to him? He walked out holding the jacket in front of
him. The fingers of one hand unconsciously caressed the tattoo on
his arm, then moved to the many scars crisscrossing his chest where
his father had taught him what fire felt like.

I'll teach you not to set fires. I'll show you what you get for being
bad. He held him down and burned Troland with a red-hot wire
hanger so he could never take his shirt off in public again.

He hated the wet feeling in his pants, needed a drink. He
unchained the bike and headed home.

9

"Do you know who this is?"

Ronnie, Emma's agent of many years, leaned over excitedly as she pointed to the name on the cover of a script she had brought for Emma to read.

They were having breakfast at The New York Deli just around the corner from Ronnie's office on Fifty-sixth Street and Sixth Avenue.

It was a big name. Emma took another bite of her eggs Benedict and grimaced. "Of course I do."

"Well, this is it. This is how it happens. You do a nothing film, don't have any expectations for it, somebody somewhere likes it. And suddenly you're a *star*. I've seen it a million times." Ronnie sighed. "It's just never happened to me."

Then she reached across the table and slapped Emma's hand. "Are you crazy? We can't eat that," she said as if she had just noticed it.

Emma looked at the Canadian bacon smothered with Hollandaise sauce on her plate. "Why not?"

"It's four-hundred-percent fat." Ronnie raked a hand through her blunt-cut red hair. The hair curled around her ears for a second and then fell back in its perfect circle around her plump face.

Ronnie was a compulsive eater. She wrinkled her freckled nose at Emma's plate with disgust and longing.

Emma shook her head. Ronnie used to refer to her as You. You do this job or that job. Now when she talked about Emma it was We or I. "We'll think about this," or "I don't want to do that."

"We have to be more careful," she said now. "You can't just eat anything you want. You can't just *do* anything you want. We have to think about what it means for our career."

"It's not our career. It's my career," Emma replied with a smile.

The pink blush lavishly applied to Ronnie's cheeks stood out strongly against her pale skin, as she blanched.

"I just don't want you getting fat," she said defensively. "I wasn't being pushy."

Emma let out a small laugh. Ronnie was extraordinarily pushy. But it never helped her, and her pushiness hadn't helped Mark, Emma's college friend and the writer/director/producer of *Serpent's Teeth,* either.

Ronnie hadn't liked the modest project, and refused to make a single call to help it. She had nothing to do with the film and now she was claiming she was instrumental in putting the whole thing together.

"It grows in the night without your consent," Ronnie said about the fat. "Look at me. I don't eat a thing. Not a *thing.* I have one tiny lamb chop at night with all the fat cut off, and a lettuce leaf. I don't know why I'm so fat." She heaved a great sigh.

"I'd be a pretty girl if I wasn't so big, wouldn't I?" She gave Emma a searching look. Emma knew that although Ronnie was deeply involved with her fat, that was not what was on her mind right then. She was really very worried that Emma would leave her.

"You *are* a pretty girl," Emma said.

She turned her head and caught sight of a couple at a table across the room. They were caressing fingers while talking and looking deep in each other's eyes. Unexpectedly, grief gnawed at her, filling her again with the overwhelming feeling of desolation that had slowly been taking her over for a long time.

"We can't eat fat. We can't eat sugar," Ronnie was babbling. "You're not going to leave me, are you?" she demanded suddenly.

Emma stared at the lovers. She couldn't remember the last time Jason had looked at her like that.

"What did you imagine happening after you did this film?" he had asked again last night.

Her reply didn't satisfy him. "It was a low-budget thing." She had shrugged. Big deal. "Kind of a lark. We had no idea anyone would pick it up."

"Some lark." He was like a stone wall. There was no getting through it.

"Oh, come on, Jason, is it so bad that people will see my work instead of just hearing me?"

For the last few years, Emma had been a voice on both TV and radio. She had acted in several of Mark's plays, but got no important work on the stage and no parts at all on TV or in the films.

"It's not just work," Jason said carefully. "It's a sexual thing. You exposed your body, you humiliated me—"

"Don't."

"Don't what? You can do it, but I can't say it?"

"I was acting in a film, that's all."

"It's more than acting. It was a *sexual* thing, Emma. You have sex. What would you call it?"

"It's work. I call it work."

"Working on your back with your clothes off and a stranger on top of you? What kind of work is it?"

"Stop it. You're making too much of it. I'm an actress. It's what I do."

"No, it's not what you do. It's not what you've ever done." He turned away, wouldn't look at her.

"I thought you were so well analyzed," she had said after a long pause. "Other husbands of actresses seem to handle it."

"Maybe, if it's part of the deal," he replied bitterly. "But I'm a doctor, a very private person. This wasn't part of our deal."

"Emma. Answer the question," Ronnie demanded.

"I have to go," Emma said suddenly.

"What? We haven't talked about the scripts yet. One of them has a sex scene in it that will knock you over." She reached in her bag for the other scripts she brought.

Emma shook her head. "Look," she said slowly. "I'm not sure I want to be known for that."

"What are you talking about?" Ronnie cried.

Emma turned away from the lovers and focused on her. "I said it isn't what I want to be known for."

"Since when are we so squeamish, huh?" Ronnie started fanning her face with one of the scripts, as if she were going to faint. It had a red cover that clashed with her hair. "Look, you have to do what they send you. If they send you prostitute scripts, you have to be a prostitute."

"Is that what they are?" Emma asked. "All three?"

"What's the big deal? What's the matter with you all of a sudden?"

"I hate films that glorify hookers. I really do. Hookers are not wonderful people. They don't end up happily ever after. I don't want to be known for my body. It's—"

"You have to read for this one next week. So look at this first and call me after two." Ronnie handed over the scripts abruptly. "Don't make me sick."

"I have a taping this afternoon," Emma said.

She was doing a Maalox moment, speaking the voice of the old woman because the old woman cast for the part sounded like a chicken.

"Then read it now." Ronnie pushed it at her.

Emma took it. It was very thin, only four or five pages. "These are just sides," she protested.

"So?"

"So where's the rest of it?" she demanded.

"Emma, don't fight me. Sometimes they just *give* sides. They don't want you to work on the whole goddamn part. They just want to see you do the scene cold, how you see the character from the few words that are written there."

"Where's the rest of it? I can't do it if I don't know what the story is."

"You're making me very upset. You've been in this business long enough to know you're not the one who has leverage at this point. They are the ones who decide on *you*. You do it, and if they like you, you get the part. You get famous, have fun, and make lots of money. What's the problem here?"

Emma gathered up her things. Right, get famous and make lots of money. Ronnie was right. She had been working very hard for this for years.

"Okay," she told Ronnie. "I'll go for it." If Jason didn't like her success, it was his problem.

She watched the lovers get up and leave.

10

"Well, what can you tell me?" Newt Regis leaned back in his chair feeling a little nervous, because Dr. Milt Ferris had bothered to come to his office instead of calling him on the phone with the information Newt had asked for. When Newt wanted a prelim, Milt usually gave him a call with the TOD and COD.

Milton Ferris had been Medical Examiner for a while in the City of San Diego, and had taught pathology for years at the medical school. When he decided he wanted to get away from it all and came out here to write his memoirs, the job of Coroner happened to be open. Milt was persuaded to take it as a stopgap until they could find someone else. So far they were lucky. Four years had passed, nobody ever bothered to look for a replacement, and he hadn't complained about the work yet.

Milt had changed a few things in Potoway Village.

Before Milt came, Newt was called Newton, which was his real name. Establishing Time of Death was just that, and nothing else. But Milton was a crossword puzzle maniac, and now everything was letters and codes. His idea of a good time was making up a cross-word puzzle with just law enforcement and forensic terms in it.

Sometimes Newt complained that Milt had turned him into a salamander and Cause of Death into a fish, but Milt pointed out the KGB, CIA, FBI, and all the other police agencies around the world were the ones that started it, not him. Hey, the FBI now had branches with names like VICAP and IMNAT, absolute necessities for any crossword on the subject.

Milt was smooth all over, bald as an egg, pale, round, not over five foot five. At sixty, his face was still unlined except around the eyes, where there was always something of a smile going on. If he had had some hair, he might have looked a lot like a small Santa Claus. But even without hair, he didn't look like someone who had spent his life cutting up dead bodies, and then studying the gruesome bits.

He sat heavily, opposite Newt, not smiling now.

"Well?" Newt demanded.

Out there where they found her, Newt and Ray and Jesse had gone over as much ground as they could, looking for some clue as to what happened. A track in the dirt, a scrap of cloth, a weapon, anything. But the girl had no clothes on, and there did not appear to be any disturbance of anything in the area around her. In some other part of the world, they might call in a botanist to examine the plant life under the body to determine, by the changes in the plants, how long the body had been there. But here there was no plant life under her. Milt had initially speculated that whatever happened to her happened somewhere else.

"It looks like she had some injuries, but she didn't die of them," he said now.

"What do you mean?" Newt frowned.

"Sometimes it's hard to tell what happened antemortem, and what might be postmortem injuries," Milt said.

"Yeah?" Newt said. He knew that.

"She could have died, and then two ribs and an arm were broken when somebody moved her. You know that sometimes happens when ambulance drivers aren't careful. It can mess up an autopsy report." Milt shook his bald head.

"But you don't think that's what happened?"

"No."

There was a long pause.

"So, what did she die of?" Newt said impatiently.

"Exposure," Milt said.

"No kidding."

"The color and condition of her skin—looks like she was thoroughly burned by the sun. Not just her front, but her back, too. That means she could have been walked around out there. Low temperatures at night. Looks like she starved, fried, and froze."

"Raped?" Newt asked soberly.

Milt shook his head. "After twenty-four hours with really first-rate samples from a living person, intercourse would be pretty hard to establish, unless there were injuries. Postmortem," he shook his head again, "not a chance. I do think she was tortured, though."

"The wounds in her groin?"

"No, that's postmortem change. That's what happens in mummification. The skin shrinks. The resulting split sometimes looks like an antemortem knife wound."

"Mummification?" Newt played with a pencil on his desk. It said *Pell's Apothecary* on the side. "Then she must have been there for a while."

"Nuh-uh." Milt shook his head again.

"Why so sure?"

"The birds just started. The coyotes hadn't even gotten there yet. A few days, and there'd only be bones left. In a way we're lucky."

"Oh, yeah?" Newt said. "How so?"

"We might still be able to get some prints."

Milt had finished and didn't make any going motions.

"What's bothering you? In particular, I mean?"

"You know that blackened part on her chest?"

"Postmortem artifact?" Newt was proud he knew the word. When he was a rookie years ago, he had seen the blackened patterns on the chest of a person who had died several days before, and thought some madman had murdered him and put them there. It didn't take long to learn the horrible truth. Humans don't fare as well as animals in the looks department after death. All kinds of colors and patterns and wounds appear on dead bodies as they go through their many postmortem changes. Sometimes, in three days if the conditions are just right, a human can swell to three times its normal size with gases and putrefaction.

"No, a man-made burn."

Milt was silent for a long time.

Newt twirled the pencil in his fingers. So, she might have been tortured and left out there. He had a mental picture of her hair, already shrinking away from her scalp, and her nails. The hair was silky and looked like it had been expertly colored; the nails were painted a delicate pink. This was no biker's girl with crudely bleached hair, roots an inch thick, and black nail polish.

"The thing is," Milt went on. "You know how ME's are when we get together. We talk about unusual cases. I have a friend down in Twenty-Nine Palms. A few months ago he had a similar case, a girl burned in the chest with something like a brand and left in the desert. Nobody took too much notice. It was a Mexican."

"Christ." Newt groaned.

"I know he photographed the burn for the pattern. In case another one came up. I'll have to get his report. Now I'm not saying two burns make a trend, but it looks like another one may have come up—" His voice trailed off.

Slowly he got to his feet.

"When can you have the data for me?" Newt asked. He wanted to get the data into the surrounding jurisdictions as soon as possible. They had to identify her before they could start investigating what happened to her.

"Soon," Milt promised. "They're working on the X rays and dentals now."

"Good." Newt was so distressed by the thought of his California desert getting littered with the bodies of tortured young women that he followed Milt out of the building and watched him drive away.

11

Troland felt bad. He didn't think he had ever felt so bad. He couldn't even go to work because of what she did to him. She had been the prettiest, nicest girl in the whole world, the only girl he ever really liked, and he had saved her. He couldn't stop thinking about how he saved her. He, Troland Grebs, saved her. And now she made a fool of him like it didn't matter to her at all that he held her in his heart all these years. He hated her.

She was the only girl who was so perfect he had to make special rules just for her. He remembered every one: He could look at her, but not when she was on the beach. He could write letters to her, but not send them. He could draw pictures of her, but not let anybody see them. The most important thing was he couldn't touch her no matter what. And he never did. He had been good all these years, and she had to humiliate him, curse him, break every rule like the worst whore that ever was.

He lay on the sofa in his apartment two, three days; drinking, staggering to the bathroom, vomiting, passing out—drinking some more. He couldn't go to work. When he finally got up and cleaned the apartment, he didn't know why it smelled, why there was vomit on the floor. He just knew he was going to take back all the things he had ever done for Emma Chapman, one at a time.

12

It took Detective Woo three days to find Connie Shagan at a friend of a friend's house in Florida. It wasn't easy to locate her with no one in the dorm or the administration office to give her names and numbers. She didn't work the case on Monday. This week Monday was her day off. She spent it studying for a psych test that evening. She had to take the subway both ways from Queens, since she was without a car, but she thought she did all right on the test.

On Tuesday April had a chance to go back to the dorm and get into the girls' room. She took Ellen's photograph with her and held it in her hand as she looked around. She had done this with another missing girl two years before. Lily Dong was twelve, and disappeared from her kitchen in Chinatown when she was home from school having lunch. The whole precinct looked for her. It was the kind of thing that got in the newspapers. A kidnapper called once. Then when he didn't call again, the family called the police. Three days after the child disappeared, April found a pile of junk in a courtyard across the street. Underneath was a dirty sleeping bag. April hated thinking about unzipping that bag, and seeing the sneakers. She didn't have to see anything else but the two sneakers to know. The girl was wearing them when she disappeared and was wearing them when she was found. She had been strangled in a panic. It took April a long time to look at any kind of sneakers without feeling terrible about Lily Dong. Very rare for an Asian to kill someone. It was the guy across the hall, Burmese.

Ellen Roane's dorm room was small, just big enough for two

twin beds with plastic cartons between them, two small wooden desks, two chairs, two reading lights, two chests of drawers. The bathroom was shared with the room on the other side. The girls seemed to have made an effort to leave the place neat when they left. Or maybe they were just like that. There were no piles of little things —hair things, makeup, trinkets—either on the surfaces or in the drawers. No nail polish, lipsticks. The drawers were stuffed with clothes. Much of it seemed to be blue jeans and sweaters. Must be very serious girls. April's own room was messier. She liked small colorful things, had a lot of cosmetics.

She found Connie's home address and telephone number in a small book in the girl's desk. Then she turned her attention to Ellen's side of the room. Ellen Roane had a CD player and many discs. She had put her name on it with one of those plastic guns that shoots out letters. She also had a computer to write her papers on, and many books. All the books she seemed to be working in were in neat stacks on the floor by her desk, and on her bed. Both beds had the same comforters on them. April wondered if the university gave out flower-printed comforters, or if the girls had bought them together. Probably bought them so the room would look coordinated. There was also a small rug of a matching color in the middle of the floor.

April tried to imagine what it might be like to have such expensive toys at seventeen, and no responsibilities but to read the books and know what was in them. She couldn't resist sitting down at Ellen's tiny school-issue desk with the computer on it and turning it on. A list of files popped on the screen. French, Biology, Psychology. Hah, something familiar. April was taking psychology. She punched Psychology and a list of papers came up.

April didn't see anything she recognized. At John Jay they taught her class psychology along with history. So she got the Napoleon complex in conjunction with the conquest of Russia. She didn't know too much about Freud, but she knew Napoleon was exiled to Elba in 1814 and came back to Paris to rule a hundred days before his final defeat at Waterloo in 1815. And she had a pretty good idea what the complex was all about.

There were no short stories or diary notes in the computer, and there was absolutely no indication that the girl didn't plan to come back. It looked like she left her best stuff.

When April got back to the precinct, she called Connie's parents. They knew where their daughter was. It took three calls to Florida to get Connie on the phone.

"No, I don't know where Ellie went. Is something wrong?" a very young-sounding voice said when April identified herself.

"We're just trying to locate her," April said vaguely.

"I don't know where Ellie went," the girl repeated solemnly. "She said she wanted to go someplace warm."

"Florida?" April asked. "I get the feeling she's running away from family troubles. Is she with you?"

"No. We asked her but she didn't want to come," the girl said quickly.

"You could get in trouble if you're not telling the truth," April pressed. "You don't want to hamper an investigation, do you?"

There was a pause. "She's not that good a friend."

"Oh." April waited for more. She glanced down at the picture on her desk. The parents had given her several. The one on her desk was a color photo of a girl in shorts with a tennis racket in both hands. Ellen Roane was a pretty girl. Lot of hair, like her mother. Only hers was much lighter. Blue eyes, big smile that showed nice even white teeth.

"Why not?" April asked after a minute.

"I don't know. She's nice . . ." The voice trailed off.

The girl couldn't say why they weren't good friends. Fair enough.

"What about a boyfriend?" April asked. "Did she have a boyfriend she might have gone away with?"

"She had one for a while, but he dumped her."

"Recently?"

"Yeah, Ellie was pretty upset. That's why she didn't want to go with anybody. She wanted to be alone."

"When did you see her last?"

"I saw her when she left for the airport."

"The airport. Which airport?"

"I don't know. LaGuardia, I think. I don't remember which airline."

"What time was it?"

"It was afternoon."

Connie told April what Ellen was wearing when she left, and they hung up. Someplace warm. That left a lot of places. Mexico, the Caribbean, Florida. California. She checked the flights going out of LaGuardia to sunny places on Thursday afternoon a week before. There were a lot of them. The airlines didn't keep passenger lists for this long. And if Ellen were running away, she might not have used her own name anyway. Checking airlines was not a useful path to pursue. It was exactly a week since Ellen had left the city. She was due back in school the following Monday. April was quite certain she would be there.

She handed in her report. This was more detailed than the initial one. Now she knew what Ellen had been wearing, and the fact that she had most probably left the city of her own volition, probably by air, during a school vacation. The assignment notebook and calendar on her desk had corresponding stars in red ink to show when papers were due and test dates. Ellen was a conscientious and methodical student. The following Thursday was starred for a test with a note to "Study hard for this one." Nothing about her room indicated a girl who didn't intend to come back.

The case was not closed, however. Sergeant Joyce had received several calls from the parents—both parents, at different times— demanding a stepped-up investigation. Joyce assured the Roanes they were doing everything they could to locate the girl and told April to stay with it.

April called Jennifer Roane with another approach. "Does Ellen have a credit card?" she asked.

"Why? Has it turned up?" Jennifer started to cry.

"No. But if she used it, it's a way of finding where she went. Her roommate says she left last Thursday for the airport."

"What?" Jennifer said, appalled. "You mean, she went somewhere?"

"It looks like it. Do you have the credit card number?"

"Just a minute."

Jennifer Roane was away for several minutes. Finally she came back with the credit card number. It was a MasterCard.

"Anybody else use this card?"

"Uh, her father. I have my own."

"Thanks."

April called MasterCard. "This is Detective Woo, NYPD. I need some information on recent charges to card number 956-1900-9424-1992."

"You'll have to talk to my supervisor."

"That's fine. What's your supervisor's name?"

After a brief discussion with the supervisor, April faxed an official Police Department request for information to the MasterCard office. An hour later, she received a printout of charges to the account for the last month. Among them was a charge to American Airlines on the date Ellen left her dorm. And a number of charges to a restaurant and shops in—bingo: San Diego.

13

Jason slammed his appointment book shut on the five worrying letters to Emma that had come in the five days since his return from Toronto. Then he masked the movement by rearranging a few things on his desk and checking the answering machine to make sure it was on. As he did this, he realized it was absurd. Harold wouldn't notice his office under any circumstances. Harold never commented on anything but himself. Jason looked quickly around anyway.

His was the usual sort of psychiatrist's office, with a leather analyst's couch, a leather Eames chair behind it, a large desk covered with papers, and a rolling desk chair, also leather. He had covered the windows to the outside world with bamboo blinds, but left open a few tiny windows into himself for those patients who truly needed to find him. Antique clocks came and went as he added to his collection and moved them about. But none in here distracted by ticking loudly or chiming the hour. A number of prints, needlepoint pillows, knickknacks, and mementos in a wide variety of tastes and quality, given him over the years by his patients, companionably coexisted with his books on every available surface in the room. Years ago he used to hide everything away, as if personal things from his patients might reveal their names and crowd the space with their voices. But now he knew therapy did not require empty spaces and blank walls to be successful.

For people like Harold, the walls were as good as blank anyway. He didn't care what was on them. Today he nodded at Jason, but didn't actually greet him, look at him, or ask how he was. As far as Harold was concerned, his psychiatrist had absolutely no life beyond taking care of him. Jason knew this, and knew that Harold didn't see the dark shadows under his eyes or the turmoil behind them.

He stood as Harold crossed the room with a loping walk and sat in the Eames chair next to the desk. Harold had always been meticulously dressed and was now. Very distinguished. He was wearing a dark suit with a gray silk tie, a white shirt, and black shoes. His hair was cut very short. He was an inch or two taller than Jason, and ten years older. His hair was almost all gray now. Two years ago when Harold first came to Jason, his hair had been black. He had been a big beefy man. Now he was caved in. His cheeks looked as if they had been deflated. His mouth had thinned out into a line. Often— several times in a session at least—he sucked his lips inside his mouth and closed his teeth over them as if to stop himself from saying or doing something. Jason had a French clock on the shelf that was a brass bull standing on a clock face. That was Harold two years ago, bullish on himself.

"I had a dream about Marilyn last night," Harold said.

Jason sat in his chair and rolled it away from his desk into the center of the room, trying to quell his anguish. Emma had appeared in a quirky and sexual movie, and now somebody was writing upsetting letters to her. He shifted in his seat but couldn't relax.

One letter came every day on the dot, very strange and rambling letters that no psychiatrist could read without being concerned. They were signed, *The Friend That Saved You.* Jason kept asking her to think, *think* about what this might mean, but Emma drew a blank on ever being saved by anybody.

"Tell me about the dream," Jason said to Harold, and thought about the letters.

There was a lot of Right and Wrong in them. Maybe they were some religious thing. They mentioned right path, wrong path, *the fire that burned but didn't consume.* In the Bible that might be the burning bush. But hellfire also burned without consuming. *Once saved, now damned to burning.* That sounded pretty vengeful to him.

Emma thought they were equal to the kind of chain letters they got as kids that threatened bad luck if you didn't copy them and send them to fourteen friends. Curses like, your mother wears army boots. Drop dead. Burn in Hell. She argued there was nothing to it. Jason knew she was wrong; there was something to this. He just didn't know what.

"How long will this go on?" Harold asked.

"A long time."

"I thought when she died I would get some relief. But, I don't know. I feel worse." Harold let his chin sink down on his chest.

"You'll feel worse for a while, and then you'll feel better," Jason murmured.

"I don't know. I can't eat. I can't sleep. I walk around at night. I can't even concentrate on a movie or anything. I just keep thinking about those nights, you know, when she was so sick. She didn't want anybody else to touch her. I told you that. I had to take her to the bathroom. And she—" Harold covered his face with his hands.

"What was the dream?" Jason asked again.

There was another letter sitting with today's mail on the table in the hall. Emma was out having lunch with someone, and hadn't seen it yet. Jason felt a deep pang of jealousy over the lunch. He never had lunch. Now she was always out at lunch, had lunch every day and was never hungry for dinner. He looked at the bull clock on the shelf. Definitely still at lunch.

"I was with a prostitute. We were having drinks. We were negotiating her price. Marilyn came in. She was very angry. Then she went into the kitchen and started washing dishes. I think we were on an ocean liner. But it had no captain. It was sort of drifting, wallowing in the water. I took the prostitute out on deck. It was, like, all foam rubber. We started, uh, doing it on the foam rubber deck. She was very skinny and small. She felt like a little girl. My dick was tiny, about as thin as a pencil. It was . . . horrible. It didn't feel like my own."

Jason sighed and shook his head.

"I mean really *numb.*" Harold frowned. "What do you think?"

He couldn't understand why Emma wasn't alarmed by the intrusion of the letters into her life. It didn't take years of training to see they came from a disturbed mind. Jason didn't like the idea of a disturbed mind fixated on Emma.

"What do you make of it?" Harold demanded.

The postmarks were all impossible to read. You couldn't see where they came from, or even the date. That didn't worry her either. Maybe it was the military upbringing. You just didn't withdraw from danger in the military.

"Dr. Frank, why are you looking at me like that?"

Jason focused. Harold's face was red. His lips were caught between his teeth, and he was breathing loudly through his nose. He was being frowned at by his doctor. He didn't like that.

"Am I going crazy? Is that it?" he demanded wildly.

"No," Jason said, alarmed that once again he had slipped away in the middle of a session. "You're not going crazy."

"Then why are you looking at me like that?"

"I'm just concentrating," Jason said. "I wasn't looking in any particular way. Tell me about the dream."

"I just did, didn't you hear me?" Harold gnawed his lips again.

Shit. Jason bit the inside of his own lip with fury at himself. He was having trouble concentrating. It was his fault, not Harold's. There was steam coming out of Harold's every orifice. Jason could see it. Harold was an important man. Very few people dared to thwart him in any way. That was one of the reasons Marilyn's death hit him so hard. Death hadn't spared him, and he couldn't take it.

"Can you remember anything else about the dream? Any other details?" Jason asked. He hadn't been listening to the whole thing and couldn't begin to comment on it. Shit and shit again.

"What does it mean? You really think I'm in trouble, don't you?" Tears filled Harold's eyes.

Jason shook his head with horror. He was making his patients cry. One after another. They were having dreams about ships without captains and rudders, about trains off the rails. Pilotless airplanes. Wallowing in quicksand. Jesus.

Jason had been thinking about the letters in his appointment book, and the unopened letter on the mail table. Harold had lost his wife. She died after a long and terrible decline. Harold was trying to get over it. But he, Jason, was the one in trouble.

"I did go to a prostitute." Harold wept. "First time in my life." He blew his nose. "And I couldn't feel it. Couldn't feel a thing. You think I'm disgusting, don't you?"

"No," Jason said empathically. Normal, all normal. "We'll have to talk a lot about this."

There was a click on the phone, the answering machine kicking in. He wondered if it was Emma, calling to say she was back from another glamorous lunch. His eyes moved to the carriage clock on his desk. He had fifteen minutes to get Harold's ship back on course. He got the ship back on course and ushered Harold out, then punched the button on his answering machine.

"*Jason, it's Charles. Listen, Brenda and I would love to have you and Emma over for a social day. We're in town this weekend. How about Sunday?*"

14

It was a hot, clear, California day with a deep blue sky and no sign of smog north of Pacific Beach when Troland took the second of his many steps to make things Right. He headed up the Five to sell his bike. Looking back, he saw a gray haze over the city.

He wore sunglasses but no helmet. He liked the feeling of the wind whipping at his face. He didn't want to go all the way to Santa Monica or Malibu, so he got off the highway at Torrey Pines. He rode around Del Mar and Mirmar for a while, then headed to the better bike shop. It was on a different planet from Stephen's Motorcycle Salvage where he and Willy used to go. This was the kind of place with ads that said you meet the nicest people on a Honda.

There wasn't another Harley like his either on the street or in the window of the shop. The only bikes he saw here were Hondas, Kawasakis—Yuppie Jap bikes with the guts all covered up. Riding a bike like that was like fucking a girl with all her clothes on.

He parked in front of the diner across the street. One of his voices told him he was hungry, so he went inside. Bikers were scattered around at a few tables drinking beer. Troland sat at a table in the front by the window, where he could see his bike prominently parked by the door.

A short, tired-looking blonde in a white bikini top and denim shorts came over with an order pad.

"Hi, I'm Jean. What can I get for you?" she said pleasantly.

"I'll have a pitcher of draft, double cheeseburger, and fries."

"Sure thing."

He looked at her retreating back. The round ass, jiggling under the short shorts, held no interest for him. He couldn't concentrate on wanting to hurt her. It made him feel cursed. He couldn't even think about taking her out on the desert where no one could see or hear anything and sticking her dry little cunt. He didn't think of this one screaming, trying to kick him with sandy bare feet, and missing. Breaking her arm. It usually made him feel good to think about it.

The little blonde put the foaming beer down. "Anything else I can get you?"

"No," he said flatly. He had been sitting very still, staring straight ahead since he came in.

She hesitated for a second. "You okay?" she asked.

"You got a problem?"

"No." She turned away quickly.

He didn't turn to look after her this time. He knew he'd been brought real low if he had no interest in sex. It was like they all got together and did something to his balls so his dick wouldn't work anymore.

The girl returned with the plate and put it down gently in front of him. She moved the ketchup bottle closer and took off without a word. Troland looked down at the plate, then drank some beer.

A kid with a cross dangling from one earlobe, stringy hair, and bare feet in holey sneakers approached the table cautiously.

"Nice scooter, man. Looks low."

Troland nodded without looking at him. "It's been stretched and lowered."

"No shit."

Troland picked up the cheeseburger and took a huge bite. He chewed and swallowed before answering.

"It's for sale," he said flatly. "Wanna buy it?"

"You're kidding."

"I don't kid."

"But it looks brand-new," the kid protested. "It's just last year's. It's not even a year old." He sat down without being invited.

"It's two years old, but I spent a year customizing it. Yeah, I guess it is brand-new." Troland poured half a bottle of ketchup on his plate.

"Stretched and lowered, huh." The kid watched him, eyes narrowed.

Troland's plate became a sea of red.

"Hey, you really like that stuff."

"Yeah." Troland dipped his hand into it and licked his fingers. "Tastes better than blood."

The boy laughed.

"The bike's for sale," Troland said flatly. He could tell by the way the kid walked he had money, probably even went to college. Poor kids didn't look like that. "Want it?"

"Well, sure I want it. Who wouldn't?"

Troland lifted the plate and stuck his tongue in the ketchup.

The kid watched him uncomfortably. "Uh, how much do you want for it?"

"You can't afford it, out of your range."

"I got enough out of my dad to buy a Fat Bob," the kid said indignantly.

Troland nodded. That meant he had eleven grand. "This is better than a Fat Bob."

The kid didn't even pause. "Let's have a look," he said.

A few minutes later he was squatting in front of it, looking the Harley over, touching it here and there, smelling it even.

Troland answered all his questions in a dead voice. Yeah it was a real nice bike. He handed over the keys and let the long-haired freak go for a ride.

"You okay?" the kid asked when he came back fifteen minutes later.

Troland's face was frozen behind his sunglasses. He had hardly moved during the whole process.

"You got a problem?"

"Uh, no," the kid said nervously. "You just seem kinda—I don't know." He paused. "Ah, is it hot?" he asked finally.

Troland reached in his pocket for the registration and the re-

ceipt from the bike shop in San Diego where he had bought it. Two
and a half hours later he was on a bus, heading back to Pacific
Beach with the kid's check in his wallet. Now he had plenty of
money. All the way home, and deep into the night, Willy's voice told
him he did good.

15

"Yes, New York is still waiting," April said as patiently as she could.

In San Diego they couldn't say Woo. When April said, "This is Detective Woo from New York," they said "Who?" She refused to play games.

"Never mind. Just tell Sergeant Coconut Grove it's the detective from NYPD."

Next to her Sergeant Sanchez laughed.

April lowered her eyes. Now he was not only staring at her, he was listening to her conversations, too.

Sanchez sat at the desk in front of hers. To stare at her properly, he had to sit sideways with his back to the window. If she sat facing the front of her desk and looked up just a tiny bit, she looked right at the middle section of his body. If she tilted her head just a tiny bit to the right she saw the upper part of him, his chest and shoulders and head.

His phone, like hers, was often plugged into his ear, but he sat leaning back in his chair, with his feet on one of the open drawers, looking at her. This was very disturbing for many reasons. One was that everybody knew it. And when people in a precinct knew things, they teased.

"Where's your boyfriend?" people said when Sanchez was out in the field, and someone was looking for him.

It drove her crazy.

Just now the room was full of people. There was a black guy carrying on in the pen. They'd just brought him in. There wasn't a mark on him; his shirt was tucked in. No one was even near him, and already he was complaining loudly about police brutality. Must be twenty-five people in the room, and no one was paying any attention to him. They always said that.

It was hard to concentrate with so many things going on. She was trying to talk to San Diego, and something had happened in Central Park so the room was filling up. She hadn't been called in on it, so she didn't even know what it was. And right in the middle of it, while she was waiting for her contact in the San Diego Police Department to get on the phone, Sanchez was looking at her so that anybody looking at him would know exactly what he was thinking.

She wished she could handle these things the way Sergeant Joyce did. Sergeant Joyce had already passed her test for Lieutenant and was waiting for her number to come up to get the promotion. She was only thirty-six, Irish, with wanna-be yellow hair cut like April's. But she was tougher and had a sharp tongue. She could swing her hips and not look stupid, make a joke back when someone flirted with her. She was decisive and powerful. Sergeant Joyce would never get stuck lowering her eyes like some caricature of the demure Oriental.

April tapped her finger on the desk and switched her thoughts to Jimmy Wong, with whom she had worked on a case once, and got to know when she was in the 5th. That was two years ago. Jimmy Wong would never let anybody know he was interested in her. Never in a million years, not for a ten-million-dollar lottery. He just wouldn't. He was on Night Watch in Brooklyn now, which meant he went out on whatever calls came in from the whole borough from eleven o'clock at night on.

April worked some days, some nights, but in the precincts the night shift of the detective squad ended at eleven. Jimmy Wong said he was waiting for a promotion to ask her to marry him, but she doubted he would ask her if she was transferred back to the 5th and got hers first. It would not stop her, though. Sergeant Joyce's police officer husband divorced her, and left her with two small children, when she went into the Academy. April wanted to be like her. Sergeant Woo, BA, MA. Some day. She wasn't sure she wanted to marry Jimmy Wong anyway.

"Yes, I'm holding," she told San Diego, looking down so she would not have to make eye contact with Sanchez.

April had a list of things she knew and did not know about Sanchez. She also had a list of things she didn't like about him. First and foremost she did not like being aware of him. And she could not help being aware of him. He draped his body in front of her and used some kind of after-shave that was very powerful. He didn't just wear it on special occasions, either. It was there every day.

Once when she was in a Cosmetics Plus store, she smelled all the men's cologne trying to find which one it was. She wasn't much of a detective; she couldn't find it. But maybe she wasn't a bad detective. Maybe the chemistry of his body changed the smell so she couldn't identify it once it was on him. She didn't like thinking about the chemistry of his body. But she couldn't help that, either. It was in front of her all the time.

She had given some thought to the fact that different kinds of men had different smells. This was the sort of thing no one would say, and she probably shouldn't even think, but she thought about it anyway, and wondered what effect things like hair and smell had on a long-term relationship like marriage.

Caucasian men had a sour smell. When she was little, she had been told this was because they ate cheese. Asians don't eat cheese. When she walked in a crowd in Chinatown, she could smell garlic coming out of the pores of Asians the way sour sweat did in other kinds of people.

Sanchez smelled so sweet she couldn't tell what his true smell was like. The worst thing was that she had gotten used to it, so she knew when he was in the room without having to see him. The sweetness was kind of comforting, and she missed it when it wasn't there.

Her thoughts shifted to the after-shave she had given Jimmy for Christmas. It was called Devin, was very expensive, and had a citrusy aroma. Jimmy made a face when he opened it and said it

smelled like urine. He said he'd never use it. But after he had
broken the cellophane on the box, she couldn't take it back. It gave
her a bad feeling about him. He was wiry and not much taller than
she was. She thought if he wasn't grateful or generous-minded before
he asked her to marry him, she'd have plenty of trouble pleasing him
after.

April gazed at Sanchez's arms as she waited for Sergeant Grove
to come on the line. The heat was too high in the building again, and
Sanchez had rolled up his sleeves. She could not help noticing the
fine black hairs he had right down to the backs of his hands. This led
April to speculate he probably had hair on his chest, too; somehow
she did not find this as unattractive and barbarian in a man as her
mother and aunts did.

Sanchez also had a mustache, which tried but did not succeed
in making him look fierce. The mustache was irritating because,
well, she wasn't sure why. Another thing was he smiled often, letting
people know when he was friendly and in a good mood. The Chinese
laughed or frowned, but rarely smiled. Everybody knew a smiling
Chinese was a troublemaker, probably a cheat and a liar. Sanchez's
smiles were confusing.

Two other items on the list were his physical type and his eyes.
April was disapproving of both Chinese body types—chubby with
undefined musculature, and thin with undefined musculature. She
disliked her own flatness so much she exercised with free weights
every night to encourage her shoulders and buttocks to become more
rounded. Nothing short of surgery could change her eyes, though.

Sanchez had well-formed eyes and a well-proportioned body
large enough to carry someone much bigger than herself from a
burning building, if the need ever arose. There had been more than
one burning building in April's childhood, so it was the sort of thing
she thought about.

She did not like being attracted to Sanchez. And the thing she
disliked about him the most was the fact that he was a fish *in* water.
He belonged where he was. He spoke Spanish on the phone. He
spoke Spanish to people on the street. He had cases that involved

his people. His eyes danced with his happiness at being where he was. April wanted her fins back in her own water. She did not want to have to study him with interest. He was Hispanic, she was Chinese. They were structurally different, and not bilingual in the same languages.

Her thoughts about Sanchez were cut off by the San Diego P.D. They had finally managed to locate Sergeant Grove.

"Missing Persons, Sergeant Grove," he said.

"Yes, Sergeant Grove, thank you for coming to the phone. This is Detective Woo in New York. I'm calling about the Ellen Roane case. Have you found anything?"

"How are you doing, Detective? Nope. I told you, we've got eight Jane Does here. Had five of them around before your girl disappeared. And none of them is a match. Three Mexican, two black. We have three Caucasians, but they're all older women."

"Is there any chance you could take her picture around in the neighborhood where she put the charges on the credit card, and see if you can locate her?" April wasn't exactly looking for the girl's body, and had counted on Grove's not coming up with it. Ellen Roane would probably be back in her dorm room in two days, mad at her parents for making such a fuss. April had seen it a hundred times before. Still . . .

"Hey, I can check out the hospitals and the ME's office. I've already done that, but you know as well as I do that our job is to match names with bodies. We want to get the dead ones buried. We can't go looking for every kid that takes off on a lark."

"Is there anybody who can go out in the field for a few hours?" April said patiently.

There was a short pause. "Look, I only tried the city. Do you want me to try the surrounding jurisdictions?"

"Yes, might as well," April said, discouraged.

"Detective?"

"Yes, Sergeant."

"How's the weather in New York?"

"It's forty-six degrees and raining."

"It's seventy-eight and real sunny here."

"Thank you for sharing that with me, Sergeant."

They said their good-byes and hung up.

"He hit on you?" Sanchez asked.

April shook her head. "I don't have a good feeling about this."

It was Friday, more than a week since Ellen had left for San Diego and used her MasterCard to buy food and clothes. There had been no new charges on the credit card in three days. Where was she eating? Where was she staying? April had checked with American Airlines on Ellen's return ticket, and found out that Ellen did not show up for the flight she was booked on. College had started up again, and she was not back. Something was wrong.

And what was wrong with the system was that the San Diego P.D. would not send someone out with her picture to find out what happened to her unless they had good reason to believe a crime involving her had been committed. Ellen had to commit a crime herself, or be abducted with a number of witnesses looking on. That was on the SDPD side. NYPD would not send someone out there to look for her under any circumstances.

It was not easy to tell parents that the network of police departments and the FBI did not actually investigate missing persons. What they did was try to match descriptions with unidentified bodies. It was terrible, but if the Roanes wanted to find their daughter, they would probably have to hire a private detective to look for her. April reached for the phone to tell them if she wasn't able to come up with something soon, a private detective was their best option.

16

Troland took the girl to the crummy house he grew up in. Back then, the streets around it had been quiet. When he and his brothers drove by, their bikes blaring a continual fart, people used to come out on their porches to see what was going on. Not anymore. The houses had gone down. Some of the porches were about falling off, and whole families were living on them, lying out there in hammocks with the Latino music blasting. Laughing, smoking, arguing in loud voices. Everywhere there was the smell of beans and frying foods. Broken-down cars were parked on the street, in the short weedy drives. Shit. His mother died seven years ago, and his aunt Lela had been living there ever since. He'd given her a trip to Disneyland to get rid of her for a few days, and offered to look after her house for her. She'd handed over the keys and taken off.

Troland unlocked the door and the girl followed him in.

"This your place, Willy?" she asked.

He was a foot or two away from her. Suddenly his hand whipped out, caught her arm, and wheeled her around to look at him.

"Hey, that hurts. What's the matter?" Tears sprouted in her eyes.

"Don't call me Willy," he snapped. Willy's voice thundered in his ear. *Only Willy is the real Willy.*

"I thought that was your name." She sniffed, trying to hold back a sob.

"Don't cry. I don't like crying."

"What's the *matter?*" She gulped a little, pulling on her arm to get him to release her.

"Nothing. Just do it right." He looked at her so intensely, she turned her head away from his eyes.

"You're not going to be weird, are you?" she said faintly. "Weird scares me."

Troland snorted. "What's weird?"

"Uh, I don't know." Her eyes were on the coke.

He had pulled some cellophane packages out of his pocket. He put one package down on the table and went to check the doors. Front door locked. Back door locked. Windows locked. He made some patterns with his foot around each entrance, to seal it from the outside. He went around the house three times, first to check the doors and windows, then to pull down the discolored old blinds. Finally he came back to the table and laid out a large piece of paper to put the lines of powder on.

"Hey, what's that?"

"What does it look like?"

She shivered. The paper was almost completely covered by a drawing, very vivid with strong reds and blues.

"I don't know." She leaned closer.

Her blond hair fell over her face, and she didn't brush it back as she tried to figure it out.

"Uh, two snakes with wings?" she guessed. "No, an eagle with two snakes in his mouth. Ugh, it has teeth, and it looks like the whole thing's burning up around the edges."

"Great, huh?"

She raised one shoulder, noncommittal.

"I drew it," he said flatly.

"Uh, no kidding. Can we have that now?"

He gave her two generous lines and watched her expertly snort every tiny grain. She breathed deeply a few times, shuddering, then turned to him.

"Your turn."

"Go away. I like to do it alone," he said.

She wandered back into the dining room and took her clothes off. She started dancing naked to music in her head. For a few minutes, Troland watched her grinding away for his benefit. She had a small flat ass, no hips, and a stomach like a board. Probably hadn't eaten anything in months. The girl was way into it. He wasn't turned on.

"Hurry up," she said. "I'm waiting for you."

He frowned at the command and turned his attention to the coke. He had to have something, but didn't want as much as she had had. Finally he turned his back to her and took a little, just enough to enjoy it. He sniffed a few times afterward, letting himself go with it. He felt better.

"Com'ere."

She danced over to where he stood by the table, humming to herself and snapping her fingers.

"Unzip my jeans."

She unbuttoned the button, then began on his zipper, opening her thighs around his legs and pressing her flat chest against his shirt with her two hands between them. He wasn't wearing anything under his jeans. She reached in and giggled.

"Ah." She rubbed with one hand and pulled at his jeans with the other.

"No, leave them on," he said.

"Don't you want to get undressed?"

She started yanking his shirt up, but he jerked away from her before she could get it very far.

"I said no. Do it right."

"What's right for you?" She sounded peevish.

"On your knees."

She looked at the worn carpet on the floor, the dining table and the chairs around it, puzzled. "Where?"

"Here. Suck." He planted himself in the chair with his legs apart. He turned his head away from her and studied the drawing as the girl got on her knees and started rubbing his inner thighs, the bare V of his stomach where his jeans were open. She nudged him out and rubbed for a while, then lowered her head over him.

"Wait. Put this on." He dropped a condom on the floor beside her.

"Geez," she muttered. She tore the foil, pulled it out, and unrolled it.

He watched her to see that she did it right, put it on so that none of her filthy germs could get inside. All the way up he wanted it. She pulled it all the way up.

He looked at his drawing some more as she put her mouth around him and squeezed· tight with her lips. She moved up and down, slowly at first and then hard.

"That's good, more tongue," he said. "Yeah." He closed his eyes and reached for her tits. He couldn't get to them. Both her hands and her mouth were working on him. He tried to get into it.

Finally he stood up, moved her aside like a piece of furniture, and went into the bathroom to take a leak. When he came back, she was on the same place on the floor. On her hands and knees wiggling her ass at him like a picture come alive from a nudie magazine.

"You didn't come, did you?"

He sat down again, ignoring her.

"Let's try something else," she said.

He looked at her. She was up, up, up, showed no signs of fatigue even though she'd been at him for thirty minutes at least. He'd lost interest. He had his true purpose in mind now.

"Hey, whatever your name is. Come on." Her tongue darted in and out of her mouth as she wagged her tail.

He laid his pens out. Then he carefully put the transfer paper over the design and taped the edges.

The girl frowned. "Hey, do me now," she said.

"Go take a nap."

"I don't want to take a nap." She stuck her tongue in his ear. "Come on, you want a good time, don't you?" She began moving against him, rubbing her pointy breasts back and forth across his arm, nuzzling his neck.

"Beat it. I'm busy."

"I wanna do it," she whined. "Come on, let's fuck."

"Later."

"I don't wanna do it later." She backed away from him so he could get a better view of her. "Hey, look." She posed, standing a few different ways, then bent over so he could see her crotch, anus, everything.

He wasn't looking, though. He paid no attention to her as she crawled under the table. Suddenly her head poked up between his legs and she had him in her hand. A firm grip on his balls and cock. He jumped a foot.

"What the fuck? Get away from me, you crazy cunt." He pushed her away furiously.

"But I'm not finished. I want to do it," she complained.

"You want it so much, do it to yourself."

She put one hand on her hip and tossed her blond hair impatiently. "Hey, don't you have what it takes?"

He reddened. She had no idea what he could do to her. The big wave rose, almost taking over. Then he glanced down at his beautiful drawing and his true purpose. Willy told him to let it go. He let the wave go back.

"I said I'm busy now. Do it to yourself."

"*All right.*" She sniffed angrily and put her hand to her crotch. She had a very small tuft of light brown hair. She started exploring it with her fingers. She became engrossed almost immediately.

For a minute or two she stood there swaying in front of him, dancing to the music in her head with both hands teasing at her crotch. Then suddenly she squatted on her heels and shoved her two fingers as deep inside as she could get them.

17

"Have you checked with Sex Crimes?" Milt asked.

Newt stirred his coffee with a bent spoon. Absently he bent it back into shape. "Yes. No burning or branding cases in San Diego at the moment. Plenty of other kinds of assault, though. They have a rapist that dresses up as Superman, even has a cape."

They were in the café down the street from the sheriff's office, talking the situation over. The coroner's report had been filed. The data on the unidentified dead girl was in the computer. Now they had to wait and see if something came up.

Milt started on his second doughnut. It was heavily frosted with glaze. Whenever he was distressed, he ate. He was silent, chewing thoughtfully.

"What about your friend in Twenty-Nine Palms?" Newt asked. He wasn't going to eat a doughnut no matter how tempted he got. They gave him heartburn. He kept that heartburn in mind as he watched Milt swallow.

"I was getting to that. I sent him the report, the photographs, everything," Milt replied, licking his fingers.

"And?"

"And he's on his way up here to have a look. He says the shape of the brand, or the object that made the burn, was not quite as clear on his victim. The appearance of the burn was altered by a superimposed bacterial infection of the surrounding skin. You know—gas formation, skin slippage."

"What does that mean to me, Milt?"

"That means the girl in Twenty-Nine Palms may have lived longer. Her wounds became infected *before* she died. He wasn't even absolutely sure it was a brand. Except that even with the swelling and blurring around the edges, it had a very distinct shape. Now we have a better picture of it. It's the only thing we have to go on. Maybe it's his totem, or something."

"Christ."

Milt swallowed some cold coffee. "Real unusual. I've never seen anything like this. There's no physical evidence at all."

Newt nodded grimly. "That's what Sex Crimes said. If they mutilate them, they usually kill them first. Very rare to torture them and then let them go."

"The girl in Palms was found only a quarter of a mile from the road. She may have walked a long way. A little farther and she might even have been saved. You have any idea what it's like to die of dehydration?"

Newt didn't answer. He watched Milt take another doughnut.

"It's a slow, agonizing death," Milt said, his mouth full. "There's military medical literature on it from American and Nazi soldiers who fought in the African Campaign in World War Two."

"I'll be sure to read it." Newt shook his head apologetically. "Sorry. I just keep thinking there might be others out there. What do we do, get a copter and patrol a hundred of miles of desert, in case he decides to do it again?"

"Oh, he'll do it again," Milt said.

"Jesus. A serial brander whose victims die of—what would you say—natural causes?"

Milt put some money down. "No, I wouldn't say that."

"Maybe we ought to get the computer people on it. Maybe it's not a local person, and there are cases of it somewhere else."

"Maybe."

"But you don't think so?" Newt said dejectedly.

"Newt, I have no idea. I don't even know if VICAP would even come in on something like this."

Milt got up and dusted the sugar off the front of his shirt. After he had been gone for a minute or two, Newt ordered a doughnut.

18

"Great lunch," Jason said.

"Yeah, it's great to be together," Charles agreed.

It was about fifty-five outside, the warmest day in months. Charles and Jason walked along the East River after lunch in Charles's elegant apartment on East End Avenue.

"Isn't this great?" Charles demanded. He pointed out to the water where a large sloop sailed between two barges. "Look at that boat. God, I'd love a boat."

"When would you use it?" Jason laughed. "With the country house and the Caribbean vacations, skiing trips to Vail . . . Must be tough."

Charles hunched his shoulders a little at the dig. Charles, who looked like he could be Jason's brother, came from an extremely wealthy Westchester family. Jason came from the Bronx, had scholarships in college and medical school, and helped support his family all through his training. They met the first day at the New York Psychiatric Center where they did their training, and had been friends ever since.

"I don't know. I'd find the time. I want to take up sailing. I didn't sail as a kid. Did you?"

"No," Jason said. The Bronx didn't have much of a coastline. And his family's primary concern had been food and shelter.

"Don't have kids," they liked to tell him. "They'll drain you of your life's blood and keep you as poor as we are."

Now they were mad because he was married to a shiksa and

were convinced God had made her barren to punish him. Jason had given them no grandchildren; what kind of son was that? They didn't know *he* was the ambitious one, the one in the marriage who didn't want life complicated by children. Until recently, Emma hadn't seemed to care very much, either. Only recently had the question of enlarging their family become an issue that smoldered away under the surface of their daily life. Now he was beginning to see how much Emma wanted and needed a child.

Charles strode along, breathing deeply. "Isn't this great? I just can't stand being in the city on weekends. I feel caged. I really do. I need to be outside." He swung his arms. "I need exercise."

"Don't you run?" Jason asked. Like Emma, Jason liked to run. It was good for the heart, made his body strong, and gave him energy. It was like taking an upper. The view wasn't much different on Riverside Drive. They had good paths and trees and a river over there, too.

"Oh, yeah, and I go to the gym and play racquetball, but that's a sprinter's game. It's not like standing back at the baseline in tennis and really smashing the ball."

"No," Jason said.

"Well, I can't complain. Brenda had my office redecorated. It's really nice now. I work a half a day a week at the hospital, to keep my hand in. Go away most weekends." And there was Rosalie. Charles didn't mention Rosalie, a colleague he popped from time to time when opportunity presented itself. He didn't tell Jason things like that anymore. "Life is a well-oiled machine these days. Everything in its place and running smoothly. We've got it made. You're the famous one. I'm the drone." Charles laughed.

Jason had been putting one foot in front of the other, listening, listening. All afternoon. Listening with empathy was what he was famous for. Now he could contain himself no longer.

"Look, Charles. Something terrible is happening to me," he blurted out. "I don't know. I just—I'm falling apart. . . ." Jason's steps faltered.

They were just at the bottom of the park, about to head back to

Seventy-ninth Street down the broad walk along the river. Charles caught him under the arm. His somewhat vacant, smug expression was instantly wiped away. The intense, searching face that Jason used to know and hadn't seen in many years reappeared.

It was the face of the young Charles who had come to work on the sixth floor of the Center one morning in their second year to find a beautiful, sixteen-year-old, acutely psychotic patient hanging by the neck on an exposed pipe in the ceiling. All her vital signs were gone, but Charles wouldn't accept her death. He had never accepted the credo that patients like her couldn't be treated with psychotherapy, either. He resuscitated her, and treated her for years after his training was completed. The girl recovered and never had another psychotic incident.

Charles caught sight of an unoccupied bench and headed for it with his arm around Jason's shoulder.

"What's going on?" he asked.

Jason sat on the bench. "It's Emma."

"Is she involved with someone else?" Charles frowned when Jason didn't reply. "Oh, man, I'm sorry . . ."

Jason shook his head. "That's not it."

"Oh, *you're* involved with someone else." Charles cocked his head. "So, you had an accident. You fell. You can get through it."

"No, no, Charles, it's way beyond that. It's something you could never believe."

"You did a foursome. What? What could be so bad I couldn't believe it?"

Jason paused. "Did you see *Serpent's Teeth?*"

"No, what are they?" Charles looked confused.

"It's a movie. Haven't you seen the ads for it, the reviews?" Jason demanded irritably.

"No, what's so important about it?"

"Emma's in it," Jason said.

"Oh, I see," Charles replied. "Emma's in a movie. That's great."

"You haven't heard anything from anybody?" Jason demanded.

"No. I haven't. What's the big deal? What's the matter with it?"

Jason took a deep breath. "It's a porno film."

"Jesus." Charles's mouth dropped open. "Emma in a porno film?"

"Well, it's not a *porno* film. It's an *art* film. But she—" Jason sniffed. "She plays the part of a young woman in therapy. With this guy who's a creep. And there's no sound in their sessions."

"Jesus." Charles shook his head as if he had water in his ears.

"It's a really disturbing film. It makes therapy look . . . evil."

"And there's—sex in it?"

"Yeah. Emma fucks this hoodlum. She's—really nude. And she really does it. Well, it looks like it. You don't see penetration. We've seen penetration on the screen."

They both pushed a little air out of their noses, remembering the sex clinic training, the films for doctors showing sex between all kinds of people—Very fat. Old. People with colostomies. Paraplegics. They had seen a number of films made to teach doctors and staff at hospitals that the desire for love and sex didn't politely go away when people were old or ill, disfigured or disabled.

"Ahh." Charles scratched his chin. "I'm stunned."

"Yeah. Well, so was I."

"She didn't tell you about it?"

"No, she didn't tell me. I don't know what happened. I don't understand how she could do it. I just don't understand. If I could understand . . ." He shook his head again. "It's a horrible thing to see your wife . . . I'm a *doctor*."

"It's upsetting." Charles sat there with his mouth open. "But it's —just a film. It's not all bad. You can find your way together." He murmured consoling words, hardly knowing what he was saying. He heard terrible, distressing things from his patients all the time, but personally he lived in a world where cheating a little on one's spouse was about as bad as a person could get.

"But it *is* so bad. She got great reviews. This horrid film where this poor girl ends up getting herself tattooed—"

"She's tattooed? Jesus," Charles interrupted.

"That's how it ends."

"Jesus, is she really tattooed?"

"Of course not, it's a movie."

"Jason, this is amazing."

"Yeah, well, it's taken over our lives. She's being pursued by these big-shot agents. She's got movie offers."

"Jesus," Charles said a fifth time.

"She's fucked her way into the big time, Charles, and I'm just —" Jason turned away.

"Afraid you're going to lose her? Of course you are, but you know you love each other."

"Oh, man, if she could do this, I lost her a long time ago." Jason covered his face with his hands.

Charles put his arm around him again. "God, this is—I don't know what to say."

"And the worst thing is nothing will stop her. Not the letters. Not anything—" Jason stopped.

"What letters?"

"Ah, well, it's not your problem. Forget it."

"Come on, Jason, look at me. We've been through a lot together. What letters? Maybe I can help."

"Not this time, old buddy." Abruptly, Jason stood up. "Come on. We've left the girls alone together long enough."

19

"They want us," Ronnie said excitedly on the phone.

"Who does?" Emma asked. She had been in the shower when the phone rang.

"I don't know. Jack does, and Albert. They want us. You."

"Oh, right," Emma said. Jack and Albert. Sure. She cocked her head. A flash of light was reflected off the mirror. "Jason?" she called.

"What?" Ronnie demanded. "Emma? Are you there?"

"Sorry. I thought there was—"

"Did you hear what I said? We got a callback on *Wind,*" Ronnie said.

"Yeah, I heard you, but it can't *be,* Ronnie. I told you I was awful, really awful. And gorgeous, famous Bill North was awful, too. His breath stank. It was the *worst* audition I ever had." Emma grimaced, thinking about it. "It was *bad.*"

"Well, Elinor said Jack said you were a delight."

Jack? Ronnie was calling the producer, whom she had never met, Jack. And the director Albert? What a business.

"Jack was so delighted he never took the corned beef sandwich out of his mouth," Emma said.

"Jack's a *great* producer." Ronnie bristled. "What's the matter with you? I thought you'd be thrilled."

"I'm thrilled," Emma said. "What time do I have to be there?"

A minute later she dialed Jason's number. His office was two walls away in what used to be a wing of the apartment. He had a separate entrance. He couldn't get into the apartment from his office without going out into the hall. He had deliberately designed it that way.

He picked up. "Dr. Frank," he said.

"Jason, were you just here?"

"What?"

"I think someone was here a minute ago. Was it you?" Emma demanded.

"Are you sure?"

"Yes, I'm sure." She hesitated. "Well, no, not really. I just thought . . ." What did she think? That her own husband was trying to scare her? That was crazy.

"I'm with someone," he said.

"Oh, sorry." She hung up. That's what they always said: *I'm with someone.* "Never need a shrink," she muttered. "They're always *with* someone."

She felt like a fool for bothering him. She dried her hair, then went out to do the shopping. The old resentment, that he was always busy, always involved with someone else, gnawed at her, making her feel both hurt and lonely at the same time. She often wondered if other doctors' wives, particularly the wives of psychiatrists, felt as isolated and cut off from their husbands as she did. Or if her loneliness had nothing to do with him and was a throwback from her childhood when help and reassurance were out of the question.

Jason came home as the hallway clock was chiming eight-fifteen.

"Come here, darling," he said. He hugged her and took her hands. He examined them carefully, as if searching for disease. The backs of her hands were still young and smooth. Her fingers were slender and flawless. He turned them over and kissed the palms.

"You shouldn't have hung up," he murmured. "You were upset. I could have taken a minute."

"What could I have said in a minute?" she asked.

"Whatever you wanted. I know these letters are getting you down. There was another one today, wasn't there?"

"They're not getting me down," Emma said, dismissing the subject.

She picked up the script Ronnie had sent her for the next day's audition.

"Well, you're very tense for someone who says she's not upset. Maybe you should take some medicine." Jason looked at her intently. She didn't put the script down.

"It's not *getting to me,* Jason. I'm not going to fall apart because of a few weird letters. I'm not built that way."

Jason got up and left the room.

"That's right," she muttered. "Walk away."

He came back in a minute and handed her a drink.

"What's in this?" she said suspiciously.

"Nice things, what do you think?" Jason looked hurt.

"I think you're trying to scare me so I won't be in any more films," she said, getting back to his view of the letters that were now yet another issue between them.

"Why would I want to scare you? That doesn't make any sense, Emma. Don't you see it's transference? You're feeling guilty about the whole movie thing: the way you went about it, not telling me the whole story about what you were doing in it. And now you're feeling guilty because you're a big success."

She didn't take the drink he made for her, so he took a sip of it himself.

"My feelings about your career and these letters you're getting are two separate things. I'm dealing with them in two different ways. Trust me on this. I'm the doctor," Jason said.

"That's a lie. You went crazy and slept in the other room," she said.

"Look, I said I was sorry about that. You caught me by surprise. I had no idea you could hurt me that way." He drank the rest of the drink and set the glass down.

"And now you're writing me letters," she said, angrily. "I know it's you, Jason."

"Why would I do that, Emma?" Jason looked shocked.

"Because if I got the part in *Wind on the Water,* I'd make a lot of money and be more famous than you. I don't think you could take that."

Jason shook his head, appalled. "That's a pretty big indictment. Is that what you really think—that I'm petty and childish, that I would hurt you because you hurt me?"

Emma looked away.

"Is that what you really think?"

She couldn't answer the question.

"Look, Emma, I trusted you; I loved you. I still love you. If you get the part, then you'll have to decide if you want to take it. It's up to you, but you have to face the fact that there's more to being a film star than what I think about it. It's a *public thing.* There are crazy people out there who don't think it's a character on the screen. They think it's *you.*"

"Thank you, Doctor." She looked back at the script.

"You have to be careful and think about what you're doing."

She *was* thinking about what she was doing, and she still thought it had to be him, writing those letters. No one else knew those things about her. She watched him go into the kitchen for another drink.

Emma was still annoyed by the way the conversation ended as she cabbed down to the same place the first audition had been: 1351 Avenue of the Americas, thirty-third floor. Then she tried not to think about it as she watched the numbers on the elevator as it went up. She tried to concentrate on the job.

The first audition had gone terribly. She couldn't believe she was called back. Emma took a deep breath and tried to calm down. She had auditioned for the soaps a number of times, but was never cast. Now she didn't know if she was glad or sorry not to have had the experience of being on one.

What happens when a good woman goes wrong? Breaks a man's heart like a wheel. Shatters everything he thought was good in the world. Knife in the water. Fire in the sand.

What did it mean? What did those crazy letters mean? It didn't make any sense. *Knife in the Water* was a Roman Polanski film. His first hit, if her memory served. Twelfth floor. Was this supposed to be some kind of a threat because of what happened to Roman Polanski?

Wind on the Water also had a bad guy and a body. Was there a connection? It occurred to her that the first letter had come almost immediately after her audition for *Wind*. Or was it before? She couldn't remember anymore. Until then, being in films seemed like a path opening up, a way made clear. It was something she could give to herself, something she could do on her way to being old.

It didn't take a rocket scientist to understand that Jason was overcommitted; he was overstimulated by all the sorrows and conflicts of his patients. And slowly Emma had come to understand that it wasn't enough for her to hang around the edge of his life, waiting for the rare moments when he could tolerate any more demands coming at him. Even if he didn't want to, she knew that was how he experienced her love, her wish for more of him, for a family. And she knew that it didn't work to ask for more than a person could joyfully give. Tears flooded into her eyes whenever she thought of growing old without ever having a child.

Eighteenth floor. She didn't think it was some crazy out there writing letters about her going bad. There were things in those letters, things that happened to her, fears she had, that only Jason knew. Jason wanted to hypnotize her to see if he could dredge up something she had repressed, some person, some event from her past that could explain the letters. She didn't like it when he said, "Trust me on this. I'm a doctor. My training has taught me to see the obsession, the threat behind the words."

Okay, okay, forget the letters. This was serious. The movie was what she should be thinking about. Katie. What would Katie think, how would she move? What does she want?

It was difficult without the whole script. How could she do a movie if she didn't have a script? Emma tried to concentrate on what she knew about the story. Not a lot. Katie's been poor all her life.

She's the girlfriend of a rich Virginia lawyer who's putting her through law school.

Katie wants to be a lawyer with all her heart. Well, Emma could relate to that. But then she has a brief fling with a gas station attendant who may or may not be a psychopathic killer. The lawyer she sleeps with likes kinky sex. These two things were harder. If the girl has a character disorder, the fact that her professor in Jurisprudence is a really nice guy—the first decent man she's ever met—will not matter a lot.

Bill North was the gas station attendant. What a sleaze. Why on earth would a heroine do such stupid things? Emma's acting teachers always said she had to find the reasons, even when they weren't in the text. The girl liked to live dangerously? Jesus, was that a reason? Emma didn't like to live dangerously. She didn't even want to take a pill to make her feel better. Her thoughts drifted back to Jason. Jason knew how to manipulate the mind. How far would he go to stop her from acting?

Emma's heart beat faster past the twentieth floor. She breathed in for four counts, breathed out for eight. Oh, shit, this was awful. Ronnie had called her twice to tell her to wear a tight wrap blouse and a short skirt. The tighter the blouse, the more she sweat. She could feel the armpits sticking to her already. Good thing she wore a dark print that didn't show the stains when wet.

Fire in the sand, the last letter said. What the hell did that mean? The elevator door opened. Emma advanced to the reception desk.

"Emma Chapman," Emma said, licking her lips nervously.

"Oh, yes, they're waiting for you. Go right in."

Blond hair tied in a knot. Rainbow ribbons. Feathers, yellow green red black. Forget it. Forget the letters. Think Katie.

Emma opened the door and looked in. Three men and a tough-looking woman were in deep conversation around the conference table. Jack, the rude producer, who ate a corned beef sandwich during her first audition and belched loudly at the end of it. Albert, the director who had asked her no questions about herself and given her no guidelines about playing the scene, but carefully described the way he wanted her legs crossed. Elinor Zing, the casting director with her stacks of glossies (Emma's included) and legal pads covered with spidery notes. Yes, no, maybe so.

"Yes, yes, come in. We like you, don't be afraid," said Elinor Zing.

Okay. Emma stepped forward. Why on earth would anyone subject herself to this? Her heart thudded as three people graded her walk.

It was then that she noticed there was someone new in the room. Oh, God. He was *so handsome* in real life. This was someone whose work she really liked. Did Katie have a character disorder? Hey, did it matter, if the script said the devastating Michael Lambert, sitting at the conference table waiting to read with her, would fall in love with her and save her from everything, including herself.

She stared at him, trying not to let her mouth fall open. By any chance did he want to be the father of her child? Yes, no, maybe so.

He looked up and smiled. Emma stumbled.

"Great. That was great," Jack, the director said. "Wonderful choice."

Glad you liked it, Emma thought. Too bad it wasn't a choice. The smile of the movie star had almost made her fall on her face.

20

Sometimes at the end of the day outside thoughts drifted over April Woo like fog, and she would walk around in it for a few minutes, looking for ways to see through the confusion.

Sai Yuan, April's mother, came from Shanghai. April wanted to go there some day. Shanghai was supposed to be the Paris of China. A foreign port, bustling with activity, and metropolitan. Not like Beijing, which was landlocked on the edge of the Gobi Desert and gray with the grit of constantly blowing desert sand.

"In Old Time all houses in Beijing gray except Forbidden City, so Celestial Sun and Celestial Moon know where to shine brightest," April's mother told her.

"Now no more Imperial family, all gray," she would say, putting down China and building herself up at the same time as she patted herself on the front of her brightly colored cotton blouse ("Look like silk, no iron. Nine dollar.") that she wore to show Celestial Sun where to shine brightest in New York. Always strongest colors best for good luck was her policy.

"No good food in Beijing," she added. "Food taste better in Shanghai. But best food in Hong Kong. No good cook in China no more." She said this with sly look at husband Woo, best cook in America, picking his teeth with menthol-flavored toothpick and reading Chinese newspaper. Pretending he did not hear the compliment.

Sai Yuan was over thirty when she met Ja Fa Woo in Shanghai where he was cook in a big hotel for foreigners.

"Best cook. He knew how to make pizzi before anybody," Sai said.

The way Sai Woo told the story, they met and got married. She said it in the third person as if she had nothing to do with it.

How Sai Yuan and Ja Fa Woo got married was a question April tried to ask many times and never got a satisfactory answer. Chinese stories had their own meaning. What was left out might be a puzzle, might be a warning, might be to teach a lesson. Might be nothing. You couldn't know the reason.

For a long time when she was growing up, April was afraid whenever she met someone that she was in danger of getting married. Every year new boys came from China into her class, and she looked around, worrying and wondering which one was the one she would meet and marry. Then she learned you had to agree to marry. You had to want to.

Well, that was not the old way. Old way was matchmaker-arranged marriages according to money and status, and no one wanted to. Married for family honor. Married for face. But Sai's family was scattered like leaves when she was young.

"All dead," she said, not showing her face or telling the story of what she did in the years of the wars and turbulence without a family to honor.

The official story was they met and got married and left Shanghai. They had many hardships before they got to golden city. They had many hardships after they got to golden city. Wasn't so golden. One hardship was no one in New York spoke Mandarin. Sai had to learn Cantonese to get along, never mind English.

Now they lived in a nice house in Queens and had no worries. Except they worried all the time. Sai Woo wanted April to make herself nice so she could meet someone and marry, and come up in the world like she did. She had a house—the whole thing, not just the first floor like Mei Mei. Not so good her daughter, closer to thirty every day, and triple stupid.

April tried to tell her things were different. You don't just meet and marry. "Ma, you have to fall in love now."

"Pah, what's that? A lily blooms only one day. So what. You marry a doctor. You have a nice house like this, best food and good clothes whole life. That's love." Sai Woo sucked best dinner out of her teeth, with the help of a menthol-flavored toothpick, behind her hand because she wasn't rough peasant woman.

These were the things April worried about at night. How she would find the time to get her degree before her hair turned gray. How she would get to be sergeant if she was stuck on the upper West Side in dry dock. How was she going to find out what happened to that college girl if she couldn't leave New York. She'd seen many sad things before, and now she was upset by the profound grief of Jennifer Roane. Jennifer Roane had only this one daughter, like her mother Sai Woo had only her. Only this kind of mother was different. She seemed to have an almost unlimited capacity for grief, and no fear of showing it. Caucasians showed their faces.

April was concluding that a comfortable life and a good-looking man in an expensive suit did not necessarily give you everything, like her mother said. Her mother talked on two sides of her face. She said April had it easy being born where they had plenty to eat and anything was possible. It sounded like hardship made her kind of superior just for suffering. But when April didn't make it easy for herself and be an accountant for Merrill Lynch or marry a doctor, her mother just thought she was double stupid. Why risk danger? Why look for bad things if you don't have to?

"You should honor your parents." Even her father, who didn't listen to women talking, nodded when Sai Woo said that.

April thought she was honoring her parents. She was just doing it the American way. She wondered if there was anything she could say to Sergeant seventy-eight-degrees-and-real-sunny Grove that would get him to move his feet a little and find out where Ellen Roane stayed, and what she did those three days when she made six charges on her credit card in San Diego.

She was thinking about Sergeant Grove when her phone rang and it was him on the other end of the line.

"Detective Woo," he said. "This is Sergeant Grove in San Diego. How's the weather out there?"

April shivered involuntarily. There was only one reason that she would be hearing from Sergeant Grove, and it wasn't for him to get a weather report. He could get that from the paper or the evening news.

"It's still in the fifties and raining," April said.

"Still?"

"That's how it is here in spring."

"That's too bad. It's still eighty and sunny here."

"Do you have something for me, Sergeant?"

"A possible match to your Roane girl just came in from a local Sheriff's Office."

"Where?" April asked.

"North of here, town in the hills. She was found by some dirt bikers in the desert."

"How did she die?"

"It appears she was tortured and left out there. Apparently she wandered around, and died of dehydration, exposure to the elements. It gets pretty hot and cold in the desert."

"Any identifying articles—her wallet, clothes, jewelry?"

"Absolutely nothing. She was found naked."

"Oh, God. You mean she wandered around naked?"

"Yes."

"Can you fax me a picture for identification?" April asked, thinking the body he had could be anybody, anybody at all.

"A picture isn't going to do it, Detective. I'm going to need her prints and dental records, X rays, whatever you can get for me."

"Is she in that bad condition?" April asked faintly.

"Well, the buzzards got to her face."

"Oh, God." April took a deep breath. "Who will be investigating the case?"

"The sheriff in the jurisdiction she was found."

"I know that," April said. "Do you have a name and number for him?"

Sergeant Grove gave them to her.

"Newt," April said. "Isn't that some kind of lizard?"

"Yes. Do you have some kind of New York accent?"

"It wouldn't surprise me, Sergeant. That's where I'm from."

She hung up and sat there. It was the end of the day. The room was stale now. Sanchez was out on a call. She felt kind of bad about that. This was the kind of situation when she felt better just having Sanchez there. He was always good making this kind of call. In Chinese she could do it just fine. She steeled herself to do it in English. *Look, it may not be your daughter, but we need the information to make sure.*

She probably wouldn't get what she needed for a day or two and, and then it would take more time to get it out there. She punched out the numbers. For some reason she made the hardest call, the one to the mother, first.

21

Troland set up the tray. Five needles, six tiny cups for the colors. A thick dab of A & D ointment. The rubber gloves. Alcohol. He laid the girl out on her back on the bed. She didn't resist at all. After running up and down the stairs and masturbating and foraging like a rat for the rest of the coke all night, she had finally crashed. He tied her wrists with thin nylon rope long enough to reach the legs of the bed.

"Troland is good, very good, he thinks of everything," he muttered to himself. Right down to the towel he tucked around her to keep the sheets dry as he shaved her from neck to thigh. He had been right. Coke addicts didn't feel a thing, not a thing, when they crashed.

He rubbed the body all over with Mennen Speed Stick, and carefully positioned the transfer, then pressed it down on the sticky surface. Perfect. The paper came away leaving the outline of the drawing on the girl's chest, neck, and stomach. He put the tattoo machine together, debating how many needles to use. It would go faster with three. He put in three needles and pressed the button. The whine sounded, but the girl didn't move. He decided to tape her mouth anyway. She didn't resist this either, and continued breathing noisily through her runny nose. Troland sat down on the stool he had put by the bed. Then he remembered he needed the jacket. The guy in the movie had his jacket on. Troland had to wear the jacket. He went to get the jacket and put it on. Then he sat on the stool with the jacket open, snapped on the gloves, and checked his watch. Willy was with him the whole time, reminding him of things and whispering encouragement.

All this was new. He could take a minute to relish the triumph of finally finding a way to make a burning last forever. He touched the flames on the wheel, on the eagle's wing. The picture he had created was electric. Richly patterned snakes, an eagle with huge wings, and two wheels were entwined in a blazing inferno that covered the girl's torso, neck, arms, and legs. She'd be on fire all the way down to her toes.

Troland picked up the machine again. Never had he felt calmer. He'd only actually tattooed someone once himself, but he'd been watching the process almost all his life. He'd even drawn the last tattoo Willy had done before he went to Nam. Tro's tattoo was supposed to be his good luck and bring him back.

He pushed the button and the contacts closed. Electricity from the battery made a magnetic field that attracted the iron armature. It moved toward the magnet against the spring and forced the needles to pop out, breaking the contact. For a fiftieth of a second the magnet lost its magnetism. The spring pulled the armature back, and the needles popped in. In and out, fifty times a second. The whine filled the room, covering the sound of the girl's thick breathing.

At first contact with her white skin, Troland held the needles too close. The black lines on the soft slippery flesh beaded with blood. A single stripe of red formed where Troland wanted it to be black. He knew it would still come out black when it healed, but it would scab instead of scale if he drew blood. And he didn't like letting the poison out. He shuddered. For a second, nausea rolled over him. Even with the gloves on, he didn't feel good with the blood of a coke whore on his hands. He didn't have to be a genius to know she was more than likely to be HIV positive.

He cursed himself and looked at her face. It occurred to him he could put her away with no trouble. Once she was dead, the blood wouldn't come out and he'd be safe. Not a twitch disturbed her features. She didn't feel anything. The fear passed as quickly as it came. No way was he going to die of AIDS. Willy told him not to kill her, so he covered the spot with ointment and went on.

The sun rose in the sky, warming the upstairs room. He didn't even consider taking his jacket off. Sweat poured down his chest and sides, but he didn't feel it. He was completely absorbed with the process. He lost all sense of time and place.

The buzz of the machine, the same as that in the movie, was the first noise he ever heard that covered all the voices in his head. If he kept it on, no one talked to him, not even Willy. Only the machine was talking, telling him how good he was, how he had found something new to add to his work.

He was an artist, an artist of the flesh. He actually trembled with pleasure when he thought of branding her at the end. That part couldn't ever change. But now the beauty of the everlasting flame and the searing punishment of the brand would be merged in a single vision. She'd be awake by then. She'd feel like she was burning alive.

Red was good. Blue and pink and green were good. Black was the most durable. Black never faded. Most of the other colors faded after time. But he liked the tattoos with many colors best. They weren't so crude as some of the bikers' tattoos that were all black, or black and blue, with only a few dabs of red. Not well done. Many were very crude. Troland wasn't crude.

He loved how the needles sucked up the ink like tiny straws, and then released it in the thousands of tiny holes he made in the skin. Several hours went by. Troland sat over the sleeping girl, deep in his work. The position he was in was far from ideal. He was sitting on a stool, leaning forward to the body on the bed. There was no resistance to the bed. She should be on a hard surface, like a table. An operating table that could be positioned would be best. He had to get one.

After three hours, he could stand it no longer. His back and left hand were painfully cramped. It occurred to him that there was something wrong with the machine, and he raged once again at the world for being backwards. He hadn't considered the possibility that the machine was a right-handed machine.

The girl's eyes were closed, and she was still breathing like a dog with a cold. Troland stood and surveyed his work. The outline of one side of her body was nearly complete. He wanted to finish it in one day. Her skin had puffed up in places. It was irritated and red. He knew that if she were awake, all the places where he had worked would be stinging badly. She must really have had a lot. He knew of cokeheads so filled with shit they had their whole bodies tattooed in a single go. Every once in a while, there was a case of someone going into tattoo shock and dying.

There were cramps in his left hand. He cursed his fate. No matter how much he worked on it, he still didn't have much control in his right hand. At his first school, they used to say left-handed people were crazy. Told him that when he was five, six, learning to write. Said it was proven without a doubt lefties were crazy and no good. His father tied his hand behind his back so he'd grow up straight. The fucker almost killed the hand that could draw beautiful pictures and write like the writing in old books.

The school people were wrong, too. It was his right hand that was a monster. It couldn't draw or form letters at all. Troland hated it. It could hold a screwdriver. It could light a match. But it couldn't do anything *nice*. He stretched, and went back to work.

22

Hi, it's Charles. I've been thinking about our talk on Sunday. Give me a call when you have a minute.

The answering machine went *click*.

Jason sat at his desk with one of his favorite skeleton clocks in front of him. The glass case was off, and he was watching the brass sunburst at the bottom of its pendulum swing back and forth as the pallet at the top of the pendulum moved back and forth over the escape wheel.

Tuesday, ten fifty-six A.M. Click, burble, doodle, doodle-oo.

Dr. Frank, I have to cancel my Tuesday appointment. My throat really hurts. Oh, and I think I left my appointment book there. If you find it, hold on to it for me, will you. I'm, like, dead without it. By the way, it's Jeff.

Something deeply satisfying about clocks. Nothing but a series of spur gears, powered by falling weights, or unwinding springs, turn the two hands.

That's right, retreat to bed, Jeff, when the going gets tough; Jason shook his head. He hated being canceled at the last minute, even when he desperately needed the time. Jeff was due in five minutes.

Jason had been tempted to leave the well-thumbed book on the floor where Jeff dumped it when he last came in. Jason had wanted to let it sit there forever, or at least until Jeff cooled down enough to come back and start looking for it. But that sort of thing always distressed the other patients. Daisy wouldn't be able to think about anything else for months. Even Harold would be disturbed. They all wanted to be only children. Jason knew that Jeff used his hypochondria to manipulate and worry him. He would never let on, but secretly he did worry over every sore throat and cold.

Tuesday, eleven-forty A.M. Click, burble, doodle, doodle-oo.

That was irritating, too. Jeff called when he knew Jason had another patient. Five minutes later, and Jason would have taken the call. He focused on the clock to calm his annoyance. Some people put pets on their laps and stroked them, or talked to them, to get their heartbeats down. Jason watched the insides of his clocks, moving the way they should. As he watched the gears engaging, he wondered what aspect of Jeff's regression he should worry about. Shit, if he might have done something to cause it? No, he decided: Jeff just didn't want to face getting well and having a future. Safer to leave the appointment book that represented his future behind on the floor.

That is your last message.

Jason sighed and pushed Erase.

I will erase your messages.

He waited a few seconds while the machine rewound the tape and then he dialed Charles's number. Charles had almost the identical message on his machine. Jason sat there while the soothing voice regretted not being with him and promised to return the call as soon as he could.

Please start speaking after the tone.

Tone.

Hi, it's Jason. I have a cancellation. I'll be taking calls for an hour. It is—He looked at the face of the clock. Now that he had made a minor adjustment, it seemed to be running perfectly.

—*Eleven forty-five.* He hung up and put the clock and its case back on the shelf between two stacks of journals.

He sat there watching the pendulum go back and forth. At eleven fifty-five, the phone rang.

"This is Dr. Frank."

"Hi, it's Charles. I've been thinking about what you said the other day."

Pause. Jason didn't help out.

"About Emma," Charles prompted. "Look, I don't know what I can do. But I can't just sit here and ignore what you're going through."

Still Jason was silent.

"I want you to know I'm here for you. I want to help. Do you want to meet and talk about it?"

One part of Jason wanted to put Charles off, send him back to his secure little niche. Another part was impressed that Charles was willing to take the time to bother.

Finally he relented and said, "Thanks, I appreciate it."

"I break for gym now. When is your next appointment?"

Jason usually jogged after Jeff, so he was free until one-thirty. Amazing. Charles was offering to give up his maintainance, and today, no less.

"I usually break at twelve-thirty on Tuesdays. I'm free from now until one-thirty," Jason replied, surprising himself.

"Great. Why don't you come here? . . . And why don't you bring those letters you mentioned?"

"You want to look at the letters?" Jason said.

"Yes, any objection?"

"Ah, no, but why?"

"The letters are what you're really worried about, aren't they?"

"Yes," Jason said, surprised that that was the case and that Charles knew it. It *was* the letters he was worried about. He checked the clock again. He could be there in ten minutes.

23

Twelve minutes later, the two men were shaking hands in Charles's waiting room.

"I brought the letters," Jason said.

"Sit down for a minute. There's a lot to this. A whole lot," Charles replied, leading the way into his office.

There was a desk, chairs, the analyst couch, the usual things. At the far end of the room was a new leather sofa. A burnished antique coffee table was positioned in front of it.

Charles headed for the sofa and sat heavily. "Would you like a drink?" he asked.

Jason raised his eyebrows. Drinking in the middle of the day now, were they? "Yes, I would," he said. "But I better not."

Charles shrugged. "Listen, I can't get a handle on this."

Jason blew some air out of his nose. He didn't have a handle on it either.

"You know I don't want to dig into places you don't want me to go. But it's a puzzle. I don't have the pieces." He shrugged apologetically. He was a big shrugger. "You know I'm here for you. I'll do anything I can, but without the pieces—" He raised his shoulders again.

"What do you want to know?" Jason smiled wanly.

Charles took a breath. "Well, I saw the film."

"I thought you would. What did you think?"

"I was very surprised," Charles said carefully. "I wasn't *shocked.* I mean, most films these days have some pretty graphic sex in them, but," he paused, "the content is disturbing. There's no question about that. It takes a dim view of therapists. But there's a lot of that going around. That's not an issue in itself. . . . You said Emma didn't tell you about this, is that right?"

Jason nodded, and then shook his head. "Well, a film doesn't just arrive out of nowhere," he admitted after a slight hesitation that he knew Charles noted.

"The script was around for a—long time." Jason could still visualize it sitting there on the table for many months. "I just didn't read it."

He hesitated again, then went on. "The guy who wrote it is a friend of Emma's. I admit I never liked him—grubby, insinuating, supercilious sort of asshole. Defensive. But he had been a friend of hers since college. Emma was in several of his plays," he added.

He smiled, thinking of the plays.

"Good plays?" Charles asked.

"She was good, but the plays were—nothing. Not daring, not involving. Just kind of dull." Jason grimaced.

"So you didn't read this one?"

"Emma says she asked me to read it, but I don't *remember* her asking me. I don't know, Charles. I just can't imagine not reading it if she asked me to."

"Well, you didn't like the guy's work. You didn't *want* to read it," Charles said neutrally, then more to the point: "I guess you've been drifting apart, as they say."

It happened all the time, happened to everybody. Different tastes, different work sent people on tangents they didn't expect when they married. Jason sucked in his lips the way Harold did when he didn't want to admit something. So the great listener hadn't been listening to his own wife. Charles's empty stomach began to gurgle.

"So what do you think her involvement was?" he asked after a minute.

Jason frowned. "Uh, what do you mean?"

"With the script. Is Emma jealous of your patients? Does she think you're involved with someone else? Did she write her own part? I mean her unconscious motivation, Jason. She may be acting, but who's the voice here? Who wrote the story and why? Was she . . . involved with what's-his-name?"

"Mark?" Involuntarily, Jason shuddered. "He's a jerk."

"He's her director," Charles pointed out. "Is he in love with her?"

"I don't know. She's attractive and bright." Jason looked away. Warm, when she wanted to be. He was feeling very emotional and was beginning to sweat. "Who wouldn't be in love with her?"

"So," Charles said. "What were the areas of conflict between you?"

Sweat ran down Jason's sides. He considered taking his jacket off. Charles wasn't wearing one, and he had loosened his tie. Jason decided not to take his jacket off. He might need to leave soon.

"I didn't think it was anything serious. She wanted more work, of course." Wanted to spend more time together. She had been talking more about having a baby, and he had been resisting. He was involved with his patients and his writing. She didn't like being left home when he went to conferences. She hated his jumping out of bed at dawn every morning. Very little morning love. He didn't say any of that out loud.

"Look, I missed it. She may have been jealous." He swallowed. "She may have been lonely, but I don't think she wrote the thing. She's not like that."

"Involved?"

"Well, she's always been *involved* with him. She knew him before she knew me. I didn't think they were ever lovers." Jason looked at the wall again. But he didn't know that for sure.

He was the one who had been married before. They talked about that. A lot. At the time, his character was more of an issue to her than hers had been to him. She was a more interesting and beautiful woman than he ever expected to get. She was deeply in love with him. Why should he harbor doubts? He hadn't. Could she be aggrieved enough to take a lover? He had seen it on the screen with his own eyes, the possibility of Emma with another man. Emma graphically showing him what she could do, what she was capable of doing, and still he had trouble believing that the woman he loved would do it.

"What about you?" Charles asked.

"What *about* me?"

"Are you involved with someone?"

Oh, so that was it. Charles had involvement on the brain. He couldn't imagine anything else. Jason frowned irritably.

"This isn't *about* that. It's not about love affairs. Look. This is something else." He took the letters out of his briefcase and laid them out on the coffee table in front of them. Fifteen of them. One had arrived each day except Sundays for the last two weeks. On Thursdays, two letters always arrived. Jason figured the second letter was the one the writer mailed on Sunday, when the mail wasn't picked up or delivered. The postmarks were all smudged. No way to know where they came from.

"Just take a look at this. I'm worried about her *safety*." Jason raked a hand through his hair. "I'm worried about keeping her *safe*, Charles. There's somebody out there who knows a whole lot about her, who wants to hurt her. It's all here in these letters. Emma doesn't see it, but anyone with training can see what this stuff means."

Charles frowned, still unconvinced about the real story. "So," he said. "You still love her."

"Of course I love her. I'll hate her forever, but I love her." Jason was surprised to hear himself say it.

"Fair enough." Charles turned his attention to the letters.

Jason had put a date and a number on the top of each one. Charles read them through, and then read them again. Then he read them a third time, going over each one very slowly. When he was finished, they sat in silence for a long time.

"Jesus," Charles said finally. "You have reason to be worried. What is this thing here?" He pointed to the drawing at the bottom of each letter. "A chariot, a Chinese symbol, a wheel with flaming swords?"

"I don't know. I've never seen it before. It seems to be a signature for him."

Charles frowned. "He's quite a poet. Listen to this: '*If you could read my mind, what a tale my thoughts could tell. Just like an old time movie, 'bout a ghost from a wishing well. In a castle dark, or a fortress strong with chains upon your feet. You'll know the ghost is me. And I'll never be set free as long as I'm a ghost you can't see. You won't walk away like a movie star who gets burned in a three-way script. Enter number two. A movie queen to play the scene bringing all the Right things out of me. I don't know where you went wrong but the feeling's gone, and I have to get it back. But stories always end, and if you read between the lines, you'd know why I can't get you back.*' This is weird."

"Gordon Lightfoot."

"What?" Charles said.

"It's a *song* by Gordon Lightfoot. But he's changed some of the words."

The blood climbed up Charles's face as he blushed. "I didn't recognize it."

"Where were you in the sixties?" Jason said lightly.

"Medical school, same place as you. What's this about amputation? And guided missiles." Charles frowned.

Jason read aloud. " 'The pathway seemed so sure. You were so pure. The pathway seemed so right. The road wasn't supposed to go left. You were meant to stay *right* and true.' He seems to have an obsession about right and left. He may be left-handed. Some people suffer a lot over that."

"Here he does it again in letter seven." Charles pointed to the phrase. " 'Do you ever wonder why the heart is on the left. You turned left. I am your heartbeat. I follow you in my dreams.' Here he calls her California Dreamin'."

"I call her that sometimes," Jason murmured.

Charles looked at him with a thin smile. "Maybe it's you."

Jason's face darkened. "Emma says that. Look at the type. It's from a really old portable. I have a really old portable."

"Then she could be writing them herself. Maybe she doesn't think she has your attention yet."

Jason shook his head. "She doesn't know how to sound that crazy, and she's right-handed. She wouldn't know how someone would express a left-handed obsession. There are more than twenty-five references to the left, i.e., wrong side of things . . . Fire in the sand. Is that a religious reference?"

Charles shrugged. "Not a specific one. Did you check and see if it's the same typewriter?" he asked. Still on the typewriter.

Now it was Jason's turn to blush. "I looked for it. I thought it was on the shelf in my closet. But—it's not around." He paused. "I must have thrown it out."

They both started at the sound of the outer door opening and closing.

Charles sighed. "Well, I think you're right. There may be some-thing to your concern. No point in taking any chances. I think you should get in touch with the police."

"It's someone who knows her," Jason said flatly.

"Obviously, it's someone who knows her, someone from a long time ago. How much do you really know about her?" Charles asked.

"I thought I knew everything," Jason said.

So much for that.

"Uh, do you mind if I make a copy of these?" Charles was already on his feet.

"Why?"

"I don't know. I want to think about it."

"I don't want them out of my hands," Jason said, shaking his head.

Charles opened the door to his closet. It had filing cabinets like Jason's, but unlike Jason's, it also had a Cannon copier. "I'll make copies. Any objection?"

Jason shrugged.

Charles copied the letters. "I think you should call the police," he said again. "Maybe they have a way of finding out where these came from."

"Yeah," Jason said slowly. "I hadn't thought of that."

"Call me later. I'll be in this evening." Charles opened the double doors carefully so the patient in his waiting room couldn't see him.

24

The shift was almost over. April studied her watch with the phone in her hand. Jennifer Roane was so upset by the possibility that the girl found in California might be her daughter, she wanted to get on the next plane to San Diego. April had to tell her several times that wasn't a good idea.

"Why not?" she demanded.

"We have no reason to think it is Ellen, and your going to California won't help." The seconds were passing very slowly.

"What do you mean?" the distraught woman cried.

"You might not recognize her," April said gently.

"How could I not know my own baby?" the woman sobbed.

She'd been outside for a while. There had been distressing postmortem changes. April didn't say that. She said they needed Ellen's medical and dental records to make a positive identification. "I'll call you as soon as I know," April promised. There, four o'clock.

"I want to go there, I want to see her," Jennifer sobbed.

"Let's make sure it's Ellen before you think about that," April said. She hung up thinking her own mother would feel the same. One child only, that's all the Gods saw fit to bless Sai Woo with. She wanted grandchildren to keep her memory alive. If the dead girl in San Diego was Ellen, who would keep Jennifer Roane's memory alive?

The phone on her desk rang.

April picked it up. "Detective Woo."

"Hi, this is Mike. I'm on my way out to the range. You haven't been there all month. Why don't you come with me? I'll pick you up in twenty minutes."

Sanchez was somewhere on the street. She could hear the traffic in the background.

"How do you know when I was there last?" she said.

"I'm a Detective First Grade. I don't miss anything. You want to or not?"

April paused to think it over. It was true she'd hadn't been to the range in a long time. She didn't like to take the time to go there and practice. It was true she half believed if she never used her gun she would never have to.

She wasn't stupid, though. She did practice pulling it out, and taking the stance with the safety catch off. She did it in the second-floor apartment of the two-family house she shared with her parents in Astoria. She had fixed up the apartment herself and paid half the mortgage for the house, but got no privacy. Her mother came up with no warning. If she caught April with the gun out, it made her crazy.

It was true she had to qualify every month. April debated taking the ride to Randall's Island.

"Yeah," she said. "Thanks, Sergeant, I would, if nothing comes up."

She called him Sergeant because she didn't want to call him Mike and have him think this might be a date or something. She was practically engaged to Jimmy Wong, and Sanchez knew it.

"I'll be there in ten minutes," he said.

April glanced at Sergeant Joyce's door. It was closed. Better hurry. Sometimes Joyce liked to come out at the end of the day and assign a new case to April just as she was leaving. It was always something that wouldn't lead to a promotion. Something like the Ellen Roane case that she didn't expect April to do anything with. Well, surprise, maybe she had located Ellen Roane.

April picked up her bag. The door to Sergeant Joyce's office opened as if by magic. Sergeant Joyce had her garish green plaid coat on, Irish as always. Her lipstick was fresh. She handed April a complaint as she left.

"This is one for you," she said. "He's waiting."

April looked at the complaint and frowned. A doctor getting annoying letters. That was a good one. Sanchez would probably leave without her. Just as well.

She went out to the bench just inside the detectives' room, suddenly a little nervous.

"Dr. Frank?" she said.

"Yes." He stood up.

"I'm Detective Woo," she said.

He surprised her by holding out his hand. "How do you do?"

She shook it briefly, further unnerved by the questioning way he looked at her. Yes, yes, she was a *real* detective, had years of training, knew what she was doing. He was tall, light-haired, medium build. Attractive look about him. Intense. She knew his tweed jacket was a good one, and wondered what kind of doctor he was as she led the way back to her desk. The room was pretty empty, the way it gets at change-of-shift time. There weren't any suspects in the pen.

Everybody who came into the precinct with a problem was different. Some people were hostile, some defensive. Most of them were shaken up and frightened. She had noticed up here that the Spanish, Caucasians, and Afro-Americans were often aggressive and demanding, wanting instant service, as if the precinct were a restaurant and the cops waiters.

The doctor with the heather tweed jacket she admired didn't show his face. He examined the room without actually appearing to, exactly the way she did when she went to new places. He settled himself in her metal chair before saying anything.

She knew by the way Sergeant Joyce told her to take care of it that this was a public relations thing. April was always the public relations detective. Downtown she had enjoyed translating the system, because she felt like a social worker with a gun. Often, when she couldn't do something for people herself, she could point them to someone who could do something. Now she had a chance to explain the system to the kind of person her mother wished she would marry.

"What can I do for you?" she asked.

He smiled, as if that were his line.

"Have you been in this precinct a long time, Detective?" he asked, surprising her a second time by accepting her authority and answering her question with a question.

"Eight months," she said. Six days and seven and a half hours.

"That's not a long time." The doctor's eyebrows furrowed.

Was that furrow a frown that meant he took back her authority only seconds after giving it to her? Did he think she wasn't up to his problem? Well, she was up to it. She had arrested very large and angry people. She could handle any situation.

"No, it isn't." She rustled the complaint sheet. In a few minutes Sergeant Sanchez would be there to get her. She suddenly wanted to get this over with.

"What kind of cases do you get here?"

What was this, a delaying tactic? He certainly was taking his time getting to the point. Maybe he didn't really want or expect her to do anything for him. He stretched out his long legs. The gray flannel trousers he wore still had a pretty good crease at the end of the day. Didn't he have patients waiting for him?

"All kinds of things, but mostly robbery, assault. Break-ins. There are a few homicides here, but not as many as in other parts of the city. You probably know that."

She looked down at the complaint sheet. "You're getting some letters," she prompted.

He corrected her. "My wife is getting letters."

"Is Mrs. Frank the complainant?" April said, turning her head a little, as if looking for her.

Dr. Frank colored slightly. "Yes. I'm making the inquiry for her."

April looked down. She had done the same thing earlier that day when a man loudly told his three- or four-year-old son in a store not to whine like a woman.

"Women don't whine," the boy retorted. "You mean, don't whine like you, Daddy."

The doctor seemed very nice, but his wife's not being there about her own complaint made April wonder. Her mother, Sai Woo, said she was suspicious. "Must have smelled something bad when baby. Always asking questions, not believe answers," Sai Woo liked to say.

April closed her face to her thought that a big part of her didn't like doctors. Her mother wanted her to marry a doctor. This one was clearly rich and looked like a Kennedy. Kennedys seemed to prey on women. He opened his leather briefcase and took out some envelopes.

"My wife and I are concerned. What can you do to stop this?" he asked, handing them over.

She took the pile and examined it. There were sixteen envelopes in all, each containing a letter. She pulled them out and quickly glanced through them. The first few had only a few lines on them, after that they got longer. The last four were several pages. All were typed on the same plain paper with black ink from a very old ribbon. On the top right-hand corner of each there was a neatly penciled number and date.

"You numbered and dated them?" she asked.

"Yes."

She studied the paper. Plain white bond. She felt its thickness with her fingers. Not bad paper, but the typewriter was very old and hadn't been cleaned in a long time. Some of the letters were filled up. The whole thing looked kind of funny to her. Why did he number the letters? She could feel him watching her as she worked her way through them.

"When did you start numbering the letters?" she asked.

"After the third one," he answered.

April read the third one carefully. *What makes a good woman go bad? Breaks a man's heart like a wheel.* She looked up at the furrowed brow and saw that he was more than watching her read the letters. He was studying *her*.

"Why this one?" she asked.

"After this one I knew they wouldn't stop."

She could smell Sergeant Sanchez before she saw him, did not turn her head. He had come back exactly on time. For a second she was aware of the gun at her waist. Why did the doctor think they wouldn't stop after the third letter?

"Why?" she asked.

"The person writing these letters has a grievance. He'll keep at it until he's satisfied."

She read on. They were kind of strange, but she didn't see a threat in them. Each one had the same drawing on it that looked like a Chinese symbol but wasn't—a semicircle with jagged edges and maybe spokes, or maybe it was swords on fire coming out of a sun going down. The last ones had other drawings on them. The letters rambled on about missiles in the Persian Gulf War and soldiers blowing things away, motorcycles with missiles on them and other weird stuff. They were all signed *The One Who Saved You.*

She paused, shuffling the letters back into order. "Do you know who it is?"

He shook his head.

"Well, do you know what the writer's grievance is?"

"My wife's an actress. She was in a film."

April looked around sharply. Sergeant Sanchez had assumed his favorite position at his desk which was no longer his because the shift was over, and Dr. Frank was blushing again. That was the way he showed his face. What kind of film would make his face red? So some loon didn't like the movie.

She squinted at the top postmark. It was illegible, as if the machine had canceled improperly, or run out of ink. She couldn't read it at all. Each of the other fifteen envelopes had a smeared postmark. The letters were addressed to Emma Chapman with the same typewriter.

"Emma Chapman?"

"My wife's maiden name."

"Does she always use it?"

"Yes."

April nodded. Okay. "Well, Dr. Frank, the thing is, there's nothing illegal about sending people letters unless there's a threat in them. It's really a postal matter."

"I see a threat in them," Dr. Frank said.

"Where?" April asked.

"All the way through. His tone is threatening, the talk about missiles and revenge, about a woman going bad. You know about the cases of disturbed people becoming obsessed with actresses and trying to kill them, or kill somebody else to get their attention?" He spoke with great intensity, but his folded hands rested calmly on the desk between them.

"If you remember the Hinckley case, you'll understand this is a potentially very dangerous situation." He lifted his hands for a second, then let them drop.

She nodded. Everybody remembered the case. So it was more than a public relations thing. Still, how did he know the letter writer was a man, and where exactly was the danger? She couldn't start investigating a potential crime, the nature of which was completely unspecified.

She pushed the letters, now ordered and back in their envelopes, to the empty space between them. "What do you want me to do, Dr. Frank?"

"I'm concerned. I want it to stop," he said, not actually asking her to do anything.

There was no return address on the envelopes. The complaint on the sheet did not justify sending the material to the lab. She looked up. Sergeant Sanchez had his head slightly cocked to one side. He didn't say a thing, but she got a message from him anyway. That was disconcerting. She couldn't read Jimmy Wong's mind; how come she could read Sergeant Sanchez's mind? The message was for her to take the letters.

"Okay," she said. "Leave them with me."

The doctor looked both doubtful and relieved. April could understand doubtful. There was no reason for people to think the police could solve anything. Truth was, most everything was needle in house-stack, as her mother would say. She gave him a receipt for the letters and took his business card. She looked at it briefly, but it didn't reveal what kind of doctor he was.

25

Troland had just about reached his favorite part, no longer feeling any fatigue, when the girl woke up. She opened her eyes and within an instant she was hysterical. Her hands and feet were tied, but the middle of her body had no restraints. She began straining and bucking. Her eyes were enormous, about to pop right out of her head. She made sounds like no sounds Troland had ever heard. It was like she was having an epileptic fit. Her skinny body went rigid. Her head shook from side to side, and she was screaming from the inside because her mouth was taped.

"Shut up." It freaked him out.

She didn't shut up.

"Look, shut up!" he screamed. "I have a gun. See, it's loaded. I have a knife, too. I'll cut you up in little pieces."

The noise didn't stop.

"You want me to finish quietly, or blow your head off?"

Snot and tears ran down her face. Troland was disgusted. After all his trouble, now she was a mess.

"Okay!" He put the gun down and roughly wiped her face with a towel.

He considered hitting her, knocking her out, but didn't want to spoil his work.

"You want me to take the tape off?" he said.

She nodded.

He hesitated. "You better not scream," he warned.

She shook her head. He reached over and pulled the tape off. For a second she breathed deeply through her mouth, and then in gulps, crying with no tears.

"What are you doing? Are you crazy? You can't do this. I'm—It hurts. What did you do to me? My whole body. It feels like—Oh, God, let me get up. I can't stand this. Jesus, are you *crazy?*" She shivered convulsively. "I'm so cold—"

"Shut up," Troland barked. "I could kill you. Understand?"

"Don't kill me!" she cried. "Don't kill me. Don't kill me. I didn't do anything. I did what you wanted. Why are you doing this?" Her words came in gulps.

"Shut up," Troland commanded again. "Can't you hear? I'm telling you to shut up. I'm in control here. You have to do what I say." He stood over her waving the gun.

"Okay, okay, okay. Don't *hurt* me," she cried.

"I didn't hurt you." He was disgusted. She wouldn't stop jerking her body around. "I can't finish like this."

"But what is it? What are you doing to me? Oh, *God.*" She lifted her head. "Ahhhhh."

"*SHUT UP!*" Troland raised the gun to strike, but he didn't want to damage his own work.

"You're freaking me out. Stop it, I can't concentrate."

"Ahhhhh," she cried, trying to look at herself. "What is it? What did you do to me?"

"It's just a tattoo. Now shut up."

"A tattoo. Jesus, a tattoo? Ooohh. A tattoo, why does it hurt all over? Oh God, it *hurts* all *over.*"

"Yeah, it's a big one," Troland said proudly.

"Ohhhh noooo. Ahhh," she cried. "Oh God, oh Jesus. Oh God, no. Oh, no, you got to let me go? Oh, no. I can't—"

It was irritating. It was good. Troland was full of rage and power, and also a feeling of impotence. He couldn't get her to shut up, but he liked it. The fear was good. The girl was out of her mind. It was good to watch, but it was getting in the way. He wanted to finish. Yeah, watch her face as he tattooed her tit, so he could think about it. But she wouldn't calm down. She was off the wall. He'd never seen anyone so off the wall.

He was like a squirrel in the road with a car coming on, that didn't know which way to run. He had time, but he didn't have time. He picked up the tattoo machine and turned it on, once, twice, three times. But each time she keened and twisted so much he couldn't continue.

"You got to let me go. Please let me *go*. I can't take it," she cried.

"I have to pee. Let me pee. Just let me pee. I'll come back. Just let me pee. I won't do anything. I won't go anywhere. You *have* to let a person *pee*."

He couldn't let her pee. He didn't have handcuffs. He didn't like them. Handcuffs made him sick. *Willy, what do I do?* He hadn't thought of her having to pee. *No!* He couldn't let her up. She was crazy. He couldn't trust her. She'd start jumping around. He made a note to think about what to do when the next one had to take a leak.

"I'm going to tape your mouth again. You want that?"

"No, no, no—"

"Then shut up and let me concentrate. I'm almost finished."

"But I can't hold it. You want me to pee in the bed?"

"I want you to lie still and shut up."

"But I got to pee," she protested. "It's not my fault."

"You can pee when I'm finished."

She started to cry. "Let me go. Oh, God, are you going to let me go? Oh, please."

He turned on the machine again and freehand, while she was moving around, made a quick question mark in the soft under part of her upper arm.

"Oh, oh, oh," she cried. "Oh, it *hurts*. Oh, *God*."

And suddenly the bed was wet. Troland jerked back.

"Shit!" The bitch wet the bed.

Now she was crying harder. "Oh, let me go. Oh, God. It's all wet. Please."

She wet his mother's bed. He could see her coming out of the wall, shaking her head with disgust. *Can't you be clean. Can't you ever be clean?*

Troland turned away from her to the girl on the bed. The girl was all wet. Wet from all the A and D ointment he had used. Wet with tears and snot and the heavy stink of sex and sweat and urine. She was still crying, begging for release. It went too far inside Troland's head for him to come back. He struck without thinking. He leaned forward with his two hands spread, his right thumb on top of the left. The left one was the strong one. He pressed hard. He was a fixer. He fixed the place where the sound came out. Easy. One two three and her larynx was crushed.

A few minutes later, when he realized she was dead, he was upset. He had forgotten he had to brand her first. Now it was too late. He had no interest in branding a dead thing. He chided himself. He hadn't gotten it right. Then he studied the tattoo. It was gorgeous. He took a few minutes to finish it. Then he snapped a Polaroid so he could see it whenever he wanted. He studied it critically. He was pleased there were no bruises on her neck. She was a little strange around the mouth. Waxy and slightly blue. And even with her eyes closed, the tension was still there. He'd never killed anyone with his own hands before. It was interesting. It was even good. She deserved it. She didn't do what he said.

See that, Willy. She didn't do what I said.

He didn't hear a word of complaint from Willy, so he ate an orange and took another picture without the head showing. That was better.

When night came, he dug a small deep hole under the huge bougainvillea where he had played as a child years ago. He put her inside several extra-heavy, garden-sized garbage bags, sealed them carefully, and placed her in a crouched position in her grave.

26

"What was that all about?" Mike Sanchez asked.

April cleared her desk for the second time, tucking the letters into her bag so she could look at them later.

"Probably nothing," she said. She didn't see any reason to tell Sanchez. She didn't want to tell him Ellen Roane might have been found dead in the California desert, either. She'd handled the parents by herself. The medical information she wanted she'd have tomorrow or the next day. She could only hope the match would not fit Ellen.

"Must be something," he said.

They headed out of the squad room toward the stairs.

The precinct was built like a school. The squad room opened at the beginning of a long, wide corridor that led to other departments. A right turn took them to the stairs.

"Why do you want to know?"

April slung her bag over her shoulder. If she had her car, she wouldn't need a ride out to the range. She didn't have it because she had lent it to Jimmy two weeks ago. He needed to drive to New Jersey and didn't want to take his own car. She had even been thoughtful enough to fill it up with gas for him. He must have done whatever he had to do by now. It was time she got her car back, and she knew she would have to take action to get it. He wasn't just going to drive it home without her making a fuss.

Sometimes she had a hard time dealing with Jimmy. He wanted what he wanted, and didn't take no for an answer. When they first met, she didn't seem to notice how bossy he was. But that was back when she was working in the 5th. She didn't know a lot of things then.

"Maybe I can help," Sanchez offered with a smile.

She still didn't know what Sanchez's smiles meant. He pushed the front door open and held it for her. There were blue uniforms everywhere, watching him hold the door for her. Why did he do that? She looked at her feet and walked out to the street.

"Hi," she responded to the greetings of some uniformed officers. "I don't need any help," she told Sanchez.

"Everybody needs help." Sanchez shrugged. "You can help me whenever you want."

They walked the few steps to the lot where his car was parked. Sanchez unlocked the Camaro on the passenger side and opened the door for her. April wasn't used to that. She looked guiltily around before getting into the car. It was low and red. It occurred to her that although she and Jimmy had done some monkey business together, it wasn't a passionate thing, the way she thought love was supposed to be. And yes, Jimmy did hold out the possibility of their getting married some day, but he had never really asked her, and never showed any eagerness for a such day to come.

"Why do you want to help me?" she asked.

Sanchez shrugged. "We're in the Bureau, on the same team. We work pretty well together. I think you have a lot of potential. Why not?"

Could be sneaky. Could be to steal her credit, make her lose face. Could be for monkey business. Lose more face. She was very quiet on the way to Randall's Island.

At the range, she took a place at the end of the line. There was already somebody next to her, and somebody next to him, firing almost at the same time. Sanchez had to stand way down at the other end. April wanted him far away so he wouldn't be able to judge how she shot. Jimmy Wong took her to the range at the Academy once, and said she was one lousy shot. He said she took too long to get her rounds fired off and would be dead already.

He seemed to enjoy saying it. "You're dead already, kiddo."

Every time she went there, she remembered his satisfaction. Wouldn't want to be her partner, he said smugly.

Now the thunder got to her before she even started. Even with the sound muffled, there was the vibration. She could almost see the air shimmer with it. It used to be hard for her to keep the gun from kicking up when she fired it. She still had to work out on her own to keep her arms and hands strong enough so that when she pulled the trigger, the recoil wouldn't make the shot fly wild every time. By now she'd had enough practice to be able to shoot into the paper torso of the man most of the time. Sometimes when she felt really mad and wasn't too guilty about her thoughts being not so nice for a girl, she could pepper the whole region of the heart. At this distance with a pistol, though, precision wasn't too important. They were .38 slugs. If you got him anywhere, he'd go down. Today she shot with concentration, and when she checked her score, she found she had done a lot better than usual.

"Thanks for bringing me," she told Sanchez. "See you," as she finished up and passed where he was still firing.

He lowered the gun and pulled the headset off his ears. "What?"

"Thanks for the ride. I'm going now."

"Hey, wait a minute. I'll take you home."

She shook her head. "It's out of the way." She knew he lived in the Bronx. She lived in Queens. They were in opposite directions, and he would have a lot of problems with the bridges. She hadn't expected him to drive her home.

"It's no problem," Sanchez assured her.

"It's all right," she insisted, heading down the line as people continued to fire around them.

"What? You'll have dinner with me," he said. "Great."

"I said I'll take the subway!" she shouted as all the shooting stopped. The other officers on the range stared.

One laughed. "You tell him."

Sanchez followed her out, and they handed the headsets back. "Yeah. Where are you going to get it?"

"Okay, you can take me to the subway," she said.

They found his car and got in.

"Why don't you tell me about the case," he suggested.

"Which one?" She rolled down the window for some air, thinking about subway stops.

"The new thing. The letters."

"I don't know yet. It's probably nothing. Wife is getting some letters. They're kind of crazy, but they don't threaten her or anything." April looked out of the window.

"So why come to us?"

"Well, the husband's some kind of doctor, and she's in a movie." They hit the bridge traffic and came to a standstill. April studied the fat man in the turquoise Toyota next to them. Why was she telling Sanchez this?

"No kidding. What movie?" He was interested, as she knew he would be.

"I don't know. He didn't say. He just thinks it might be some kind of Hinckley thing. You know, like a stalker."

"What do you think?"

"I don't know. I just got it. I'm not supposed to do anything anyway." Maybe that would shut him up.

Sanchez was quiet for a minute. "So, who're they from?"

"I told you they don't know."

"*Where* are they from?"

"Don't know that either." The traffic started to creep forward.

"The postmarks, I mean."

"They're illegible. There must be something wrong with the machine. It's not canceling right. Where are you going? This isn't the way to the subway."

Sanchez headed out to Queens.

"I know a really great Mexican restaurant. It's near you. We could talk about the case. And then I could find out where these letters are coming from."

"Thanks, I can't."

"What's the matter, don't you like Mexican food?"

"I really can't." April looked out the window.

"Why not?"

"Are you asking me for a date?" April said, still looking out the window.

"What's the right answer? I like being with you. Is there anything wrong with that?" She had her head turned away and didn't see it, but she knew he was smiling.

"I guess you're involved with someone," he said when she didn't answer.

"Yeah, that's it."

"Oh, because the way you treat me, I kind of get the idea it might be something else. Like from your point of view there might be something wrong with me."

"I don't know you that well, Sergeant, but as far as I can tell, there isn't anything wrong with you."

"You're just not interested."

"I, uh, wouldn't be interested in anybody in the Department," April said. "It wouldn't be professional."

"I thought your boyfriend, what's his name—Jimmy? Isn't he in the Department?"

"This is close enough. I can get out here," April said angrily.

"Okay, I'm sorry. I shouldn't have said that. I just get the feeling that things between you aren't so—How shall I put it?"

"You know something I don't?" April snapped.

"Me?" He shook his head. "I don't know a thing. Look, I'm sorry. I just wanted to help, that's all. It's better when you work with someone you like."

April was silent, thinking it over. He was clearly checking on her, and possibly checking on Jimmy. But then, she'd done some checking on him, too. She knew he'd been married and it didn't work out, knew he lived with his widowed mother in the Riverdale section of the Bronx. Having to check everything out seemed to come with the territory. She couldn't exactly blame him for it. And suddenly he was making her wonder why she hadn't bothered to do a little investigating herself into what Jimmy was so busy doing that he couldn't return her car or even call her in over two weeks. And she knew that was what Sanchez wanted, because she could read his mind.

"Okay, so what could you find out about the letters, then?" she demanded, finally turning her head to look at him.

"I have a friend at a lab. You never know. He might be able to tell you where they're from."

April hesitated for a long time. "There's probably nothing to it. But thank you."

They rode in silence.

"It isn't all tacos and burritos, you know."

"What?" April looked straight ahead.

"Mexico. It isn't some little island in the Caribbean like Puerto Rico. Mexico has thousands of years of history. A whole culture. Art, literature, everything. I mean, does Puerto Rico have a whole wing in the Metropolitan Museum?"

April didn't know. "It's not the food. My mother expects me," she said softly. "Anyway, Puerto Rico's okay. What's the problem?"

"Everybody thinks I'm Puerto Rican. Does Puerto Rico have Carlos Fuentes? Diego Rivera? Huh?"

April didn't reply. She had no idea who Fuentes and Rivera were. "I don't have anything against anybody," she said finally.

"I'm Mexican-American. My father fought in the Second War. I have a proud history." She could see he felt strongly about it.

He turned the corner, and headed down her street. She had planned to tell him to stop on the corner, but his speech about Mexico made that impossible. The red Camaro stopped in front of her parents' house where she lived in the upstairs apartment, and where her mother expected her to live one day with the long-dreamed-of Chinese husband and children. Shit. Now she had insulted him, and her mother was probably standing at the window watching her arrive with a Mexican. It was all very difficult.

"I'll tell you about the postmarks tomorrow," Sanchez said, holding out his hand for the letters.

"Thanks," April said. She opened her bag and gave him the first five. She didn't know what she thought about it all, as she headed up the steps to where her mother had already opened the door to the smell of Chinese food and a thousand questions.

27

Jason called Charles as soon as he returned to his office. Charles got back to him in twenty minutes.

"I spoke to the police," he said gloomily, "and I think I'm going to have to handle this myself."

"How are you going to do that?" Charles asked. "You don't know who the guy is or where he is."

"I'll do a profile. I'll find him," Jason said.

"So?" Charles said worriedly. "Then what?"

"I'll go talk to him."

"I don't know, Jason," Charles muttered. "That doesn't sound like a good idea. Why don't you do the profile, give it to the police, and let them take care of it? I'll even help you."

"We'll see," Jason said.

"Come on, it'll be like the old days. Remember the old days?" Charles pressed.

"Yeah, I remember them."

Jason wasn't quite as nostalgic about the past as Charles was. He'd been unhappily married during their training when they were part of a team and worked long hours at the Psychiatric Center. He remembered the stints they did in different parts of the hospital, meeting every day for endless evaluations and reports on the psychotics and potential suicides that came in to the ER every day.

Charles remembered it enthusiastically because he had been wealthy then as now, and none of his patients these days were very sick people. If he was so interested in this, he must not have a whole lot to worry about, Jason thought.

"We'll work on the letters together," Charles said. "Maybe we can get Emma to help us. She must have some idea who it is."

"I told you she thinks it's me," Jason said.

"Do you want me to talk with her?" Charles asked.

"Maybe later."

"You want to start in the morning?"

Jason looked at his watch. Did he want Charles involved? Yeah, he guessed he did. "Okay," he agreed.

At six-thirty the next morning Charles leaned back against the leather sofa in his office and stretched. His jacket was on a chair and his sleeves were rolled up.

Jason looked up from the chart he was making.

"Tired?"

"No, no, I'm fine," Charles said, yawning.

They had been working since Jason's arrival forty-five minutes earlier.

"When do you think the police will have something to tell you?" Charles asked.

"I don't know if they'll ever have anything to tell me. I told you the detective wasn't very impressed with the case." Jason checked his watch. He had a seven o'clock appointment.

Charles took a sip of his cold coffee.

"*Breaks a man's heart like a wheel.* Was that a movie or something?" he asked after a minute.

"I don't know." Jason shook his head. He wasn't sure they were getting anywhere with this. They had never had to put together a profile based on written material alone. The kind of writing samples they got always came from people they knew, who were desperate to explain, to clarify what they felt, who they were, what was wrong. These letters were from someone who didn't want them to know who he was and what he intended to do. They were in code. The signature drawing showed that the writer liked to decorate things, had some artistic outlet. Others, added to the last few letters, were illustrations of his fascination with power and motion and fire.

"Yeah, with Sally Field. Wasn't that the one where they lose the farm?" Charles persisted with the line.

"I don't *know*," Jason repeated. He didn't go much to the movies, probably never would again. He pulled himself together and tried to concentrate.

It looked to him like the guy was becoming more focused, at the same time as he was coming apart. His thinking was confused, but his drawings were precise and painstakingly done. Jason knew there were experts who could predict by letters and past behavior what a psychopath was likely to do next, and even what he would be wearing when he did it. But he and Charles were not experts. Not only that, they had no idea what kind of background this guy had and what kinds of acting out he had done in the past. They were trained for clinical evaluation, for living people in front of them talking their hearts out. They couldn't do a history with none of the facts.

"I don't think that's the tie-in," Jason said about the movie. "The references to wheels start here."

"*Chariots of Fire.* Wheels of fire," Charles murmured. "Humph, Lear?"

"Jets of Fire?"

"No, *King Lear*—'I am bound by a wheel of fire that mine own tears do scald like molten lead.' "

Oh, *Wheel of Fire,* of course. All the psychiatric analyses of King Lear were called *Wheel of Fire.*

"Do you think he's a fan of Shakespeare, or fire is like a child's tears to him?" Jason asked.

"Who knows. Fire's only one thing. What about motion and power? Here he talks about *running with the wind and two legs gone.* Maybe he means the cruise missiles. They run with the wind with two legs gone, don't they?"

"Uh-uh. I think he's talking about amputation there."

"Maybe he's missing something," Charles speculated.

"Or thinks he's missing something," Jason murmured.

"Could be." Charles made a note. "He could have been in an accident, and was injured. Maybe there's something physically wrong with him. . . ."

Jason tried to console himself with the thought that Freud had analyzed Leonardo da Vinci based on the "Mona Lisa." The problem with that was da Vinci was long dead when Freud did it, and it didn't matter whether he was right or wrong. He looked at his watch again. Better start making some hypotheses. He had to go soon.

"What do we know?" he asked.

"We know about his obsessions," Charles said. "He's clearly obsessed with good woman/bad woman. He has a virgin/whore fixation. Emma was a good woman who is now a bad woman. He believes in punishment for wrongs done. His drawings indicate a great deal of technical skill. Maybe he does something graphic for a living. He's educated enough to be able to handle the language pretty well. He talks a lot about speed and motion and power. His signature drawing certainly seems to have a wheel in it, as well as fire, but that could be feathers. And, of course, he's left-handed. Left-handed people are often tortured about it when they're kids, made to change over."

"He's angry that the world is set up for right-handed people," Jason added. "Emma was on the Right path and went off it. He wants to make things Right again."

He frowned. About six percent of the population were left-handed. That was a whole lot of people.

"Air power versus land power. He talks about the Apache being sloppy," Charles went on. "It's got some design flaws and can't stay up in the air. Maybe he's in the military. Air and land. Air and land. Angel and whore. Right and left. Everything is an opposite. He's probably conflicted about the good/bad in himself."

They looked at each other over the empty coffee cups. If the good side of him wrote letters and drew pictures, what did the bad side of him do? Jason turned away first.

"I met this bone surgeon on a plane once, wouldn't shut up." Charles changed the subject. "Know what he told me? Eighty percent of his emergency cases were amputees."

"What?" Jason was startled out of his speculation on what the guy might do if he started acting out.

"Bikers."

"Jesus. So here he's speculating about missiles on a motorcycle taking out a tank."

"Yeah, so what's he telling us? Want some more coffee?"

"Yes, I'll get it. What about you?" Jason got up to pour it and was distracted again by Charles's setup.

Charles had everything in his office. Tiny, immaculate kitchen in a closet with a two-burner stove top, sink and refrigerator in one unit, and a coffee maker and microwave on shelves above. Had Charles thought of this himself, or was Brenda responsible for all the luxuries?

Jason and Emma didn't even have a microwave in their apartment. Jason wasn't absolutely certain what they were good for. He felt another pang. Emma liked to cook for him, and he rarely had the patience for candlelit dinners. There were a lot of things he should have thought more about, tolerated with better grace.

He poured the last of the coffee into two matching mugs and reached into the refrigerator below for the fresh milk that was in there. Who bothered about all this? Who got the milk and the excellent coffee? There was smoked salmon in there, brown bread and butter. Capers and chilled champagne. It was unimaginable to Jason that Charles had the energy to think of all this. Who did he eat the smoked salmon with?

Jason looked over at him, on the leather sofa with his copies of the letters, his notes. What was going on with him? Charles had the frown of concentration between his eyes. Jason felt another pang. He didn't have much doubt about the salmon and champagne. Charles, married to Brenda for less than the five years he was to Emma, seemed to be playing the same old games and getting away with it. While he, who had been so responsible and faithful, was losing everything he cared about because the woman he loved didn't scream at him when she wanted something. The sounds Emma made when she talked were not loud or insistent enough to make him

listen. He felt the knife in his gut again. Whatever made him think
he could escape the most basic and non-negotiable biological need a
woman has? No matter whether she was quiet or loud about it.
Really stupid.

The coffee burned his tongue. He sat down again and went over
his chart of what they knew. The guy was obsessed with things not
turning out Right. Emma was bitten by a snake and poisoned. He
was going to make things Right again. *There* was the threat. But
where was he, and what was he likely to do? He was into motorcycles
and air power. He himself was off the path of Right. The guy was
furious about being left-handed in a world of right-handed people.

He talked about her—about Emma—being branded. By appearing in the film? By having herself tattooed? By having sex, or
showing her body? Or was it the whole thing? And branded as what?
Somehow Jason thought the guy writing was the one who was
branded. But in the film they were both branded, if the brand was
the tattoo. Jason shivered. Great. Really great. There was just too
much he didn't know. He looked at his watch and then gathered his
notes together. It was time to go.

28

At exactly eight o'clock in the morning, Sanchez dropped the envelope with the three letters April had given him the night before on her desk. He smiled. "Guess where they come from?"

"New York," April said promptly. She bet it was the husband. He looked just like a Kennedy. She didn't like the way he came in by himself, talking about his wife's problem. Maybe it was his problem.

Sanchez shook his head. "Guess again."

"What is this, a guessing game?"

Sanchez raised a shoulder slightly. He was wearing a gray shirt, a darker gray jacket, and a black tie. April couldn't decide whether she liked the combination or not. Wednesday and Thursday she worked the eight-to-four shift. So did Sanchez. They were on the same schedule. She was forced to think about that half the night because her mother had a lot of questions about the red Camaro.

"Why don't Jimmy drive you home in white Baron?" Sai asked.

"LeBaron," April said. Her mother knew very well he was at work in Brooklyn and couldn't possibly get to Astoria at that hour. But she was wondering about a lot of things herself. Why didn't Jimmy care about her enough to give her her car back? If Jimmy had returned her car, she could have driven to the range herself. No, wait a minute. Why did he have to take her car in the first place? She loved that car, really loved it. She frowned. Apparently he loved it, too.

"You want to know or not?" Sanchez asked, noting the frown.

"Sure I do." She forced herself to look at him square in the face. What was it about that face that was so compelling? The man was *nice, gentle?* How could a man be nice? That just didn't make any sense.

"Well, they've been handled too much to get even any partials, but they come from San Diego," Sanchez said with a note of triumph.

"What?" She must have been distracted by the thought of her mother or the subway ride or something.

"I said San Diego," Sanchez enunciated elaborately.

"No!" April's breath caught. In six years on the force that name had never crossed her lips. Now she had two cases with a link there.

Sanchez stood beside her desk, a hand on his hip and a smile under his mustache. "Oh, yeah, why not?"

"That's where that girl dead-ended. Ellen Roane. That's where they're trying to make a match with her on a girl's body that turned up yesterday. I'm waiting for her medical data right now."

"No kidding."

April shook her head. The letters couldn't be from there. It was too weird.

"Are you sure?" she asked.

"Of course I'm sure. I took it to this buddy of mine in the lab at Jay. He popped it under the microscope, and a few minutes later he had a reconstruction. High resolution microscopy. Most of the letters were there. You just can't see them with the naked eye. Canceling without enough ink," he added. "The post office out there must be going broke like everybody else."

April's eyes widened with amazement. Sanchez went back into the city for her last night? Why did he do that? She shook her head again. San Diego. What did that mean?

"Piece of cake to trace the machine," Sanchez said helpfully.

"Thank you." She knew very well how to trace the machine, but who was going to send her to San Diego to do it?

He didn't move away from the corner of her desk. She could smell the soap and the after-shave he used. Okay, so he got a piece of information for her. Why didn't he go and do something of his own?

Her temper flared, but it didn't show because she lowered her eyes demurely. "I can take it from here," she said.

"Sure." He sat down at his desk, swiveled away from her, and played with his stack of case folders. Then he swiveled back.

"That drawing he's got on the bottom. It looks Chinese, doesn't it?"

"It's not Chinese," April said flatly.

"I know. It's a Harley symbol," he said.

April took one out and studied it. "It doesn't look like it." A biker? Couldn't be. Bikers didn't sit around writing weird, menacing letters to women three thousand miles away. It didn't make sense.

"Yeah, inside the fire part is a wing and a wheel. See it?" Sanchez said.

April nodded doubtfully. "Sort of."

"The eagle is the Harley-Davidson symbol, and there's its wing."

"Maybe," April said noncommittally.

"I'd bet anything on it," Sanchez said.

"Well, you don't have to. It's my case."

"True," he said. He swiveled around so he was facing his desk again. "Just thought it might help."

It did help. It helped a lot, but she didn't want him in her head so much. It was hard enough as it was. She switched her attention to the two cases, both from the same place far away but with no connection to each other. She probably wouldn't have another one that connected with California for the next six years. She checked her watch. It would be hours before she could start trying to reach Sergeant Grove in San Diego to ask if anyone out there was getting letters with a Chinese-looking Harley-Davidson symbol on them. Then he would tell her he was in Missing Persons and didn't do letters. He'd tell her to check the post office; he'd ask her about the weather again and laugh.

29

Jason was right next door. Emma knew it because she heard the door open and close on a patient at five-thirty. Then at six-fifteen there were two sets of openings and closings, one immediately following the other. She wanted to look through the keyhole to see who it was, but was too far away to make it there in time. Finally she could restrain herself no longer. She moved swiftly into the bedroom and started going through Jason's drawers.

"What are you looking for?"

"Aaah." Emma jumped.

It wasn't a patient going in. It was Jason coming out. He was standing in the doorway watching her.

"Jesus, you scared me," she gasped. "What are you doing here?" He had his suit jacket on, and looked like he was on his way out. Why had she waited all day to start looking?

He frowned, peering past her at the open drawers. "I wanted to tell you I have to go out of town unexpectedly."

"Why?" She rammed a drawer shut guiltily.

"I have to speak at the medical school in San Diego day after tomorrow." He colored as he said it.

She stared at him, stunned. "Why?" she said again.

"What are you doing with my things?" he asked.

"Nothing." She rammed the drawers closed one after another. "Just putting your clothes away."

He didn't move. He was able to stay absolutely still for long periods of time, as if in suspension while his patients talked. Emma hated it when he did it with her. She shook her head impatiently. His lecture arrangements were made months in advance. She studied his face.

"Why don't you just tell me what's going on with you and get it over with?" she said. "I know you're not going out to San Diego to speak."

"Yes," he said testily, "I am. I was going to go later in the summer, but now is a better time. I'll go see your parents. Would you like that?"

Emma closed the last drawer and headed out of the bedroom. No, she wouldn't like that. She didn't think for a minute he was going to San Diego. Why would he go there?

"Why don't I come with you?" she said lightly. "I haven't been home in ages."

He followed her down the hall. "What were you doing in my things?" he asked again.

She turned, trying to catch him off guard. "Looking for those letters. What did you do with them?"

"I told you, I gave them to Charles." His face didn't say a thing. He had spent years learning how to appear invulnerable. He looked hard as nails now.

"Why?" Emma shook her head at him and moved into the living room.

It had been the dining room when the apartment was much larger. Although it was the living room now, it was lined with books and looked like a study. The former living room had been made into a separate office and waiting room for Jason years before she met him, during his first marriage. The letters were probably in there, she thought. She wasn't allowed to go into his office unless she was specifically invited. He was a doctor; everything there was confidential.

She looked out of the window. She had wanted to live somewhere else when they got married. Jason didn't like hearing her voice lessons, or seeing her around during office hours. He said patients got distracted easily and asked intrusive questions about his life that didn't help their therapy. He wanted anonymity. It made her feel like she was in hiding all the time. She shook her head at the old wound. Why did he marry an actress, then?

It was raining again. She shivered and glanced at a clock. In the living room alone there were nine of them, evidence of Jason's passion for the keeping of time. Two skeleton clocks, a regulator, a grandfather clock, a mantel clock, a desk clock, and two carriage clocks. They were all at least a hundred years old. All chimed on the hour, and half-hour, though none exactly at the same time. Jason kept them in working order, but they were old and unpredictable and sometimes did what they wanted.

"Why?" she said again. It was almost six forty-five.

"Why what?" Jason asked. He was poised by the door.

"Why did you give Charles the letters?" Emma demanded. The typed words kept going through her head, even when she was sleeping. *Dear Emma: You were my white spirit. You were my purity. You make me think of poetry.* Funny drawing at the bottom. Not so very different from the tattoo in the movie. She didn't know what to make of it.

The first letter was a list of weres. *You were all the good things Faith Hope and Charity.* He called her "California Dreamin'," like the song. The second letter was a list of whys. *Why did you do it? Why don't you want me to love you? Why do you want to hurt me? It's not Right what you did.*

The blood rushed to her cheeks. There was something about Jason in the suit, now studying her face. He was looking at her in a way that always made her feel she was some kind of inferior being for not having gone to medical school and knowing the meaning of everything as he did.

"I gave the letters to Charles because they worried me," he said, with his shrink mask still firmly in place.

"Please don't start trying to scare me again." Emma looked away. Didn't he have to go back to his office and tend to somebody? All these years he was too busy to stop for a minute and be with her, and now he was spending hours on those stupid letters. Why? Were they really so menacing?

He reached out to take her hand, his brow furrowed. "I don't want to scare you, Emma, but I want you to be careful while I'm gone. Really careful."

She looked down at his hand holding hers, and her eyes filled with tears. "Why don't I go with you, Jason? We're never together." Her voice trailed off. "And I haven't been home in a long time. I wouldn't mind seeing my mother."

He put his arms around her and frowned over her shoulder. "Wouldn't that be stressful?"

"Not as stressful as this. What are you hiding?"

He stroked her hair. "It's only for a couple of days."

They moved to the sofa and sat in an uneasy silence. Emma thought of her mother.

"Did I ever tell you my mother used to shake her finger at me and say, 'You've made your bed, you lie in it,' every time we picked up and moved to another base? I thought it was my fault she married him and chose to be a navy wife."

"I know," Jason murmured. "Did you ever go out with anyone in the navy?" he asked suddenly, as if the question just occurred to him. All day he had been trying to figure out where tattoos fit in the picture. Now he remembered they were a navy thing. Emma was a navy child. Why hadn't he thought of that?

"I was too young in Virginia and Hawaii. But I did in Alaska, when I was sixteen. Did I tell you I worked the night shift in a crab plant because I hated being called a spoiled officer's kid?"

She put her head on his shoulder. "He was the lowest-ranking officer, and we had *no* money. None. How could someone be spoiled who never had more possessions than could fit in a knapsack?" She looked down at her wedding ring. She still didn't have much jewelry, and no offspring. Jason's family had been poor, too, and he couldn't help saving for the future. It was true what the shrinks said about background being everything. Nobody ever got over where they came from, or what happened to them when they were kids.

"I know." Jason put his arm around her. It was very quiet. He could hear the soft chime of the first clock in the room to herald the hour.

"The only bike I ever had came from the dump. I painted it myself, and then I had to put it back when we moved," Emma said. "People went crazy in the navy, but no one ever complained. Every time I went to a new place I thought the old one ended."

"We're not so very different," Jason murmured. "I was lonely, too. I worked nights in a gas station. My mother thought if I knew what it was like to work with my hands I'd choose to work with my head." He laughed. "I still hate the smell of gas."

"I was covered with crab slime in twenty-below temperatures at three in the morning," Emma said. "And had to go to school the next day. I don't like fish of any kind."

"We're not in competition for who struggled most." Jason smiled tenderly.

"My parents were mortified. I hung the rubber suit by the back door so everyone could see it."

"I guess you like mortifying people," he remarked. "Goes back a long way." The bitterness crept back in his voice.

"Well, I never liked people telling me what I can or can't do." She pulled away from him, her face tense again. Shouldn't have married an actress. Did he secretly think she'd fail and never be seen by anybody, just be a voice behind somebody else's body for the rest of her career?

He changed the subject. "But what about California? Did you date anyone from the navy there?"

"What difference does it make?" Emma sighed. "I only lived in California one year, my senior year in high school. We didn't live on the base then. It was my first house in a regular neighborhood. I thought I was in heaven. There was no way in the world I would have gone out with a navy man then. I wouldn't even go to the club."

"The club?" Jason murmured, confused. She'd said they were poor.

"Officers' Club."

"Oh. Did you have a boyfriend that year?"

She frowned and shook her head. "Not really. Why are we talking about this?"

He shrugged. "You said you wanted to go back."

"What's going on, Jason? Why won't you tell me?"

"Nothing to tell. I'm going out for a couple of days. You have a movie deal pending. You have to stay here and negotiate a good deal."

"I thought you didn't want me to do it," Emma said in surprise.

"Well, I was wrong. You have to do what feels right to you." He leaned forward and put his face in her hair.

There was the slight aroma of brass cleaner on him. She thought he must have been polishing the insides of a clock during a break earlier in the day.

He put his fingers under her chin and turned her head to make her look at him. "Look, I might have been angry at you for not telling me what you did. But you're all I have. I love you, Emma, and I'm here for you. Don't forget it." He held her face between his hands and bent to kiss her.

She shivered at his touch. He'd been avoiding her ever since the film opened and the letters started coming. But even before that, he had been withdrawn from her. He'd been married before. Sometimes she thought he had someone else. She didn't know how long she could endure marriage without a physical life. The kiss went on for a long time. Maybe he really did love her. The clocks were bonging now, one after another, striking the hour, each in its own rhythm.

30

The air was sharp and cool when Jason got off the plane in San Diego and headed for the baggage area. He had left New York in the early evening, and now six hours later in California the sun was just going down. Somehow the feeling that he was not losing time made him think the trip out here was the right thing to do.

It made sense to him now. It clicked into place after Detective Woo had phoned to tell him the letters came from San Diego, not New York. Emma was right. It was someone who felt close to her, someone who knew her. Only it wasn't someone with any recent knowledge. It was someone from a long time ago, he was certain of it.

He kept going over his last conversation with the young detective, and brooded all the way out on the plane about whether he should have told Emma about it.

"There's nothing I can do," the girl had said over the phone. "Even if we knew who it was, it's not against the law to send unpleasant letters, Dr. Frank. It's a free speech thing," she added.

"So, that's it?" Jason had demanded, his anger growing. "What if he gets tired of writing letters and decides to pay her a visit?"

"Look," Detective Woo had said. "I'm not saying I'm not going to check into it. But I have no authority right now to make any kind of, you know, official investigation."

Jason's next move had been to call his travel agent.

Now he walked slowly, checking his watch several times. He passed a bank of telephones on the way to the car rental and hesitated as he debated calling Emma. What was the point in worrying her? He didn't usually call her the minute he arrived somewhere. He switched his briefcase, with the charts he and Charles had made, from one hand to the other and moved toward the baggage claim. Better just to find the guy, take care of it, and tell her about it afterwards, he decided.

A thin woman in a short gray dress hurried past him going the other way. She had a hard, lean face full of fury that reminded him of his first wife. He figured the image of Nancy throwing things at him in one of her frenzies rose out of his anxiety about doing the wrong thing with Emma.

"You're just a man," Nancy had kept shrieking at him, until he couldn't stand it anymore. "You're not the king of the world, Jason. You're not *God.*"

He turned away from the woman in gray with a familiar shudder, because Nancy had been right. There were a lot of things he just couldn't fix, and the most painful one had been her. The old failure weighed on him. No sign of any baggage yet. He headed for the Budget counter. It was seven-thirty.

Fifteen minutes later he was on the road with the windows of a new Ford open and the California wind blowing in his face. The sun was down, but there was still a vivid glow on the horizon in the west, like a halo over the city. The airport in San Diego was a strip of land almost in the middle of the city, with the ocean on one side. Even though he couldn't see it yet, Jason felt a surge of energy from the briny smell of the sea. He was suddenly optimistic about his and Emma's future. He vowed to practice what he taught and listen more. He was committed to working it out. He'd go back to New York, and they'd work it out. He turned his thoughts to things she had said about her year here.

Emma had often told him she felt free in California. Now he could understand it. It felt good to be behind the wheel of a car, instead of in the backseat of a taxi so old and redolent of unwashed foreigners it was painful to have to go somewhere. He thought about leasing a car for the summer. Maybe after Emma finished this new film, they'd start looking for a house out of the city and go away for

the weekends. Have a family. It was very radical, suddenly considering things he had resisted all his life. But he knew that, quite often,
everyday things people were afraid of were what they wanted most.

A small smile twitched at the corners of his mouth as he considered what it would feel like to buy a car, a house, a crib, and then
actually have all the paraphernalia of a successful husband and
father. He had no excuse for avoiding it any longer. He would do
whatever it took to make Emma happy. He further surprised himself
by getting on the Five heading north to Coral Beach instead of south
to the Meridien where he had gotten a businessman's special for two
nights.

He had planned to see Emma's parents anyway, but the sudden
acceptance of the possibility of having a family together made him
want to be near her. Understand her better. It was only a ten-minute
drive and he had been there once. He had a pretty good idea where
to turn off.

He exited at Coral Beach. It was a pretty community, not as
aggressively affluent and stylish as La Jolla, a few miles to the north.
He noticed that the streets were quiet even this early in the evening,
and the air was charged with eucalyptus, bougainvillea, and the
slight beginning of a salty mist. Not such a bad place to live. He
turned left off of Grand Encinada, fully lined on both sides with
royal palms, onto Encinada Drive. Four blocks west of the ocean and
five houses in on the right. Yes. The lights were on.

Jason pulled into the short cement drive and walked across the
cement path in the lawn. It wasn't a very big lawn, but definitely big
enough to be called one, and to merit having a small lawn mower in
the garage. He knew it was in there because his father-in-law, Brad
Chapman, had shown it to him on his and Emma's one and only visit
several years before. Brad had been as proud of the lawn mower as
the house. Jason rang the bell and looked across the street as he
waited.

The houses were all pretty much the same. Eighth-of-an-acre
plots with small, but nearly gracious, two-bedroom ranch-style
houses, each with slightly different design accents apparently cho-

sen at random from favorite styles around the world. Columns in front, wrought-iron curlicues around the windows, a two-foot cement wall in front of the door. Frosted or stained glass insets. All well cared for and tidy as could be.

No one answered the bell. As Jason considered ringing it again, Martha finally peered anxiously through the sidelight to see who would stop by without calling. She didn't live on a navy base anymore, and resented invasions on her privacy.

Then she saw Jason and her face lit up. She opened the door so fast he realized it hadn't been locked.

"Land sakes," she cried. "Emma told us you were coming, but we didn't expect you so soon. Come on in."

Martha stepped back to let her famous son-in-law in. "I just spoke to Emma. I mean just—um." She frowned anxiously. "Did you just get here?"

Jason smiled. "Yes, within the hour. Am I disturbing your dinner?"

"Oh, no, no. We finished hours ago. Oh, my—are you hungry? I could fix you something—"

"I had dinner on the plane. I'm fine," Jason assured her.

"Oh, well, then." She nodded happily, then less happily, in case she had done something wrong or misunderstood her famous daughter about when her famous son-in-law was coming and what she was supposed to do about it.

To Jason, Martha looked like an older, buttery version of Emma. Her hair was still light, almost blond, but with a silvery cast to it, and her body seemed fluffy. She had filled in around the edges in a gentle way, like a marshmallow, pale and soft. She was as tall as Emma, but had an apologetic air that diminished her. The smooth pink-and-white skin on her face broke up in a thousand tiny lines as she repeatedly excused herself.

"The place is a mess." She pointed to the pristine living room with its unused sofa and chairs in pale colors, and pottery lamps that gave off hardly any light. "Skipper, look who's here," she cried.

Martha led the way to the kitchen where her husband was sit-

ting at the table with a glass of Scotch in front of him, studying the
fan of cards in his hand.

"Who's here?" he demanded.

"You know very well who's here," Martha said with a determined playfulness. "You old dog, you heard me talking to him. It's
your favorite son-in-law."

Jason advanced with his hand out. "How are you, sir?"

Brad, the Skipper, got up and offered his with a show of reluc-
tance. "My only son-in-law," he said grumpily. He was a meteorolo-
gist, a weatherman, smaller than both his wife and daughter, an
unhappy fact he compensated for with a brusque, almost bullying,
manner.

"What are you doing?" he demanded, as his wife gathered up
the cards.

"You can't play now that Jason is here," she scolded.

"Who says so?" He turned to Jason again as if trying to decide
how disagreeable to be. "How are ya?" he said finally. "Have a good
flight?"

"Yes, thank you. It was fine."

"Treating our baby all right?" he demanded.

"I try."

"You don't have any children," he argued.

Martha turned the color of the chairs in the living room, dusty
rose. "Good Lord, Bradley, have a heart. Maybe they want to and
can't."

"Looks like he can." Brad's hairline mustache twitched with
emotion over Jason's looks. Jason was much bigger than he and had
a lot more hair. "Never mind," he conceded. "Not everybody's the
same, heaven knows. Have a drink. What are you doing out here?
Emma's quite the star, isn't she?"

He rambled on as he poured Scotch into a glass for Jason. He
didn't seem to care much about getting answers to his questions.

"Have you seen the film?" Jason asked finally.

"Yup, yup." Brad nodded, sipping at his own Scotch in earnest.

"Yup." Martha nodded. "We sure did."

There was silence.

Then Martha cocked her head. "She says she's got another part but she doesn't know if she wants it. Isn't that just like her? First she does a thing and then she has her doubts."

Jason nodded, wondering if Emma had ever voiced any doubts about him. *They* certainly must have. He, too, colored a bit. Now they were all a little pink.

"You two look fine," he said.

"We're fine," Martha agreed heartily. "Just fine."

"Great. What have you been doing?"

"Lot to do." Brad shook his head. "A whole lot."

"He goes to the Club," Martha said. "And he has his bridge." She nodded at the cards she'd laid aside.

"Got to mow the lawn. You'd be surprised how fast it grows," Brad added.

"Get many visitors, many inquiries?" Jason asked.

Martha frowned. Visitors, inquiries?

"About Emma," Jason prompted.

"Oh, that. Of course people are just thrilled. Everybody loves Emma. All our friends ask about her." Martha beamed.

"Any of her friends ask about her?" Jason asked.

"Her friends?"

"People she used to know."

"Oh, she doesn't keep in touch, never did. Even that guy who called from the high school said she was lost, remember that, Martha?"

Martha shook her head angrily.

"Course you do. They wanted to invite her to the reunion and couldn't because she was on the 'lost' list."

Martha clicked her tongue against her teeth. "You're not supposed to give her address. She wanted to be lost, Skipper. You know that. She went away and didn't ever want to come back. It's hard." Martha shook her head, sadder this time.

"But you don't argue with Emma. She does what she says. She's a sweet girl," she added apologetically, "but if you hurt her, she'll just cut your heart right out."

Jason nodded. She would indeed. And what had hurt her here in Coral Beach that she hadn't told him about?

"Don't go on about it, Martha. If the girl doesn't want to go, she just won't go. What about it, Jason? She coming to that reunion or not?"

"I don't think so, Skipper. Was there anybody else who wanted to get in touch with her recently?"

"Other than the guy from the school, uh-uh." Brad shook his head.

After a while, Jason had a glass of orange juice fresh from the tree in the yard, thanked them, and headed south to his hotel.

31

April had been sitting in a booth at Noodle Palace, looking at her watch, for nearly an hour. Jimmy was now so late she had to conclude something must have come up. Something coming up in police work was a fact of life no one who knew anything about the police department could argue with. But today there was the smell of something bad in her nose, as her mother would say. Only it wasn't really her nose. Her nose and every other part of April felt good being in Chinatown.

Almost as soon as she got off the subway, she saw somebody she knew. A woman she had helped a long time ago trotted up to her on the street and showed off her grandchild.

"Very pretty," April said, stroking the child's petal-smooth cheek with one finger.

"No, no. Not so pretty." The woman frowned critically at the exquisite three-year-old, dressed in an expensive padded silk jacket and embroidered shoes. "But very smart. Smart more important than pretty."

April nodded. "But she's pretty too. Pretty doesn't hurt."

"You nice girl. Why I don't see you no more?"

"I work uptown now," April said.

"Oh, too bad."

April agreed, as she went into the Noodle Palace on Mott Street and chose a booth in the window so Jimmy could see her right away. Often someone walked by and smiled at her, showing they still remembered her even though she hadn't been working here for nearly a year.

As she wondered where Jimmy Wong was, and analyzed his behavior lately, she watched what was going on outside on the street. She'd been a cop so long now she couldn't look at people without memorizing their faces, watching their movements, looking for trouble.

She observed a brownie, a traffic cop, stop a van and pull the driver over. She couldn't witness that kind of thing anymore without thinking of the last case she had down in the 5th. A traffic cop just like the one out there now, a Hispanic, had been threatening newly arrived Asians with jail, or deportation, or both, as a result of his giving them a ticket, if they didn't pay him off. She asked around and found four or five victims, persuaded them to testify. They got him. It felt good thinking about that even though it wasn't so hard to find out things down here. People had trusted her.

It was a whole different thing Uptown. She had so many things to learn. She pushed the teacup away with irritation, as she thought how hard it was to do things right. A lot of the cases they had Uptown she couldn't even begin to solve. She had faxed Ellen Roane's dental records to Dr. Milton Ferris, the Coroner of Potoway Village. He probably had them by now. She also faxed Ellen Roane's prints and everything that could be transmitted through the wires. The few X rays there were had been sent by overnight mail and would be there tomorrow.

She wondered what kind of place Potoway Village was. Was it some old Indian site where they once threw their pots away, sacrificed them to the Gods for rain, or something? She had talked briefly to the sheriff. He had a rich, rumbly voice and said the country around it was hills and high desert. The village was several thousand feet up. There was no hotel or motel in town, no place for transients to stay. The people who had houses there were pretty well off, generally older, he told her. What was a city girl like Ellen Roane doing there?

Sheriff Regis told her that bikers liked to ride out there on the rough terrain. He also said they had a similar case three months before about forty miles south, and both dead girls appeared to have been branded and abandoned. It was an unusual sort of situation. More commonly in crimes of this nature, the girls would be killed and then mutilated. This guy seemed to be a mutilator, but not a killer. They didn't know if he was a rapist.

Well, if the body in Potoway Village turned out to be Ellen Roane, April would send Regis more pictures of the girl so he could start looking for people who had seen her.

Only seventeen days had passed since Ellen's last credit card charge. April had called the stores to check the receipts and find out what each one was. The last charge was a bathing suit, a skimpy red-and-gold Cole of California bikini, on sale for $34. The salesgirl actually remembered Ellen. She told April that Ellen had a gorgeous body, but no, she had had no idea where the customer was staying. The other items Ellen had charged were three San Diego T-shirts from San Diego Tee for $38.69, a white leather belt from Fashion City for $46, a lipstick, shampoo, and conditioner from Kay Drugs for $15.76, and two dinners at the Beach Café on the night she arrived and the next night, for $19.42 and $15.73 respectively.

April had spent a lot of time studying the two photographs Jennifer Roane had given her of Ellen. Ellen's fine Caucasian features framed by her golden mane of wavy hair, her unclouded eyes and perfect figure, troubled April. All her privilege showed in the eyes. Ellen Roane had had no reason to be afraid of anything when those pictures were taken. There was no tension in her anywhere.

She had the kind of curves and curls April would give a lot for. Also the room at college with its printed bedspreads and no mother around to nag. There was a time April would have given a lot for that, too. But her parents wanted the house in Queens, so she went to work instead of to college.

Well, maybe Ellen was all right. Maybe she did know enough to be afraid. Anyway, with those looks there were sure to be other people who remembered her. Her luggage had to be somewhere. It wouldn't be hard to find if only someone tried.

And then there was the Chapman case. How could there be a biker's symbol on all the letters from San Diego, and a whole lot of references to branding? The coincidence of two women in her precinct both being involved in different cases with bikers from San Diego was too freaky. On the other hand, a connection between them didn't make sense. Writing and branding were not the same kind of activity. It occurred to April that he might have written Ellen Roane, too.

Her heart started beating faster as she considered the possibility that the biker might not come from San Diego. He could be from here. Two women in this precinct pointed to the possibility that he knew them from here. Maybe he even went *with* Ellen Roane to San Diego, had a fight with her, branded her, and left her in the desert.

At the same time as he was writing letters to Emma Chapman? Not so likely. *And* three months before that he had done the same thing to another girl, also in San Diego?

No, it couldn't be the same guy. But April made a note of calling to ask the two California coroners for a rendering of the burn on the two dead girls to see if it was anything like the drawing on the letters. She would also go back to Ellen Roane's room at the dorm and check out if she had received any letters there. Her roommate would know that. With a jolt April realized that she didn't know what Emma Chapman looked like. She hadn't seen the movie. She was working without any sense of the woman at all.

The smells of cooking oil, garlic, and roasted meat finally overcame her desire to give Jimmy a chance to redeem himself. She simply wasn't going to sit there starving for any man, especially one who had less than six hairs on his entire chest and had never had a truly sexy moment in his whole life. She got up, her head lowered a little with shame for drinking a whole pot of tea and eating the whole bowl of fried noodles and then leaving without ordering a thing.

She shook her head at the waiter. "Guess my mother got lost," she told him. "I'll go find her and come back."

April took her usual position on the subway going uptown. She stood on one end of the car by the door. Even though she wasn't on duty, she took the demands of her job seriously and didn't consider herself ever off duty. On the street she watched the parked cars and who was standing near them. In the subway she kept an eye on people's hands, where they were, what they were doing. But today, even as she studied the scene constantly playing before her, she was thinking about getting her car back. She had decided, without even knowing she was thinking about it, that there would be no more monkey business with Jimmy Wong. She'd tell him today. The decision cheered her up.

She was further elated when she found a message waiting for her from Sergeant Grove. Her desk was occupied, so she had to take an empty desk to make the call to San Diego.

"Yeah, Sergeant Grove speaking."

"This is April Woo in New York."

"How's it going, April."

"The sun is out, Sergeant."

"That's very good news. The name is Bob, April. You can call me Bob. Do you have a positive ID on that girl in Potoway Village yet?"

"No. I've sent out the data. They're probably working on it now. But I'm not calling about the Ellen Roane case. Something else has come up. It's probably not connected. But maybe it is."

"All right, April. What do you have?"

April waited while a suspect in handcuffs, screaming obscenities, was led through the detectives' room into an examining area behind it.

"April, you still there?"

"I'm having a little noise interference. Can you hold for a second?"

Two doors slammed on the curses. A few phones rang. "It might be kind of a Hinckley case," April told Grove when it was finally quieter. "An actress is getting some threatening letters."

Anyway, her husband said they were threatening. April hadn't
been so absolutely convinced about any of it until the postmark on
the envelopes came up San Diego.

"Uh-huh," came the noncommittal reply from the other coast.
"So what can I do for you? I'm in Missing Persons."

"I know that, Bob. But these threatening letters are coming
from San Diego."

"No kidding."

"Yeah, I was surprised, too. Six years on the force and I've
never had a case with any ties to San Diego. Now I've got two."

"So, do you figure they're a conspiracy?" Bob gave a little
laugh.

"No, I think they're just a coincidence. But the thing is . . .
that other unidentified female body you've got out there, the one that
has a similar burn on it?"

"You got me on that, April. What Jane Doe?"

"Don't you talk to each other?" April asked. "There's another
case of a girl, tortured, burned, and apparently left in the desert to
die."

"There's no desert in San Diego."

"What?"

"I'm in Missing Persons, San Diego Police Department. We
don't have desert areas in the City of San Diego. You're talking about
other jurisdictions, and I wouldn't hear about missing persons in
other jurisdictions unless other authorities like you ask me to check
them out." Grove was peeved.

"Well, if there get to be a few more of them, I guess you'll hear
about it."

"You talking about some kind of serial thing?" His voice sharp-
ened.

"I really couldn't say. I'm a detective here in New York. It's not
my jurisdiction. I'm just trying to put a few pieces together, and I
thought you could give me some advice." She let that sink in.

"All right, April, I have to admit you're persistent, and let's say
you've caught my interest. What can I do for you?"

"Okay, at the bottom of these letters there's a—kind of a biker symbol."

"Uh-huh."

"I need to know if anybody out there is getting threatening letters with a signature drawing like it. I need to know, maybe from Sex Crimes, if maybe anybody's been branded with a symbol like that and lived to talk about it."

"You don't want much, do you?"

"Look, your computer may have come up with the first missing person I was looking for, Bob. Now I'm looking for a guy who's writing letters. He's kind of a missing person, too, isn't he?"

"Uh-uh. Doesn't work that way. But did you say this was a brand or a drawing? I'm a little confused."

"The letters have a biker's symbol drawn on the bottom, kind of like a signature. The guy writing them talks about branding. The two Jane Does you got out there in other jurisdictions appear to have been branded. See?"

"So you think there might be some connection?"

"I really don't know," April confessed. "But both cases seem to involve bikers."

"Uh-huh," Sergeant Grove said. "Bikers aren't usually big on letter writing. But I'll ask around and see what I can find out."

"It might not be a biker," April said quickly. "It's just a biker symbol. Harley-Davidson."

"Lot of Harley fans out here."

"I'm sure there are, Bob. I appreciate your asking."

April took his fax number and sent off copies of the two strangest letters Emma Chapman had received. She hadn't had the delicious Chinese lunch with Jimmy she had hoped for, and her stomach was growling ferociously. She decided to ignore it. She'd go up to the dorm to look for Ellen's roommate.

32

Ronnie's broad face puckered with rage. "What's the *matter* with you? What's going on? A whole week goes by and I can't get a straight answer from you. What kind of shit is this?"

She covered a block of Sixth Avenue with quick little steps, her heels pounding the uneven sidewalk. It was the last day of April. The sun was finally out. Tomorrow was May Day. Ronnie went on without an answer.

"I've been telling Elinor Zing every day for more than a week that we want to do this film, and now you say you're not sure you do. How much longer do you think I can hold them off? I can't hold them off." She stopped and turned to Emma. "Are you listening to me?"

Emma had her eye on the street behind her.

"What's the matter with you?" Ronnie demanded fiercely.

"Nothing." Emma shook her head, looking puzzled. "It's weird."

"You know what Elinor told me? She said they like you very much, but just between us, she doesn't think Jack and Albert have a long attention span."

Emma took a few steps forward and then turned around again, frowning.

"What *is* the matter with you?"

"I don't know. I have the strangest feeling. . . ."

"Emma, look at me. Elinor told me not to jerk them around. She told me to tell you that no one who turns Jack down gets a second chance."

Emma studied the array of people behind Ronnie on Sixth Avenue. Nothing out of the ordinary. The usual mix of business people and street people. There was a crowd around two huge black men playing three-card monte.

"I told her you *adore* Jack," Ronnie went on. "I said you're dying to work with him. What are you looking at?"

"I told you, I have a funny feeling someone is—Oh, forget it." She shook her head.

"So Elinor said, 'What more could anyone want?' She could tell you liked Michael. God! *Anybody* would kill to work with him. I told her *you* would kill to work with him. You're crazy about him, aren't you? Can you imagine being with him for six weeks in a small hick southern town, huh?"

"I liked him," Emma admitted. "I liked him a lot."

"So she wanted to know what the trouble was and I couldn't think of a thing. So she, I don't know how, she got the idea you wanted more money."

"Jesus." Emma muttered.

"So she said she'd call me today and see if they can do any better." Ronnie pointed to her watch angrily. "Look at this. You waited too long, you asked for too much, and now they may not want you anymore. Do you think she called me back? Huh? Do you? No. She did *not* call me back."

"It's only twelve-thirty," Emma muttered. "It's still early in California."

"Yeah, but they may be talking to other people. I could just kill you. Hey, where are you going?" Ronnie protested. "I have a reservation at the Tea Room. Don't you want to be *seen?*"

Emma had continued up Sixth Avenue and was heading toward the park.

Ronnie huffed after her. "Speak to me," she demanded. "You finally got what we wanted, and now you're teetering on the edge of losing it. What the fuck's the matter with you?"

Ronnie stopped in the middle of the sidewalk by Café De La Paix and planted herself in Emma's path. Her face was red and angry. "Don't do this to me."

"You're my agent. You're supposed to represent my best interests," Emma said, "not just yours."

"But mine *is* yours," Ronnie insisted.

"Then you'll understand it isn't so simple." Emma started walking again.

"Oh, for God's sake, stop. I can't walk anymore. Where do you think you're going?" Ronnie protested helplessly.

"I'm going into the park. I don't want to eat. I want to sit on that bench over there in the sun." Where she could see the people around her. She started to cross with the light.

Ronnie plunged after her, puffing with the effort of keeping up. "You're making me crazy," she muttered.

"I can't *make* you crazy." Emma replied sharply, because it was a sore point. She wasn't exactly sure whether she could make someone crazy or not. Jason said she could do something that could trigger a crazy reaction. And now he was out of town. But she had a very strong feeling that he was still around. It was extremely unnerving.

"Look, I may be thwarting and frustrating you, but you're already crazy."

"Don't give me that shrink shit!" Ronnie cried. "I'm sick of that shrink shit. Just talk normal."

Emma made for the newly painted green bench just inside the park wall. It had no homeless person on it, no bird droppings. And just at that moment it was in the sun. Emma sat, and Ronnie collapsed next to her. Ronnie's red-and-blue silk skirt rose like a tent as she sat down, then gently deflated around her.

"You're already crazy," Emma repeated.

"Maybe," Ronnie said, more gently. "Maybe I am, but I know a few things, and you're making a big mistake here. What's going on with you?"

Emma paused for a long time. "Maybe I don't want to change my life," she said, starting cautiously. "Being so—public isn't all terrific."

"What are you talking about? Of course it's terrific."

"Something's happening, Ronnie."

Ronnie scowled. "What are you talking about?"

"I've been getting . . . letters." Emma's lips trembled.

"So? Everybody gets letters. It's part of the game. You get famous, you get letters. Forget it. Let's go have lunch. You'll feel better." Ronnie stood up.

Emma's face was white. "Not like these. It's somebody who knows me."

"How do you know?" Ronnie was irritated again.

"How do I *know?* He talks about things that happened in high school. I was the ghost in *Blithe Spirit.* He knows what my costume looked like. He talks about how pure I was. There was an incident in my senior year with the captain of the football team. . . ."

You were the Ice Queen no one could touch you.

"What kind of incident?" Ronnie was curious now.

Emma looked at a squirrel running up a tree. "It happened so long ago."

"What?" Ronnie asked again.

"Oh, nothing. Just . . . I don't know."

Ronnie sighed. If Emma were a big star, then she, Ronnie, would be a big star's agent. Other actors would come to her. She'd make a lot of money and be thin. She screwed her face up with the effort of looking for the right thing to say.

"Um, so, you're kind of freaked by these letters."

"It isn't *just* the letters," Emma said, looking at some serious scuff marks on the toe of her new shoes. *It was Jason.*

"Actors are recognized and talked to on the street all the time. They get thousands of letters. It's the price you pay for fame."

"What do they do?" Emma asked after a long moment.

"They don't open the letters. Give me the go-ahead, Emma. They're not going to wait for you forever."

Why did you become a piece of shit?

"It's not so easy," Emma said. "I'm scared."

"I don't believe this," Ronnie said. "What's there to be scared of? Do the damn film. Don't open the fucking letters. What's so hard?"

"You don't understand," Emma said. Somebody knew how to scare her from the inside.

She rubbed at the scuff mark. She didn't want to believe that she could do something that could make a person go crazy. But what if it was true? What if seeing her naked in a film made her own husband crazy?

Jason said he left town. Her parents said they saw him when he arrived last night. But she had the distinct feeling he was back. He had come back without telling her and was following her around. She shook her head. How could that be?

Planes flew all night. That's how it could be.

"Aw, shit. I'm going to call Elinor. So what if we leave a few thousand on the table." Ronnie put her arm around Emma and gave her a squeeze. "Come on. Come, let's go eat something. You'll feel better," she said soothingly. "Come on, Em. You know I love you."

The words struck a chord. Emma put her hands to her face.

Ronnie leaned over, concerned. "Jesus, what's the matter?"

They were surrounded by sunlight and springtime and the glow of a golden future. They should be eating caviar and drinking champagne in The Russian Tea Room, and Emma was crying her eyes out.

33

"Newton, honey. You got to do something about that dripping tap."
That was the last thing Rose said to him as he walked out the door
that morning. *You got to do something about the faucet.* It left a bad
taste in his mouth as he headed to work. She had been saying the
same damn thing for weeks, and she knew she could get it done just
as easy as he could, maybe easier.

Sometimes he couldn't understand why she didn't see he had
something on his mind—didn't sleep the whole night, worrying—
and leave him alone about faucets.

He didn't like got-to-dos.

If Milt got a match on that body, and it turned out to be that girl
from New York, then he'd have a big got-to-do. She died in his
jurisdiction. That made it his case. He couldn't just close it up
because there was no physical evidence. He'd have to investigate it.
But hell, there were not really enough of them to start running
around asking questions. Shit.

Newt half hoped Milt and his friend, the coroner from Twenty-
Nine Palms, would get together on this and find the same MO on the
two bodies. Then they could inform the FBI at VICAP and let them
deal with it as a serial murder thing. Never mind that it was just two.
More than one was good enough. Those guys had the experts and the
computers. They were used to checking and cross-checking every
kind of killer and every kind of bizarre twist the human mind could
think of.

But even though Milt and his friend agreed there was a striking resemblance between the injuries on the chest, even though the two girls did appear to have been tortured and were found in similar circumstances, that's all there was. They had not been murdered in the usual way. For homicides, you needed more than a body. You needed a murder weapon. You needed a place of death, some indication someone else was there.

Newton Regis certainly couldn't go to the FBI and say he had a serial killer. *Yes, sir, and by the way, sir, the desert did it.*

Maybe the guy hadn't worked his way up to killing them yet. Maybe he would, maybe he wouldn't. In any case, at the moment it was some kind of sex crime thing. And they certainly didn't have a Sex Crime Unit in Potoway Village. So Rose should understand he had a problem, if the girl Milt had on ice was the girl from New York.

Newt got in at eight and sat at his desk gloomily until ten, when Milt finally called him. They had a positive ID.

34

Jimmy leaned against the driver's door of the white LeBaron. His hair had gotten quite long, and his face was lean and narrow. Even in its best moments, it was not a generous face. Now it had kind of a pinched look about it, as if he had just eaten something sour.

April knew the sour thing he had to swallow was her insistence that he come into Manhattan right away. She called him every place she could think of, and someone must have given him the message.

"What's so urgent?" he said on the phone when he called her back.

"Hello," she said.

"What?"

"You skipped our lunch. The least you could do is say 'Hello, how are you, April,'" April said.

She had gone up to the dorm at Columbia to look for letters, and had found Connie Sagan but no letters. Connie was sure there had been no letters. She was sure Ellen hadn't been seeing anyone since she broke up with her boyfriend, and certainly didn't go to California with someone. Connie was absolutely sure she would have known that.

"I guess you haven't found her yet," Connie said. She was the opposite of Ellen, a fat girl with a lot of pain in her face.

April shook her head. "No, I don't have any information on that."

She had gone back to the precinct instead of home to wait for Jimmy's call. She was in a bad mood and didn't care who knew it.

"Look, I'm sorry about lunch. Something came up," Jimmy said. It didn't sound like he was in a good mood, either.

"You haven't called me in two weeks." She was sitting at her desk. Everyone was out. For some reason she felt strong.

"I've been on a case. What's the big deal? Are you my wife or something?"

"You have my car, Jimmy."

"You gave me your car. You told me to drive carefully."

"Now I want it back."

"Huh? I'm on a case right now. You called me for that?"

"You're off duty right now, Jimmy. Today was your day off. We were going to go to lunch. You stood me up."

"Look, you asked *me.* I told you it wasn't convenient. So just because I couldn't get there you want the car back. That's not a nice way to be."

"Jimmy, I want the car back because I need it to get around."

"I'm disappointed in you."

Yes, she'd heard that before. Whenever she opened her mouth to disagree with him, he either called her a crazy woman or said he was disappointed in her. She thought she used to be a crazy woman. Now she was a sane woman.

"You've changed since you've been Uptown," he complained, like she was contaminated in some way because of it.

"How soon can you be here? I'm not leaving here without my car. I'll let everyone know you have it. I want it now."

He showed up in an hour and had to wait outside the building because there was no way he would go in and look for her. He was leaning against the car scowling when she ambled out of the building and crossed the street.

"I told you I'd be here. Why'd you have to make me wait on the street?" he grumbled.

April held out her hand for the keys.

"I kept you waiting three minutes. You kept me waiting for an hour and a quarter. You knew where I was. You could have called. Now you know what it feels like."

His face turned red. There were some blue uniforms watching him lose face.

"Uh, get in. I'll drive you home," he said.

She shook her head. "I'm not going home."

"Then I'll take you where you're going."

"I thought you were on a case," April reminded him.

"I have time to take you where you're going." He cocked his head at her, telling her to get in the car.

"Uh-uh. You can't take me where I'm going, Jimmy."

"Why not?"

"Because we're not going to the same place anymore. So we're not seeing each other again."

"What, just like that?"

His thin face was very red.

"Not so just like that. It's been coming on for a long time. You don't love me, Jimmy, and I don't love you. I guess that about covers it."

"How do you know I don't love you?" he said very quietly, with daggers coming out of his eyes.

She wanted to get away from those angry eyes before he found a way to curse her for all time.

"Because of the way you act," she replied.

"I don't know what you're talking about. We've been together almost three years."

"And that's about long enough." Too long.

"Look, I said I was sorry about the lunch." He was very angry now. His voice was tight. His eyes had all but disappeared into their Mongolian folds.

She looked around for someone she knew. "Give me the keys, Jimmy. I have to go now."

He saw her nod at a uniform, a big guy, probably Irish. He handed her the keys.

She got in the car and closed the door very gently. "Have a good life," she said, careful not to curse him.

It was more than he would do for her. He sloped off toward the subway without a word.

35

Troland knelt on the floor and lifted the blind just a few inches, so he could peer out sideways at Mrs. Bartello's living room window. He did this every few minutes. She never seemed to be in there. That was good. Sometimes he thought she was dead. There was no sign of life in her house.

When she came to the door the first time, the old lady was wearing a stiff black dress and said, "What do you want? I'm in mourning."

That was good. He switched his attention to the front window. Out on the street the traffic was backed up. A jet thundered in over the roof, heading for LaGuardia.

"I want to rent the place," he said. He pointed to the hand-lettered sign in the window, GARAGE APARTMENT FOR RENT.

He had seen the sign as he wandered around looking for the way into Manhattan the first time, and knew it was there for him. He exited to the service road and parked in front, just like he had lived in the neighborhood all his life. It didn't feel good, though. He breathed in the air and felt dangerous particles entering his body. It was gray and damp. He didn't think much of New York.

"You can call me Mrs. Bartello." She was a small, thin woman. She looked him and his rented Ford Tempo over. "I guess you'll want the garage, too."

"I have to have the garage," he said.

She shrugged. He had to have it. It was the only way into the apartment.

"You don't have wild parties with loud music, do you?" she asked, looking him over again. He was blond and not too big. He had blue eyes, was wearing a leather jacket, black jeans, and boots.

"I don't like music," he said.

"What about drugs?"

He shook his head.

"Okay." She took the two hundred in cash he gave her, counted the bills with surprising speed, and shut the door.

He liked that about her. She wasn't interested. She let him look at the place alone because she didn't like going there. Reminded her of her dead husband, she said. For days after he took it, he kept looking for a flaw. He couldn't find one. It was a perfect setup.

He could drive into the garage and go upstairs without being seen from the outside. He had two rooms, one with a sofa, table and chairs, a little kitchen, and a telephone; the other, a tiny bedroom with a single bed and a skylight. He didn't like the skylight. He saw faces looking in from above. Airplanes and faces.

There were windows on three sides. Troland checked the back and the side. When he got restless he took the rental car into Manhattan. The first few times he did it he had a map with him. He experimented crossing different bridges and working his way across town to the West Side. Then he tried taking the subway. The subway was faster, but an old crazy lady pulled up the two skirts she was wearing and urinated in front of him, squatting between two cars, as the train speed along. Crazy people made him upset.

He got there early in the morning and sat in the car down the block, looking up at the window and waiting for her to come out. Sometimes he parked the car far away and walked around the neighborhood, getting the feel of it. He hung around the next block over, trying to figure out the buildings.

Half of the block, from west to east, was built around a sort of garden that was part of a larger building on the other side. Sometimes the iron gate to the garden was open. She lived on the fifth floor.

He'd seen her about six times now. The first time it was like being hit by a blast of cold air. Like when he rode the scooter at seventy-five on the freeway with no helmet. Cold, exhilarating beyond anything, and almost out of control. It was a shock. The bitch he'd taken all the trouble for didn't look like her. She looked like somebody he wouldn't even look at. It almost took his breath away. Sixteen years and she was someone else.

She was wearing a tan skirt and loose tweed jacket with a kind of purple blouse under it that didn't show her figure at all. Her hair was not as blond as it used to be, was hardly blond at all now. Not blond by California standards. Even from a distance he could see she was quite thin, and her face was—different. She was not like the girl in the movie. This one was not the kind of woman he would talk to. He didn't like her. That upset him. Then he told himself, so what? He wasn't supposed to like her.

He saw her stop at the wrought-iron doors and talk briefly to the doorman, a guy so small he couldn't stop a child from getting in. Then a tall man came out with a dog. The dog jumped up on her like it knew her, and she leaned over to pat it. A small hairy thing. She smiled. Yeah, it was her. The smile made him mad.

The second blow came when he delivered a pizza and found out she was living with a man. A doctor.

"Chapman, or Dr. Frank?" the doorman asked.

"It says Chapman here." Troland showed him the receipt where he had written Emma's name and address. He saw the doorman ring up 5C.

"There must be a mistake. She's out."

Course she was out. He saw her go out. Shit, he hadn't considered a man. What kind of man would let her do that?

"Look, I can't help you," the little doorman said. "I'm not supposed to ring the Doc under any circumstances, okay? You'll have to take it back."

"Nah, you keep it." Troland handed the pizza over and walked away.

What kind of doctor wouldn't let the doorman ring up under any circumstances? He wanted to get a look at the doctor. He wanted to get inside and look around where she lived. But it didn't take a genius to see the inside was a problem. It was a really old building. He didn't like the see-through elevator, or the center staircase. Anybody coming in or out could look up the middle of the building and see all the front doors. It didn't take a genius to see it was a problem.

The man came out of the building early, as Troland was walking by in a windbreaker and baseball cap, with a newspaper under his arm.

"Morning, Dr. Frank," he heard the night doorman say. The night doorman went off at eight.

"Morning, Pete."

The doctor didn't look like a doctor. He was at least an inch taller than Troland and probably a few pounds heavier. He was wearing white shorts and a plain gray sweatshirt, had muscular legs. No gray in his hair. Not a bad-looking guy. He felt himself getting upset.

Troland slowed down and passed him when he stopped to stretch.

"Nice day," the doctor said to the doorman who stood outside with him, looking.

"Perfect day."

The doctor took off at a brisk jog and passed Troland, heading for the path along the river. At a slower pace Troland followed him. Much later in the day, he couldn't believe his luck when he saw him come out of her building with a suitcase and get into a taxi.

36

After breakfast, Jason drove around until he found North High School, which turned out to be south of both South High and Central High. It was a three-story brick building that looked only a few years younger than the municipal buildings nearby. It had a lot of steps going up to the entrance, green stuff that wasn't ivy growing on the walls, a huge parking lot in front, and playing fields in the back. It was a real old-style American high school, the kind that's always in the movies.

As he pulled into the parking lot, he tried to picture Emma as a lonely senior in this tight community, where the rest of her class had been together for years. What he saw instead was himself and Emma, talking so many times in a coffee shop, a half hour stolen here and there, between his patients and her jobs. He had interviewed her for a paper he was writing on adults who had been constantly uprooted as children. And they kept meeting.

He remembered the way she sat leaning slightly forward, with her hands relaxed in her lap as she told him how the Navy liked to move people as far away from where they had been as possible, preferring to move them laterally around the world, rather than up and down a coast. She had spent second and third grades in Jacksonville, fourth and fifth grades in Seattle. Sixth and seventh in Norfolk, Virginia. Eighth and ninth in Hawaii. Tenth and eleventh in Kodiak, Alaska. San Diego was her father's last post.

The parking lot was nearly full at ten, on another in an endless succession of golden mornings in southern California. The cars

parked here showed no sign of a recession in the country's economy.
This was clearly not a deprived area. Corvettes, Mercedeses, Miatas,
a few Hondas and Toyotas were tightly parked side by side, all
polished and shiny. It made Jason think again of maybe getting a
car.

He parked in the area reserved for visitors and started toward
the building. Earlier he had debated what to wear, and finally decided to stick with what he had come in. Khaki pants and a sports
jacket in the kind of muddy colors women don't usually like, but
men find unchallenging and comfortable. He noted some temporary
classrooms on what had been another parking area.

It didn't take long to find Guidance, which was in the same
office as College and Career Counseling. There was a list of names
on the wall outside. He studied them for a second before going in.

"Can I help you?"

A plump woman with heavily rouged cheeks, red lips colored
outside the lines, fluffy orange hair, and a purple blouse looked up
from her computer screen.

Jason almost said "Wow."

"Ah, yeah," he replied diffidently. "I'd like to see Dr. Londry.
Would that be possible?"

"Anything is possible." She smiled, showing off a set of whiter-
than-white teeth to prove it. "Especially now with all the students in
the middle of third period," she added. "He's right in there."

She pointed at a closed door behind her with frosted glass in
the top half so nothing could be seen through it.

Jason tapped on it softly and obeyed the equally soft reply,
"Yes, come in."

He found Dr. Londry sitting at his desk with his feet up, reading a newspaper that he put down as soon as he saw his visitor wasn't
a student. Londry had long lifeless hair that grew unashamedly
around a large circular bald spot on the top of his head. Rimless
glasses magnified the lines around his pale eyes. His short-sleeved
plaid shirt was open at the neck, and he promptly took his suede
shoes off the desk.

"Hi." Jason held out his hand. "I'm Frank Miln. I'm out here doing an article for *New York Magazine* on rising stars from California who make it in film in New York. It's kind of a reverse coast thing."

"Good lord," Londry said, blinking. "Yes, I heard something about that. You want to come in?"

"Yes, thank you," Jason said.

"Big film industry in New York, right? I've heard of people going down to Florida, too. What brings you here?"

"Well, Emma Chapman is going to be in the article, and she was at school here. She graduated thirteen years ago. Were you here then?"

"Oh, yes, somebody told me something about that just a few days ago." He narrowed his eyes at Jason. "I was here, but I couldn't tell you anything about her even if I had a file on her, which I don't."

Jason laughed comfortably. "Oh, I wouldn't want to see what's in the file. That would be—" he hesitated, "unethical, of course."

"Well, they do," Londry said disapprovingly, pulling his lips into a thin line. "Reporters ask for anything they can get. Sometimes it makes good reading." Londry swiveled back and forth in his chair. "But I don't have a file on her. I'd remember if I did."

"Well, I wasn't looking for a file. I just stopped by to see if you knew where I might find some of her friends. She's lost touch with them."

Londry sneaked a look at his bookcase. Jason followed his gaze.

"I talked with her, and her parents, of course. She said she didn't mind who I talked to," Jason said. "But she couldn't remember the names of the people she knew then. You probably don't either. I guess a lot of kids pass through."

"I remember them when I see their faces." He got up and crossed to the shelves of yearbooks. "Seventy-eight, you said?"

"Seventy-nine. She mentioned one person in particular. A guy, of course. Had a Harley-Davidson."

Londry took down a book and opened it, searching for a face to attach to Emma Chapman. "Ah, yes, the actress. Yes, I remember. There was something."

"What?" Jason asked too quickly.

"Oh, nothing. She was in a play. Noel Coward." He turned pages. "I don't know," he murmured, shaking his head. "There are always a few kids in every year with motorcycles."

"This guy might have gone into the military, or the defense industry."

"Okay, then you must mean him." Londry pointed at a small square picture that was slightly out of focus. "Great guy. You'd think he was running for president. Yeah, talk to him. He knew everybody."

"Do you know where I might find him?" Jason asked, making a note of the name.

"Sure I do. He's at General Defense."

"Where's that?"

"Lindbergh Field."

"Of course." Jason put out his hand with a broad grateful smile. "Thanks. Thanks a lot."

"No problem." Londry turned his attention to the book he'd left open on Emma's page. He was studying the faces on it as Jason left.

Out in the sun again, Jason began to tense up. He could feel the muscles tighten in his neck as he thought about how he would handle the thing. He was going to get the guy. He was going to get him in his office where he felt safe, and nail him to the wall. He liked that image.

There was a nice breeze off the ocean. Jason realized he had left his objectivity back in New York somewhere. He wanted to know what happened between Emma and this guy all those years ago that made her leave the only home her parents ever had. And he wanted to kill the guy for torturing her now. Son of a bitch. He was so tense over this thing he had broken out in a cold sweat.

He drove back down the main highway to Lindbergh Field and was directed from one building to another in the sprawling complex where jet engines and airplanes and rockets were made. Finally, in a new office building, he was shown into the office of Bill Patterson.

Jason glibly repeated the story that he was a reporter from *New York Magazine* to the secretary guarding the door, and asked if Mr. Patterson could spare him three minutes.

"Well, he's here, but he won't talk to you." She looked Jason over with vague distaste. "You might as well forget it. We have a rule here. We're not supposed to talk to the press about anything. Not the government contracts, not anything."

"Tell him I'm doing a story on a girl he knew in high school," Jason said evenly. "He'll see me."

A few seconds later, not bothering to hide her surprise, she ushered him into the office.

"Hi, what can I do for you?" Bill Patterson was a fit young man with a conservative haircut, in a white button-down shirt and striped tie. He looked up from some papers on his glass-topped desk, and examined Jason with unguarded, curious blue eyes.

"Thanks for seeing me. I'm Frank Miln. I'm doing a story on Emma Chapman."

Patterson nodded and scratched his chin. His expression didn't change.

Jason looked around. The walls of the room were covered with prints of airplanes. The man was pure middle management. He was wearing loafers. On his desk were pictures of a sailboat, two golden children in bathing suits, and a smiling woman. Jason got a sinking feeling.

Patterson moved his scratching on to his temple, worked on that for a moment. "Who is she?" he asked finally.

"She's an actress in New York. She was in your class in high school."

"Oh. Emma Chapman." He paused, as if doing a computer search of his memory. Then he shook his head. "I'm not sure I remember her."

"That's very surprising, because when I was talking to her, she mentioned a guy with a motorcycle who works for General Defense."

"Really?"

"Yeah, she specifically wanted me to say hello."

"Gee, I haven't been on a bike in years," Patterson said nostalgically. He pointed at the photos of his family. "Well, say hello right back, but it must be some other guy. I didn't know her."

Jason nodded and got up slowly. Before he got to the door, Patterson stopped him.

"Hey, wait a minute. There is a guy who works for us. But he wasn't in our class. He was a year behind us. Matter of fact he still rides a bike. I see him in the field lot sometimes."

Jason's throat constricted. "What's his name?" he said carefully.

Patterson scratched his face some more. "Funny name." He reached for the company directory and started flipping the pages. "Here it is. Grebs, Troland."

Jason leaned forward to look at the page. Grebs, Troland was in Technical Drafting, Building 4. The guy drew. It sounded right. For the second time that day Jason felt a surge of adrenaline shoot through him. He checked his watch. If he hurried, he might still be able to get home to Emma that night.

37

Sanchez had a hit-and-run on Amsterdam. In broad daylight a van running the light hit a woman with a dog and a baby carriage. Mother and child were squash flat, as Sai Woo put it when April told her about it. The dog, which had been tied to the carriage, managed to escape injury. Sai liked hearing stories like that. Happen to other people, not happen to her.

"I had a dog once, long time ago in China." She reached for the story, offering it up to April as favor for favor.

April nodded seriously, accepting the gift she'd already received a hundred thousand times.

"One day dog gone. I very sad," Sai said. "Look for it and look for it. Ask everybody." When she paused to shake her head, April knew she was thinking about how everybody said they didn't see a thing. Didn't remember ever seeing any dog. And that was how Sai learned she couldn't trust anybody.

"Neighbors ate it," she said now, playing it for all it was worth.

"Serve dog right," she added, "for going outside without me." She looked at April slyly out of the corner of her eye. She was eating melon seeds, cracking the shells open delicately with her teeth at the kitchen table after dinner. The TV was on, but neither of them was watching. Sometimes Sai left the picture on and the sound off, just for company when Ja Fa Woo and her daughter were both at work. Now it was on for show. To show April she didn't have to be there and could go home whenever she wanted.

"Probably dog's fault. Why he tied to carriage anyway?" she

asked. She couldn't stand the sight of a dog now, didn't like her neighbors either. She brushed an errant shell off her lap impatiently.

She had given April perfectly good story. Very good story about her life. And now April's turn to tell something. Dead baby and mother not enough. Sai wanted to know important things, like what happened to red Camaro, and why white Baron was back with no sign of Jimmy Wong.

April was writing something and wouldn't say. Sai leaned over to see what it was, but couldn't see a thing without her glasses. She never liked Jimmy Wong. Not so good as a doctor or dentist. Jimmy Wong wore a gun in a shoulder holster and walked like gangster. Had no good future. *Boo hao.* "*Ni*, you listening to me?" she said.

April nodded without looking up.

"Main thing is, lose innocence but not hope," Sai said pointedly.

"Okay, Mom." April rolled her eyes because she had no idea what that meant and her mother still called her "you." Like, hey you, you listening to me? How could she avoid it?

April looked her mother over critically. Desperate to be "new style" right up-to-date, Sai Woo always wore extravagantly colored blouses which she tucked into matching tailored pants. Her hair was still black as patent leather, and though she swore up and down she didn't touch it, April knew she dyed it promptly at the beginning of every fifth week.

In spite of these details, she was "old style" in her soul. No getting around it. She ate melon seeds, cracking the shells with her teeth, gossiped like an old woman, and sometimes hunkered all the way down on her heels without warning. Just the way they did in China, because not so many chairs there. Nobody who was born in America would dream of doing that. No one could. Well, cowboys maybe. But there weren't many of those in Queens.

"You should be the detective," April said.

"Not so good detective, not find out much," Sai replied disgustedly, ending the discussion as usual on a sour note.

By the time Sanchez found the van, it had been sold. But he didn't have too much trouble getting to it. The person who bought it lived only a few blocks away from the suspect, and hadn't had time to get the bumper or the broken headlight fixed. It was after four when he came back from the indictment.

The squad room was always pretty empty between four and four-thirty. Day shift going or gone, night shift coming in.

"I was afraid I'd miss you," he said.

April was sitting at her desk, tying up a few loose ends. Sergeant Riley was already there and hassling her to get out so he could have her desk. She looked up at Sanchez. It was nowhere in her thoughts that she might be waiting for him.

"Why?" she asked. Then lowered her head with some confusion because he seemed tired and discouraged.

"Why what?" Sanchez asked.

"Why were you afraid of missing me? Did something come up?"

"No. Just wanted to know what was going on, uh, with you. Bad day." He said it as fact, not a question.

"Had a DOA on Broadway. Homeless. Poor guy sat there on the bench for nearly thirty hours before the neighbors were willing to admit he hadn't moved in a long time."

They didn't look at him when he was alive, but a crowd had gathered to watch him bagged and taken away. But that wasn't what Sanchez was asking about.

"The positive ID came in on Ellen Roane," she said at last.

"I heard."

"I had to talk to the mother."

"Rough."

"Very rough." April looked away. That was the worst part of the job. That and collecting more pictures and information about Ellen to send to Sheriff Regis. She would have liked to follow up on this case herself, go out to San Diego and follow Ellen's tracks all the way to Potoway Village in the hills to see if she could come up with anything resembling a suspect. Now Sheriff Regis would have to do it. She'd found her Missing Person. For her, the case was closed.

"I see you got your car back," Sanchez said after a minute.

"Yeah, last night."

It was in the lot downstairs. April took a lot of flak for it. Very flashy car for a cop. Couldn't miss it coming, couldn't miss it going.

"That have any special meaning?" Sanchez asked.

"Why don't you two woo somewhere else," Sergeant Riley said with a leer. He'd already been married twice, had the white hair to show for it, was now engaged to be married for the third time, and still didn't think much of women. "Ha, ha. Woo woo, get it?"

April saw the words "fuck off" jump into to Sanchez's mouth behind the mustache, and then saw them jump out again when he looked at her.

"Hey, man. We're doing business, got a problem?"

"Yeah. I want to sit down."

"Fine. Let's go." Sanchez put his hand up to touch April's arm, then checked the gesture.

Good. She didn't want him embarrassing her. She picked up her bag. It was heavy. It had mace and a .38 in it. He followed her out.

"So, ah, what's happening with this Hinckley case of yours?" he asked as they headed down the stairs. "You got plans? We could talk about it, eat some Mexican." He looked at her slyly.

So he knew about Jimmy. April didn't say anything until they got downstairs and punched out.

"Nothing to talk about," she said. "No one's getting letters like that in San Diego. I tried to call the husband to find out if they were still coming, but he's taken off."

"What do you mean, taken off?"

"I don't know. He's out of town. I guess he doesn't think it's so important anymore. On his answering machine, he gives the name of another doctor to call in case of emergency."

April caught sight of the LeBaron right away, even though it was parked in the back. Sanchez's red Camaro was right next to it. Yeah, he came in just around four. Maybe someone was pulling out right then. The red Camaro was flashy, too. Even her mother remembered it.

"It's kind of weird." She unlocked her car door but didn't get in. "Maybe it's like this. One time we went up to this lake when I was a kid. Upstate somewhere. In the middle of the night there was this helicopter with a big searchlight flying back and forth over the cabin. Everybody jumped up and got really scared and thought there was an escaped convict out in the woods gonna kill us." She laughed, remembering it.

"So what was it?"

"Well, we couldn't call the police, because Chinese, well, you know how the Chinese feel about the police."

"No." Sanchez moved over and leaned against her car, smiling. "How do Chinese feel about the police?"

He was close enough now for her to smell him. His after-shave was not so strong after a whole day of sitting around a stale courtroom. But even now he didn't smell of sweat. More like shirt starch. She wondered if he took his shirts to a Chinese laundry, or if some woman ironed them for him. *Boo hao, ni, ni,* she scolded herself in her fish-in-water language. No good, you.

"They think police will steal what's left in their house after they've been robbed, and take their favorite son to jail," she said. "I have to go."

Sanchez's face fell enough so she kind of felt sorry for him.

"I have a class," she added.

"So what was it doing there?" he said after a second.

"What?"

"The helicopter?"

"Oh, that." He got her so mixed up she couldn't remember what she was talking about. "Turned out there's this wife and husband staying on a boat. They get drunk. Wife jumps off the boat. Husband gets scared and calls the police. Police spend three hours searching for her. They get cars, park them all around the lake with the lights on, send up a helicopter. Everything. Then when they get all ready to start dragging the lake with nets, she walks out of the bushes where she's been watching the whole thing. Know what? She gets right back on the boat. Wouldn't go to the station, make out a complaint against him. Nothing."

"So you think it might be something between the two of them?" Sanchez asked. "The husband and wife?"

"Well, I haven't heard a word from her. It's kind of weird, isn't it?" She cocked her head toward the car, so he would move.

"Yes," he agreed. "Sometimes you think they're going to add up to something, and then they just go away." Sanchez shrugged and moved away from the door of her car.

What? Cases or people?

A few days before, on the way back from a call, Sanchez had told her his father was a cook in a Mexican restaurant before he died. He worked in a restaurant in El Paso and then when it failed, someone offered him a job in New York. It was at a red light in a lot of traffic. They were sitting in the car. April had to close her eyes for a minute to keep the Mexican ghost out of her soul. Her father and his father did the same thing. She didn't want to hear that. Sanchez put his arm out on the seat so his hand was not too far from hers. She knew he was showing her they were the same color. But she wasn't sure they were the same color underneath, so she didn't say anything.

"The thing is there's still the San Diego thing. I have a feeling it's not over." April smiled suddenly. "You know, Sergeant, I've never had Mexican food."

Then she looked at her watch in alarm and realized she'd been talking so long she was going to be late.

38

The lights were off, and Jason was not in the apartment when Emma returned from her long lunch with Ronnie. There was no sign that he had been there, and no messages from anybody on her answering machine. That was strange. Usually there were three or four. She wondered if it had stopped recording again. Sometimes it did that for a day or two. The heads or something got stuck. She took off her jacket and, with her heart pounding, she started going through the stack of mail she had picked up on the way in. She knew she was doing this to take her pulse, to see if she was all right. There hadn't been one of those letters in the mail for three days and she was afraid to hope there would be no more.

Because of their two addresses in the building, mail was a little confusing. Some of it was put on a table outside Jason's office door, and some of it was left on the mat outside their apartment a few steps away. That day Jason's mail, the thick pile of envelopes, checks from patients, correspondence, books and periodicals, was still on the table. If he had come home, he would have gone into his office taking it with him. There were only bills, no personal letters to Emma in her and Jason's joint mail. Not a sound came from the other side of the wall where his office was. She was still not all right.

A profound sense of aloneness overwhelmed her. The silence in the apartment was even more unnerving than the menacing sights and sirens on the street below. She was upset that Jason wasn't there spying on her after all, and wondered if the creepy sensation she'd had outside, of being watched and followed around, was her own wish that he really had come back.

She shook her head. The truth was Jason wouldn't take time off to spy on her. Time was everything to him. A lawyer could work at home, could work at the office when the client wasn't there, would bill more hours than there are in a day, and no one could ever know. Heart surgeons could charge ten thousand dollars a day, could set their fee at whatever someone was willing to pay for a life. But a psychiatrist had only a few forty-five-minute periods in a day. And someone like Jason, who wrote and spoke, and did research, had to give away the price of every hour he spent on scholarship.

He didn't waste his time without a good reason, and rarely had any for her anymore. It was a gift he used to give her, but not anymore. He was so involved with his work he didn't enjoy the few occasions he had to cancel his evening patients to go see her in a play. For an opening night in Philadelphia, he had to miss much of the afternoon as well; he'd complained about it the next day. She hadn't been at all surprised that he didn't even consider giving up a three-day conference in Toronto to be there at her first screening. Often when she was alone in the evenings she dreamed about being a rich movie star, and buying some of Jason's hours so he wouldn't always feel he was losing something when he was with her.

Apprehensively, she flipped through the envelopes, mostly bills, a few invitations to events they would never in a million years attend. Nothing dangerous so far. Maybe she was just being nuts, afraid of success, afraid of making things worse with her husband, like Ronnie suggested.

"Everybody goes through rocky periods in the business, you know that," Ronnie said.

Emma nodded. In marriage, too.

"Look, better face it now. Success is harder to manage than failure. The *least* of it is nasty letters."

Emma came to the last envelope. It was from Save the Wilderness. Maybe Ronnie was right and this thing with the letters had played itself out. No more were coming in. The incoming fire was over. She picked up her jacket from where she had tossed it on a chair and wandered around the apartment, checking to see if it was in order. Everything was exactly as she had left it.

She was feeling all right and then without warning, anxiety about Jason welled up in her again. Where was he and why hadn't he called her all day? It wasn't like him. Was he just so mad at her he finally turned to one of his many fans, some woman, like himself terminally nice and comforting, from the 'caring profession'? Someone who both sympathized and empathized with his needs?

That's what they always asked her whenever she met one of them. "Are you in the 'caring profession'?"

"No, I'm in the uncaring profession," Emma was always tempted to retort. For Jason's sake, she never had.

In the kitchen she found the slip of paper Jason left for her with the hotel number in San Diego on it. She never called him when he was away. He frequently made her feel guilty, but he didn't like it when she made him feel guilty. She studied the number for a minute. Then she dialed it to see if he was really there.

The operator at the Meridien said there was no answer in his room. In a moment of pique at his secrecy, Emma didn't care about the probability of bringing on his guilt. She left a message asking him to call her right away.

39

Jason had his hand on the doorknob and was desperate to get away when Bill Patterson offered to call Technical Drafting and tell the guy a reporter from New York wanted to talk to him.

"No. Thanks anyway," he said as casually as he could. "I'm sure I can find it."

Patterson crossed his legs the other way and did some more scratching of his short brown hair. "Not a chance. You won't get anywhere near it. Security is pretty tight over there."

"Oh." Jason fell silent.

"They don't let anybody wander around asking questions." As he said that, Patterson's eyes became suspicious for the first time.

Jason looked at his watch. It was way past time to get out of here. This was a defense company. Of course there would be security. Of course they wouldn't like reporters. He cursed himself for not thinking of a better cover story. The last thing he wanted to have to do was say he had left his press card home.

"Well, I've got to get back downtown. I'm running late. Thanks for your help. I may give this guy—what's-his-name—a call later."

He swung the door open, and once again Patterson delayed his exit.

"Grebs," he said, halting Jason's progress.

Jason stopped and nodded. "Yeah, Grebs."

"I'll write it down for you." Patterson picked up a pen and neatly printed the name and number on a piece of his monogrammed memo paper, then handed it over. He was right-handed.

"Thanks." Jason returned to the desk to get it. "Thanks a lot."

"You're not going to try wandering around here, are you?" Patterson said. "You reporters—"

"No, no," Jason assured him. "It isn't that kind of story."

"Well, good luck then."

Jason found a telephone in a restaurant a few blocks away and dialed his hotel to see if there were any messages. There was one from Emma. He called his office answering machine and took some notes of the messages left there. Nothing that had to be responded to immediately.

He looked at his watch, then dialed the home number and waited. On the fifth ring Emma's voice told him she was not available to take his call, but if he would leave his name, his number, and the date, she would get back to him very soon.

His shirt was soaked and he was getting a headache. It wasn't a lot of fun pretending to be a reporter. He wondered what time Emma had tried to reach him and what she wanted.

She knew he had a policy of checking in every few hours. If she wanted to talk to him, why couldn't she stay put and wait for him to return the call?

He punched his telephone credit card number into the phone and dialed the number Patterson had written down for him. It took a long time for someone to answer the phone.

"Drafting," a woman's voice finally said.

"Hello, I'm trying to reach Troland," Jason said.

"Who?" she said.

"Troland Grebs."

"Oh, yeah." Pause. "He's not here."

"Not here forever?" Jason asked. "Or out to lunch?"

"He wasn't here yesterday. He's not here today." The sound became muffled as she called out, "Anybody know where Willy is?"

She came back on the line. "He's sick," she said.

"You have an address for him?"

"You kidding?" There was a pause. "Who is this anyway?"

"Friend of a friend," Jason said. "I have a gift for him."

"Well, that's a first. Can't help you." She hung up.

Jesus, he thought everyone in California was supposed to be so friendly. He tried Information. Nobody listed by that name in the San Diego area.

Shit, the San Diego area was a big place. Where else could Grebs be? He tried dialing Emma in New York again. She still wasn't there.

The cashier frowned at Jason when he asked for the phone book, so he had to sit down and order a cup of coffee and a corn muffin to appease him. He realized as he studied the book and ate the muffin that he was hungry.

There were only two Grebses in the phone book. Gloria Grebs was way north and west according to Jason's map. And the road going there was the merest squiggle that actually looked like it thinned out to nothing in places. It didn't seem worthwhile going all the way out there first, when Esther Grebs lived on Twenty-eighth Street, right in the heart of the city.

Jason nodded absently at the offer of another cup of coffee. It was only one-thirty. He still had all afternoon. He wrote down the two addresses and studied the San Diego map he had bought in the hotel gift shop. Twenty-eighth Street was not far from downtown. It was on the west side of the highway, at least in the direction of his hotel. He paid the cashier the dollar fifty for the coffee and muffin and left two dollars on the table for the use of the phone book.

Before he went out into the sunshine, he tried Emma one more time. Still no answer. He shrugged. Couldn't have been too important if she didn't leave a number. He got back in the car, all too aware that he was wandering around a strange city like an idiot for reasons that were not entirely clear, and hadn't really learned a thing.

40

He drove south and after a few exits got off. He was amazed at how quickly the neighborhood changed. South of the airport and west of the highway was shabby enough to qualify as a slum. Turning off Martin Luther King, Jason saw a huge open water or sewage pipe dripping into a culvert. The structures around it were more like shanties. Some of the cracks in the streets and sidewalks were big enough to have small trees growing out of them. There was graffiti everywhere.

But even here was the powerful smell of California. Bougainvillea, oranges. And now beans and garlic. He studied the streets. A row of warehouses with the back halves of trailer trucks parked inside a chain link fence on one corner. Spare parts shops. Then rows of tiny houses, all dilapidated. Weeds everywhere. Not many people around.

On Twenty-eighth Street he pulled to a stop in front of a faded wooden house, a little bit different from the others on the street. It had gabled windows on the second floor. All the rest of the houses squatted flat on the ground, with no more than three rooms.

At some time the house had been painted yellow, but now the color was left only in patches. Where the paint had come off it was all gray. The porch in front sagged around the steps. The railing looked loose. Four wicker chairs made a straight line across the porch, but looked too fragile to sit in. The number on the door read 3525. The last number had lost a screw and was tilted sideways.

Jason got out of the car. Some boys in jeans with the arms cut out of their shirts were gathered on the other side of the street around a junker that was missing a couple of wheels. They were smoking, and watching him sweat. He locked the car and walked around an ancient Pontiac parked in the field of weeds that was the front lawn.

By the time he walked up the creaky steps, there was a woman standing by the window. She, too, was smoking a cigarette, scowling.

"They've already been here," she said, cracking the door just enough to get her words out. "I told them to go away, and don't send no one else."

"Who?" Jason asked, thinking right off that she was either drunk or insane.

"Don't make it hard on yourself. I hate you Jesus people. No way I'm going to let any of you in. So beat it."

"I'm not a Jesus person," Jason said. "I'm a journalist."

"You can't fool me. You look just like that man who was here last week. Had a pretty little girl with him. You people ought to be ashamed of yourselves, using little children like that."

Jason considered telling her she'd won a trip to Paris, or a washing machine or something, then decided that was not such a good idea. "Are you Esther Grebs?" he asked.

"Esther Grebs is dead," she said flatly. "Dropped dead years ago. Who's asking?" She peered at him through the crack in the door.

"Frank Miln. I'm a reporter. I'm looking for a man named Troland Grebs. He used to live here." *I hope.* Jason smiled in a hopeful way.

The woman stepped back and opened the door. She had a lot of extra weight on her and was shaky on her feet. "That was an awfully long time ago. How'd you find out?"

"It's not a common name." Jason felt elated, but didn't want to take credit where it wasn't due.

"What's he done?" she asked peevishly.

Jason smiled encouragingly. "Nothing. I'm just doing a story, looking for background material."

"Background. What kind of background?" She backed out of the door so he could come in. Her curiosity, or her loneliness, or his unthreatening way of grabbing people's attention got her.

He smiled encouragingly as he came in. "My story's on North High School graduates of his year. '80. Just picked a few at random to see where they came from and what they've done with their lives. That kind of thing."

"Well, that's *something*."

"Do you know Troland Grebs?" Jason asked.

"Course I know him. I'm his aunt. His aunt Lela. How do you think he got to North High School?"

"I don't know," Jason said.

"Not from here." She spat out the words as she led the way to the front room, which was crowded with some surprisingly good furniture, all very dusty and too large for the space. "Couldn't get anywhere from here. I took him with me that year after his brother died in 'Nam."

She looked confused for a minute and then found her glass. It was empty. "Would you like a drink?"

Jason shook his head. "No, thanks."

She considered it, then put it down. Obviously had some restraint left. Jason couldn't miss the tired old housedress and slippers, the slack discontented mouth. The room smelled of bourbon and cigarette smoke. But the woman's hair was carefully combed, and she had lipstick on as if she had been expecting someone. She sat heavily on a worn, tufted sofa with her feet planted far apart. "Have a seat. What do you want to know?"

Jason sat in an armchair catty-corner, so he didn't have to struggle not to look at the rolls of puckered flesh on her thighs.

"Well, I know Troland has done pretty well for himself. Has a good job, drives a good car—"

"Since when?" Lela interrupted.

"Uh, I assume he's had it a long time."

"Well, smarty, he doesn't drive a car. He still rides a bike, like a kid. Hah."

Jason took out a small notebook. Whenever important information came to him his face went blank. His face was blank now. "What kind of bike?"

"Oh, Lord. There was the old panhead, that was Willy's. Willy died in 'Nam. Willy's Tro's brother. Tro rode that a long time. Then he started trading up. He told me the bike he has now took a year to customize. Cost over fifteen grand. Can you believe that? Any motorcycle costing that much?"

It was too much for her. She got up and went into the other room with her glass.

"All Harleys," she shouted.

"What was he like as a kid?" Jason asked.

"I didn't know him much then. My husband and I lived in Coral Beach then." She returned. Her glass was half full now. She fluffed her hair. "It's nice there, in Coral Beach," she said wistfully.

Jason nodded. "Troland," he prompted.

She looked into her drink, then took a tiny, ladylike sip. "My sister complained about him. He was always kind of wild." She fell silent for a second, thinking it over. "All the boys were wild, but Tro was the worst. Can't really blame them, having the kind of father they did."

"What was his father like?"

"Well, he couldn't hold his—" She held up her glass. "Some people can and some people can't. Him, he'd be all right, and then he'd have a few drinks—Get out of the way." She sniffed. "I wouldn't go there unless I absolutely had to."

"He was violent?"

"I guess you could say that. Beat up my sister pretty bad. I guess you don't need to know about that."

Yes, actually that was exactly what he wanted to know. He needed to know how dysfunctional the family was. He needed to know how badly damaged Troland Grebs was.

"What about Tro—was he violent, too?"

"Violent?" Lela narrowed her eyes.

"Was he in trouble a lot? Was he ever arrested?"

She sipped again, taking her time to think about it. "Well, Tro was a funny kid. And not ha-ha funny. He was strange. I always thought he was a little—" She touched her finger to her head meaningfully.

"Crazy, huh. How was he crazy?" Jason kept his voice neutral.

She shook her head. "He has brains, you know. But there's something kinda different about him. He gets an idea—still makes my blood run cold. Aw, you don't want to hear all this."

"Sure, I do. It's very important background, you know, sheds light on what he's become." That was the truth.

Lela stared at him, then nodded. "Well, there was this *pretty* girl. She had hair, oh, my God, all the way down to her waist. Must have been third grade. She was the president of the class. Somebody squirted a water gun at her hair. Only it wasn't water. It was gasoline. And there were some matches." Lela opened her pale eyes wide.

"Her hair caught on fire." She was silent for a long time.

"What happened?" Jason asked.

"Oh, she could have died, but she was all right. They had a big investigation, and they just couldn't prove anything. Years later Tro told me he knew how to make people do whatever he wanted. He used to tell the kids he'd kill them, and their parents, and their brothers and sisters. Cut them up in little pieces so nobody could ever find them. Poor suckers. They believed him."

She remembered the drink in her hand, took a greedy swallow. "He was always talking about getting even, about revenge, you know. And the thing was she didn't do a thing to him. That little girl didn't keep him out, or do anything to him. He just wanted to hurt her because she got too much attention."

She peered out the window at the overgrown bougainvillea that was the view. It was so big it wrapped around the back of the house as if it were going to take over. Jason followed her gaze. The blossoms were the deepest purple he'd ever seen.

"I didn't know that when I took him in. I knew he set fires, of course. Went kind of wild when his brother died. But he seemed better when he came back from—you know where. And he never *hurt* anybody. I thought if he went to a *good* school and made friends with some nice people, he'd be all right. . . ."

"Where's you-know-where?" Jason asked.

"I know where, but you can't know where. See, I was right. He went to a good school, got away from some bad influences, and he turned out, like you said. Write that part." She gestured at his notebook with her glass.

"Sure I will," Jason said. "Thank you for talking to me. You helped a lot." He had to go now. "Could you give me Troland's address?"

"Course I will." Without hesitation, she went to a book by the phone that had faded blue flowers on the cover, and read out the address. "It's a nicer place than this, but do you think he'd help me? —I shouldn't say that. He sent me to Disneyland last month for three days. I think he wanted to stay here. Cleaned the whole place. I couldn't believe it." She shook her head, still couldn't.

"Well, he's something of a mystery. Keeps to himself." Her eyes suddenly filled with tears. She waved at the dusty furniture with one hand. "This was only a tenth, a *hundredth* of what I had."

She fell silent, turning her unfocused eyes back to Jason. "All that time I thought my *sister* married the jerk. He hurt her bad and she died of cancer. But the truth is all men stink. Hah, you could write a *book* about my story," she muttered.

"I'd like to hear it. But I have to go." Jason looked at his watch. Now it really was getting late.

"That's what they all say." Her face crumpled.

Jason put his pen away. He was always telling his students you have to listen to the things they don't say as well as the things they do. Poor woman. She'd probably been drinking all morning. She couldn't even get up to walk him to the door when he left.

41

Emma got off the treadmill when the odometer read three and a half miles and hobbled to the fridge. There wasn't much of anything in it, and most definitely no club soda. She was covered with sweat and shivered slightly, annoyed at herself for not stopping to pick up some water on the way home.

Checking the clock on the wall, she was also irritated that she had left a message for Jason hours ago, and he hadn't called her back yet. She was sure she hadn't heard the phone ring. And the machine still didn't have any messages on it. If the machine wasn't working, she'd start getting complaints pretty quickly from people whose calls she hadn't returned. She hoped Ronnie hadn't tried to reach her.

She loved to run, always had, even as a kid. It was a natural high, gave her energy, made her feel exhilarated. That afternoon she had run farther and faster than she ever had before. She was now exhausted.

Where the hell was Jason? She drank some water from the tap. People said there was bacteria in it now from all the sewage in upstate towns leaching into the city's reservoirs.

It didn't taste too bad, but Emma didn't like drinking it. She went back to the fridge with the glass in her hand. Although she'd had lunch, she knew she'd be hungry again soon. All that exercise. Even after she stopped, the perspiration was still pouring off her. She opened the door and studied the contents of the refrigerator, distressed at the way it seemed to symbolize her life. It looked like the refrigerator of someone who didn't have a family. There were some tired lettuce and carrots in the crisper. A lot of half-used jars of things scattered around on the shelves. Some unopened, out-of-date yogurt, and cottage cheese she always bought but never ate.

The problem was they didn't eat many meals together, and when they did, it was never anything she liked. Jason complained when she brought home cheese, or any kind of dairy product, salami, baloney, liverwurst or pâté. Red meat was out. So was duck, foie gras, chicken or calves' liver. They had bread, but no butter. Pasta with tomato sauce, but no shellfish, no squid, no sausage, no anchovies.

Other forbidden foods were omelets with bacon—omelets with anything in fact—osso buco, artichokes with hollandaise. Emma liked hollandaise so thick a spoon could stand straight up in it. She began to salivate thinking about all the foods she liked and Jason felt would kill him if he so much as encountered them in his refrigerator. She had eaten a lot of strange things in her childhood. Her mother was always leaving the base to find the markets where the local foods were sold, unlike the other wives who stuck to the Kellogg's Frosted Flakes and Campbell's Tomato Soup they could find from home in the canteen.

Food was the way her mother kept the evenings civil. Every night a food surprise. Emma bought the same way. She went to the markets on Broadway, and always bought things fresh: arugula, a chicken breast, a few bananas. Only healthy things, and just enough for one night. If she tried to slip in anything interesting, Jason left it on the plate. He didn't want to die of clogged arteries before he finished the work he was meant to do.

She sipped at the water. Well, Jason wasn't here now. She could go out and get anything she wanted, have a fat fest and run the extra calories off tomorrow. She closed the refrigerator door and went into the bedroom. The muscles in her legs were a little trembly. She probably hadn't given herself enough cooling-down time. If she walked slowly to the store, it would be better than sitting down.

She showered, considering it. Should she sit and wait for Jason, who might not call her back for many more hours, or go out for club soda and forbidden food before it got dark? She put conditioner on her hair and combed it through, rubbed body lotion into her skin. As she pulled on faded jeans and a sweatshirt, she decided to go out. She stuffed her money and her key in her pocket. She didn't bother to take her handbag with her driver's license and credit cards in it. She left the apartment, closing the door carefully.

As she waited for the elevator, she ran her fingers through her damp hair. She had been too hungry to take the time to dry it. She looked up at the elevator, which she could see on the top floor. It was the old-fashioned kind, an open cage that hadn't been changed from the day it was installed decades ago.

The stairs going up went around in a big square, so everyone could see everyone else coming in and out of their doors, and what they were carrying. From any level one could look all the way up to the top of the building where there was a stained-glass skylight, like a kaleidoscope with only one picture. While she waited for the elevator, Emma looked up at it. When she reached the lobby she looked at it again. She could tell what kind of day it was and sometimes the hour, too, by the way the light came through the colored glass.

The doorman opened the heavy wrought-iron doors for her.

"Hello, Mrs. Frank, going for a jog?"

Emma shook her head with a smile. "I did that already. Just going to the store."

"I'll watch you down the street."

"Thanks."

He always said that. He was missing most of his teeth and was hardly five feet tall. But he had been a marine and kept a baseball bat beside his chair. Emma had no doubt that he would use it if something happened. It was quiet now, though. No sirens, no homeless.

Emma stepped outside and greedily breathed the fresh salty air from the river. Her building was on the corner of Riverside Drive, two long blocks from Broadway where all the stores were. She began walking slowly, testing the muscles in her legs. The ache went very deep. It was hard to imagine people running in the marathon for twenty-six miles at a stretch.

She wondered how it felt as they were doing it, and if it felt anything like this afterwards? After running only three and a half miles, she had to admit she didn't feel all that wonderful. As she walked, she glanced at the trees which were in full leaf now, noticed the few cars that passed. Riverside and West End Avenue were quiet streets. Broadway was where all the trouble was. She considered what she would buy. Something really bad, with a crusty French bread.

As she got to the corner of West End Avenue, she decided to open a bottle of wine. She passed the thick old tree that partially blocked the view to the intersection. A car was parked in the space in front of the fire hydrant. Emma watched the traffic light change to green, and had prepared to speed up to make it when an arm snaked around her from the back.

"Hi, Emma."

"Wha—" She jerked back and the arm tightened, wrenching her shoulder.

"Don't get upset. I'm not going to hurt you." The voice was calm, very polite.

"Ow." A hard object was shoved into her stomach, pushing the air out of her lungs.

She saw it. It was a gun.

"Ah—" Her knees buckled.

"Get in the car, Emma, or I will shoot you."

Now she could see that the car door was open. Blue car. Her knees sagged. She couldn't stand up. A scream gathered in her throat trying to take shape, but she had no breath. Her mouth wouldn't move.

"Uh, ah—"

"Not a sound," he said. "It's gonna to be fine. It's gonna be great. Don't worry about a thing."

He moved her into the car as if she were a sack of laundry, then hit her on the head with the butt of the gun, hit her maybe a little harder than he meant to. The thunk was quite loud and startled him. She slumped over in the front seat.

He checked her pulse to make sure she was still alive, then covered her with a pale blue blanket, tucking it in carefully so it wouldn't fall off. Then he looked around quickly, closed the door, and walked around to the driver's seat.

"Say good-bye, Emma," he murmured, patting the blue blanket as he drove off.

42

Sometimes April was so busy she didn't have time to think about Sanchez, and sometimes, like right now, she found herself listening to his voice. He was on the phone having some kind of conversation with his mother. He was speaking in his fish-in-water language, and said her name.

"*Sí,* Mama."

Sanchez had a special tone of voice when he talked to his mother. April had mixed feelings about it. Sanchez told April that when she talked to her mother, it always sounded like they were arguing, no matter what they were talking about. When he talked to his mother, it sounded like she was center of the earth to him.

Spanish people were not so different from Chinese, April thought. Both spoil their sons rotten, give them everything, and never get mad at them. Fix it so when they marry, their wives sound like scolding nags and can never make them as happy.

"*Sí,* Mama," he said again.

And then something something else about *la casa* and something something else she didn't get at all. They were on the four-to-eleven shift that day. Maybe he was telling her when he was getting home.

By now April was beginning to pick up a few of the words. It wasn't a hard language like Chinese, which had a lot of different dialects and words that changed their meaning just by the register and tone in which they were spoken. She had a lot of paperwork to do and tried not to listen. Soon she was thinking about it again.

It was a good thing that Sanchez had respect for his mama, but a bad thing that he hung on her every word. Pretty soon she was speculating about how Spanish women were lower than Chinese. Chinese kept their pride in their face. Men and women, same thing. Both had pride, both had face. All Chinese spent time on saving face, protecting face, building face. It was kind of like face was money in the bank, and you could accrue interest on it, or lose it all, if you didn't watch and protect it every day, and invest it just right. Jimmy lost face when his girl dumped him and he had to go home on the subway.

Spanish had their pride in a different body part. They didn't care about face. Spanish had their pride in their penises. So only men could have it. You could see by the way they walked and talked that was where the pride was. Women were lower, had no pride. They walked around with their clothes too tight and their big behinds bouncing up and down to get men's attention. Lipstick too bright, eyes too dark. All so they could attract a man and get some pride from him. Pah. And *then* when they got one, if he was a true Spanish man, he'd have the red-eye disease, be crazy jealous over her big, jiggling bottom, afraid every minute some *other* man would take it away.

Still, Sanchez went home to take care of his mama after his marriage broke up and his father died. And he was not ashamed of it. That was like Chinese, but not like Caucasians, who ran away from their parents in a big stampede as soon as their hormones changed. Other people just did their sex business and went home, didn't have to make a big deal about it.

April couldn't help wondering about Sanchez. Why did his marriage break up? Why were all the women he knew named Maria? It was hard to tell if they were sisters, or aunts, or cousins, or girlfriends, or what. Even Sanchez's ex-wife was called Maria. That was another difference between the two cultures. Each Chinese had his

own name, not like anybody else's name. Parents put together whatever words they wanted. Happy Face. Free of Sorrow. Jade Luck.
Tomorrow's Chance. Chinese named their children like round-eyes
named racehorses.

April's Chinese name was Happy Thinking, as a kind of coun-
teractive against the way she wrinkled her nose just after birth, as if
she came into the world with a bad smell in her nose and was thus
fated to spend her whole life questioning everything. Her mother
liked to tell how she called her daughter Happy Thinking to trick the
Gods into changing April's fate.

"Didn't work," Sai lamented. Her unlucky daughter was still
sniffing out the worst in everybody. She also liked to say she was
afraid her only child had too much untempered *yin* to get married,
which April believed was a contradiction in terms.

"You can't be too much woman to be woman," April told her.

"Not woman like person," Sai argued. "Woman like down
thinking. Settle for less when you could have husband, babies. Not
gun in hangbag."

"Handbag."

April's phone rang just when she was wondering which Maria
Sanchez was now having his sex business with before he went home
to his mother.

"Detective Woo?"

"Yes, speaking," April said. It was a voice she knew, but
couldn't place.

"This is Jason Frank."

"Oh." The doctor who didn't call himself a doctor.

"I'm calling from San Diego."

San Diego again? "What are you doing there?" she asked with
surprise. It was nine o'clock at night. What made him think she'd be
on duty?

"I'm doing your job, Detective. Do you have anything new?"
The edge to his voice made her bristle. Curiosity wrestled with insult
as she struggled for an appropriate reply.

"I can't do a job that I'm not authorized to do, Dr. Frank," she said more sharply than she meant to. What did the man think he was doing in San Diego? He must be crazy.

"I'm sorry," he amended hastily. "I meant the police, not you."

"Okay." She accepted his apology. "Then the answer is no. I tried to call both you and your wife, and neither of you has returned my calls."

"You called my wife?" Now he was surprised.

"Was that a wrong thing to do, Doctor? I thought it might help to get *her* opinion of who might be sending her these letters."

"Well, I think I might have something. . . ."

"Oh? What do you have?" Crazier and crazier. How could he have something?

"I have a name, but I can't locate the guy. He doesn't seem to be around. Do you have any suggestions?"

"What do you think you're doing?" April demanded.

"I thought I'd pay him a visit, but he doesn't seem to be around."

Pay him a visit? Was he crazy? April's heart constricted with anxiety. This was her case. Sergeant Joyce had given it to her and told her to be diplomatic. She had failed, and now the doctor was out there looking for some letter-writing lunatic on his own. What if he found him and got his head bashed in?

"You can't do that," April said loudly. "Come home, get a lawyer. Get an injunction against him. Dr. Frank, please listen to me. You can't help your wife this way."

"There may be more to it."

"What do you mean?"

"He may have done some . . . other things."

April took a deep breath. "What kind of things, Doctor?"

"I talked with his aunt. He has a psychological profile that definitely indicates he was a troubled boy. He set fires. He threatened other children. He may have been institutionalized somewhere. Maybe nobody's been paying any official attention to him for a while. Maybe they have."

"Okay," April said, quickly pulling herself together and making up her mind. She didn't like the urgency in the doctor's voice. When civilians got involved in police business, things always went wrong. "The thing to do is call Sergeant Bob Grove of the San Diego Police Department. I've been in contact with him. Ask Grove to check if this guy has a sheet, a criminal record. . . . But, Dr. Frank, even if this man doesn't have a sheet, *don't* go to talk to him. Get a lawyer, get the court to deal with this. You can't just charge around taking things into your own hands. There could be legal consequences. You could get hurt."

"Uh-huh. Sergeant Grove? What's that number?" Dr. Frank asked.

April looked up her notes on the Ellen Roane case and read the number to him. "Uh, Dr. Frank. What's the man's name? The man you think is writing the letters. I'll try to work on it from here, see what I can find."

He told her the name. She wrote it down on a fresh sheet of paper. Troland Grebs. She hung up and looked at it. What kind of name was that?

Sanchez had long since finished his conversation with his mother. He leaned over April's desk. "What's going on?"

"Can you believe this? That crazy doctor went out to San Diego," she said, her nose wrinkling up with deep suspicion and concern. "And unless the wife doesn't like the police or doesn't return her calls, I bet she's gone somewhere, too." It was all very difficult and out of control.

A few minutes later a call came in about a robbery on Central Park West, and Sergeant Joyce sent them out on it.

43

Jason broke the connection, then dialed the number Detective Woo had given him. Her advice not to look for Grebs came too late. He had already gone to the address the aunt gave him. He had driven all the way up the coast to Queen Palm Way, off Crown Avenue. It wasn't easy to find. He had to cross the small bridge over a dry gully twice before he located Queen Palm Way, so well was it hidden behind a short street of slightly dowdy stores and restaurants, not too far from the beach. When he got to Grebs's apartment building, the manager told Jason he hadn't seen Grebs for nearly a week. There were no lights in the place, no sounds of running water. No Harley-Davidson.

   Jason was in his room at the Meridien, puzzled now. He had called Emma a dozen times all afternoon, and she still wasn't home. It wasn't like her. Six hours had gone by since she left a message for him to call her right away.

   He had his notes spread out on the desk. In the mirror he could see out the window behind him to the bay and the docks on the other side of the water. Funny city. The skyline was dominated by the view of navy shipyards and warships of various sizes. He had no idea which were which.

   The fact that he didn't know which ship was which suddenly pierced him with sadness for Emma. He felt a lot of sadness out here. Emma had spent her childhood watching these ships, drawing pictures of them when she was little, counting the days she was allowed to visit on them as the most exciting of her life. All she ever wanted was to be the one to get on a ship and sail away from those faraway places she didn't choose to be. He reached for the phone.

"Missing Persons, Sergeant Beasly."

"Uh, I think I've got the wrong department. I'm calling for Sergeant Grove," Jason said.

"Who's calling?"

"It's Dr. Jason Frank from New York." He added, "Detective April Woo of the New York Police gave me his name."

"I'll see if Grove's here."

Missing Persons. Why did she give him the name of someone from Missing Persons? Jason tapped his pen against the table nervously. Where was Emma? Emma waited for him. That was what she did when she wasn't working. She waited for him to come home, or call. Occasionally she went to the theater with a friend, but she didn't go out alone at night.

He wanted to kick himself. He always assumed Emma was all right because she never complained and whined the way Nancy had. Acid roiled around in his empty stomach. The corn muffin was long gone, replaced with burning guilt for neglecting his wife and insisting all was well in their world because all was well in his.

What if Grove wasn't there? What if he was wrong and it wasn't this Grebs person? What if it was somebody else and he was wasting his time? What the hell did he think he was doing? Was he altogether crazy to be out here?

He shook his head, ran his hand through his hair. Had to be this guy. But where was he?

"Grebs takes off for days sometimes," the manager at Grebs's apartment building had told him. It wasn't at all unusual.

"Takes off? Where does he go?"

"I think he likes to go down to Mexico." The manager was a small freckled person with a red nose and thinning red hair.

"Why?" Jason asked.

"Who knows?" The man looked off into the middle distance. "I just get that feeling. Strange fella."

"Strange in what way?" Jason's anxiety escalated, but he kept his features neutral.

"You know, those eyes, like marbles. See right through you. Pays on time, though. And he's a terrific mechanic, always out there working on that bike. Hell of a bike, ain't it?"

Yeah. Jason nodded. He'd heard it was a hell of a bike. He wondered where it was. And where was Grebs, with the eyes like marbles.

"Sergeant Grove speaking."

"Hi, this is Jason Frank. April Woo told me to get in touch with you. I have a name of someone who needs to be checked out."

"You want to fill out a Missing Person report?"

Great. Another frosty, unresponsive voice.

"Uh, no, not exactly. I need somebody checked out for a criminal record. Arrests, convictions." Jason's tongue felt thick with the words he wasn't used to saying.

"We're not an information service. We don't do that."

It was a definite, cold dismissal.

In hospitals people did whatever the doctors told them to. "I have a reason," Jason said, getting very frustrated now.

"I'm sure you do, but this is Missing Persons. You want to make a complaint about somebody, you'll have to come in and talk to a detective."

"Are you a detective?"

"Yes, but I'm a detective in Missing Persons. If you have a Missing Person, you come to me. Otherwise, you go to someone else."

"So, Detective Grove, how do you know April Woo?"

"Detective-Sergeant Grove," Grove corrected. "April had a Missing Person. We found her."

"Well, Detective Woo told me to call you about this. She said you could help me." Jason wondered if Detective Woo was also Sergeant, and if her missing person was found alive.

"Okay, well, April must be quite the girl. What's the problem?"

Jason told him succinctly.

"Oh, you're the guy with the nutcase letters. I know about you, Dr. Frank. Look, I asked around. Came up with zip on this one. What makes you think there's anything to it?" The voice warmed up, but only a little.

"I talked to this guy's aunt, and she implied he had a record. If so, he poses a threat to my wife. All I want to do is find out what there is on him."

"All right, I'll pull the sheet," Grove said reluctantly. "But you'll have to come in."

"When?"

"Now. I'm supposed to be out of here at four."

Jason looked at his watch. It was after six. "Tell me where and I'm on my way."

A few minutes later he was loping through the lobby of the Meridien again. The place was very luxurious, very quiet. He didn't think it was meant to feel like a mausoleum, though. There wasn't anybody around.

After telling him to hurry, Detective-Sergeant Grove, or whatever he was, kept Jason waiting for nearly twenty minutes. He sat in a metal chair and looked around. The police station was not so different from the one he had gone to in New York. Both looked like public schools. There were a lot of signs in Spanish here, too. In fact it looked like there were more instructions up on the wall in Spanish than there were in English.

"Dr. Frank?"

Finally Grove stood in front of him. He was a very tall man with blond hair, not in uniform. He looked like many years ago he might have been a surfer.

"Yes." Jason was glad to escape from the hard chair he had taken next to a woman with an infant who needed to be changed.

"Sorry, it took some time." Grove led the way to a corner of a big room. On the wall was a sign that said "Missing Persons, Sergeant Robert Grove."

His desk was a lot messier than April Woo's. Thick files were stacked on both sides. In the middle half a dozen partially filled

Styrofoam coffee cups were surrounded by a snowfall of empty sugar packets. Grove sank down into an ancient swivel chair clearly left over from an earlier incarnation, pointed Jason to the wooden chair opposite, and sat back.

"Okay, exactly what do you want to know?"

Jason had chewed up a couple of Maalox tablets on the way over. But the pain came back with the skepticism in Grove's framing of the question. He felt around in his pocket to see if he had any more. He didn't. He could see the package on the dashboard of the car. Shit. He let it go.

"I talked with Troland Grebs's aunt," he said, pulling himself together. "And she described the kind of family background and personality problems that suggest to me he had some encounters with the authorities."

"Like what?" Grove shifted in his seat so he wasn't sitting on his gun. He seemed to be arranging his defenses against unwanted, outside influences. One hand reached into his desk drawer and pulled out a paper. He angled it in such a way that Jason couldn't see it.

"Like he set fires." Jason knew he didn't want to challenge the man, but the pressure was building to get up and snatch the damn paper.

"Yep," Grove said, glancing down. "Quite a few. They put him away with some other nice boys for a while. It seemed to do the trick on arson. That's going back some, though." He sounded bored, as if the man's record was old, old news and had no bearing on his current activities.

"What else is there?" Jason leaned over. Grove leaned back.

"Like I said. What are you looking for?"

Jason's stomach churned. "Why can't you let me see the damn thing?" he asked, trying to keep calm. "All I need is a minute or two and then I'll be out of here."

Grove's expression did not change.

"What do you want the information for? Are you making a complaint? Let's get this out in the open."

Jason spoke slowly, biting off his words. "I'm trying to establish if the person with this criminal record on your desk that you won't let me see is a violent person capable of harming my wife."

Why else would he want the information? He needed to protect his wife. No one else would. It wasn't a hard one.

"Will you be making a complaint?"

Jason snapped. "I don't fucking know. Is he a psychopath? Has he been hospitalized? Has he been in prison for any violent crimes? Come on, Sergeant Grove. If my wife is in danger and it turns out you withheld information from me, I'll have your fucking ass—"

"All right, I'm with you," Grove said coldly. "But let's get one thing straight. We don't do things this way, Doctor. We don't make people's records available just because someone *thinks* a guy could be dangerous. It doesn't work like that."

"Are you telling me all you do is bag bodies? Is that how it works?"

"I'm in Missing Persons. I try to match unidentified bodies with people who have been reported missing."

"Fine." It occurred to Jason that Detective Woo would give him what he needed. Fuck this. He got up to go.

Grove looked down at the paper he'd been guarding so carefully from view.

"Well, there's no record of any hospitalizations," he said casually, "but that doesn't mean he hasn't had any. There are a couple of real old arrests for assault and battery. No convictions."

"What does that mean?"

"It means Grebs here used to get a little carried away with ladies of the night. Whores."

Jason was silent. Then he asked, "What did he do to them?"

Grove looked at him. For several long moments Jason was afraid Grove would stonewall all the way. Then he looked down at the paper again as if whatever he had in the way of a brain just clicked into gear.

"Jesus H. Christ," he muttered.

"Tell me," Jason insisted.

Another brief silence. Grove's hand came down on the paper, protecting it from any onslaught.

"For God's sake!" Jason exploded.

"You want to know? Okay, he burned them with cigarettes, Doctor." Grove got a little defensive. "But that was a long time ago, and the charges were dropped. You know, sometimes they just grow out of it."

He was saying one thing, but his face said something else.

"Yeah?" Jason said. "They grow out of it?" The bile rose in his throat. "The guy set fires, and then moved on to burning people. Prostitutes. You're right. Sometimes they learn how to control it, or cover it up. A lot of things can happen with sick people. Sometimes they move on to new kinds of acting out. Sometimes something can trigger them into violence. Or they can get disorganized with stress —trouble at work, a loss of some kind—and just break down. But they don't just grow out of it, Sergeant. They're *sick*—It's not a bad habit."

The deep tan receded from Sergeant Grove's face as he listened.

"The girl from New York April was looking for was burned," he said when Jason was finished. He didn't look bored or disinterested now.

"Burned? Is she—?" The acid from Jason's stomach bubbled up into his mouth. He swallowed.

"Oh, yeah, she's dead. But she wasn't a whore. She was a college girl on vacation."

The two men looked at each other. Then Grove handed over the sheet. Jason reached for it with a tremor in his hand. Well, now they had a suspect with a history of burning people that went back to third grade, and a dead girl from New York. The guy they should be looking very hard for was a draftsman in a defense company, rode a motorcycle. He knew Emma from high school, and hadn't been seen for over a week. Emma needed immediate protection.

"Can I use your phone?" Jason asked.

44

The blanket didn't move all the way out to Queens. Troland watched the dashboard clock and forced himself to look at the blanket only every two minutes. The traffic was so heavy on Second Avenue around the bridge he started muttering to himself. What if he hit her too hard. What if she was dead. If she was dead, she wouldn't know anything. She wouldn't even have met him. Shit. Then he couldn't make things right. Not ever. He fumed at the gridlock. Thousands of cars trying to get into a single lane to get across the fucking bridge. And the fucking bridge was falling down. He didn't want her dying before he fixed her.

The inside lanes were completely closed. There was one outside lane on each side that seemed to be outside of the bridge altogether. Getting across meant hanging over the water in a single lane that didn't even have a solid roadbed under it. Looking down, Troland could see the water in the East River. To his left, the Roosevelt Island tram passed by on its wire string, high in the sky. It passed the one going the other way. The traffic was going only three miles an hour. Sometimes it stopped altogether.

He had been feeling so good. And now when he looked out at the cars halted around him and down at the motionless bundle he had gone to so much trouble for, he started feeling bad again. He put his hand under the blanket on the seat beside him. Touched a piece of bare flesh. Arm, he thought. He stroked it with his finger and was excited by its warmth.

It took nearly an hour to get back to his place. A very pale light shone from the front room, which meant the old woman was probably sitting there in front of the television with her back to the window. It gave him an unpleasant memory of his grandmother who died last month. He pushed the thought aside as he got out to open the garage door. It wasn't automatic. He had to pull it open and shut. The light was automatic. It came on when the door went up. No one saw him.

Still, he was almost jumping out of his skin when he carried her up the stairs at the back of the garage. He had hit her hard. She was a dead weight, still out cold. He almost staggered at the top when he had to get the door open.

And then he was inside with the door closed. He put her on the sofa in the living room. This must have been where the old man had his studio, because the skylight was in here. He had noticed none of the other houses in the area had a skylight. The skylight bothered him because of the planes coming into the airport. They did that in San Diego where he worked, but there they were friends. Here, they seemed to hover directly over the house, casting a huge shadow like a giant evil bird. They seemed to be watching him somehow, getting ready to dump a load. He wasn't thinking of that now, though. He was high again with how great this was.

Yeah. He studied her on the sofa, looking for the girl he knew. He didn't see the soft smile, the golden hair. He started pulling at her clothes. First the short boots, then the jeans. Yeah. It was the body in the film. He frowned, studying her legs and the tiny bikini briefs she was wearing. They were white, a silky material, and looked new. She looked good like that.

He struggled to get her sweatshirt off and was a little disappointed because she made no effort to wake up. The bra matched the panties. He took them both off and held them in his hand. They had a strong fragrance he didn't know, some kind of flower. The body looked good, real good. Well kept, clean. He liked that.

The hair wasn't blond, but wasn't so bad. At least her breasts were bigger than the other girl he tattooed. He liked that. And there was no excess flesh around her stomach and thighs. He liked that, too. Fat women disgusted him. On his knees, he sniffed her shoulder and then her breast. The fragrance was stronger there. He wanted to sniff all of her, but he was getting too excited. He had to pull out the Polaroid of the other girl to remind himself of his mission. He didn't want to fuck her before she was right. Yeah, he had stuff to do.

He got up and walked into the other room with her clothes, put them in his suitcase and the suitcase under the bed. He went into the bathroom and urinated for a long time, then carefully combed his hair. Wanted to look good for her. Then he figured he better get the ropes and tie her up. He put the gun down on the table in case he had to scare her. He had a whole collection of ropes. They were all thin nylon, the kind that would cut deeply into her flesh if she struggled too much. He had planned to put one around her neck with a slip knot. Now he thought that might be a mistake. He wanted her perfect, beautifully decorated, but not marked by anything else.

Looking at her, lying on her back with her eyes closed and one arm flung out, it occurred to him that just doing the torso like the other girl was not enough. He could do all of her. Her hands, her feet. He'd even seen people with the inside of their lips tattooed, their armpits. He started sweating as he thought of tattooing her cunt. He could put anything on it. It was so exciting he had to remind himself over and over to cool down or he'd never get it done.

He tied her hands and feet loosely, considering places he could work on her where no one had ever tattooed a person before. Too bad he didn't have a table to put her on. The sofa was low. Lower than the bed. He didn't want her on the bed in the other room, though. The black bird was on the other side of the wall. She might hear something.

Finally he was ready. He was cool. He slapped her face a few times.

"Emma, Emma. Wake up."

When she didn't wake up, he put a few drops of ammonia on a paper towel and waved it under her nose. She started coughing.

"Wake up, honey."

After a long time, her eyes fluttered.

"That's right. Come on. Look at me. Look who it is." He dabbed a wet towel on her forehead the way a nurse had once when he was in the hospital. He still remembered how good it felt.

Dabbed at her cheek with cold water.

Emma groaned and opened her eyes.

"Hi, Emma. Guess who." Troland leaned over so she could see his face.

She closed her eyes again.

"Oh, come on. You're all right."

"My head," she mumbled. "Car crash."

"Hi, honey. Look at me. Say hello." When she didn't respond, Troland got some more water and sprinkled some on her neck and forehead.

She opened her eyes and tried to focus. "Car crash, get me out," she cried, fighting the ropes.

"Hey, stop that. You weren't in a crash. Look who it is."

Her eyes moved around, trying to make a picture. "Car crash. My head . . ."

"It's Tro—remember me?"

She stared at him, tried to lift her hand to touch her head. It wouldn't move. It was attached to something.

Her forehead wrinkled with puzzlement. "Hospital?"

He laughed. "What kind of hospital looks like this?"

She groaned. "My head." She shivered. "Where are my clothes?"

"I guess I've changed a lot since you saw me last." He was wearing his leather jacket. The one like the guy in the movie had. "Don't you recognize me?"

"I can't . . . move."

A jet thundered over the house. She looked up at the skylight. "What's . . . ?"

"Maybe I wasn't so hot then, but I've come a long way." He squatted next to her on his heels, ignoring her confusion. "You know the Patriot missiles. I built those. And the cruise missiles, too. I've done a lot for this country. Won the whole war."

Emma groaned, frowning some more. "Car crash . . ."

He shook his head. "Uh-uh. Tro."

"My head."

It upset him that she didn't seem to know him. He had to get up and walk away in frustration. Maybe she had a stupid concussion. He snapped open his lighter, flicked it on and off, watching the flame spurt and die. That calmed him.

Emma lifted her head and looked down at her naked body. Her hands and feet were tied. Her forehead wrinkled with puzzlement.

In a second he was back. "I'm a whole other guy. I used to have some trouble with my temper, but I got that under control. I'm a terrific guy now."

Emma closed her eyes. She swallowed. When she opened her eyes again, he was still there, standing over her.

"And I got a better bike. Remember my knucklehead? Rigid, straight-leg frame, with a six-inch springer and a set of full apes?"

"A bike hit me?"

"No, I guess I already had the panhead, right? Yeah. Well, I got a twenty-thousand dollar bike now. You should see it. Nessy engine, everything custom made, custom painted." He had forgotten he sold the bike.

Another jet thundered over the house. She looked up again. In the dark, the lights of the plane twinkled in the skylight.

"Where am I?" she said thickly.

"A special place."

"Well, how did I get here?" she mumbled.

"I picked you up off the street and brought you here."

Emma's blue eyes closed.

"Wake up," Troland demanded.

"Bike crash," she muttered. "Bike crash?"

"No, honey. I picked you up off the street and brought you to a special place for a special reason."

"What? What reason?" Her voice was still slurred and puzzled.

"My reasons. You'll see."

There was a moment of silence, and then she started to cry with her eyes squeezed shut. "My head hurts. I want to go home."

"Don't cry," he snapped. "I don't like crying."

Her eyes popped open wide and stared at him, stunned.

"I'm sick. I have to go home." Her voice came from a long way away.

"No, honey. You're mine now. You're not going anywhere."

"Going home," she said thickly. There was a pot of glue in her mouth. Cement in her legs.

"No, honey. You're mine now. You gotta remember that. Just completely mine."

She shook her head, her whole body trembling uncontrollably. She moved her hands and feet around in the ropes, as if to check if they were attached to something.

"Remember me? I'm Tro. You don't ever say no to me again. Got it?"

He watched her face change. It went through a lot—deflated, paled, reddened. For a second it almost looked like she was going to choke on fear. He liked that, smiled with encouragement.

"Good, now you know me," he said with satisfaction. "Keep it up. It's going to be great."

He turned around to show her the gun. They liked that kind of thing. He was sorry his bike was in California where she couldn't see it. Still, he had photographs of it. He could show her those. He headed for the bedroom, needed the switchblade, too. He wanted to show her the switchblade.

45

Sanchez pulled up next to Dr. Frank's building and parked the car in front of a hydrant. It was eleven-thirty. Their shift ended a half hour ago. The call from California had come just as they were leaving. Sergeant Joyce was already gone.

April took the call and talked to Dr. Frank for a long time. He was still at the San Diego Police Department with Sergeant Grove. He was extremely worried about his wife. He had been out of touch with her for nearly twenty-four hours. She had left a message at noon his time to call her immediately. Now it was almost nine hours later and he still hadn't heard from her. He had called the apartment, her agent, her friends. No one knew where she was. Grove faxed April the sheet on Troland Grebs.

As the husband talked to her long-distance, April felt sick with anxiety. It was possible that she had not done the right thing from the very beginning with this case. Maybe she had waited too long to call the wife. If she had called earlier, she might have found out the real story then. Why had she accepted the doctor's request that she not call? And when she did call and the woman didn't call her back, why didn't she just go over there and talk to her? Now she, April Woo, would be to blame if she went in there and the woman was dead.

April felt sick, sick all over. People weren't supposed to just run around on their own, checking things out. There was a system for doing everything. April followed the rules. She always followed the rules. There was a reason for every one. Cases had to have complainants, or they weren't cases. Cases that came in after eleven had to be referred to Central. If she let it go until tomorrow, then the doctor would come home. If his wife still wasn't there, he could fill out a Missing Person Report, and Sergeant Joyce would assign the case.

But it was her case. She'd already been assigned this doctor, and she'd messed up. She should have followed through. She should have talked to the wife before. What if she was dead on the floor? April had been trained just for this kind of thing, to look around and underneath what people were telling her for the real story. Why hadn't she listened more carefully, asked more questions? It seemed to be about letters, but she knew it wasn't always what it seemed to be.

Every day she tried to remind herself about the robbery call that came in when she was so green the sap was still leaking out of her every pore. She got to the address and climbed three floors to find a hysterical young Chinese woman covered with bruises, dressed only in a robe, hitting herself and wailing in Chinese that it was "My fault, my fault."

After talking to her for a long time, April finally persuaded the woman to tell her what the crime really was. She had been raped and sodomized by two men for three hours. And the only thing that had been stolen was the woman's whole life. No way the man who was engaged to her would marry her now.

April never waited until tomorrow for anything. Why had she not gone to see this Chapman woman sooner? My fault, she told herself. She had been intimidated by the husband, the doctor. Now she couldn't go into an unknown situation by herself. They didn't exactly have partners in Detective Squads. When big cases came in, they all worked together, each trying to find a tiny piece. In small cases they usually worked on their own. They certainly could work together if they wanted to.

"Mike," April had said when she hung up, "I need your help."

The car had stopped, but she wasn't in a hurry to get out. She looked at Mike.

"All set?" he asked.

They had hardly spoken on the way over. She was tired, and apprehensive about what she was going to say and do. They had an understanding. This was her case, and she had to handle it. But she had no real sense of these people. All she knew for sure was that the husband was a doctor, a shrink he finally told her. And the wife was an actress. But what did that really mean? She had no idea what it meant, no idea at all what their lives were like. She had never met any people like that.

For months after being transferred up here, just walking into one of these buildings on the upper West Side was a shock to her. And she was still trying to get used to it. She didn't know about buildings with doormen to guard the entrance, back elevator men to take away the trash, drugstores, dry cleaners, and grocery stores that all delivered. She didn't know people who wore fur coats and had dog walkers to walk their tiny dogs, who went to the Caribbean islands in winter and passed through Queens only to get to the airports or the Hamptons.

She'd never been to the Caribbean or the Hamptons. She was born in a building where the toilet out in the hall was shared by three families. And the tub was in the kitchen. All she ever wanted was to grow up, get her degree, and help people like her mother and father survive. She had never asked to come uptown, to have to look in the mirror and wish her eyes and bottom were round. Never in ten thousand years would she have wanted to have to learn to walk and talk and think like educated Caucasians. And now she had to. These people were coming to her as if she knew how to solve their problems.

The shrink, with all his years of education and training, had come to her, as helpless and terrified as any illiterate Asian just off the boat.

She glanced at Sanchez and nodded. "Yeah, let's go," she said.

"Jesus, what a place," he remarked.

April looked up at the extraordinary canopy made of some kind of carved metal. She had found that even in buildings like this, she was still afraid of what was behind the door. They had taught her that, but the fear must be from another life. She had always been scared to open the door. April couldn't get the thought out of her head that maybe there was a reason the wife never called her back. Maybe she was already dead.

She glanced at Sanchez again. He was waiting for her to go in first. She straightened her shoulders. She didn't want him to know she was scared.

46

"Hi, I'm Detective Woo, and this is Sergeant Sanchez from the police." Usually when she said it, the sound of the two names together made her want to laugh. Tonight it didn't.

April pulled out her badge, and Sanchez did, too.

The night doorman stubbed out his cigarette and looked at them dumbly. "What's going on?"

"We've have a request from Dr. Frank to check his apartment," she said. The name on the pocket of the man's uniform was Francis. It was probably his first name.

"He's away." The man's eyes looked dimly out at them from puffy lids. "Do you want me to ring his wife?"

"Is she here?" April asked.

"Could be," the doorman said.

"What do you mean, she *could* be here?" April said.

"Well. She ain't in the book, and I ain't seen her since I come on. She could be out. She could be in."

"What time do you come on?"

"Eleven."

That was only forty-five minutes ago. So, Emma Chapman could be there or she could have left any time since yesterday. April nodded. "Please call her."

"I'll have to ring the apartment . . . ." The doorman gestured at the old-fashioned intercom, one of those ancient telephone switchboards with the plugs and buzzers. There were no names by the holes, but there was a thick ledger on the table with a list of apartments and people who were out. April leaned over to look at it. Dr. Frank was listed as away. Emma Chapman wasn't on that day's list or the one for the previous two days.

"Well, go ahead. Ring up," she said.

Sanchez moved out of the way. Francis stuck a plug into a hole and pushed the knob down. There was a faint hum as the connection was made.

No answer from upstairs.

"Where does it ring?" April asked.

"In the kitchen."

"Is it loud enough to hear in the bedroom?"

"Depends."

"Try again."

He pushed the knob down a second time.

"What's the procedure with the ledger?" Sanchez asked as the man rang over and over.

"Front or back?"

"You have two books?" April watched the board. Nothing. She hadn't expected anything. God, she hoped the woman was at a friend's house.

"Two doors, two elevators. Two books. Guess she must be out." Francis gave up ringing and lit another cigarette. "What're you looking for?"

"We're looking for her," April said. "Emma Chapman. Do you have a key to the apartment?"

"Well, yeah." He frowned. "But I'm not supposed to give it to anybody."

Everything always took forever. April took a deep breath. Everybody took persuading. Without a warrant, this guy might not let them in.

"You don't have to give it to us. You can open the door and stay with us," she suggested, keeping her voice casual.

"We'll only be a minute," Sanchez added.

"I can't leave the door," the man hedged.

"Oh, come on, not even to take a leak?"

Sanchez was good at making people do what he wanted. April's face didn't change when he took charge of the situation. She was a detective. He was a sergeant. She never forgot that.

Francis eyed them suspiciously. "The Doc is a real particular man. How do I know you're really cops?"

Sanchez pointed out the glass door to the blue-and-white police car parked by the fire hydrant. It had their precinct number on it.

"By our squad car, Francis. You going to take us upstairs or what?"

Mike had left the lights flashing on top of the car. He did that sometimes, even though it ran down the battery. It did the job now.

Francis considered it only for a second. Then he moved away from the switchboard and locked the front door. "Okay, two minutes. But you better not touch anything."

Sanchez held his hands up to show he had no intention of touching anything. As they headed to the elevator, April looked around. Twelve floors up at the top was a stained-glass skylight in the middle of the ceiling. The elevator was a big metal cage. The stairway went around the building in a square so you could walk all the way up if you had to. This place was . . . She didn't know exactly what it was. She let out her breath in a little whistle.

They stopped on the fifth floor. April stepped back as the metal door accordioned closed. She wondered how many kids had gotten their fingers caught in it over the years.

They started around the square landing. There was a little indentation, not quite a vestibule, for every apartment.

"This is the Doc's office. I don't have a key to that." Francis stopped at a vestibule with two doors. One had a table beside it piled with letters and packages.

"This is the apartment."

Sanchez held his hand out for the keys. Francis handed them over, shaking his head. "The Doc won't like this."

"Stand back, will you," Sanchez told him. His voice was very friendly.

Sanchez rang the bell repeatedly, then fiddled with the two

keys, locking the top lock at first, and then unlocking it, while Francis muttered disapprovingly out on the landing.

April's heart beat faster. She hated going through unknown doors. She looked at Mike and saw that he, too, noted this one hadn't been double-locked. Without a word, they each took a side, moving away from the door as it swung open.

Inside the lights were on and there was the sound of voices. Someone was home. For a long moment neither of them moved. Then April stepped forward.

"Police," she called. "Anybody home?"

No answer. She went into a square entry hall. A table on one side had a green marble clock with a gold cupid perched on top, and another huge stack of mail. To her right was a darkened room that April figured was the living room. Ahead was a long cream-colored hall with prints on the walls. She could see the frames of the prints. They were dark green. The noise was coming from the kitchen on her left. April headed through the door.

Her heart thudded and her mouth was dry. She just couldn't get used to the fear of what she might find on the other side of an unknown door. She moved through this one quickly, on an angle, her body out of the frame before anybody could make it a target. Her hand was on her gun even though she was absolutely certain no one was in the old-fashioned kitchen. She saw at a glance the glass cabinets, wooden countertop, and new-looking appliances. It was well cared for and big enough to eat in.

On the counter was an empty cracker box with cracker crumbs around it and a half-filled glass. April sniffed at the glass without touching it. Water. A small TV by the window was tuned to CNN, which was airing a report on the stock market.

A salad bowl in the sink had a head of lettuce soaking in it. Mixing tools and a small jar of what looked like vinegar and oil sat beside it. She took a tissue out of the tissue box on the counter and turned off the TV. It looked like the woman had started a meal and left it.

April started at the faint *dong* of a clock in the other room, striking the quarter hour. She went out to take a look. Another struck with a different sound, and yet another. She switched on the lights and looked around with amazement. Every surface in the living room had some kind of working clock on it. It was like they were all alive, with their hearts ticking at different speeds. And there were books in neat stacks everywhere. There were so many books in the room April thought the clocks must be the Caucasian way to trick the Gods into getting more time to read them all.

She returned to the kitchen. Down the back hallway was a room with a washing machine, dryer, and treadmill. The ceiling light was on in here, too. A light on the panel of the treadmill showed it was on Pause at 3.5 miles.

Sanchez came out of the bedroom shaking his head as they met in the hall. "The tub and towels are wet in the bathroom, and her handbag is on the bed. Wallet, credit cards, fifty bucks. Everything but her keys."

April followed him back into the bedroom, and did a double-take at the bed. It was a king-size bed with a pale blue-green brocade bedspread and a lot of pastel satin pillows on it. It looked like a film star's bed. She sneaked a look at Mike to see what he thought of it. He caught her eye and raised his eyebrows. She turned away to check the closets.

They were both the walk-in kind. She walked in and looked all the way in the back. The doctor's closet smelled a little musty, but there was nothing in either one that had ever been alive except the shoes. The wife had nice shoes, nice clothes, too, if you happened to like tans and beiges. Everything was understated, except the bed.

April was beginning to feel something for the woman. You couldn't go through someone's things and not have some feelings. This woman had the kind of taste you couldn't really get without being born with it. Everything was rich and smooth, the colors subtle. Husband and wife both seemed to be neat almost to a fault. April wondered what it would be like to live in a place like this. Beautiful clothes. Beautiful kitchen. Monkey business every night. On the table by the bed were some pictures of her and him together, smiling. Both of them American good-looking, like people out of a magazine.

April picked one up with a sinking feeling. The photo was the first image she had of Emma Chapman, and it was disturbing. The picture showed another Caucasian beauty—a woman with long blond hair and clear blue eyes, the kind of well-formed lips models had, curved into a happy smile. She was on a beach somewhere, her arm around her husband, the man April had met, Jason Frank. People like this seemed always to be on vacation, wearing shorts. They always looked graceful and at ease with their long, suntanned legs hanging out. April felt hot all over and realized she had broken out into a sweat because Emma Chapman looked a whole lot like Ellen Roane.

She handed the photo to Mike. "See anything that bothers you?" she asked.

He studied it for a second, then put it back. "Yeah, there's your connection."

The two women looked alike. It was eerie, and somehow it didn't feel like a coincidence. April's attention shifted to a flashing light on the answering machine. There were messages. She pushed the play button. Francis came into the bedroom.

"Hurry up. I got to open the door for somebody. I can't stand around here all night. People want to come in."

"Just a second," Mike said. The tape was rewinding.

"I got to go," Francis insisted.

"Well, then, go. We're cops, remember."

"Yeah. Well, if you're not out of here in five minutes I'll call more cops. And don't forget to lock the door."

The machine clicked and started playing. No sound came out. April frowned. There was another click, and it reset itself with the message light still flashing. She did it again, and the same thing happened. Mike fiddled with it.

"It's not recording," he told her.

The solution always turned out to be the thing April hadn't thought of. The woman wasn't getting her messages because her machine was broken. She shook her head. How did that fit into the picture?

"Well, she went out for something," Sanchez murmured; "some time before eleven, without turning the lights off or taking her purse with her. And she didn't come back."

"She intended to come back." April cocked her head in the direction of the laundry room where the treadmill had been on Pause and the news still played in the kitchen.

Mike nodded. "Looks like it."

April felt sick. Even though statistics showed most missing persons returned, the last two cases she had been assigned had turned up dead. Lily Dong came home from school and opened the door to a neighbor. Ellen Roane went to California for spring break. Now there was Emma Chapman. What did she do?

April could tell Mike desperately wanted a cigarette and couldn't have one because he quit smoking two months ago.

"Let's go," she said.

He flicked off the lights with his elbow and headed for the door. "Let's get something to eat and talk about it."

April nodded, looking down at her feet. Didn't want to show her face. She was a cop, wasn't supposed to get freaked out by nasty surprises. She couldn't imagine chewing something and swallowing right now, couldn't imagine closing her eyes and getting any sleep in what was left of the night. But a lot of times there was nothing else to do before morning. All the way downstairs she tried not to think about where Emma Chapman was, concentrated instead on the car battery, praying it wasn't dead.

47

The gun was on the table. Emma could just see it through the slit between her closed lids. She could see his lap, too, because of the way he was sitting in a chair next to her, his legs apart. The knife was in his hand, some kind of switchblade. The blade popped in and out, flashing silver as he played restlessly with it.

She was shivering all over, freezing. The pain in her head was severe, but she couldn't reach up her hand to touch it. In her mind's eye she could see nails in her head piercing the nerves.

"Come on wake up, honey. I want you to know what a good friend I was to you at North. You never had a better friend."

Terror shot through her. The guy with the knife was talking to her like he knew her. She had trouble concentrating. Sometimes she thought she was in a movie, but she couldn't move her hands or her head. The sound of her groans came from a long way away.

"Come on, wake up. Your best friend is talking."

Never had a friend. She slipped way back to the smell of Virginia. Salt and seaweed filled her nose, like sand packed in a bucket. Her head hit a rock and she fell down, sliding on the mossy stones into the water. She could feel the water filling her mouth and dragging the dress down with her. "You got to watch what you wear, Emma. You're not the pink, girlish type." Her best dress, green, all tangled up and heavy, dragging at her while people shouted, "Pull her in. There, get her arm." Ripped the dress. Mommy, don't be mad. What navy kid can't swim? Stop the shouting. "You bad girl. Made a spectacle of yourself. The whole navy knows, all the way to

China. You're not getting another dress." *Oh no! Mommy. Please listen. I didn't fall. He hit me with a rock and knocked me down. Liar, liar, stick your hand in fire.* "You know better than to say things like that, Emma Jane. His daddy's a captain. You don't say such things. You don't lose your self-control." Paramount. Paramount importance. Now Hear This. Now Hear This. "Navy juniors ride waves. They don't make them."

Emma drifted in and out of consciousness while the guy in the chair talked to her.

"Where's my stuff?" she whimpered. "I lost my hat."

The guy touched her arm with the point of the switchblade. "Yeah, you're okay."

She opened her eyes. "What's going on?" She had no idea where she was or how she got there. It didn't even sound like her own voice speaking. It was so hoarse and slurred it could have been someone else's.

"You're some slow learner. I already told you."

He made the blade flick in and out again, trying to keep her attention.

Don't do that. She started to say it, but he began talking again, playing with the knife, touching her with it. The point pressed into her nipple. Fear poked at her from every side. Animal sounds of alarm jumped out of her mouth before she could stop them.

He smiled. "I already told you. I'm your old friend. I did a lot for you. Now I'm going to do something real special. Like nothing ever before."

He wiped the switchblade on his knee and looked at her through a square he made of his fingers.

Nausea pushed up into her throat. "It's wrong," she said thickly.

"No, it's right, baby. Just right."

"No. All wrong." A whimper of protest escaped her. "No," she mumbled. *Need a cup of coffee.* "Gotta to go home. Feel sick."

"You don't say 'No' to me." He stood, taking the switchblade with him. "Are you stupid or something?" He started walking back and forth, furiously flicking the blade open and closed. She twisted her head so she could see him. "I could cut your nipple off. You want that?"

"Uh." Emma grunted in terror.

"Now say no."

"Nnn." She tried to get her lips around the word. Sound came out of her stomach and not her mouth.

"NO!" He stopped pacing and shouted the word. "I could rape you. I could stick this knife right up your cunt."

"Nuh." The sound wouldn't come out.

"Say it," he screamed.

"Nn, no."

"Okay." He backed off, his hand in his pants. "Don't give me problems. Don't wire me. I got a schedule. I'm making it right, see. I did that for you before. You should have been better. You shouldn't have messed me up."

He raved, one hand in his pocket and the other clutching the knife. She got it in one tremendous, horrifying piece: He was turned on. It felt like a wave the size of Hawaii crashing over her. He wasn't an actor acting. He took her clothes away. He tied her hands and feet. She couldn't get up and walk out of the frame he was making with his hands. He wasn't in a movie. He was a lunatic. And she was his prisoner.

Sounds of pure terror came out of her mouth. She didn't recognize them as hers. She had to push them back the way she did when her mother told her not to show a thing. *Don't cry, Emma. Don't let them know they can get to you.* Never. Never, never, never. Just do the job and don't ask questions.

He kicked the sofa. It jerked backward. "You messed me up."

She had to gulp it back and listen now. Push it way back in her brain before it could take control of her. Fear had a shape of its own. It could fill her mouth and throat, fill the whole cavity of her body. She knew all about fear. It was something she was trained to master a long time ago. *Strength comes from fear* was her motto from the day she started school. Only this time it wasn't about being shunned or humiliated. This time, if she didn't concentrate and find a way out, fear would kill her.

She could see him rubbing the bulge in his pants with the handle of the knife. She could see it clearly. Her terror turned him on.

"I'm sorry," she mumbled thickly, her eyes closing again. "I'm sick. I don't remember."

"You don't remember Andy?"

"Andy?" She didn't move, but the eyes in her brain shot open. Andy. How did he know about Andy?

"Yeah, Andy the Animal. The Football Star, Big Man on Campus?"

Emma chewed her lips to keep from crying.

"Yeah, you remember Andy the Animal." He paced back and forth. "Maybe you don't know enough about me. I take care of things. I took care of that for you."

There's never a good reason to lose your self-control, Emma Jane. She could hear her mother's voice from a long way away.

Sometimes when someone got too close to her on the street, coming from behind, she could still feel Andy's breath on her neck. Smell the beer. All these years later. And the panic bubbled up all over again. Big guy, drunk at a party. She didn't even know him.

Her eyes squeezed tight, pushing it away, but she saw it anyway. The blood suddenly coming out of her at a dance; running to the girls' room. Realizing that the machine was empty. Coming out of the girls' room and running upstairs to her locker, where the long hall was dark. Hurry, hurry so no one would see her with blood on her dress. She didn't hear a thing until he was on her, breathing on her, his hands all over her. On her breasts, up her skirt. Big guy, sweaty and drunk, dragging her into the dark classroom, mumbling how great he was, how lucky she was he wanted her. Stop it, get off, get away. No way he would stop. He was on top of her, all his weight trying to shove it in her around her bloody panties.

"No, no," she whimpered, telling him to stop even now.

"Yeah, you remember."

And suddenly the fire alarm was ringing and all the lights were on. People everywhere. Blood all over her and her dress torn. Asking what happened to her. So humiliated about her period. So ashamed that someone would do that to her. Don't tell, captain of the football team. No one will believe you.

"My head hurts," Emma moaned.

"I took care of him," he said impatiently, "and you never thanked me."

"Wha?" She had to think.

"I saw it. I could have let him nail you. So what?"

Emma moved her wrists in the ropes, just a little. "Hurts," she cried.

"So what? I took care of him."

"My hands. My head. I'm so dizzy."

"Listen to me. I took care of him. I'm your best friend, see."

"If you're my best friend," she muttered, "get me some aspirin."

"Forget the fucking aspirin."

"If you're my friend, untie me." She didn't dare look at him.

"Oh, Christ."

He checked the ropes around her wrists. Her hands were white, but they weren't blue. There was no color in her face at all, but she was a little blue around the lips. Like the flake in California. It worried him. She was so out of it and confused he was afraid she might die.

"Ah, shit. You better not die on me." He played with the knots, loosening them just a fraction.

A little scream escaped her at his touch. He touched her breast with his finger, then with the tip of his switchblade.

"Shut up." he cried.

"No circulation, I can't breathe."

He started pacing again, his hand in his pants. "Look at what you're doing. I got a schedule. Don't mess me up."

Her heart was hammering so hard she thought it had lost its rhythm and was out of control. She could feel herself dying of fear. She let go. If fakirs could stop their hearts, so could she.

"I'm getting tired of this. Look at me, you stupid bitch. It wasn't an accident. I offed the guy. It was easy. A little gasoline in a condom. The condom in a toilet paper roll. Fits right in the pocket. You don't even have to get under the car. Just reach down in the parking lot and put it in the exhaust manifold. Know what kind of heat is generated a few minutes after a car is turned on? Burns the toilet paper tube and starts a nice big fire. Bye-bye, Andy."

Emma's mouth fell open; her head lolled to one side.

"Say thank you." He slapped her face. Nothing happened. She was out of it, again. He didn't want to do her like the flake who slept through the whole thing. He kicked the sofa again.

"Shit. I got a schedule," he muttered.

He paced back and forth in front of her, framing her with his hands and mumbling. When she showed no signs of reviving, he grabbed a few things and slammed out the door.

48

There were a few vital inconsistencies in the information Detective Woo, calling him from New York, was giving him. Jason sat in the chair by the bed, looking out at the lights on the navy ships in San Diego Harbor.

"Dr. Frank, from the appearance of your apartment, there is no indication that anything untoward happened to your wife," she began.

He sensed another message behind her words. "What do you mean by that?" he asked.

"Ah, there are no signs of anything being disturbed," she said.

There was some crackling in the background. The connection was not a good one. If nothing was wrong, why hadn't she waited until morning to return his call? Jason looked at his watch. It was way past midnight her time. He had asked Detective Woo to check his apartment, but he more than half expected her not to do it until the next day.

He had pegged her as a bureaucrat from the moment he saw her, from her very first words. There was a lot of tension around her mouth and eyes, a rigidity in the way she held her slender body. Her precisely layered haircut was extremely controlled, and the navy blue blazer and red-and-white blouse she wore buttoned all the way to the neck took no chances. Everything about her indicated a person who walked a straight line in the middle of the path, afraid of risk-taking, or of veering from the rules in the slightest detail. Jason had known a lot of bureaucrats, still did. Bureaucrats were the peo-

ple who had accidents in hospitals, who let little things by them that
resulted in very big consequences. There were times people died
because bureaucrats were just doing their jobs. That's why Jason
didn't trust them.

"But she's not there, and you tell me the lights and television
were on. That's already very untoward," he said.

"That depends on your wife," Detective Woo said.

What did that mean? What was the real story here? Jason
shifted the phone from one ear to the other. He didn't like the
vibrations he was getting from the detective's voice. He could feel
how tightly wound she was. Clocks wound too tightly sometimes
froze up and stopped working altogether.

"What did you see, Detective?"

"There were wet towels in the bathroom," April said. "Some
lettuce in the sink. The lights were on in the kitchen. She may have
started to make herself something to eat and then changed her mind
and gone out to visit a friend."

There was a slight hesitation before her next question that made
Jason think the detective didn't have any faith in that theory.

"Do you think she was likely to do that?" she asked.

"No, she wouldn't do that. She wanted to talk to me."

But how badly did Emma want to talk to him if she didn't pick
up all the times he rang? Now it was really late and she was still out
somewhere. She couldn't be out negotiating a movie deal at *midnight*.

"No," he said again.

"Maybe somebody from business you don't know."

He pondered the heretofore unconsidered possibility that
Emma was indeed out with some producer or movie star, and that
was what she wanted to tell him when she called more than twelve
hours ago. Just that she was going out with someone wonderful that
night. He walked around in the idea for a minute. Emma didn't know
what he was doing in San Diego, what was going on. She might have
gone out in all innocence. Maybe she took the afternoon off and went
to the hairdresser first.

None of it worked for him. And it was clear the theory wasn't working for the detective, either, or there wouldn't be so much strain in her voice.

"Were you aware her answering machine is on the blink?"

"What?" Jason started. "No, I wasn't."

"It picks up, but it doesn't record."

So maybe Emma didn't know he returned her call.

There was another small, telling hesitation on the New York end. Jason was sure the detective was keeping something else from him. What was it?

"I'm coming back," he said suddenly. "There's no point in trying to talk like this."

This time there was no pause on the other end. "That's probably a good idea, Dr. Frank," Woo said. "You have to be here to file a Missing Person Report."

"What?"

"I can't investigate without a complaint," she said.

"So you don't think she's just out for the evening." Jason had known it from the beginning.

"Well, she left her purse with her wallet in it on the bed."

Oh, shit. Oh, no. No. Emma wouldn't leave the apartment for more than a few minutes without her bag. He knew her habits, knew what she did. She must have gone out to pick something up at the store. And something prevented her from coming back.

Jason swallowed. "I'm leaving now."

He hung up, and started furiously throwing the few clothes he had brought into his suitcase, gathering his notes on Troland Grebs, all the time reviewing what he knew.

There wasn't a thing on Grebs's record that was recent. No hint of hospitalizations, no way to find if there had ever been a psychiatric evaluation of him without calling every in-patient and out-patient facility in the state. Grebs didn't have a file at North High School, which meant he hadn't been in trouble there. Jason didn't even know the name of the school Grebs attended in third grade where the little girl's hair was set on fire. The aunt didn't remember it, and she couldn't remember the name of the technical school he went to after high school, either.

What the record confirmed was that Grebs's obsession with fire went well beyond letter-writing. It confirmed there had been many occasions in his life when he acted out his desire to burn. Another significant thing about the record was the fact that there was nothing recent on it. That meant he had a high degree of intelligence and had learned from his mistakes. Grebs had found ways to avoid being caught. He may have killed the girl in San Diego by burning her and leaving her in the desert. What was he likely to do in New York?

Jason now had no doubt Grebs was the guy who had written the letters to Emma. Whether or not he killed the college girl was another question. His last letters to Emma indicated he was becoming disorganized. The more disorganized he became, the more unreachable and dangerous he was.

Fire, the guy was obssessed with fire. Jason shivered. Fire was permanent, the damage it did irreparable. Oh, God, help Emma, he prayed. Then stopped himself short. *Fuck praying.* There was no God to help her. He took some deep breaths, forcing himself to calm down. He had to think clearly, must not let his panic over Emma get in the way of finding her. He might have some time, but he was certain now that he didn't have much.

He slammed the small suitcase shut and looked at his watch. It was a Cartier Tank watch with a brown alligator band that Emma had given him when they got married so he could treasure their time together. The watch told him he could probably make the ten o'clock flight.

49

Troland was disgusted with her. She didn't seem to remember anything, wouldn't even make an effort to wake up and do it right. It
made him mad, reminded him of another girl, a really young one,
who just wouldn't make a sound no matter what he did. And he did a
lot. Finally he got tired of it, had to dump her. This one got him so
worked up he couldn't even stay in the place and do what he was
supposed to do.

He pulled the car out of the garage and headed into Manhattan
for the third time that day. The traffic going into the city was lighter
now, and it didn't take long. Twenty minutes, by the clock on the
dashboard. He got off the bridge and headed downtown. He figured
he better stay away from the West Side, even though he'd seen a lot
of girls over there and knew that part of town best. Several had
talked to him in the bars where he'd stopped for a few beers at night,
when he was tracking her and knew she wasn't coming out again. He
didn't like it when girls tried to pick him up. He was the one who
had to choose.

He cruised down Second, and then headed up First. There
was a gang of girls on the corner of Fourteenth Street. They looked
Spanish. He passed by, didn't want a Puerto Rican. On Forty-
second Street there were some black girls hanging around a coffee shop. They were too tall, were wearing elaborately braided wigs
and had big asses. He didn't like it when they were heavier than he
was.

In the Fifties he found what he was looking for. One girl on her own, covering the same stretch of block over and over like she was waiting for somebody who was late. She was wearing tights and a rainbow-colored shirt so short it barely covered her ass. There wasn't much flesh on her body, and she had the kind of fearless strut in her walk and swinging, little-girl blond hair that turned him on.

He cruised past her two, three times to be sure. He didn't like to get it wrong. Finally, he parked the car a block away and walked back because he was embarrassed by the navy Ford Tempo. Didn't want to be seen in it. If he had had his bike with him, he would have just roared up to her and told her to get on.

When she looked him up and down and changed direction to walk his way, he figured she was okay. Pretty much like him, didn't have much to say. In a few minutes she had already accepted one of the cellophane envelopes left over from the flake, and was taking him someplace he didn't catch.

It turned out to be at the end of the block in a run-down brownstone with a shabby shoe repair on the street level and an equally shabby locksmith above.

He nodded with approval. Yeah, it was right. The steep flight of stairs sagged so badly in places someone could slide right off the steps and tumble all the way down without a thing to get in the way or stop her from breaking her neck. Her two-room dump was in the back on the second floor, behind the locksmith that was closed for the night despite the sign in the window urging customers to "Come In Anytime. We're Open Twenty-Four Hours A Day."

It was grubby and dark. The one window was covered with a piece of faded cloth. A bare light bulb hanging from a socket in the ceiling illuminated the sagging couch in the center of the room. The sofa, though older and in worse condition, was not unlike the one the real girl was lying on in Queens.

"Take off your clothes," he said as soon as they were inside. "I want to tie you up."

She shrugged. "Whatever turns you on." She took the coke out of the pocket of her rainbow-colored shirt and waved it at him. "I got to do something first."

He looked around coldly. "Hurry up," he told her. "I'm on a schedule."

50

It came every few minutes, a sound like thunder. The roar, like an undertow, pulled Emma back to the place she didn't want to be. It was a noise she knew. What was it?

She opened her eyes cautiously. It roared again and didn't seem to be in her head, even though a lot of other things were. Terror all the way through, and a fog so dense she couldn't figure out what had happened, or how long she'd been there. Her throat was dry, and hurt so much she thought he must have tried to strangle her. She couldn't stop shivering, just couldn't stop.

He had left the light on. Now she saw the skylight in the ceiling. It had been covered with garbage bags and carefully taped around the edges so no light could get in. What else could she see? She lifted her head. He wasn't sitting beside her. He wasn't pacing around the room with the knife or the gun in his hand. He must really have gone.

His face was empty and hard, like a robot's. She shuddered. There was nothing remotely familiar about him. She still didn't know who he was, or if she had ever known him. North High School was a long time ago. A year in hell with people she had struck from the record of her life, as she had so many times before. Every time they moved to another base, the life they had before was gone. Everyone they knew and saw every day disappeared, and the system was replicated in another setting. Emma grew up believing that people left behind were erased completely, and that she alone had memories of things that happened.

Her heart wouldn't slow down. He was going to come back. She was so scared she could hardly breathe. All these years she thought she'd been alone, and she'd never been alone. He had been there all along, following her down the dark school hall that night and watching what happened. He was the only one who knew. And he killed Andy.

She believed him. She had never thought for a minute that Andy's death, a few days before graduation, was an accident. But she thought she was the one who murdered him. She had made a wish on a star, asked some almighty power she hardly believed existed to kill the bastard. End his life before he got to college. She hated him so much that when he died, there was no doubt at all in her mind she alone was responsible.

Her head hurt. Bits of story lines from plays and movies drifted through, along with her own memories, confusing her. She thought of *Equus*, the play about a troubled boy who blinded horses because they'd seen him making love. Was this that? There was a psychiatrist in that, too.

It was horrible being naked, unbearable having him look at her and touch her with the gun and the knife point. She tugged desperately on the ropes around her wrists, had to get away. What had Jason said about people who were really crazy, so crazy they couldn't be reached at all?

When he was in training, he had a patient who got on all fours and barked at him. For months he got on the floor every day and barked back at her. One day the woman got up and sat in a chair.

"You have to enter their world," he said, "but you can't go in there with them."

"Don't go in there with them," she muttered. *I'm in there with him.*

"Oh, God, help me." She was afraid to scream.

When she was little, her bones were so soft she could get out of any ropes, any wrestling hold. The kids practiced all the time, playing military games. "You're my prisoner, try to get away."

"You're a POW, hung by your wrists with a hundred and twenty rats gnawing at your feet."

Emma pushed through the pile of images, trying to find the right one. She saw herself sitting on the floor and sobbing as each hostage hit American soil. This wasn't that.

She didn't know how he got her there, or when. What did she hear? She heard street noises, the growl of traffic, a truck backfiring. But she also heard the sound of a garage door opening and a car pulling out.

She must be in a house. There it was, the roar again.

She screamed. "Help!"

Screamed again.

"Help me!"

Silence. She had to get out herself, must find a phone.

She turned her head. She could see windows on both sides, but the shades were drawn. There was no clock in the room. The stove in the corner next to the sink was an old one, didn't have a clock. How much time had passed? The table was bare except for a paring knife. She focused on the paring knife. She had to get out of here. How long did she have before he got back? Five minutes, ten?

Drip, drip, drip.

She lifted her head. The sound of a dripping faucet reminded her that she needed water. The room spun as if she were drunk, or dying of thirst in a desert. She closed her eyes. When she opened them again she had no idea how much time had passed or what she was doing there. Her throat was very sore. She thought about water, then concentrated on the ropes.

The ropes were loose, loose, loose. So loose she could pull right out of them if she moved the right way. Her wrists were covered with Vaseline; and she saw her hands, small as a baby's, slipping out of the loops. She saw Billy Budd hanging by the neck on the mast. They all went to the same schools, played together, but officers' kids sat on reserved benches at the movies. Movies every night, from Kodiak to Norfolk to Barber's Point, Hawaii. Only officers' kids were allowed in Officers' Mess with the silver and starched napkins. "No, don't die, Billy Budd," she had screamed at the big screen outside, making everyone laugh.

"Slip out." Before you choke. It's easy. She folded her left hand in half, squeezing her thumb into her palm and her little fingers together. Her fingers were long and thin. Her hand pulled out. She swallowed back the terror that he would catch her.

Better to move. The other hand was more difficult. The nylon rope bit into her wrist. Then, after a brief struggle, her right hand was out. She sat up. After all these years, Billy Budd was free.

51

The tours of duty were eight in the morning to four in the afternoon, or four in the afternoon to eleven at night. Every week they had two days of one and three days of the other. Periodically the days and hours were switched. April yawned into her napkin. There was a reason the Department organized the duties this way, but she didn't know what it was.

It was nearly one-thirty in the morning. She could see the time on a clock that hung between two lurid posters of bullfighters. She had to be back at work in five and a half hours. Her car was a few blocks away, still in the precinct lot. After she picked it up, she figured it would take her half an hour to get back to Astoria. Tomorrow morning it would take a good forty-five minutes to return over the bridge and make it across town. That left her with four and a quarter hours of sleep only if she didn't count the time it would take her to shower and dress in the morning.

Still, she didn't make a move to close her notebook.

"Finished?" Sanchez asked, eyeing her plate. Still uneaten was a pile of refried beans, some rice, and at least half of a seafood enchilada with guacamole.

April picked up a sprig of cilandro and chewed on it, nodding. "You liked it?" he asked.

They were in a tiny restaurant in the neighborhood that April had passed a hundred times. It was dark and quiet, looked to her like it was likely to go out of business soon. The front window had a bead curtain in it and some spearlike sticks with ribbons on the end that Sanchez said they used in Mexico to irritate the bulls at the beginning of bullfights.

"I liked it," April said, not entirely certain that she did. There was a heaviness in her mouth that she had a feeling would not go away for a long time.

In fact her mouth was actually quite sluggish and foul as a result of eating Mexican food. This was probably because of the cream and cheese that the scallops and shrimps were cooked in before being wrapped up in the pancakes. Tortillas. More cheese on top. Humh. Twice-cook pancakes. Every dish in Chinese cooking had a name. April silently named this dish Sluggish Mouth Pancake.

But it wasn't only the pancake bathed in cheese that was somewhat unpleasant. The raw onions in the mushy green stuff he called guacamole tasted like soft soap with bite-the-tongue bits of sharpness in it. April couldn't think of any textures in Chinese food that were similar.

Refried beans were smooth but tasteless. The Chinese used fermented or sweetened beans for flavorings, but did not eat them alone. Not even the rice was the same. Chinese rice was put into cold water and not stirred or seasoned until it was done. It came out white, and was for mixing with the tastes and textures of all the other dishes on the table. Mexican rice was cooked with oil and spices. Interesting, but heavy in the mouth.

She chewed on the cilantro, hoping to purify her mouth. This reminded her a little of the time she tried goat cheese and felt like she was eating vomit. But Sanchez was studying her with such intensity she knew it was a matter of national pride to him that she approve of it. His father did this kind of cooking. His mother must be very fat. April smiled at the thought of a waddling Maria scolding her son the police sergeant on the phone. *"Hola, Miguel, es Mama."*

Both April's mother and father were very thin, the kind of thin that always looked unnatural to her in light of the number of dishes piled high with food that appeared on the table every day. It almost seemed to her like they were starving in the midst of plenty.

Maybe if she ate more of this kind of food, her bottom would become plump and round in the American style. April realized she was thinking all these things about food because she liked sitting there with Mike, listening to him talk about his family and the cases he'd worked on. And she felt better talking to him about the ten thousand things she had to do in the morning than she would if she had gone home to brood about it on her own.

"You liked it," he said, "but what did you really think of it?"

April ducked her head, considering how to approach the subject. "Very good combination of tastes," she said seriously. "I think I liked your fish the best. What's that green stuff, kind of spicy on the side?"

"Tomatillo. It's like a green tomato with an onion skin over it. You have to peel it."

"The fish was very fresh." She nodded her approval of the snapper. "And I think avocado tastes better plain. On your dish it was plain."

There was a brief silence as they thought about avocado. They had talked about it earlier. It was another food the Chinese didn't have. Like thirty different kinds of chilis and sauces made with chocolate.

"Do you like to cook?" Mike asked.

No one to cook for. April bit her tongue. Her mother or father did all the cooking. "I know how," she said. "What about you?"

"I like it. Does that sound weird to you?"

The waiter cleared off the table.

"No. It runs in the family." April reached for her bag.

"You want me to drive you home?" he asked suddenly. The table was cleared and a check put by his water glass. "They want to close."

"Yeah, it's late. Let's go." She reached into her bag for her money. "How much is it?"

He shook his head.

"It's not a date. I have to." She objected in such a passionate way he had to smile.

"Of course it's not a date. But—" He cocked his head in the

direction of the kitchen. "It's only a token. If they saw me letting anyone else share it, I would get a bad name."

April fell silent. She liked the fact that he didn't make it a man-woman thing. He said anyone else. She wondered if this was where his father was a cook before he died, and that's why the bill was only a token. She understood about tokens. Everybody save face. She didn't feel she could ask him right then, though.

"I'd like to drive you home," he said when they were out on the street.

It was a warm, clear night. April looked up at the crescent moon. Her mother used to torture her with a story about a girl child whose angry parents sent her to the cold, empty moon as punishment for her disobedience. April grew up thinking the world's favorite symbol of romance was a prison whose walls closed in to nothing every thirty days. No romance for her. She smiled at fish-in-water Sanchez.

"Thanks, but then I'd have to take the subway back."

They turned up Columbus, heading for the precinct.

"Not necessarily. I could come and get you. We could talk about the case," he said.

April shook her head. "That's a very hard way to get from the Bronx to Eighty-second Street."

"I get up early," Mike argued.

"I thought this wasn't a date," she said more sharply than she meant to.

"Who said it was a date? We're working a case together. So I drive you home, what's the big deal?"

They debated about the bigness of the deal all the way back to the lot. Fine to work with each other. Maybe okay to have Mexican food. Not okay to drive back and forth in red Camaro making everyone in her neighborhood and everyone in the precinct think just what April didn't want them to think. She drove herself home, stewing about the trouble she was in with this case, and with Mike who wasn't going to be happy just working together for long, no matter how nice he could be when he wanted to.

She was not surprised to find the light on in her parents' part of the house when she got back at two o'clock. Nor was she surprised when her mother opened the door loudly demanding, in Chinese, explanations from her thoughtless daughter. How she could stay out so late without letting her worried mother know where she was? Who was she with, and what kind of no-good person would let her come home at this hour all alone?

"Mom, I'm a cop," April said wearily. "I'm on a case."

"What kind of case at two o'clock in the morning? I know what kind of case. Humh. *Boo hao* case."

"I'm a cop," April protested. "Just doing my job."

"Maybe a cop, but still a woman." Sai stood there with a hand on her skinny hip, resolutely blocking the door, as if she would not budge an inch until her every question was answered, including what her daughter had been eating to make her mouth smell so bad.

52

Emma sat on the edge of the sofa for many minutes, fighting the nausea and dizziness that came from the effort of leaning forward and untying the ropes around her ankles, knot by knot, with shaky fingers. The pain from the blow to her head was intense, and her legs trembled so much they didn't support her when she finally tried to stand up. She sank down on the hard sofa again.

"Help." Her voice sounded pitifully weak.

She looked around. Must be a phone. Everyone had a phone. Where was the phone? She saw a window by the sink with the dripping faucet. Maybe she could open the window and call for help. Maybe she could jump out.

She organized herself enough to get on the floor and start crawling toward it. How many feet was it?

"Help . . ."

She couldn't seem to make much noise.

The window was just above the counter. She pulled herself up to the counter and grabbed at the shade covering the window, missing the cord on the first two tries.

She sagged against the sink. Don't fall down, she told herself. She grabbed the cord again and this time succeeded. When she pulled on it, the shade snapped all the way up with a ferocity that startled her. She cried out and looked behind her, certain the door had opened and he was back. Everything was the same.

She turned back to the window, panicked. She had to get out there to the other side. She was on the second floor, pressed against the glass, naked in the artificial light. There were cars but no people on the street below.

She could tell by the sky that she wasn't in Manhattan. There were no skyscrapers with lights that cut pieces out of the sky here. In fact it was a long way across a maze of roads with walls to the row of low buildings on the other side. Where would the street be so wide she could hardly see the houses on the other side? The skyline was a map for anyone who knew the buildings.

It was dark, but there were a lot of streetlights. It seemed that the window fronted on a number of streets parallel to each other. Emma desperately tried to think. What was she looking at?

She pounded on the window at a man in a passing car. He didn't turn his head.

The latch on the window was too high for her to reach it without climbing up on the counter. Her muscles ached from having been stretched so long over her head. She shuddered. How long had she been lying there with him looking at her? Had to get away. She struggled to get up on the counter. She could hardly stand, much less pull herself up.

She stopped suddenly, confused by the roar that kept pushing through the haze in her brain. Through the thunder she could see lights and a dim shape in the sky. She frowned, struggling to name what she saw, tilted her throbbing head to one side.

Looking at it this way, she suddenly realized that although the street in front of her was flat, the street beyond that was on an angle. It was going up a hill to a Christmas tree of lights. Strings of lights out there like lace in the sky. That made no sense.

She inched down the counter. There she could see the side of a house. The light was on in the room opposite her, but there was no one in it.

It was then that she saw the phone. It was a white wall phone, a few feet to her right, almost hidden by the refrigerator. If she hadn't been standing right next to it, she might never have seen it.

"Oh, God." She reached for the phone and almost collapsed with relief when she heard the dial tone.

She tried her own number first. The receiver shrilled three discordant notes in her ear.

This number is not in service in area code seven-one-eight.

Oh, God, where was she? Emma fought back her panic and tried two-one-two, then her number. Was flooded with relief when it began to ring. *Please, Jason, be home.*

The phone rang and rang. Had she called the wrong number? She dialed again, more carefully this time. Two-one-two and then their home number. It rang again, a series of hollow echoes in her head. What was wrong? She was sure she had left her answering machine on. Had he come home and turned it off?

"God, Jason, pick up," she cried.

Maybe he was in his office. She tried two-one-two and then his office number. The machine picked up on the second ring. His cool, reassuring voice said he couldn't be with her right now, but if she would leave her name, date, and time of the call, he would get back to her as soon as he could.

I can't be with you right now. I can't be with you right now. I can't be with you right now. Those were the most powerful words she knew. Her father couldn't be with her because he was always in the middle of some ocean. Her husband couldn't be with her because he was always with someone, with someone, with someone. Always someone in trouble. The words had an echo that resounded all the way to the depths of her soul.

Jason was always telling her he'd be there if she needed him, but he was always "with someone, with someone, with someone" whenever she felt she did. No needs that she'd had were ever sufficient for him to consider it necessary to be with her right now.

She was sobbing uncontrollably by the time the beep sounded.

"Jason. Please come home," she sobbed into the receiver. "This man—He's cra—crazy. Please. He took my clothes. He has a gun, and he said he'd shoot me. Oh, please, help me."

The thunder sounded again. She couldn't stop crying. "My head hurts. I can't think. I'm in a house. I don't know where it is. Low houses, somewhere in Brooklyn, or the Bronx. I see a—lights and a ramp. I think it's a bridge. Oh, God, Jason, he tied me up," she cried hysterically. "He's going to kill me."

Beep.

"Oh, God."

She clutched the receiver in her hand, staring at it dumbly. The tape machine clicked. She was cut off. She was alone. She started sobbing again.

Then a shape moved in the window opposite.

Someone was standing there looking at her. Emma's eyes widened.

"Help!" she cried. She banged on the window. "Help me."

The person stood there stolidly, all in black, studying her grimly. Maybe it was a ghost.

"Oh, God," Emma cried.

A nun, or a Russian patriarch.

Without knowing what she was doing, she dialed 911.

"Police Emergency."

In the window across the way, the mouth began to move.

"Help," Emma cried. "Help!"

"All right, miss, calm down. Are you injured or is there an injured person with you?"

"Uh," Emma gulped.

"Try to calm down, miss. Where are you located?"

The mouth was moving across the way. The narrow black figure was making hand motions. It was too confusing. Emma started to cry.

"Help . . ."

"Okay, take it easy. Let's take it one step at a time. Can you tell me your name?"

Nausea swept over Emma. She gagged over the sink. She couldn't talk. She needed something to drink.

"Miss, are you there? I need some information to help you. Give me something—a location, a phone number."

The words dribbled out of the receiver that Emma had dropped on the counter. "Call back later," she muttered, hanging up the phone. Moments later her head hit the edge of the counter as her legs gave way under her, and she sank to the floor.

53

The girl came out of a bathroom so small and filthy Troland would not have used it under any circumstance.

"That's better. What's your name?" She tossed her blond hair and started to unbutton her shirt.

"Willy." He said it flatly, looking around the room.

It had a table with only one chair, a hot plate with a pot on it that clearly wasn't used for food. No sink or refrigerator. A sofa with very old fabric on it. There was nothing female in the place, no clothes or lacey pillows or soft objects of any kind. No makeup or hair ornaments. It occurred to Troland he better be careful. This place didn't seem to be hers.

"Willy? Like Willy Smith?" She giggled. "You a Kennedy?"

Troland turned to her and snorted. "Yeah." He snorted again. She was high already, didn't know what she was talking about.

"You live here?" he asked.

She shook her head. "Nope. It's a friend's." She had her shirt off now and was peeling her tights down, like she was in a locker room getting ready for a game.

Troland watched her with little interest. The pressure he felt before had eased with the trip into the city, and the cruising up and down in a car. He didn't like driving a car unless he had to. He didn't feel that great now. He wanted to get back to the real girl and get started.

He sat down at the table, suddenly disgusted. Although it seemed right at first, inside the place had a lot of things wrong with it. It was dirty. Troland didn't like dirty. His lip curled at the smell of glue and old leather that leaked up from the shoe repair downstairs. The guy from there was probably the one whose place this was. Troland didn't like that, either. He might come back in the middle and give him some trouble.

He switched his attention to the body that was now fully naked in front of him. He was turned off by a number of blemishes on its neck and arms. There were a few black-and-blue marks on the thighs, too. In fact, except for the thin, pale, young-girl hair, this body wasn't as good as the one he already had. That made him feel a little better. He had a real prize waiting for him. Something that was well kept and smelled good, didn't have any diseases like this probably did. He had a real movie star, all his own. He snorted, and instinctively reached for the items in the pocket of his leather jacket.

"There's a bed in there." The girl pointed to a closed door.

"You have somebody coming back?" Troland asked.

There were four lengths of the thin nylon rope he had specially cut to size, his knife, his Zippo lighter, and several marking pens with medium points. The feel of the familiar items comforted him. He fondled the lighter, pumping himself up.

"Not for a while. What do you have in mind?"

She came over and sat on his lap. He pushed her off. "Do it my way," he snapped.

"Hey, just being nice." She retreated through the half-closed door into the other room.

It occurred to Troland the guy might be in there, and the whole thing was a scam. That made him mad. He jumped up and kicked the door open with a bang, the switchblade in his hand.

"What's going on?" he snarled. He didn't like scams.

The girl was dancing on the bed. "Nothing," she protested. "Hey, you're really wired."

"I'm not wired. I don't get wired. Look at you, you're the one that's bouncing off the wall."

He kicked around for a minute, looking for a hiding place, or a mirror someone could be looking through from the other side.

"Why don't you chill out and have a good time," she said.

"Get out of there," he commanded.

"What's the matter?" Now the baby voice with the New York accent was offended and a little scared. That was good.

"I don't like it in here," he said.

"Okay. That's fine."

She got off the bed. The sheets were grimy. He didn't like the setup. When she got close to him he grabbed her arm. "Okay. I'll tell you what we're going to do. You lie down over there. I tie you up. You try to get out."

"Okay. I can get out."

She walked the short distance to the sofa and sat down.

Troland clicked his tongue against his teeth with annoyance. "You don't get out," he said. "That's the whole point."

She made a little half-shrug with her shoulders. "You won't hurt me, will you?"

"I don't hurt people."

She lay back on the sofa. "Okay, so you tie me up, and I don't get out. Then what?"

"Then I draw some pretty pictures on you and I fuck you." Troland took one of her wrists and started to tie it to the sofa leg.

The girl popped up, wrenching her arm away. "No kidding," she said with interest. "What kind of pictures?"

He grabbed the arm and yanked it until she squeaked. "Don't do that. It's not a game."

"Ow."

"Do it right."

"I just wanted to know what kind of pictures," she whined. "You can't mess me up."

"I only do good pictures. Now hold still." He tied her hands together over her head.

She giggled. Then he went to the other end of the sofa and grabbed a foot. She stopped laughing.

"Hey, don't tie my feet. I got claustrophobia."

"Shut up. I'm doing this." She didn't look so bad like this. Now he was feeling better.

She kicked with the free foot. "Hey. I said not the feet."

He pulled the switchblade out of his pocket and flicked it open.

Her eyes bulged at the knife. "Oh, shit. You said you weren't going to hurt me."

"You're supposed to give me a good time," he said angrily. He kicked the sofa. "Now do it right. Act like you're in a movie."

"I'm going to need another hit," she wheedled.

"When I'm finished." He grabbed the other foot and tied the ankle down.

She pouted.

He was satisfied at the picture she made. This sofa was not as good as the other one. He had to tie her hands over her head, but she was spread-eagled from the waist down. The sparse tuft of pubic hair showed she was a real blond. He cursed himself for not thinking of bringing a razor to shave it off. He knew just what to draw there. He pulled up the chair and laid out his equipment: four pens—red, blue, black, and green—rubber gloves, the switchblade, the Zippo, and two condoms.

She giggled nervously when he put on the gloves. But he had already forgotten her. He was planning the picture. Snakes going up the inner thighs with fangs darting into her cunt. Then the torso would have a new addition, the doctor's staff, since he was the Doctor of Death. The flames would curl out of the staff, burning it up.

When the first pen tip touched her thigh, she jumped back in alarm. But after he unzipped his pants, and had her suck on him, she got into it. By the time he began shoving rubber fingers into her, and his double-sheathed penis, and biting the pictures he had drawn, she was way out in outer space.

54

In the early hours of the morning, Jason pulled himself out of the taxi and headed for his front door. As he rang the bell for the doorman, he was seized again with the same wild, unreasonable hope that had been nudging at the corners of his mind all the way across the country, the hope that his instincts had been wrong all along. Emma was not really threatened. She had just moved into another life without him. The letters were just an excuse for him to develop an elaborate fantasy of a madman's retribution for his wife's transformation from teen angel to movie-star whore. In this scenario he was the one who was threatened by it, and the hurt and anger were his alone. Nothing else was acceptable. He desperately wanted to be the crazy one, so caught up in the fantasy of retribution that he went all the way to San Diego to find himself an imaginary serial killer.

Francis wasn't at the door. Jason had to ring twice. Maybe Emma had come home, and he would be proven a fool. Rumpled and exhausted, with dark circles under his eyes, he thought about that as he waited for Francis to appear.

Not many people actually did what they dreamed of doing. Even Charles had suggested more than once that there was a big difference between writing letters and acting on the rage and hatred expressed in them.

Francis shuffled across the lobby and started at the sight of him. "Oh, Dr. Frank, Dr. Frank. Thank God you're back. The police were here," the doorman cried as he swung the heavy door open.

"I know," Jason said.

"What do they think happened to Mrs. Frank?" he demanded. "They just didn't give me no choice. They forced their way in. What did they expect to find anyway?"

"It's all right." Mechanically, Jason went through the motions of calming him down. He was a stoic and a doctor. Staying in control when people around him were bouncing off walls was what he did. He had managed his raging panic on the plane and continued to do so now without thinking.

"It set me off for the whole night, I'll tell you." The man followed him to the elevator. "I didn't leave them alone for a minute. Stayed with them the whole time," he insisted.

"Thank you." Jason got on the elevator, hardly knowing what he was saying. The acid had begun eating away at his insides again. Emma had not magically returned. He refused to let himself think about Troland Grebs.

Upstairs, he went through the apartment carefully. He saw the towels, still damp in the bathroom, and her purse on the bed. Nothing of hers seemed to be missing. Not a coat, not a dress, not a credit card, not a hairbrush or a toothbrush or a lipstick. There was no way in the world that she would voluntarily go anywhere without those essential items.

He went into the kitchen. There was the lettuce in a bowl in the sink. The treadmill in the laundry room was still on Pause. In the bedroom he turned on the answering machine and fiddled with it. Detective Woo had been right. Several messages had been counted by the machine, but not recorded. Only blank tape played back. This had happened with the machine before, but it had righted itself before Emma had gotten around to getting it fixed.

Just like the police, Jason saw an interruption in life in the apartment. But he did not want to jump to any conclusions about it. There could be more than one explanation for Emma's disappearance. She could have gone out to the store for something and had an accident. Only a month ago an old woman crossing Riverside Drive had been struck by a van when the driver ran a red light. More recently a taxi jumped the curb and smashed into the window of the

video store on Broadway. The driver had been distracted by a homeless man waving a stick at him. And other things happened, too.
Bicycle messengers, silently racing the wrong way on one-way
streets, knocked people over all the time.

Emma might have been sideswiped by a bus, or a car, and was
in the hospital. There were a thousand unexpected, freaky things
that happened to people every day in New York City.

Jason took his jacket off and went back into the kitchen. He
made himself a cup of strong coffee and started calling hospital
emergency rooms and morgues. No Emma Chapman or unidentified
woman who fit her description had been admitted anywhere that
night.

When he could think of nothing else to do, he went into his
office and played back the messages from his own answering machine.

55

April had arranged to meet Dr. Frank in his office as soon after eight o'clock as she could get there. She had that in her mind as she spent several precious minutes placating her angry mother.

But even after she got away from Skinny Dragon Mother late at night, April didn't sleep. She spent nearly an hour writing up her notes on the Chapman case. As she worked, she tried to put out of her mind the unrelated incidents her mother insisted on telling her as tit for tat about jealous lovers and humiliated husbands in long-ago China. April hadn't wanted to hear about it. It was after two in the morning, and had nothing to do with now.

"That's what you think," Sai said huffily, blocking the stairs. "People crazy like fox everywhere."

Her mother was offended, but April had to sleep. What did a kidnapped young noblewoman locked up in a farmer's cave in a mountain because she was pregnant and his only wife was barren— ninety years ago—have to do with anything?

Still, April kept thinking about the young woman in the cave for a long time before she could fall asleep. What was the meaning of the story? There was no way to know if it was true, or the myth of anxious mothers-in-law, made up to prevent unhappy young wives from straying far from home. Women had to be obedient or suffer terrible consequences in China.

It came to April later, in her troubled sleep, that her mother might be telling her the actress was a runaway. The same thing April herself once told the parents of the missing girl, Ellen Roane. She forgot to tell her mother missing girls and wives in America don't leave their credit cards behind on the bed. There had to be another meaning.

It seemed like only five minutes passed before the alarm went off and April was up again, pulling herself together and heading back into the city. Luckily, in the morning her mother was too busy with her father to come upstairs and knock on her door.

Luckily, too, Sergeant Joyce was already in when April got into the precinct a full ten minutes early. April went into her office to fill her in on what had happened, except for the part about how she and Sanchez went out for dinner. She was a little uneasy about that.

Sergeant Joyce made a lot of listening faces and frowned when April asked if she could go out to take Dr. Frank's statement on his missing wife. Nothing was happening right then, and no one else was around yet, so Sergeant Joyce reluctantly said okay.

"But we'll have to review the case when you get back," she said ominously.

It was April's turn to frown. She knew that meant her coming back might be the end of the case for her. Sergeant Joyce would reassign it to someone with more experience, maybe even take it for herself. And April would be stuck doing foot-soldier work in the wrong part of town. She might even have to learn Spanish. That was a horrible thought. She stopped at her desk for a minute. Sanchez wasn't in yet. Humph. So much for his being an early riser.

She took a Missing Person form from the color-coded stacks of forms on top of a filing cabinet. Then she checked her bag for the notebook with the long list of questions she had prepared last night, for the investigation she probably wouldn't be allowed to finish. Finally she drove the few blocks over to Riverside Drive and parked by the same hydrant she and Mike had parked in front of the night before.

In the building, as she waited for the elevator that was like a cage, she stood looking up at the stained-glass skylight which was brilliant with color in the morning light. More than once she felt in her bag for the hard shape of her gun to reassure herself that she was meant to be here and knew what she was doing. Her confidence fell apart when Dr. Frank opened the door.

"She's been abducted. She's been kidnapped," he cried wildly, hustling her inside his office.

"What?"

Waiting room, empty of everything except a few chairs and some bookcases, all filled with books and periodicals. Brown rug on the floor. Two floor lamps gave off a lot of fairly harsh light. His office was much more crowded with objects and furniture, the desk cluttered with papers and notebooks. There were three clocks in the room, all ticking away. Like the ones in his apartment, they looked pretty old.

April tried to take everything in all at once, the way she was taught. How he looked. How the room looked. What he was saying. Most important, *what* he was saying. She was aware from her first second on the scene that above all she had to keep her wits about her and find the real story.

"My wife's been kidnapped," he cried. "What are you going to do about it? It's been a whole night. We've got to find her right away. We don't have much time. It may be too late already. Grebs threatened to kill her. He will kill her. We have to hurry."

He stood in the middle of the room talking rapidly, as if he thought he could propel her right into action without going through any of the preliminaries first. His appearance was alarming. He was large and pale, and so shaky April was terrified he might topple like a tree from the stress.

She'd seen Chinese do that. Before the questioning even got underway, they'd fall right over. And then April had to pick them up and calm them down. But very rarely did Asians kill the people they kidnapped. Kidnapping was just business. She thought of that as she asked herself for the thirtieth time what mistake had brought her to the upper West Side where people were movie stars and psychiatrists, not immigrants from Asia.

"Sit down," she said quietly, trying to calm her own hysteria as well as his. The voice inside said, *I can't do this. All I know is caves*

in mountains. Another voice told her it was all the same thing. She
did know what to do.

"Take a minute." She put her hand on the doctor's arm. "I know
how it is. Sit down for a minute, Doctor. What makes you think she
was abducted?"

She thought quickly. It couldn't have happened up here. There
was no way to get in or out without the doorman seeing. Maybe the
day doorman saw something, or knew something.

"I've been calling every hospital. Nothing on her," he said,
looking at April as if he already knew she was useless.

"It took me hours to come in here. I didn't think of it until just
now, when I came in to meet you. I just didn't think of it." Furious,
he hit his forehead with his palm. "Oh, God. I can't tell you how
serious this is."

What was he talking about? April wished he'd get organized
and tell her what was going on.

"Did you get a ransom call?"

He shook his head miserably. "Worse than that."

"Why don't you sit down and let me ask you some questions,"
she suggested.

She had to get him organized. No different from Chinese. Except he didn't take directions. He had to do everything his own way.
Went to California, found his own suspect. What kind of person
would do that?

He was shaking all over. "Listen to this," he commanded. He
went to his desk and pushed the button on his answering machine.

The voice of Emma Chapman jumped out, crying for help.

April's face didn't change, but inside every part of her started
screaming, too. He was right. The shrink had been right all along,
and she hadn't been paying the right kind of attention. Here was the
voice of the person she was supposed to protect, and hadn't. She
should have contacted Emma Chapman a week ago. Never mind if
the woman didn't return the call. Why so shy? Why so afraid to come
and check it out for herself? Now look what happened.

My fault, she told herself. She let him scare her into staying away from the wife. My fault. The others weren't her fault. Not her case until after they were gone. She'd heard a few pleading voices on the phone. They had all scared her, but this voice was on her head. It was slurred in places. The woman sounded hurt as well as terrified. It was horrible. Horrible to listen to. He played it four times, while they concentrated in silence. By the second time April had already begun taking notes.

Finally he switched the machine off and looked at her hard. April knew he was trying to see inside of her. Trying to determine what she might know. She was very aware that he was a head doctor. Head doctors knew what people were thinking before they said anything. Her pen was poised above the pad. She did not let her hand tremble with fear.

She was not a head doctor, but she knew what he was thinking, too. She knew he was thinking what can this Asian woman do, nothing. But she could do something. She could make sure he wasn't right at her expense any more.

His office answering machine clocked the call from his wife at just before midnight. April was in the apartment next door about then, but not just then. If the woman had called the apartment only a few minutes earlier, April would have picked up and talked to her. They might have found her by now.

"She was alone at midnight," April said.

"That was eight hours ago. What are you going to do?"

He kept demanding the same thing. She was going to do her job. What did he think she was going to do?

"She was able to make the call. She was by a window, looking out," April said. "That means she wasn't restrained."

"What are you getting at?"

"It's possible she got away."

Dr. Frank looked at her like she was stupid. "Then we would have heard from her."

"Maybe not yet."

"She says the guy's going to kill her. What are you going to do to find her?"

The way he demanded this sounded like he really thought she was going to drag her feet on the matter. April was determined not to bristle.

"I'm going to ask you a lot of questions, Dr. Frank. And when I leave here, I'm going to make a report to my supervisor. Then there will be many people in this neighborhood asking questions."

"Why this neighborhood? She said it was the Bronx or Brooklyn."

"It's going to take a while. Why don't you sit down," April said firmly.

She could see he wanted to do it his way. He had been standing all this time by the machine. He seemed to have to think it over for a minute before sitting down at his desk.

"The doorman last night didn't see her leave. That means she left before eleven," April said patiently. "We'll talk to the day doorman. We'll try to find someone who saw her leave the building, set a time. If she met anybody, or someone stopped her on the street. If she got in a car. This is a busy neighborhood. Someone must have seen her. We'll get a description."

"But I *know* who it is, and he's not going to keep her around while you're busy setting times," Jason said bitterly. "We're talking about my wife and a man with a violent history. He's going to kill her or rape her, or burn her." His voice caught on the words. "Look, I'll find her if I have to do it myself."

April couldn't help being impressed by him. He loved his wife, and he was professional. Like her, he was thinking all the time. He had been thinking from the beginning. He wasn't completely helpless like everybody else. She watched him pull himself together. It took only a few seconds.

"Can you trace her call?" he asked more gently.

"From the tape?" April shook her head. "The phone company does have the technology to print out the number a call is coming from, but it isn't available to the police yet."

"He's from a lower-class neighborhood," Jason said suddenly.

"What is the significance of that, Dr. Frank?"

"People tend to gravitate to what they're used to."

"Yes," April said, still not getting what he meant.

"I've seen where he comes from. He's very compulsive. That means he does the same things over and over."

April nodded. How did that help? She raised a delicate eyebrow, afraid to seem stupid by asking the question.

"He's quite regressed right now. He's likely to be in a place that looks to him like the place he came from."

"And you know what that place might be?"

Jason nodded. "The Bronx or Brooklyn sound right, where the houses are small and right next to each other."

"Does your wife know the Bronx and Brooklyn at all?"

"No."

"Well, it's more likely to be Queens or maybe New Jersey," she said.

Jason's face fell. "New Jersey? What makes you think so?"

"Because of the sounds on the tape. She's near an airport. She might see a bridge and hear an airplane in Newark. Or Queens. Not the Bronx or Brooklyn."

"Jesus. Of course. He works at an airport. Lindbergh Field in San Diego. Yes, he'd be near an airport, but which one? There are at least three."

April sighed. He was not going to follow her line of questioning. She decided to let him do it his own way.

"Why don't you tell me about what you found out in San Diego, and we'll take it from there."

It was nearly two hours before April met with Sergeant Joyce again. She had the tape and a recent photo of Emma Chapman, as well as some yearbook pictures and a mug shot of Troland Grebs. She'd gotten the rap sheet of Grebs the day before and already knew what was on it: two convictions for arson and three arrests for assault. One was a bar fight and two were battery cases against prostitutes. It occurred to April that she might check to see if any prostitutes had been beaten up in the last few days.

56

The key turned in the lock, but Emma didn't hear the door open or Troland come in. He was very tired. He was moving slower now. His plan was to go to sleep for a few hours and get started on her after breakfast. He was a methodical person, always did things the same way. He liked to have a shower and eat something. Then he liked to start his work. He could work as late as he wanted, but he always had to start in the morning when he was fresh.

He had already forgotten about the girl in the city. He was thinking about making it right. All the way back in the car he had been thinking about the brand. It was in his knapsack, very light aluminum. Airplane material. He'd had it made by one of the welders in the plant. He was very proud of it. He liked thinking about how he'd designed it, how he'd worked out the difficulties. He wanted something that would get very hot and was light. Not everybody could think of such a thing or get the wrinkles worked out.

And it hadn't been so easy to get relocated in New York. He had important stuff that couldn't be moved around just like that. He had had to think about the best way of moving the torch and the gun. He had to decide whether to put the compressor in the suitcase or buy a new one here. He left the gun and the torch behind. He took the compressor in the suitcase, heavy as it was. What was easy was getting another gun and small butane torch here. He had a plan. He knew what he was doing.

He had thought about the whole picture, and he thought about each little piece of it. For a while he considered getting some handcuffs. Handcuffs were the professional way to go. But he didn't like them. After what happened to him when he was a kid, he didn't want to touch them ever again. Decided against them. Anyway, even though they looked professional, you couldn't kill somebody with handcuffs, couldn't get them positioned right on a sofa, or a bed.

Willy agreed the nylon ropes were better. Troland told Willy how he liked knots. Liked wrapping the package. He talked to Willy about things like this, arguing the case for and against the different ways to carry out the plan. He was talking to Willy now, telling him he was all ready to go. He just needed a few hours of rest before starting.

He had decided he wasn't going to tattoo the whole, whole torso, like he did the other girl. Because if he did that, he might get to the end and not want to spoil the tattoo part with the brand part. Better plan to leave a place for it right at the beginning. He decided to draw it in so he'd know exactly where it went.

He didn't look for the girl. He wasn't thinking about her. He was thinking about the transfer paper, about leaving a place for the brand, getting everything just right when he was setting up. It wasn't until he almost tripped over her that he realized she wasn't where he left her.

"Oh, shit."

She was on the floor, lying there face-down like she was already dead.

"Fucking shit!"

He was horrified, couldn't believe it. Had he fucked up and killed her before he left? He didn't remember killing her. Why would he do that when he had a plan, wanted her awake for the whole thing? He wanted to talk to her and show her everything. That was the important part to getting it right. She had to know how good he was.

No way he would kill her first. Maybe somebody else killed her. He squatted down, furious with her for dying, himself for leaving her, and whoever might have killed her while he was gone. Who would do such a thing?

He leaned over and put his hand on the back of her neck. Her skin was warm. Now that he looked at her he could see that she was still breathing. He couldn't believe this. What the—He looked back at the ropes. Four pieces, three lying on the floor and one on the sofa. What kind of shit was this? How did she get loose, and what was the matter with her now?

Jesus. The bitch was making trouble for him. "You stupid bitch," he said. "What'd you think you're doing?"

He turned her over and got even madder. Her mouth was slack, and she didn't move at all. She wasn't dead, but she might be dying. Jesus, he didn't need this after all his trouble. Maybe she was faking.

"Get up, bitch," he told her. "What the fuck do you think you're doing? I got a plan. I'm doing you a favor here. I'm taking care of you. You're not going to die on me. Just get that straight."

All the time he was talking to her, he was looking her over for injuries, poking at her warm body. It was a little clammy now, not as fragrant as before. This irritated him. He didn't want her dying and releasing all that body stuff for him to clean up. That was all he needed. For her to die and make a mess before he had the plastic laid out. Before he was ready.

He moved her around carefully. If he bumped her on the edges of things, she'd bruise and the tattoo wouldn't look good. That was what he liked about her right from the first, the expanses of fresh, well-cared-for flesh. Now he had to clean it up before he even got started.

He examined her all over and got excited again handling her. He wanted to do some stuff to her, but wanted her awake. Shit. He didn't see anything wrong with her. Except for the bump on the head and a little scratch on her forehead, there wasn't anything.

He decided the sofa was no good. He had to move her. He picked her up and moved her to the bed in the other room. Laid her back against the pillow so she looked like she was just sleeping. Yeah, that was better. Now he could sleep with her. That was good. He hadn't thought of that before. If he kept her with him all the time, he could keep her alive. He could touch her whenever he wanted.

He started thinking about biting her and shoving it in her and making her scream. It made him desperate to wake her up.

He got some water and poured it down her throat. After a while she started choking.

"Hi, honey," he said when she finally opened her eyes. "We got a busy day. Don't do that again."

57

Sanchez rewound the tape and turned to April. There was a long silence. Already there were eleven people on the case, combing the neighborhood with the photo of Emma Chapman and hastily made sketches of Troland Grebs. The blowup of his photo in the yearbook would take a little longer.

"You know what I don't understand." He swiveled around in his chair, facing her and the small tape machine on her desk that was closer to him than her. He was wearing a blue shirt with a darker blue tie, gray trousers of some undefinable fabric, and the sad expression that always made April feel she'd done something really wrong.

She lifted her shoulders a tiny bit to indicate she had no idea.

"I don't get you," he said. "One day we're working a case together, hanging out on a limb a little bit, and I think maybe we're onto something."

She frowned. What was he talking about? They weren't onto anything. As of last night, they didn't know a thing except that the woman was not where her husband wanted her to be.

"I mean, trust. Working together like a team." Sanchez looked at her intently, his mustache quivering just enough to show he was agitated.

Her brow furrowed even deeper. Trust was not a word she was comfortable with. She had a lot of trouble in those training sessions where you had to fall down and let somebody catch you. Not so good to let somebody stand behind you, even a cop.

"You don't get it, do you?" he demanded.

"What?" Her phone rang. She let it ring.

"We go out on something," he said. "We have something to eat. We're talking about it, working it over in our minds. Like the two of us, you know? And the next day I come in, you're already out of here. Not a note, nothing. What am I supposed to feel, huh?"

He looked offended. Angry, too.

She tried to look angry right back and almost immediately had to look down. Angry right back was not something she was good at. "Feel?" She wanted to scold him. You don't have feelings when you're a cop. She shook her head. "You have two things mixed up." She reached for her phone. "Detective Woo," she said.

"It's Jason Frank."

April looked at her watch. It had been only twenty-five minutes since his last call. "Yes, Dr. Frank."

"Were you able to get those pictures duplicated?" he asked.

"We're working on it," she replied.

There was a pause.

"Is there anything new?" he asked.

Sanchez moved restlessly in his chair while she focused on her conversation.

"I know how you're feeling, Dr. Frank," she said soothingly. "It's terrible to have to sit around waiting for news, but I promise I'll call you as soon as I have anything to report."

"Listen, I've been thinking. Is this something the FBI should be getting involved with?"

"Do you think you'd have better luck with the FBI than the New York City Police Department?" she asked without a trace of a smile.

"I wasn't questioning your expertise. I was just thinking that kidnapping is a federal offense."

"Yes, it is. But the FBI doesn't step in on every missing person case, even if there is a suspected abduction. Have you received a call asking for ransom?" April asked, suddenly.

"No."

"Then try to give us a little time, Doctor. We have a lot of people working on it." She looked up at Sanchez. At that second he wasn't looking at her.

"I can't. I told you it's too serious. We don't have much time," Jason Frank was saying.

"Believe me, Doctor Frank. We know how serious it is. We've brought people in." A lot of them. Right then the squad room was filled with blue uniforms and detectives, rushing around, coming in and out of the field. Coffee cups everywhere. It was hard to breathe, much less hear anything on the phone. The place had become a war room.

"We have to find her soon," Dr. Frank pressed. "I'd like to come and help."

That was the last thing she needed. "You *are* helping. You're helping a lot," April said, trying not to get annoyed. He couldn't just come in and help. It didn't work that way. And the more he distracted her, the less time she had to concentrate on it.

"I'll meet with you very soon," she promised. "But right now you have to let me do my job."

"One hour?" he said.

"I can't give you a time. I'll call you when I have something. That's all I can promise."

He had no answer for that. April finally had the space to hang up.

Now Sanchez was looking at her.

"What are you looking at?" she demanded, exasperated.

"We were having a conversation."

"Mike," she said, lowering her voice. Right above her head two blue uniforms were distributing the sketches of Troland Grebs to new arrivals. "You got two things all mixed up."

Sanchez poked the smaller uniform, an earnest-looking female, bulging out of her pants. "Hey, why don't you do that over there." He pointed across the room toward the door.

"Oh," she said. "Sorry, sir." And moved away.

He turned back to April without skipping a beat. "No, lady, I don't have two things mixed up. You trust somebody one way, you got to trust them another way. It's not about anything else. You're not together with me one minute and then going it alone the next."

April was silent for a second, thinking it over. "You weren't here," she said finally.

"What are you talking about?"

"I went out alone because you weren't here."

"Well, I would have been here if you'd let me pick you up." He poked a finger at the air. Ha, got her.

She narrowed her eyes, furious at him. "Look, don't confuse things. You listened to the tape. That's all there is to think about. Finding her. If we find her, then we can talk about trust."

He shrugged. Okay. "So what angle are you working? You know what that noise is in the background?"

"Of course I do. Do you think I'm stupid?"

"What is it?"

Oh, they were playing guessing games again. "An airplane," she said irritably.

"So is it landing or taking off?" he demanded.

"How do I know?" April said.

"You should know," he said grimly. "Well, where's your map?"

April looked startled. Sergeant Joyce didn't mention any map.

He looked at her with disappointment. "We need to pinpoint all the bridges and airports."

"I was just on my way to do that," she said quickly, frowning because she thought that was just a little bit premature. The woman could just as easily be in New Jersey or Connecticut. They had airports there. But no bridges near enough to be able to see the bridge and hear the planes directly overhead. Scratch New Jersey and Connecticut.

"Did you get an audio person to tell by the sound of the engines if the planes are taking off or landing?"

April nodded vigorously. Oh, yeah, she'd had many hours of free time to think of all these things. Why did she listen to him? He just made her feel bad.

"Does that make a difference, if she's looking out at a bridge?" she asked, without sounding as annoyed as she felt.

She wanted to do things her own way, but he was looking at her accusingly again. She hated having him mad at her.

"Okay," she said, relenting. "I'm sorry I didn't leave a note. I didn't think of it." There, she said it.

"But you don't leave me notes." She modified the apology. Who leaves notes? Nobody. Anyway, if she started leaving him notes, everybody would see them and think they were involved.

"I would have today," he said.

April had to look down again, away from his eyes. He meant today after last night. She hated herself for looking down to hide her true thoughts. It was so Chinese, and she couldn't seem to help it. Must be genetic.

"Did you get a list of all her friends?" he went on, ever so helpful now that she was confused and sorry.

"Yeah, why?"

"Maybe when he wasn't home, she called somebody else."

She also hated it when he thought of things before she did. And he thought of a lot of things before she did. Yeah, the lady could have called somebody else. She could even have called the police. Somebody would have responded to the call.

"You want a cup of coffee?" she asked. "I was just going to get one." Stupid woman. That was the biggest concession she could make. He said he did, and even went with her to get it.

58

As the sun rose, Claudia counted the minutes until the big cop she was pretty sure was Irish by the color of his hair would drive by. Once on this side of the street, once on the other side of the street. She knew how long he'd cruise around before parking outside the diner down the block next to the corner store.

It was one of the many things about the neighborhood Claudia Bartello knew that nobody else bothered about. If she had a name for herself it would be "watcher in the night," because that's what she did. She kept an eye out, knew who was coming home drunk at what hour, knew things about the kids in the houses around her that their parents would never know. Even before Arturo died, she'd never been a really good sleeper, but now she was hardly taking the time to go to bed at all. She took a few hours here and there when she felt like it, slept on the sofa or in her chair by the window.

In fact she was "watcher in the daytime," too. She had to keep an old enemy in sight all the time. The unresolved conflict between her and her husband about living on the approach to the Triboro Bridge kept Arturo alive for her.

She sat in her chair going over and over how she hadn't wanted to live near that bridge, even though the house Arturo found was brand-new, in a nice neighborhood. Three bedrooms, two bathrooms. A little place to grow roses and tomatoes in the back. Everything a person could want. Except for the bridge. You could always tell what day it was and what hour it was by the amount of traffic heading on and off the ramp to the bridge. Even with two panes of glass in every window Claudia could still feel the vibration.

She was having her usual argument with Arturo about it, as she sat in front of her window half the night, waiting for that big Irish cop who stopped at the diner every day. He went in to get something to eat and then sat in his car for twenty minutes afterward pretending he was doing some kind of paperwork. But she knew he was not really doing anything. Now he could do something.

He was there at eight-thirty. What Claudia Bartello wanted to do was call out to him, have him come to her so she could point out to him the problem. How close it was to her and how offensive.

But there was no way the cop could hear her. And maybe it wasn't such a good idea to attract attention and let everyone see a cop coming to her house. She didn't think she had any choice in the matter. She had to struggle down those steps that always made her feel like her heart was going to give out on the way back, like Arturo's did. And then after she got down the steps, she'd have to hobble down the block to the diner. She didn't like it, but she did it.

When she got there, the way the big cop looked down at her from a great height made her feel like an old, old woman.

"I'm Mrs. Bartello." She peered up at the name tag on his chest but couldn't make out the letters.

"Good morning, Mrs. Bartello," he replied pleasantly.

"It's not a such a good morning," she snapped. "I didn't sleep at all."

"I'm sorry to hear it." They were standing outside, by his car. He looked down at her with a big friendly smile, like she was his great grandmother with a hip complaint. Well, she had a complaint all right, but it wasn't about joints.

"There's a woman in my garage apartment, walking around naked for all the world to see," she told him angrily. "I don't like that kind of thing."

"Hmm. What's she doing there?" he asked.

"That's a good question. He said he wouldn't have no women or parties." Claudia was indignant.

"Who's that?"

"My tenant."

"You have a tenant, and he has a girl in there. Is that the problem?" he said, smiling just a little bit.

"My name is Mrs. Arturo Bartello," Claudia said. "That's my house, right there. Fourteen twenty-five Hoyt Avenue. I don't want no women there."

"Have you talked about this with your tenant?" the cop asked.

"No, I have not. How can I with her still there?"

"How do you know that?"

"I watched the door. He was out. He came back. She didn't leave. That young man was out half the night with the woman in there. She's got some kind of thing on her forehead. I don't like it at all."

The cop frowned. "What kind of thing?"

"I don't know. Like blood or something. Maybe he beat her, too."

"And you could see all that?" he said, like maybe she was making something like that up.

"Course I could see it. She was standing right in front of me, no clothes, waving at me like some kind of crazy woman. Probably taking drugs. I won't have that. I have my rights." She paused for a breath. "You're a cop. Take care of it for me."

"What would you like me to do? Do you have any reason to believe he's doing drugs? Or is it the woman in the house that's bothering you?"

She hesitated. It was both and everything that was bothering her. His head was tilted like he was really waiting for her answer. But then he didn't wait for one.

"Maybe you should just wait for the woman to go, and then have a talk with your tenant. Tell him how you feel."

Claudia was getting tired standing there getting nowhere.

He tried another tack. "If you think he's doing something illegal, like drugs, you can make a complaint. You want to do that?"

"I'll think about it," she said. "What's your name?"

"Police Officer O'Brien," he said. "Let me know if you have any trouble."

She turned around and started hobbling back. Fat lot of good that did. She saw that he made a note and then sat in his car for a while just like he always did, digesting his breakfast without a worry in the world.

59

There was not a clock anywhere. That scared Emma as much as some of the other things. She had lived with so many clocks for so long, not having a single one to look at now made her feel her time was running out. When she was awake she was thinking all the time. *Gimme a clock and a machine gun. Please God give me a knife, just a little one.* Half the time she was too terrified almost to breathe, and then she got angry. The air was stale and stuffy. The guy had all the windows closed. Every breath she dared to take was foul. The brown curtains were tied back, but the roller shades were down. She couldn't see out, couldn't see the light.

What she saw was a lot of peculiar stuff laid out on a table the guy put by the bed. What scared her most was the black box that looked like a car battery. You could kill someone jump-starting a car. He must know about that, too. It happened to some boy just after she moved to California. It was in the papers. Emma shuddered. It happened miles away, in another county, couldn't have been him. Don't let it have been him. It was hot in the room, but she couldn't stop shivering.

She didn't like looking at him. He wore a motorcycle jacket and tight black jeans. He kicked the furniture with his motorcycle boots, his face twitching with rage.

She had to close her eyes to get away from him. The guy was crazy, and furious at her for untying the ropes he thought were secure. If she had a chance of survival before she untied the ropes, she didn't have one now. Her hands were tied tighter now. He moved her around angrily, twisting her arms, and pinching her breasts, trying to make her cry. He flicked his lighter on and off, teasing her with it like a kid torturing a frog. Only she wasn't a frog. The switch-blade terrified her, too. It seemed to be his second-favorite toy. He had a name for it. He called it Willy. Sometimes he put the lighter in his pocket in the tight black jeans and fondled it there. But the switchblade was always out. He stabbed at the air with it when he got frustrated.

What was the worst thing that could happen? Emma asked herself the question the way she had as a kid when they played war games. What was the worst pain a person could take? How many hours, how many days could pain last? What could they do to stop it? On navy bases all around the country they used to play the game. What if Daddy were caught and put in a tiger cage? What would he do? What would I do if it were me? What if I were a captured spy? What if our ship went down in the ocean, and there were a thousand sharks circling our lifeboat? Survival. How did survivors make it out? There were a hundred hundred hero stories from a hundred hundred battles, and every story absolutely true. Navy juniors knew them all, and in all their stories the hero always got away. Now she was a captive who'd had a chance and didn't get away.

Why didn't she get away? In the movies the heroes got away. Only the walk-ons were strangled, got their throats cut. What was the battery for?

Emma wanted to keep her eyes closed and miss her death. Let him kill her in her sleep. She'd kill herself first, if she could. Heroes did that, too, when there was no other option. She wanted to scream and cry because no one had given her a cyanide capsule. She was the prisoner of a madman and she didn't have the capsule. But she couldn't cry. It turned him on.

"What'd you do that for?" he demanded when she woke up. "I'm taking care of you."

He was wearing his leather jacket and smelled of beer. His blond hair was all messed up, his eyes red and puffy. They were like stones, harder than any eyes she'd ever seen.

She coughed so much he had to loosen the ropes and let her sit up.

"Don't barf on me," he snapped.

She tried to catch her breath.

"What'd you do that for?" He wouldn't let it go, kept asking her until she answered.

"I—"

"Yeah? You what?"

She swallowed. Her throat hurt. "I saw the sink. I needed some water."

"Well, you got some." He laughed. "Want some more?"

He had poured water down her throat until her lungs filled up, and she thought she was going to drown. She concentrated on breathing. Her throat hurt. Her headache was worse. He had put her in a different place. On a bed. How to get out. How to get out.

"Want some orange juice? I got some for you. It's morning. You want some eggs?" he said. "See, if you're nice, I'm nice." He tweaked a nipple. "Hey, I'm talking to you."

Her face didn't change. "Eggs?" she muttered.

"Yeah, like from a chicken. I'm nice to you, see."

Emma didn't say anything.

"I said I was nice to you."

"Then let me go. Let me go. I'll pay you. How much do you want?"

He shook his head.

"I have some money."

"I have money, too. You think I'm some kind of bum that I need your money?" he said furiously.

"I don't know."

"I'm a friend, remember. Friends don't take money."

What was the right line? She searched desperately for something that might get to him. But he was out of his mind. What could she say?

"Friends don't tie each other up," she said at last.

"Yeah, sometimes they do."

"Why? Why are you doing this?" Her throat was raw. She eyed the water. She wanted it, but was afraid he'd start suffocating her with it again.

He was sitting beside her on the bed, making a strange noise from the back of his throat instead of answering why. The noise didn't sound human. He adjusted the wick on the Zippo so the flame flared higher. He flicked it on and off. He held the switchblade in his other hand. He was trying to scare her.

Emma had the terrifying feeling she'd played this scene before. Only last time it was an acting improvisation, an exercise. This time she didn't have to imagine what it felt like. Her whole body really did ache, every joint, every muscle. And the point here was she couldn't just pretend to be brave. She couldn't afford to be a coward. This was the real thing. She had to survive.

She closed her eyes to get into that place where she could think about survival.

"Don't do that," he snapped.

She waited for a second before opening them.

"Damn it, fucking bitch. You're not dying on me." He smacked the bed with his hand. "You hear me? You better not die."

He seemed to think she had some kind of choice in the matter. If he stabbed her with the knife, or electrocuted her with the battery he had down there on the floor, she'd die all right. But maybe not today. She opened her eyes.

"I'll take the orange juice," she said.

He got up to get it for her, then held it up to her lips so she could drink. This encouraged her. When she finished drinking all of it, she had another idea.

"I have to go to the bathroom."

"Sure." He put down the glass.

She heard it *clink* on the floor when he set it down. He leaned over her to untie the knots. She could smell the beer more strongly now, and old sweat. It made her want to gag up the orange juice, but she kept it down.

When all the knots were untied, he helped her up. She shuddered when he touched her. His hands were all over her as he pulled her to her feet. She hated herself for moving so slowly. Everything took time. She had thought that when she was free she'd find a way to get him. Maybe grab the knife. Her heart started beating faster. She was going to make a move.

But before she was even up and on her feet, he wrenched her arms behind her back so hard she gasped. Then he tied her hands. He was behind her. She had no chance to get him. He guided her to the door with one hand around her neck, squeezing just enough to let her know he could end it right then. In the bathroom he stood there in the doorway, watching her pee. Even though the pressure on her bladder was great, it took a long time to get it out with him watching. She struggled to reach for the toilet paper, couldn't reach it.

"Dirty bitch," he cried. "Didn't anybody teach you to flush the toilet?" He laughed suddenly. "Don't move." He set the knife on the floor.

The window was behind her, high over her head. He started filling the tub. The knife was on the floor beside him. She eyed it. What now?

"Get in the tub," he commanded.

"What?" She couldn't move.

"Are you deaf? I said get in the tub." He grabbed her and shoved her into it, knocking her legs against the cold porcelain. He turned on the taps and adjusted the temperature carefully. Not too cold, not too hot. Water splashed into the tub. He closed the toilet and sat on it, waiting for the tub to fill up.

Emma's eyes widened with the sudden terror that she would not live through the day, after all. He was going to drown her as soon as there was enough water in the tub. She started to gasp and pant.

"Take it easy. Don't you want a bath?"

Emma whimpered. A bath?

He reached for a bar of Irish Spring and started lathering up her chest and arms.

"Don't! I'll do it myself," she cried. "You're hurting me."

"Shut up." He was getting hard. She could see it. She went limp and closed her eyes.

"Shit! Get up. I told you, don't do that." He pinched her.

He didn't like it when she fainted. That was a good thing to know. She groaned a little.

"Get up," he ordered.

Water sloshed around her chin as she sank deeper. Maybe he'd drown her now and put her out of her misery.

"Get out."

She opened her eyes. "Huh?"

"Get the fuck out. Are you stupid?"

That was it? That was the bath? She struggled to get out. It wasn't easy to move with her hands tied behind her back. He had to help her up, and wrap her in a towel. Out of the warm water, she started shivering again. She moved so slowly, staggering as he held her up. He swore at her.

"You're no good at all," he said.

"Let me go," she said weakly. "I may die. Then what will you do?"

"Uh-uh. You are not going to die."

He put her back to bed, tying all the knots, one by one, just as he had untied them before. When he was finished, he tucked some towels around her and squirted some menthol-scented shaving foam on her from neck to ankles, concentrating on the crotch area.

"Hey, what are you doing?" she cried. "Don't do that."

He picked up the razor. He didn't hear any protests. He was tired of her. He put her out of his mind and began shaving her all over, muttering to Willy. He could see his hands get bigger and bigger. He felt a lot better when she started screaming.

60

Newt Regis couldn't really afford to send two men down to San Diego, but he did it anyway. The image of his own daughter, Clarissa, so happy with her husband and new baby, wouldn't leave him alone. He thought about what it would mean to lose Clarissa, all the time he was talking with Jennifer Roane, the mother of the dead girl, who'd come from New York to get her.

Without any warning, she'd come in a rented car all the way to Newt's office in Potoway Village, and Raymond had to lope across the street to get Newt at the café where he was having a late lunch.

"I thought I told her that wasn't necessary." Newt shook his head with disbelief.

Raymond looked at the half-eaten hamburger in Newt's hand. "She wanted to see where it happened," he muttered. "Said she needed it for *closure.*"

"Closure, huh." Newt put down the hamburger and wiped his hands on the too-small paper napkin in his lap. He got up, shrugging. "I'll be back," he called over his shoulder to the surprised waitress.

Mrs. Roane was sitting stiffly on a chair outside the sheriff's office. She was wearing a khaki bush jacket, as if she'd come to Africa, a wrinkled matching skirt, and huge sunglasses. She was working at the large wad of tissues balled up in her hands.

"Mrs. Roane? I'm Sheriff Regis."

She stood up and held out the hand without the tissues. "You were the one who found her?"

Newt took the slender hand, nodding. "No one told me you were coming."

"I didn't tell anyone. The policewoman in New York said I didn't have to. . . ."

"No," Newt said gently. "You didn't have to." He held the hand sympathetically, taking a minute to assess the situation, then let it go.

The woman's dark hair was pulled back in a ponytail. Her white skin was puffy. She wore no makeup and sniffed back tears Newt guessed had been pouring out nonstop for days.

"Would you like a cup of coffee?" he asked. Coffee was all he could think of to offer.

She shook her head. "Where is she? I want to see her."

"We've—taken good care of her," Newt said slowly, ushering the woman into his office.

"I want to see her."

"I understand."

She looked around the office, at the cheap furniture, the cluttered desk, the window with its dusty venetian blinds that didn't prevent the afternoon sun from streaming in between the slats. He couldn't see her eyes behind her dark glasses.

"What was Ellen doing out here?" she asked.

Newt didn't respond to that question.

"Tell me. I loved her so much. . . ." She let go and sobbed.

Newt never could bear to see a woman cry. He took a deep breath. Right under his fingertips was a folder that contained all the photos he had of the dead girl who was this woman's child. Before a madman, the desert, and the vultures got to Ellen Roane, she had been a beautiful, healthy, much-loved college girl. If the suspect was ever apprehended and went to trial, Mrs. Roane might hear the testimony and see the photos of what happened to her daughter. As far as Newt was concerned, that would be too soon.

"Mrs. Roane," he said, "if it were my daughter, I'd hold onto that love. I'd hold onto it real tight."

She shook her head vehemently. "I need to see her . . . to say good-bye."

"No. You got her whole in your heart. Keep her that way. Take her back home with you and say good-bye when you bury her."

Since she didn't want to do that, it took Newt a long time to convince her. It wasn't until the next day that he could send Raymond and Jesse down to San Diego with the photos of Ellen and Troland Grebs that Sergeant Grove had supplied. They also had copies of the six credit card charges Ellen Roane had made, sent by the detective from New York. There was no hotel or motel charge, so Newt figured Ellen never checked out. He had the sheet on Troland Grebs. He couldn't tell from the old arrests on it why the detective in New York was so sure it was Grebs. But one witness tying Grebs and Ellen Roane together would do it.

"Find out where she stayed first," he told his officers. "They're probably still holding her things at some hotel. Maybe they saw who she was with."

The two men started early. They planned to cover the area around where she had shopped and eaten. There had been no car rental charge on her credit card. It seemed fairly clear that Ellen Roane hadn't had a car. There were two hotels, three motels, and one bed-and-breakfast within walking distance of the places she had made the charges. The beach was only a few blocks away from the shopping area.

After an hour, they found Ellen's possessions at the sixth place they tried. The Coral Reef Bed and Breakfast was one of those quaint places with no phones in the rooms. On the second floor, a large patio overlooked the ocean just across the street. They served breakfast there, and iced tea, wine, fruit, cheese, and crackers in the afternoon.

The owner, a tall, very thin, overtanned woman in her forties, took one look at the two deputy sheriffs in their khaki uniforms with their hats in their hands and asked them to sit down at one of the tables.

"Would you like a glass of iced tea?" she asked.

It was a hot day. Raymond, who thought he knew how to handle women, glanced quickly at Jesse, then nodded. Jesse was the elder, nearly fifty now, and looked tired. He sat.

The woman came back in a moment with a fluffy blonde who was clearly her girlfriend. The blonde carried a pitcher.

"I'm Gena Howard. I'm the owner. And this is Roberta. Roberta cooks."

"Hello." Roberta poured out two glasses of dark tea with lots of frosty ice and handed them over.

"What can we do for you?" Gena Howard had clearly dealt with cops before.

"About two weeks ago, did you have a young woman staying with you?" Raymond asked. The iced tea was cold and strong and very sweet.

Roberta nodded. "Debby," she said. "This is about Debby, isn't it? Where is she? What happened to her?"

"Debby?" Raymond said.

"Shh, Bobbie. Let him ask the questions."

Raymond took out the picture. "We're looking for this girl. Her name is Ellen Roane."

Bobbie and Gena took the photo of Ellen Roane in shorts with a tennis racket in her hand, and a big happy smile on her face. The two women held it together, their heads almost touching as they bent over it. The recognition was immediate, but they continued holding the photo as if they didn't want to let it go.

"Debby," Bobbie confirmed.

"Such a *nice* girl," Gena Howard said, still studying the picture. "She wanted a room where she could see the water. We put her on the third floor. She was just crazy about the ocean. . . . You know, I was really worried when she took off without her things. . . . But sometimes they do that when they don't want to pay—"

"You thought she left to avoid paying the bill?" Raymond asked incredulously.

Gena looked at Bobbie, then shook her head. "We didn't want to think that of her. And she had expensive things, more than the room was worth. It didn't seem likely."

"We were afraid something happened to her," Bobbie said softly. "But . . ."

"Don't you read the newspapers?" Raymond interrupted.

Gena put her hand protectively on Bobbie's shoulder and shook her head again. Bobbie kept her eyes on them, clearly frightened.

"It's always such bad news," Bobbie explained.

"We've got a lot of things to do to keep this place going," Gena added defensively. "We have ten rooms, and it's just us. We don't really bother with the news." She changed the subject. "We did keep her stuff in case she decided to come back. Like I said, it's good stuff, worth more than the room. We hoped she'd come back."

"What happened to her?" Bobbie's face was very pale.

Raymond told her as gently as he could. "Somebody took her out into the desert and left her there."

"Oh." She put her hand to her mouth.

Jesse sat there drinking his iced tea. His expression hadn't changed since they walked in. Raymond glanced at Jesse and wondered if he'd ever get to be that cool.

"She was a pretty girl," Gena said, still studying the photo. "Real pretty."

Raymond nodded. "Why don't you tell us about her," he suggested.

"What do you want to know?" Gena finally relinquished the picture. Raymond took it back and reached for his notebook.

It took some time to hear everything the two women had to say. They had never thought Debby was her real name, Bobbie said. She didn't always answer to it. She kept pretty much to herself. Yes, they could see her on the beach from here, and they did see her, Gena supplied. But when they were looking, she was always alone.

Raymond handed over the two old photos of Troland Grebs.

Gena laid them down side by side and studied them doubtfully for a long time.

"Those were taken a long time ago," Raymond said helpfully. "He's a lot older now."

"I don't know," Gena said.

Bobbie lifted a shoulder diffidently. "Does he ride a motorcycle? There's a guy hangs out at the beach that looks kinda like this. Same build, same blond hair."

"Oh?" Jesse said. It was the first time he had spoken. His glass of iced tea was empty now, except for the ice, and he was smearing the circles of moisture the glass left on the table with his finger. "Where do you see him?"

"Around the beach. He hangs out."

"Are you sure he's the one?" Gena asked. "This guy's so *young.*"

"Look, same mouth," Bobbie insisted.

The two women thought the guy who looked like this lived somewhere around here because he liked to come to the beach in the evening and watch the sun go down. He had a motorcycle. He'd probably be out there tonight.

The deputies waited around until nine that night, but no one like Grebs showed up. They questioned some regulars who hung around the beach. A few of them thought the boy in the photo was someone they knew as Willy. One guy, an aging surfer who didn't put on a shirt even though the temperature had dropped to the fifties, said he saw a girl who looked like Ellen get on Willy's Harley-Davidson and drive off. He wasn't sure when, thought maybe it was two weeks or so ago. As far as he knew, Willy hadn't been around since.

After he got this information from Raymond and Jesse, Newt came down out of the hills himself to try to establish Troland's whereabouts. Grebs wasn't at his apartment. The manager of the building said he hadn't seen him in days. His office said Grebs was on vacation.

61

"Nine-one-one Emergency, can I help you?"

"Yes, this is Detective Woo up in the Two-O," April said. "I'd like you to check and see if you got a call last night from a woman, name of Emma Chapman."

"I'd need an official request, Detective—"

"Woo," April said. "Okay. Who shall I send it to?"

Fifteen minutes later, April faxed a request for information downtown to Headquarters, where the 911 calls from all five boroughs came in, were recorded, and were dealt with.

An hour later she tried again. "I'm trying to locate a call from a female, name of Emma Chapman."

"Okay, Detective. I can check that now. Would that be Manhattan?"

"We don't have a confirmation on that. We're trying to locate her."

"You want me to run them all?"

"Yes," April said.

"Any particular time?"

"Yes, we'd like it right now."

"I mean any particular time last night?"

"Oh." April thought for a minute.

"Where do you want us to start, Detective?" The operator sounded impatient.

April didn't let it bother her. Emma had called her husband at just before midnight. Would she call her husband first, or the police first?

"Start at eleven-thirty," April said, just to be safe.

"All five?"

"Yes."

"Manhattan, too?"

"I want them all," April said. How many times did she have to say it? Yes, she wanted five, all five boroughs, from eleven-thirty on. She sat back in her swivel chair.

"It's going to take some time."

"Why?" April asked.

"You want last night. That isn't even twenty-four hours ago."

So? What did that mean? Didn't they have some kind of printout of who called on what complaint? April tried to imagine what it looked like down there at One Police Plaza where all 911 calls in the city came in. She'd certainly been sent out on enough calls to know they were dispatched through the closest precinct.

But the calls were organized by borough. Did they have one huge room in the basement of Headquarters with dozens of operators answering the phones? Or did they have a different unit for each borough? She had never been there. She had no idea what the setup was. Probably a different unit for each borough, she guessed.

"How long will it take?" she asked, careful not to sound impatient herself.

"A while. There's no one to do it right now."

April looked at her watch. Maybe she should go down there and do it herself. Then she looked up. She saw Sergeant Joyce in a new green-and-black plaid suit that was ugly in the extreme, talking rapidly to Bell, Davis, and Aspiranti. Even from here, she knew they were discussing the case.

Bell had located the afternoon doorman of the building and gone to talk with him. The doorman was able to set the time of Chapman's disappearance at just about six P.M. He had watched the actress walk to the end of the block. She crossed the street and he didn't see her again after that. Now they had a description of the clothes she was wearing: jeans and a gray sweatshirt. She sure wasn't going out to dinner dressed like that.

For a second, Joyce turned and looked in her direction. April didn't like the look at all. "I'd like to talk to your supervisor," April said, to irritate the voice on the phone.

She always hated it when people did that to her.

"Certainly. What was your name again?" the operator said sweetly.

"Woo," April said. "Detective Woo, from the Two-O. You already have my ID."

Ginora waved at her. "Dr. Frank on the line," she called. "Want him to wait?"

"Tell him I'll call him back."

April sighed. Frank called every thirty minutes. He just wouldn't let up. She repeated her request to the 911 supervisor. The supervisor said the calls from last night hadn't been printed out yet. That meant someone would have to listen to every single tape for calls that came in during the time frame in question. Problem was, at the moment no one was available to get the tapes together and run them.

"Look, this is an emergency—" April pressed. "Can I come there and do it myself?"

"No—but . . . I'll get someone on it—What's your name again?"

"Woo, Detective April Woo, and thanks." April hung up.

A few feet away at Aspiranti's desk, Sergeant Joyce was waving at April to come join the discussion.

62

Jason dialed Detective Woo's number for the tenth time. For the tenth time a woman's voice answered the phone and informed him Detective Woo was busy. Would he like to leave a message? No, he would not. He had something to say all right, but it couldn't be said in a message. He wanted to get Woo's attention, get her so involved she'd let him tell her what to do.

He'd been studying a map of New York City and his notes, but he needed more information. He needed the kind of information a person could only get from the police, and he needed a police car to take him around so he could see what different neighborhoods looked like. He was certain that if he could look around, he could find the right one.

It didn't occur to him that New York was a very big place, and his thinking might be unrealistic. N.Y.P.D. was not going to give him a car and driver to make his own investigations; and even if it did, he was not likely to find what he was looking for.

He wasn't thinking about the odds. He was counting on Woo's doing what he asked because the alternative was unbearable. He had no way of knowing if any of them were doing the right things, going to the right places, asking the right questions.

Apparently Woo had been sitting there on the phone for hours. How could she find Emma if she hadn't left her desk all day? And what were the other detectives doing? Probably nothing.

Sitting there in his office waiting for someone to get back to him was unbearable. Jason had canceled all his patients, but the phone kept ringing. There were still eight unreturned messages on his answering machine, three of them from Charles, wanting to know what was going on. Jason had spoken to Ronnie, Emma's agent, three times already. Ronnie had been contacted by the police. Now she was hysterical. She wanted to come over and be with him, wanted to call in the army and the FBI. She had other suggestions, too. Jason couldn't face calling Charles back and hearing more advice.

There were a whole lot of things bothering him. One of them was that the phone kept ringing and none of the voices on his machine was Emma's trying him again. What did that mean? Did that mean she was already dead, or that the guy caught her making the call and—And what? What would Grebs *do?*

Jason knew what the trigger was to coming after Emma, but he simply didn't have enough personal data about Troland Grebs to know what he planned to do to her once he had her. He had threatened to kill her, but as of midnight last night he hadn't done it yet.

Even though he tried to avoid checking the clocks every few minutes, the ticking went on. There was no relief from them. The clocks were driving him crazy.

What was Grebs likely to do? Without a detailed history of his illness, it was impossible to predict. And there was no way to get a history of his illness. His parents were dead. According to his aunt, one brother, Willy, died in Vietnam. The other brother dropped out of sight years ago. She didn't remember Grebs ever having counseling, and his company had no record of insurance claims for therapy. That much Jason had been able to find out.

Troland Grebs had grown up on Twenty-eighth Street in downtown San Diego. Not far from the Gas Lamp district, the old red-light district where Grebs had once picked up prostitutes. Twenty-eighth Street was not far from the airport. Grebs liked familiar things, Jason knew. He worked at an airport. There were planes overhead all the time. Where he lived now, on Queen Palm Way, just off Crown Avenue, he had to cross a small bridge to get home every night. He probably ate in the fifties-style diner at the end of his block. These were the elements they had to look for here in New York, Jason was

certain of it. The number, the names. The layout of the neighborhood. All these things would have special meaning for Grebs, and he
would need them around him to feel safe.

Grebs might never have been treated. But even if he had been
hospitalized numerous times, it would take too long to find out
where. There was no sheet for the mentally ill that listed how many
times a person sought help for what symptoms, the way there was for
felons and their arrests. Mental illness was a private thing. No central place stored information. A person could be hospitalized a dozen
times, in a dozen different places. Each hospital kept only its own
records, and none could tap into the records of the others just by
hitting the right computer button.

The danger of bureaucracy reminded Jason of Margret. He
hadn't thought about Margret in a long time. Margret was an out-
patient of his at the Center when he was in training. He worked with
her for a year, then she was assigned to someone else when he was
rotated out. He took only two patients with him. That was two more
than most people, but Margret was not one of them.

He wouldn't have kept her as a patient even though she didn't
want to work with anyone else. It was not surprising that she was
assigned to someone who was not right for her, someone with no
sympathy for her, a bureaucrat who did therapy by the book. Few
people got better with therapy by the book. What made people get
better couldn't really be taught.

It wasn't surprising, either, that Margret didn't get better. Margret was a difficult case, not because she was so very sick, but
because she was an awful person. It was uncomfortable to be with
her. Margret was fifty-seven years old when Jason met her. A badly
aged former beauty, she had been married for thirty-two years and
had no children. Her problem was her inability to deal with growing
old. Her husband had only recently left her for another woman, even
though she had been cruel to him for years and told him countless
times that she never loved him.

Margret couldn't stand losing her looks and the status and attention that went with them. How many male doctors of any age

could relate to a woman who was deeply depressed because she lost her one weapon, the considerable sexual power that she had always used to control and humiliate the men in her life? She had attempted suicide more than once. It was all documented in her records. Jason had carefully briefed his replacement. He warned him that although Margret appeared stable at times, she was deeply depressed and very much at risk. But the young man, now practising on Fifth Avenue, was a bureaucrat, a man without imagination. One evening, Margret called him at five o'clock and left a message saying she had to talk to him. She didn't say she was desperate or suicidal, so the young doctor interpreted her call as another attempt to control him. He heard only what she said, and didn't take her seriously. He had seen her earlier that day. She had seemed fine. He didn't check on her that evening, and she slit her wrists and bled to death sometime in the night.

Jason kept thinking about Margret because he knew the young doctor never felt he had done anything wrong. He still believed he had an unblemished record. He didn't count Margret as a personal failure.

It was when Margret killed herself that Jason realized he could never leave anything, not the smallest detail, to anybody else. Nobody under his direct care had ever died of anything but natural causes. Margret had been somebody else's responsibility at the time of her death. But Jason couldn't help seeing a connection between her and his situation with Detective Woo and the police. He had no hope of finding Emma without them. But police were bureaucrats. They did the minimum. He couldn't let it go at that. Emma's life depended on very fast action. Jason didn't care how many times Detective Woo put him off. He would keep banging on her door until she let him in.

In the deep quiet of his office, where the only sound was the ticking of his clocks, Jason decided that enough time passed since his last call. He allowed himself to check the clock. Twenty minutes was close enough. He dialed Detective Woo's number again.

April picked up. "Detective Woo."

"It's Jason Frank."

"Hello, Dr. Frank," she said cautiously.

"Call me Jason,"

April Woo did not respond to the invitation.

"I want you to think of me as a colleague," Jason said in his warmest voice. "We can work together. I can help you."

"You are helping," April replied in her own warm and reassuring voice.

He knew that voice. He had one just like it, professional and distance-making. He was the doctor. He didn't let patients tell him what to do—unless they were right. He was flexible that way. He had to make her flexible. Emma's life depended on it.

"Look, I've been thinking about the tape. I can help you pinpoint places where he might have taken her, landmarks to look for. I've worked up a psychological profile of him."

"Okay," April said. "I'll take anything you've got. What do you want to tell me?"

"Before I get into that, is there anything new?"

Again she paused before answering, as if trying to decide whether or not to tell him. His heart jumped. There was news.

"You can tell me. I'm a professional. Whatever it is, I can take it."

"It might be nothing."

"What is it?"

"I had the nine-one-ones checked out."

"Emma called?"

"No, but there was an incomplete."

"What does that mean?" Jason cried.

"It means someone called in and asked for help but didn't give a name or location before hanging up."

"Oh, God . . ."

"Sometimes they're potential suicides. Sometimes they're pranks. We get a lot of pranking, you know. It may be nothing."

"What are you doing about it?"

"We're having the voices on the tapes compared to see if it's your wife's."

"Do you know where the call was from?"

There was another long hesitation before she finally told him. "Yeah," she said with a note of triumph. "Queens."

Queen Palm Way. Queens. Jason's heart leapt. "Look, Detective, I'm coming over. I need to talk to you right away." He hung up before she could protest.

63

Sergeant Joyce studied the photographs of the burns on the two dead girls in California and an enlarged version of the drawing on the bottom of each of the sixteen letters Emma Chapman had received. The pictures were inconclusive. There had been such discoloration of the skin in one case, she found it surprising the coroner could even tell the wound had been a burn. The other one was clearly a shape, a similar sort of shape, certainly, but as far as she could tell, not the shape of the drawing in the letters.

Joyce threw them on the desk in her office, where April had assembled all the documents and photos that represented her case against Grebs, and shook her head. "I don't know. I don't see anything to help us in these."

"I just got a call from that sheriff in California," April said. "They have a witness who says he saw Ellen with Grebs the afternoon she disappeared."

"We still don't have anything that helps us with *this*," Joyce replied coldly.

April had placed Emma Chapman's yearbook picture next to the photo of Ellen Roane in her tennis shorts. The two young women both had long blond hair and classically beautiful features. They could almost be sisters. April had a connection in the looks of the women. She had a connection in the guy's obsession with burning. She had a suspect with a sheet that fit. And still, Joyce didn't want to connect the two cases. April wondered if her supervisor just didn't want to acknowledge her work.

She pushed aside the gruesome photos of the corpses found in the desert, so the two smiling girls were on top again. "Don't you see a resemblance here?"

Joyce didn't reply.

"Look, he *knew* the Chapman woman from high school, and he's taken off." What else did the woman want?

"That doesn't mean he's *here.*"

April shrugged. "It *could* mean he's here."

"This isn't his MO," Joyce said flatly.

"Maybe not," April agreed. "But sometimes they do it differently each time. And he *knew* her. Of course it could be a coincidence that he knew her. . . ."

"You know it isn't a coincidence." Joyce glanced down at the two lovely, golden-haired girls. "But we don't have a desert here for him to leave her in."

Talk about lack of imagination. Didn't have a desert. April suddenly remembered her first case in this precinct. Sergeant Joyce had sent her into a townhouse where the worried owner had been afraid the Chinese cook might have murdered the Chinese maid and hidden the body somewhere in the house. There was a horrendous smell in the place, unbearable, and the maid had disappeared under suspicious circumstances several days before, leaving all her possessions behind. The owner couldn't find the source of the smell. It seemed to be coming from the very core of the house.

It was a big house, four stories high, with a huge basement kitchen and laundry room. The place had marble stairways and marble bathrooms with gold faucets in the shape of dolphins. April had talked to the Chinese cook for a long time. He confessed he hated the maid. He had a lot of grievances. The maid had turned down his advances. It made him mad. She was eating their employer's leftovers. That was no good. No one gave her permission to eat the leftover food.

Then she got hungry, but he wouldn't let her into the kitchen to make her own food. It was his kitchen. So she took food into her room to dry it like in China.

"What kind of food?" April asked him.

"Fish," he had replied with disgust.

"She tried to dry the fish in her room?"

Yes, that was it. "Only this New York, not Hong Kong. Fish no dry."

When he talked to the maid about getting rid of the fish, they had a screaming fight, and she lost face, wouldn't come back, not even for her things.

"Not many things," the cook had said scornfully about her possessions.

April located the result of their feud in one of the heating vents in the basement. The smell of rotting fish was being pumped everywhere. She found the woman in New Jersey with a friend. She refused to come back.

This New York, not Hong Kong: Fish no dry. It made April think Grebs had something else in mind for Emma Chapman. He meant to kill her and hide her somewhere.

"Maybe he plans to change his MO on this one," April told her lack-of-imagination supervisor.

"Maybe." Joyce had taken her jacket off and was sweating in her green blouse. April noted that it was too dark a color for her. Joyce looked sallow, and the sweat rings under her arms revealed that she was worried, too. It made April feel better.

"I have a dozen people out there with his picture. Better get it to every precinct in the city," she said.

April nodded. Yes, Sergeant. Right away, Sergeant.

"Do you have a voice match yet on that nine-one-one to Queens?" Joyce switched focus.

"They're working on it." April tapped her fingers on the desk. She was in a hurry to get away.

"Where's Sanchez?"

"He went down to the lab to sit on them." April still stood in front of Joyce's desk. She didn't like to sit down in there. "I want to talk to the husband again," she said after a minute.

"Oh, what does he know?"

"He's a shrink. He found the guy in the first place."

"Yeah, you told me."

"He knows where he works. He's seen where the guy lives, where he grew up, even talked to his aunt. He knows Grebs's background."

"So?"

"He's a *shrink*. He's done a workup on Grebs, a profile of his habits that might help us find him."

"So talk to him again."

Sergeant Joyce's phone rang. She picked it up and began to speak. April stood there. After a minute Joyce put her hand over the receiver.

"What?" she demanded.

"He wants to go for a drive," April said.

Joyce shook her head. "What are you, crazy?"

"Just checking."

April left the office.

Dr. Frank was waiting for her downstairs.

64

Claudia Bartello felt uncomfortable. She had a feeling there was another vibration in the house, something more than the traffic at the height of the rush hour on the bridge. Sometimes it sounded like a hum. Sometimes it sounded like weeping. Twice she thought she heard screams. She moved around the house, upstairs and downstairs, looking for the source of the noise, as if it were an odor she could ferret out and purge.

Since Arturo died a year ago, there had been times when the lights had been funny. They made a crackling kind of noise, or flashed on and off for no reason. She did not question the possibility of there being a ghost in the house. He died there. Right on the front steps while she was in the kitchen making dinner. Without a sound or anything. He just fell over on the way up the stairs and died on her. Maybe he was still mad at her for not knowing, for letting a neighbor find him almost a whole hour later. That would be something he'd be mad about.

But more likely it wasn't a ghost. It was that man in the garage with his naked girlfriend. The woman hadn't left yet. Claudia was pretty sure of that. No one had been outside of that garage door. She considered going in and complaining. She considered calling that Irish policeman and telling him something funny was going on. What was his name?

The problem was she didn't know how to call the police, what number to dial. It wasn't the number they flashed on the TV screen for emergencies. Arturo tried that once when the car got bumped from behind. After he told them no one was hurt, they promised to send someone over. But no one ever came.

How to get the right number? Her eyes were not good enough to struggle with the phone book. She wouldn't know where to look in it anyway. And he didn't seem like he was very interested. She wanted another policeman. An Italian she could talk to, explain about Arturo and the man in the garage. Sometimes the hum seemed like voices arguing.

Claudia could have a whopper of an argument with Arturo right now. What did he mean building a little apartment upstairs that you couldn't get to without going through the garage and up the stairs at the back? It didn't make sense. But Arturo never had any sense. He said he wanted to make it hard for people to bother him. Nice.

One thing she could say about herself. She might be old, but there was nothing wrong with her hearing. Claudia could hear dirty things happening on the other side of her wall. She'd heard things like that before. She just hadn't heard it at eleven in the morning. At twelve.

At one o'clock she decided to do something about it. She shuffled to the front door, remembering first to put her sweater on because it still felt chilly to her. She didn't put her heavy shoes on because she wasn't going far, and her feet were swollen. The soft slippers were easier to walk in.

She left the front door unlocked. She didn't want to have to struggle with the key, and she was coming right back. Finally, for the second time that day, she grabbed the railing and carefully maneuvered the steps that killed Arturo. There were only three of them, and they were not very steep, but Claudia was afraid of falling and did not like them.

When she was on level ground at last, she shuffled down the path to the sidewalk in front of the house. She couldn't take a shortcut across the tiny patch of grass Arturo called his lawn because it had grown in. Soon the neighbors would start complaining again.

Claudia contemplated the garage door. One thing she could say about herself. She might have arthritis in her fingers, but there was still some strength in her arms. She leaned over, her old bones creaking, and lifted the garage door. It swung open easier than she expected. The guy living in there must have done something to it, oiled it maybe.

When the door opened, the light came on automatically. Claudia walked inside. For a minute she thought the car was Arturo's car, that no time had passed, and she was going in there to catch him at it. But then she remembered. This car was a Ford. She was in here to scold somebody else. She almost tripped over Arturo's lawn mower that was so old it didn't even have a motor. She climbed the stairs slowly, holding the railing, and when she got to the top, she banged on the door three times. No one answered.

She knocked some more.

"Hey," she said. "I know you're in there."

There was a long silence and then a reply right on the other side of the door. "What do you want?"

"You said you weren't going to do anything," Claudia cried peevishly.

"I'm not doing anything."

"I *know* what you're doing. You have a woman in there."

"No way."

"Yes, there's a woman in there," Claudia insisted.

"What makes you think so?"

The voice on the other side of the door sounded reasonable. That sound of reason reminded her of Arturo. It irritated her.

"I'm not stupid. I have eyes and ears. I saw her. I won't have this." It was an old argument. "I'm not running a whorehouse. You'll have to get her out of there."

"What are you talking about?" The voice was angry.

"I said you'll have to take that woman and get her out of here. I won't have no dirty stuff in my house. You should be ashamed of yourself."

"There's no woman in here, I promise you."

"Yes," Claudia cried. "Oh, yes, there is. I saw her."

"Okay, okay. There was a woman, but she's gone. I'm sorry. It won't happen again."

"Open the door. I can't talk like this."

"I can't, I'm not dressed. I was sleeping."

"This is my house. If she's gone, I want to see she's gone."

"I told you I was sleeping. I got no clothes on."

"Then put some clothes on."

There was a pause, and then the voice was soothing again.

"Lady, I think you're all excited for nothing. So I had somebody here for a while. It's a free country. I told you she's gone now. Forget about it."

"I want to see she's gone," Claudia insisted. "It's my house. Do you want me to call the police? I'll call the police. I got a friend in the police. You want him to take care of it?"

There was another lengthy silence.

"You hear me?"

"Yeah, I hear you."

In a second the door opened, and Claudia shuffled in. The door closed after her before she had a chance to protest.

65

April sat with Dr. Frank for over an hour in an empty questioning room downstairs. She could see that the doctor hadn't taken the time to shave or change his clothes since she met with him at eight that morning. She figured he probably hadn't eaten anything since then, either. It was three o'clock. She ordered him a sandwich.

He shook his head when it came. "No, thanks. I'm not hungry."

"It won't help to starve," she said. She opened it and left it there. Tuna fish and lettuce on white toast. It smelled pretty good to her.

"Coffee?"

"Thanks." He took the coffee and drank some. Eventually, without appearing to be aware of it, he started eating the sandwich.

Between bites, he described where Grebs had lived when he was a kid. On Twenty-eighth Street in downtown San Diego. He described the plant where Grebs worked as a draftsman for jet engines at Lindbergh Field, San Diego's airport. He told April that Grebs now lived on a street called Queen Palm Way, off Crown Avenue.

"He could be in Crown Heights."

April shook her head. "Crown Heights is in Brooklyn. Too far from the airports. More coffee?"

"No, thanks." He pushed the cup away.

April closed her notebook. "Well, I think we've about covered it." He'd finished giving her everything he had. A quarter of the sandwich was left, but she didn't think he was going to eat it.

The clock on the wall said it was three forty-five. Sanchez had been gone for nearly two hours. Why hadn't she heard from him? She'd left word upstairs for someone to come get her if he called.

"Well, let's go." Dr. Frank gathered up his notes.

"Where do you want to go?"

"I've given you enough. Let's get a car and go find her."

"Dr. Frank, it doesn't work that way. Hiding places don't just pop out at you from the street."

April lived in Queens and knew it very well. She could visualize a number of things he described. The entrance to the Triboro Bridge was only a few blocks from her house. Airplanes flew overhead day and night. Still, you had to have more to go on. It was a huge city. You couldn't just run out to a place you thought a killer might be without knowing what you were going to do when you got there.

He shoved the papers into his briefcase furiously. "Are you telling me you're just going to sit here? You're not going to go out and look for her?"

He didn't get it. Nobody was sitting around. The whole precinct was taking this case very seriously. When a person receiving threatening letters suddenly disappears under suspicious circumstances, there's reason for investigation. Emma Chapman's desperate message on her husband's answering machine saying she was held by someone planning to kill her was reason for a major investigation. That's what they were doing, a major investigation—on April Woo's case.

And the only reason three thousand reporters weren't outside hounding them for pictures and information was that not a word about it had gone out on the police radios. It wouldn't be long before someone got a tip, but for now no one in the press knew a famous actress had been kidnapped. Everyone at the Two-O wanted to keep it that way. Word from the top was to keep their mouths shut. They didn't want Grebs killing her in a panic because he saw his face on TV.

April was very well aware of all the time factors. A life-and-death situation was bad enough without the press lowering their odds of saving the woman.

"No, I didn't say I wasn't looking for her, Dr. Frank." April got up and threw the garbage from his lunch into an overflowing wastebasket in the corner. "But there's no point in going out in the field until I have my ducks in a row."

"What ducks?" Jason demanded. "Every second counts if we want to find her alive."

"I know that. There are a lot of us working on this. We're waiting for some information before we make a move."

"Jesus, what information?"

"I'm waiting for a voice confirmation on the nine-one-one call from Queens. Remember, you listened to it, but weren't able to make that confirmation for me?" The tape and the tape machine were still on the table.

"What's taking so long?" Dr. Frank looked at his watch.

April shook her head. She didn't know why it was taking so long. "Why don't you go home for a while? I'll call you as soon as I know."

"I can't go home," he said miserably.

"Well, you can stay here, but when I go out, you can't come with me. Look, if I learn something, I'll call you."

"I want to be there when you find her."

It wasn't so easy. It didn't work like that. April stared at him. They might find Emma Chapman soon. They might not find her for days. By then the press would be involved. Dr. Frank would be on TV. The precinct chief would be making statements. Emma Chapman would probably be dead, and there'd be a media free-for-all. She didn't want to say any of that.

"Look," she said, "you've done a lot. You broke the case. Don't tell anybody I said it, but it's the truth. Now you have to let me do my job."

"Please, April. She needs me." Jason was pleading with her. "I have to be there."

So, now they were friends. He was calling her by her first name.

She shook her head. "I have no choice. This isn't my call. You can't come in the car with me. It could endanger you. It could endanger me or your wife. You have to go home. As soon as I have something, I'll call you. As soon as we locate her, you'll be there. I promise."

"No. That isn't good enough."

"Dr. Frank, I understand how you feel. *Believe* me, I understand. You're a professional in your field, and you don't think anybody else knows how to do anything. But I'm a professional in my field. I've been well trained to do what I do."

"But this is different—"

"Dr. Frank, would you send a civilian out on a battlefield?"

"*This* is *different.*" He was still protesting.

"Look, here you're an untrained civilian. Do you want to get in the way of the investigation and waste time?"

"No, but—"

"Then go home and take a shower. Call me in an hour, okay?"

"Do I smell that bad?"

April didn't smile. "You look like you'd feel a lot better, Doctor, if you stood under the shower for a while."

"Twenty minutes," he said, looking at his watch again.

April went back upstairs. Everybody was out in the field. The squad room was nearly empty, and Sanchez wasn't back. She beeped him. He called in a few minutes later.

"What's going on?" she asked.

"I'm not exactly sure. Either there are other priorities ahead of us, or the machine that does voice matches is down, or the person who runs the machine left early. I could try another lab," he suggested. "Too bad she didn't say a few more words. Then we'd be able to tell it was Chapman's voice calling from Queens and wouldn't have to be going through all this. Any luck with the husband?"

"About the voice match? I played it for him five times."

"What did he say?"

"The only recognizable word on the tape is 'help.' He said the woman sounded drugged. He wasn't sure it was his wife. He got really upset because he couldn't be sure."

"Should I try another lab?"

"Look, the husband's panicked about time, and so am I. He seems sure the guy isn't going to keep her around for long. He thinks if he hasn't killed her already, he'll do it soon. I'm going to go out to Queens with the pictures."

"You're not going to wait for confirmation on the nine-one-one?"

"I can't sit here waiting. . . . Anyway, I think it's Queens," April said.

"Any particular reason?"

April thought for a second. She trusted the shrink. That was the reason. "It fits the profile," she said finally.

"Okay, I'll leave now and meet you. Where are you going?"

She told him, picked up her bag and the stack of photos, and went to tell Joyce what she and Sanchez were doing.

Joyce gave her a sour look. "Okay, but keep it quiet. You heard what the chief said about leaking the story."

Actually April hadn't heard what he said. Sergeant Joyce reported what he said. The chief hadn't spoken to April in the nine months she had been there, and probably had no idea who she was. But all the same April knew what he'd have to say to her now. Detective Woo and Sergeant Sanchez were on their way out to Queens, fine. He wouldn't limit their investigation to the neighborhood. But if the missing woman turned up in Queens, it better be those detectives from the Two-O in Manhattan who located her. And they better do it without alerting the whole world.

"You want me to call in?" April asked.

Joyce looked at April as if she were some kind of moron.

"Yes, call in. Just be cryptic. You know what cryptic means?"

A flush of outrage at the insult spread across April's face as she nodded that she knew what the word meant. Sure, her supervisor had put a lot of other people on April Woo's case without reassigning it away from her. But that wouldn't stop April from hating Joyce anyway.

66

"Hey, April Woo. What the hell are you doing out here?"

April stared in surprise at the large red-faced desk sergeant. She had just stepped into the Astoria precinct near where she lived and was startled to hear her name. She didn't think she knew anyone here.

"I don't believe this. We go to school together, through the Academy together, and you don't remember me," the sergeant said, throwing up his hands. "I'm really hurt."

She struggled for a second, trying to fit the familiar voice into the chubby form in front of her. The guy was fat. Nobody in the Academy was fat. Nobody she ever knew was that fat.

"Come on, April, it's—"

"Oh, my God, it's *Tony.*" She moved forward to shake his hand. "God, Tony, you've put on a few pounds."

"Yeah," he said sheepishly. "It happens."

"What are you doing sitting at a desk in Queens? Last time I saw you you were on foot patrol in Little Italy."

"Yeah, you got out of that faster than I did. Weren't you in a car in Brooklyn?"

"Oh, God, has it been that long? I was a detective in the Fifth for four and a half years after that," she said proudly.

"The old neighborhood. Hey, that's great. I've been here for three years." He shrugged. "Can't complain."

"Better not," she said with a smile. "I live around here."

"No kidding? You never stop in. Where are you working now?"

April made a face. "Upper West Side, the Two-O."

He whistled. "Manhattan. You have all the luck."

April ducked her head. She had known he would say that. There were over thirty-five thousand cops in NYPD. Once people got posted in the hinterlands, it was like they were filed away in a drawer and forgotten. It was real hard to get into Manhattan after a few years in Queens or the Bronx. Only way was to be in some special unit. April spent a second of spiteful satisfaction thinking of Jimmy Wong, not ever likely to come out of Night Watch in Brooklyn. Ha. She was going to be sergeant before him. Make him lose face twice. Double stupid Jimmy Wong.

This was amazing. She had been standing there talking to Tony for almost three full minutes without a single interruption. Boy, this place was really quiet. She'd probably shoot herself if she had to work out here. She had left the car double-parked outside. There was hardly any traffic, and nothing much going on outside the precinct on the street. Really quiet.

The building was more like the 5th in appearance than the Two-O. The Two-O was big, a blue brick building that looked like a school. This was made of sandstone that was dark with age. It was low and squat, old and shabby.

"So, if you didn't know I was here, to what do we owe the honor of your visit?" Tony said, attempting gallantry.

April had a quick vision of the captured noblewoman in the cave and shook her head. "Have you had a complaint last night, or maybe today? A woman, thirty-three, white, name of Emma Chapman?"

He shook his head. "What about her?"

"She disappeared from the street last night in Manhattan."

"What makes you think she's out here?" Tony looked unimpressed.

"It's a long story. There was an incomplete nine-one-one from Queens last night. Might have been her. There are a few other indications."

"Look, April, you better go upstairs. There's a shift change in a few minutes. I'll ask around when the guys come in, see if anybody knows anything."

April pulled the sheets with the photos of Emma Chapman and Troland Grebs out of her bag and handed some over. The face of Emma Chapman jumped out at her again. The high cheekbones, the generous mouth, Caucasian eyes, blue as the sky on a sunny day. The colors of the woman that didn't show in the black-and-white repro were summer colors. She had white skin and hair the color of sand, pale sand, red lips. April wore red lipstick, too, sometimes; but her colors were winter. She had black hair and black eyes tucked deep in Mongolian folds, brown skin. The kind of beauty Emma Chapman had was not just in the eye of the beholder. She was beautiful to anybody who looked at her. In the picture Emma had a wedding ring on her finger and a gold chain around her neck. April had no good jewelry except some pearl earrings, and a jade ring for good luck. It wasn't a very good piece of jade. It was too dark a green, and it didn't give much luck.

"These are the people we're looking for," she told Tony.

"Who's the guy?"

"He's the suspect in her abduction."

She turned and headed up the stairs to the detectives' room. They were always on the second floor and looked pretty much the same. A lot of desks, filing cabinets, a questioning room with a big table where the detectives sometimes had lunch. The obligatory lockers in the back. The only difference was this one had a wet patch in the ceiling from which a steady drip was falling into a half-filled pail on the floor. The room was empty. As April studied the drip in the bucket, a voice came out of nowhere.

"If they don't come and fix that soon, the whole ceiling will come down on us. I hope it happens after eleven. I'm Detective Bergman. What can I do for you?"

April took two steps further into the room before she realized that Bergman's desk was hidden behind a bank of filing cabinets. Very clever. He could see her, but she couldn't see him. She crossed the room toward the voice.

"Detective April Woo, from the Two-O," she said, showing her ID. She tried not to be startled when she finally got a look at Bergman. He was a burly man with intense dark eyes that seemed to jump right out of his briar patch of a beard.

"We need some help with a search," she added.

"Who you looking for, Detective?"

April pulled out her copies of the two tapes and the photo sheets and settled into the hard metal chair by his desk.

"You have a tape machine?" she asked.

Bergman with all the hair on his face nodded curiously. Yeah, he had a tape machine. It was just after four. April hoped Sanchez would hurry up and get over the bridge before the traffic got worse.

67

Claudia Bartello looked up in surprise at her tenant in the leather jacket, the jeans, and the motorcycle boots.

"I thought you weren't dressed," she said accusingly, looking sharply around the room.

Troland glared at her. He couldn't believe it. Her head seemed to come out of her neck at a funny angle that he hadn't noticed before. There was something wrong with her. Maybe that was why she stood inside the door the whole time that first day when he came and didn't even ask him in.

Now she looked like a joke to him. She looked like some kind of enraged comic book crone with a lumpy body, swollen ankles, and a mouth that seemed to be shaking a stick at him.

"Where is she?" she demanded, turning toward the closed bedroom door. "I want to see her."

What should he do? Troland didn't feel like moving his mouth to talk to her. She was an ugly thing that was upsetting him. He had work to do, a whole lot of work, and he hadn't slept the night before. He could feel the muscles cramping in his neck and hands and shoulders. He was so deeply into it he hadn't felt any fatigue until now.

He wanted to punch her in the mouth for interrupting him. His face was impassive, but his hand closed tightly around the lighter in his pocket.

"Why don't you answer me? You never answer me."

Suddenly the old lady launched into a full-blown tirade with a

whole list of complaints that made no sense. She was screaming and
carrying on like the crazy woman who had upset him so much in the
subway. He had walked out of the car, and she had followed him,
hitching up her filthy skirt and urinating between cars as he tried to
get away.

"I want you out of here. I want you *out.*" The crone jabbed her
finger at his chest. "I won't have dirty business in my house. I told
you that before. You don't listen. You never listened."

The finger kept jabbing at him. He backed a few inches away
from it, trying to decide what to do. He couldn't believe this. She was
hardly four and a half feet tall and didn't seem to get that it wasn't a
good idea to scream at him. He couldn't hear when somebody started
screaming at him. The pressure to do something about it was building up.

His gaze shifted uneasily to the bedroom. He'd left all his stuff
there. He didn't want to leave the witch alone in there with his stuff
too long. She was tricky. Sometimes she seemed to be fainting and
she really wasn't. She just went somewhere else for a while and
wouldn't talk to him or listen or groan or anything. He didn't like
that.

He had a feeling she got some kind of power when she passed
out. Like she was charging up from some outside evil source he
didn't know about. It was clear to him now that coming to her here
was an even more important thing than he had thought. She was
more than a fallen angel who had betrayed him. She was actually a
witch he had been sent to burn. He couldn't leave her for a second.
The last time he left her she got the ropes untied. No one he ever
tied up got out before, which more than proved she was a witch. He
had to get back to her right away.

He was trying to figure it out, how he was going to get it all
done. And the old woman was still shrieking at him, distracting him
from what was important.

"Get your stuff and get out now," she was screaming.

"Shhh," he said, opening his mouth for the first time.

There was just no way he was ready to get out. He had stenciled the whole body, thighs, crotch, breasts, everything. But all he'd actually tattooed so far was the area around the navel.

It was coming out pretty good, if you looked beyond the puffiness and irritation of the skin. In some places it had blown up pretty bad. It occurred to him that she might be allergic to the ink, even though he had gotten the best kind, the one with the brightest colors. But he wasn't going to let the possibility of an allergic reaction worry him. What difference did it make?

Well, the difference was that here he had come all this way to do something special on this particular body, and she turned out to be some kind of witch that was trying to fuck it up. Well, she wanted to puff up, that was fine. He'd burn her up. He just had to get her decorated first.

She was married to a doctor, but Troland was the Doctor of Death. Troland had decided to incorporate the doctor's staff down the middle of her body with the twisted snakes and the flames around it. Except that he'd leave a space on her chest for the brand. Then the Harley-Davidson wheels and the eagles' wings would come out of the snakes' shoulders and spill out her sides while the serpents' teeth devoured her nipples. He had only gotten that far. He hadn't decided yet what to put on her neck and cheeks. And now this bitch was telling him he had to get out. No way he was going to get out.

"Don't tell me to shhh," she cried. "It's my house. I'll say what I want."

It became clear that the crone wasn't going away. She took two steps toward the bedroom. "I'm going to see what kind of dirty stuff you're doing in there—"

The pressure had built up so much he wasn't thinking any more when he grabbed her. He just wanted it to stop. At first he took hold of her and shook her as if she were a sack of laundry. But she wasn't quiet. Her bones made cracking sounds like they were all breaking at once, and she squawked with surprise.

"Shut up!" Even now she was infuriating.

His hands went around her scraggy throat. The skin hung down from her chin, crepey and soft. He almost gagged with disgust. Now she was off balance, hanging by his hands, heavy and inert. Not so hard to kill, but hard to handle.

The package continued making gurgling noises while he wrung her neck, trying to get it to stop. He flung her away from him when her bladder emptied, wetting his boots.

"Fucking shit!" The bad ones thwarted him even in death.

He rushed into the bathroom to wash his hands and clean off his boots. When his hands smelled like soap, he went to check the witch tied up on the bed. He was calmer now.

For a second after he opened the door, he was completely dazzled by his work. It was an awesome sight, the woman covered by his extraordinary drawings in colors so vivid they looked like an oil painting. The only thing that marred the picture was the part he had actually tattooed, which didn't look like it should at all. Never mind.

Her hands were tied. He had covered her mouth with tape so she'd be quiet.

"How's it goin'?" he said pleasantly.

Her eyes were wide open, and kind of stunned, focused behind him at the bundle on the floor in the other room.

"Oh, don't worry about that. I'll take it away."

He closed the door. He was moving slower now, wanted to take a nap. Maybe he'd take a nap. He promised himself a rest after he cleaned up. Yeah, that sounded good. He took some of the plastic he had planned to use for the witch and lined the trunk of the rental car with it. He didn't want to leave the body in the house where someone might come by and find it. He didn't want to pick it up either, so he dragged it to the stairs and kicked it step by step all the way down. At the bottom of the stairs, his foot glanced off the bundle. His heavy boot dislodged the ancient lawn mower propped against the wall, setting it in motion. The blades whirred as it rolled over the end of the corpse, severing a brittle toe as if it were a twig in the grass. He hoisted the bundle up and threw it in the trunk. Now he didn't have to think about it any more.

68

Emma lay there with the tape over her mouth. The door was closed. For a long time after the old woman stopped screaming it was profoundly quiet. Then she heard Troland go to the refrigerator and get something to drink. She could hear the pop of a can opening.

Troland. She could not visualize him as he must have been as a teenager, seeming normal enough to be in school, but doing things no one could even imagine. Her heart felt huge, big enough to burst.

She could hear him moving around out there. She tested the ropes. They were tied so tightly now there was no way to get out of them. She kept opening and closing her hand, trying to keep the circulation going.

Earlier, she had shivered uncontrollably for hours. All she wanted to do was warm up. Then he turned several lights on her so he could see better, and started working on her with the concentration of a surgeon. He shaved her, painted her body with Mennen Speed Stick, and stuck transfers all over it. It was then, before he even set up the table with the inks and the needles and the rubber gloves and the tattoo machine, that she knew what he was going to do. He was going to tattoo her. She knew how it was done. She knew about transfers.

She didn't even realize she was screaming, totally out of control. She thought the sounds were in her head. He was going to mark her perfect body, and there was nothing she could do to stop him. He was crazy. Nothing would stop him. He'd seen the fake tattoo in her film, and now he was doing one for real. But this wasn't just a little thing on the shoulder. This was her *whole body*. He was going to tattoo her *whole body*. Oh, no. No! *Can't take this*. Emma couldn't stop screaming.

He didn't seem to hear it.

"No. No, no. No!"

Was this what her daddy described, what it felt like when bombs were falling everywhere, your buddies were dead all around you, your legs were blown off? You were bleeding to death in a muddy swamp, and *still* you didn't give up.

"Nooooo."

She could hear her daddy's voice behind her, in her ear. *Be a soldier, Emmie. Take what they dish out and be a man about it.*

"No," she screamed.

"Shut up, or I'll tape your mouth," he said finally. "That's enough."

She shut her mouth. And still the screams came out. She felt the ropes with her fingers. They were low on her wrists, too low for the game. *Untie the knots with one hand, Emmie. Show me how good you are.*

Not good enough.

The first time the needles touched her skin was like a jolt of lightning. She was dead. She knew she would not survive this. The sting and burn, coming both at the same time on the sensitive skin of her stomach, told her life was over. Yet it went on and on, and she was still alive.

Years ago, when she first came to New York, Emma had a long tussle with a young man at the end of a date that had seemed pedestrian and safe. He was a Wall Street lawyer, and he jumped on her in the middle of a conversation about depositions. He didn't care that she was unwilling, and would only seem to stop for a minute or two to calm her down, before attacking her again. Her body was covered with black and blue marks by the time she finally got rid of him. And even at the door he tried tackling her one last time.

"Hope springs eternal," he said when he called her two days later for another date.

"I don't want to die," Emma whispered now.

Now, instead of freezing to death, she was burning. Her stomach was on fire where he had tattooed it. She could feel the heat radiating outward. He was going to tattoo her whole body until she was burning all over, and still she didn't want to die.

On the floor by the bed was a butane torch. She stretched out her fingers, wiggling them to see if she could reach it. It worked like a big lighter. Push the handle down, she knew, and a flame would shoot out. What was that for? I have to pee, she thought. He put packing tape on her mouth because she couldn't keep from making noises. Now she could only make grunting sounds.

On the other side of the door she could hear him muttering to himself. Then she started hearing other noises, thumpings and scratchings. A car door opened and a few minutes later slammed shut. Later, he came back and started fiddling with something in the wall. At one point there was the sound of a hammer hitting metal. What metal? What was he doing?

Her terror was like a wild animal. Her pulse seemed to be everywhere, as loud as the hammer on the other side of the wall. What hammer? What metal?

Then silence, for a long, long time. Maybe an hour. Maybe more. She shifted her body, trying to get closer to the torch. Way above her hand, on the table, was the switchblade. She couldn't reach that, either. She knew he had a gun somewhere, too, but she didn't see it. She was sure the old woman was dead. Maybe someone would come looking for her. Emma started pushing at the tape with her tongue. She closed her eyes.

69

Waiting for a red light on the street in front of the Greek diner, April felt a mounting excitement. The sight was amazing. Next to her was the diner, exactly as Jason Frank had described its unrelated twin in California. In front of her was the ramp to the Triboro Bridge. Way ahead she could see the bridge, long rather than high, spanning the East River. Just about a block behind her, Twenty-eighth Street bisected Hoyt Avenue. The houses on either side of the wide street were all attached, single-family dwellings. None was more than two stories high.

The stoplight was taking forever. April had some very long seconds to sit there gaping. Right there, all in one place, were the landmarks the psychiatrist had told her to look for, and didn't think she'd be able to find without him. Ha, she wasn't so stupid. If Grebs and the Chapman woman weren't right around here, she'd eat her badge. She gripped the wheel tightly to stop her hands from shaking.

The light changed. She moved forward slowly, taking a moment to look down at her notebook where she'd copied the house number the old lady had given to Officer O'Brien.

Checking out the local precinct had yielded exactly the results she had hoped for. Every investigation was about as successful as the contacts one made. This time April lucked out. The desk sergeant was an old friend from grade school on the Lower East Side. He took the time to ask every uniform coming off duty from the street if there had been any disturbance, any complaint, anything that could help with a case from Manhattan. He displayed the photos of

Grebs and Emma Chapman. Nobody could identify them, but Officer O'Brien had an old lady with a complaint about a rowdy tenant and a naked lady in her garage apartment. Maybe the old lady could make the ID.

Bergman had thought there was enough in O'Brien's story to give April backup when she went in to check out the Bartello house. April had told him what Troland Grebs did to women, and Bergman liked the idea of nailing a possible interstate serial killer on his turf. His proposal was to give April three men for an hour or so, gratis. Just to be on the safe side in case Grebs was there and tried to bail out before her people were ready to grab him. They both understood it was a case from the Two-O, however, and the best thing was for the Two-O squad to follow it through. April appreciated his understanding. Then, because she was getting this much support from Queens, she took a big leap off the deep end. She called Sergeant Joyce for backup without knowing she absolutely needed it. If she was wrong Joyce would kill her.

April could see the house now, halfway down. But it was a one-way street. She had to drive around the block to get to it. She made the turn and headed around the block. On the next block over not all the houses were attached. It was possible to see through a driveway to the backyard of the house that interested her. Overgrown shrubbery hid most of it. But, upstairs, on the garage side, the shades were drawn. She paused for a stop sign even though there were no cars in the four-way intersection. Everything looked quiet. She cruised to the end of the block and turned the corner.

Slowly, April drove back to Hoyt Avenue and finally stopped in front of the house two doors down. Mrs. Arturo Bartello's house was pink brick with some decorative painted tiles set in here and there to make it fancier. April had seen this block and noted this particular house a thousand times. Maybe ten thousand times. It had a trellis with wisteria on it. The wisteria was in heavy bloom right now. Even two houses down she could still smell it. She wondered if there was wisteria, or any fragrant plant like it growing on the house Grebs lived in in California. Probably was. She got out of the unmarked car she had taken from the Two-O lot and locked it. Then moved in closer.

The house was staked out. One stringy-looking kid was in the backyard abutting the Bartello yard. April saw him down the driveway of the house opposite, hacking away at the air in the neighbor's yard with a large pair of pruning shears. Now, a shabbily dressed man called Renear, with a baseball cap on backward, pulled an unmarked, mud-colored Chevy into an empty spot down the street. Two minutes later a huge bearded man lumbered up to the phone booth on the corner.

Where the hell was Sanchez? She'd called him over an hour ago. April looked at her watch. Four thirty-eight. After a few minutes, with her stakeouts around her, she had such a powerful feeling about the house the four of them were watching, she decided to displace the beard in the phone booth for a minute and call Dr. Frank.

70

Jason took the time to listen to the messages on his answering machine. Just in case Emma had tried to call him again. There were seven messages on it: three worried patients, and Ronnie and Charles, each twice. He returned the calls from the patients.

Then, reluctantly, he left the office and went into the apartment. He didn't want to go back in there. The noise of the clocks was like hearing Emma's life tick away. He closed the doors to the living room to silence some of them. He headed down the hall to the bedroom where Emma's purse was still on the bed. He left it there, took his clothes off, and went into the bathroom.

He had just gotten into the shower when April Woo called. He jumped so fast at the sound of the phone he forgot to grab a towel.

"Where are you?" he demanded, dripping on the bedroom floor.

"I'm in Queens at the entrance to the Triboro Bridge. Hoyt Avenue around Twenty-eighth Street. Do you know where that is?"

"No kidding, Twenty-eighth Street. Did you find her?" Jason cried.

"No," April said. "Not yet. But I wanted to tell you. It's just like you said, right down to the diner on the corner."

"What are you going to do?"

"I'm waiting for my partner." April surprised herself. It was the first time she had called Sanchez her partner. "Look, we may be wrong. This may be nothing. It just fits, that's all."

"You don't think it's nothing, or you wouldn't have called me."

"I didn't want to leave you in the dark."

"I appreciate that," Jason said. "Where can I find you? I'm on my way."

"I'll tell you when I have something. I have to go."

"Tell me where to meet you."

"It's staked out. If you come anywhere near us, you could blow the whole thing."

"I won't blow it," Jason promised.

April hesitated, then gave him an address at the end of the block. "Hang around by the diner," she said firmly. "If you come any closer, I'll lose my job. Understand?"

"I understand."

April cut off.

Jason went into his closet and started pulling on his clothes without bothering to dry himself. Twenty-eighth Street in Queens. He passed that whenever he took the shortcut to the airport. He knew exactly where it was.

His hands trembled so much he could hardly button his shirt. If Emma was alive, she was going to be burned. He tried not to think about that as he reached for his wallet and stepped into his shoes. All that mattered was to get there before Grebs burned her.

The elevator was up at the top of the building. He could see someone struggling with packages. To hell with it. He started running down the stairs. The elevator door clanked shut and started moving toward him. He kept running.

71

In the booth on the corner, April hung up and turned to the detective with the beard. He was huge, probably six five.

"Anything?" he asked softly. His name was Paccio, but he had introduced himself in the squad room as Pac.

April shook her head. "Not yet." She checked her watch. It was nearly five o'clock and beginning to cloud up.

Where was Mike? The Queensborough Bridge traffic was very heavy. That's where Mike was. She was getting more anxious as the minutes passed. There was no sign of life in the Bartello house. What if Emma was in there, already dead? What if Grebs had taken off, and she was too late?

On the other hand, what if the old Bartello woman had overstated the case, as O'Brien had initially believed, and there was no woman in the garage apartment with blood on her head? O'Brien said Mrs. Bartello was old and upset about the sex. He didn't take it too seriously when she told him the naked woman may have been beaten. It never occurred to him that maybe she was locked in, too. April looked at her watch again. If she was wrong about all this, Joyce would have her head.

April decided to show the photos to the old lady without waiting for Sanchez. Just see if she could make the guy. That's all.

"Tell my partner I went to talk to the old lady. You'll know him by the mustache and gray jacket."

"It's your call," Pac said, taking the receiver off the hook.

April headed down the street. It was oddly quiet. Except for

Renear, with his backward baseball cap ducked deep under the hood of the dented and rusting Chevy, there was nobody out. No dogs, no children on tricycles, nobody returning from the store carrying plastic bags of groceries. April passed the house and looked up at the windows over the garage where O'Brien said the woman's tenant lived. The shades on those windows were still pulled all the way down. April frowned, as she searched for a door into the space. She didn't see one.

Upstairs in the main house the blinds were open, but there were no lights on. There were no signs of anybody being home in either place, but that didn't mean anything.

Three shallow steps led to the front door. April went up the steps. Here the smell of wisteria was as sweet as anything she had ever smelled. It was almost impossible to imagine anything wrong in this sweet-smelling house. But she'd had that thought going into places before. The flap of her purse was open. She reached in and rested her hand on her off-duty pistol. Her other one was strapped to her waist. She rang the bell.

There was no answer. April rang the bell again. Maybe the old lady was hard of hearing. Still no sign of life. She rang the bell a third time and turned the doorknob. The door was unlocked. April's hands were sweaty as she stepped inside.

The hallway was empty. To one side, she could see the living room. Wow. Ornate, heavy furniture like the kind she used to gape at in the windows of the furniture store next to Ferrara's in Little Italy. The dining room table was absolutely unbelievable. The four chairs around it were carved swans. The room she stood in smelled of old garlic, fried to the burning point.

"Hello, anybody home?"

No answer. She drew her gun and walked inside. *I'm just looking for the old lady,* she told herself. She moved down the hallway, hugging the wall. *Don't make a target of yourself.* Shit. She had walked through the open door and entered the premises. Maybe that wasn't so smart.

Nothing in the kitchen. Nothing in the living room. The door to the next room was closed. She stood on one side of the door and nudged it open with her foot. Nothing jumped out at her waving a gun. The room looked like a sitting room. Bookshelves, armchair, daybed, TV. It was empty. April climbed the stairs. Cautiously, she searched the bedrooms one by one, looking for the old woman and a door to the apartment over the garage. She found neither.

Where was the door? And what about the old lady? Did she always go out leaving her front door unlocked? April closed the door on her way out and slipped the gun back in her bag.

Outside nothing had changed but the clouds in the sky, moving in for the showers predicted later that night. The street was quiet, and there was still no sign of Sanchez. April checked her watch. Ten minutes had passed. What the hell was going on? He should be here by now. She was annoyed. Where was the old lady? She went around to the garage again. The entrance to the upstairs apartment must be in the garage. That meant there was no other way out. She didn't like this waiting.

She turned the handle on the garage door. It swung open with hardly any effort, and a light came on. She could see a car, a dark blue Ford Tempo, late model, rental. It was cool and dank in the garage. She shivered. Several pieces of old lawn furniture were folded up and stacked against one wall. An umbrella. A lawn mower. She crouched low and inched toward the stairs, careful to use the car as a shield. The cement floor was gritty under her feet.

At the back of the garage, she almost tripped on something soft. She looked down. It was a pink felt slipper, worn and gray at the edges. She bent to examine the slipper. There were three small red droplets on the floor, and some brownish spots on several of the blades of the lawn mower that stood nearby. She crouched down. What the hell—? Underneath the mower was a lot of dust, spider webs and dead flies, and something white. What the hell was it? April examined it curiously. What was that?

It had a toenail on it. It was a human toe. The toe was old and gnarled, the nail yellow and deeply ingrown. It looked not so very different from the dried sea slugs in large jars in Chinatown. The

Chinese prized them as a delicacy, served them only on special occasions. But this was no sea slug. April's thinking was automatic, deeply ingrained with years of studying unpleasant things. She knew instantly the toe on the dusty floor did not come from Emma Chapman. Emma Chapman was young and beautiful, well cared for.

A footstep sounded outside. April pulled her gun out of her bag a second time.

72

"Wake up." Troland stood over Emma. "Want some soup before we get back to work?"

"What?" Emma struggled to focus. Everything was numb except for the fire on her stomach where he had been working on her.

"Soup. You have to eat something."

She could see him now. Still wearing the leather jacket, open with nothing under it. And the jeans. The gun was in his right hand.

She shook her head, couldn't make a sound with the tape over her mouth.

"Oh." He remembered the tape and ripped it off.

"Ow." Tears jumped into her eyes.

"Don't start that. I'm being nice," he said.

She didn't reply.

"You got to be hungry. You want soup or not? I got Campbell's Tomato."

"No, thanks." She didn't recognize her own voice.

"Good—anybody touches the stove, and the place blows up." He laughed like he'd pulled a good joke. She could have the soup, but couldn't touch the stove. He kept laughing.

"Huh?" Emma was shivering uncontrollably.

"What's the matter now?" Abruptly he sounded angry.

"Place blows up?" Emma tried to stop her face from twitching, her body from trembling all over. She wasn't successful. He was trying something new to scare her. He liked to do that. She didn't want to believe him.

"Yeah, it's brick on the outside. Well, not this part, up here is aluminum siding. But it won't go without some help."

He was telling her he planned to blow up the house. Emma had to keep focused. She couldn't play his game.

"Relax," he said, genial now. "There's nothing for you to worry about. That's for later."

"My wrists hurt," she said faintly. "Could you fix the ropes?"

He bent to check them, adjusting them just a little. "You're all right," he told her. "Want some juice?"

"What about the fridge?"

"What about it?"

"Will that blow up, too?"

"Ha ha, you're very funny." He sat down and pulled on the rubber gloves, forgot about the juice.

"I thought you said I could have some juice," Emma complained. "I want some juice."

"Too late. I was nice, but you weren't nice."

"I'm sorry. Please may I have some juice."

He ignored her. "You should see my work. It's great. You've never seen anything like it."

Emma took a deep breath. "I'd like to see it. If you let me go to the bathroom, I could see it."

Troland turned on the machine, and the whine filled the room. He dipped the needles into the ink and bent over her.

"I have to go to the bathroom," Emma insisted, grimacing when the needles bit into her skin.

He had begun to spread out lower now, along her pelvis. Her eyes filled with tears. They spilled over and ran down into her mouth and hair. "Please."

He ignored her.

She had the end of the rope in her left hand. It had always been harder with her left hand. She worked at it, trying not to think of his blowing up the house. He said a lot of weird things. Half the time he didn't know what he was saying.

Emma closed her eyes against the dipping of the needles into the ink, the dabbing of the Vaseline on her skin, the whine of the machine, and the excruciating sting that quickly heated up into a steady burn. She concentrated on the rope in her left hand. She stopped thinking about the machine. She was a soldier working the second knot.

Then suddenly, without warning, Troland tensed all over and turned the machine off.

"What—?" she asked.

"Shh," he said sharply. "One sound, and you're dead." He was out of his chair and in the other room in a second.

73

A man appeared briefly at the corner of the Bartello garage door. He kept himself low, angled out of view. April choked back her fear. For a second she thought it might be Grebs, returning on foot from the corner store or something. Then the familiar crouch-and-dodge moves betrayed a cop. She hoped some clown wouldn't come in and blow the whole thing. She stayed put.

It was cool and damp in the garage. From where she was crouched behind the back wheel of the blue Ford Tempo, April could see the pink felt slipper she had dropped in her haste to duck out of sight. Her Aunt Mei Ling Lily Chen had slippers just like it. Most older Chinese women liked to wear the same black canvas shoes, made in China, that their ancestors had worn for centuries. But Mei Ling Lily Chen said, felt was more comfortable on feet, easier to get off.

Yeah, they came off real easy if you were dead. The severed toe was still on the floor near the lawn mower. Only a few brown spots led to it on the cement floor. If the stains were blood, the person was dead when the toe was chopped off. All was quiet upstairs.

April thought of Dr. Frank, stuck on the bridge with the rest of her team. She knew it was a highly irregular thing for her to call him like that, but he had broken the case for her. She figured she owed him. She prayed that his wife Emma Chapman, whose features were so different and superior to April's, was not already dead, too. She shivered, her sweat now chilled and icy under her arms. She wondered where the old lady's body was.

Suddenly the overhead light went off. April looked up, startled. The light was attached to the garage door. Must be one of those automatic gizmos that came on when the door opened, and then went off after two minutes. The neighbors next door to her parents had one. The gloom settled instantly. Still no sound from outside or the apartment upstairs. In the dim light, the smell of mold seemed to grow stronger. It assaulted April's heightened senses. The bushes rustled. April held her breath.

An elbow edged around the corner of the garage door. April recognized the shiny gray fabric of Sanchez's sharkskin jacket.

"April?" It was barely a whisper.

She let out her breath with relief, then stood, her finger to her lips. He gestured for her to get out of there. She inched toward him, down the wall farthest from the stairs. She reached the door, and they moved away from the building, out of sight of the upstairs windows.

She wanted to say something, but Chinese were unsentimental, undemonstrative. Cops, too.

"You all right?" Sanchez asked.

"Yeah, sure." She didn't ask what took so long. It was a stupid question. Everything took so long.

"Looks quiet. What's going on?" Sanchez asked.

"The car's a rental."

"Yeah, I saw that."

"I think he's up there. I don't know about the Chapman woman. If she's alive, she sure isn't making any noise. . . ." April changed the subject. "There's only one way in, up the stairs in the back of the garage. You can get to the backyard through the house. I have someone out there."

Sanchez nodded. "Pac filled me in. What about the old woman?"

April shook her head. "She's not in the house. She left the front door open. She may be dead. . . . I think I found one of her toes."

"No shit, where?"

"On the floor in the garage." She looked away, didn't want him to criticize her for going in there alone.

"We need more people," was all he said.

"I know. I already called."

"I heard the dispatch." Now he looked away. "Go cover the backyard. We'll wait till they get here."

April shook her head. "Unless he jumps out the window, there's no way out."

"Go cover it, anyway, Detective," Sanchez snapped.

"What? Are you pulling rank on me? You're not my supervisor," April protested angrily. "I've taken it this far. I'm not covering the back now."

Sanchez bristled at the outburst, then relented. "All right, then cover me."

"No, you cover me," April insisted. Hadn't he seen her shoot?

"Look, you want to get this done, or do you want to stand here arguing about it?"

"I thought you wanted to wait for backup."

He nodded toward the garage. "We'll go in *there* and wait."

A car backfired on the street. As Sanchez walked over to check it out, April slipped back inside the garage.

74

Emma heard a car backfire on the street. She had one knot to go. She turned her head toward the door. He'd taken the butane torch but not the gun. What now?

He'd been gone for a long time. With each knot she untied, the ends of the nylon rope had become more frayed. They were badly tangled now. Emma worked one thin strand out at a time, holding her breath without realizing it. How much time did she have left? She had to hurry, but her fingers were stiff. Her body was slick with Mennen Speed Stick and A and D ointment, smelled of menthol and fear. But there was another odor in the room, deep and persistent. Way under the surface, vague and teasing, like a feather stirring the air, was the faint smell of gas. Emma tried to ignore it. The rope had to be her only concern. She couldn't worry about what he was up to now.

Emma worked at the last knot, her eye on the gun that lay on the table among half a dozen little paper cups filled with colored ink. She hadn't heard the outside door open and close since he left the room. She was pretty sure he was still in the house. She couldn't let him get her this time.

The last strand pulled free of the tangles. She sat up, shivering and rubbing her arms. Her fingers were stiff. Her arms were numb. She was shaking all over. For a second the sight of her naked body, shiny and colored all over, stunned her. She looked like an eighties poster for a heavy metal rock group. Between her breasts, the skin was white, but her shoulders, her stomach, her arms and legs were a madman's sick fantasy of a woman tormented by devouring animals and flames. *Get a grip. Get the gun,* she told herself.

She rubbed her arms with the stiff fingers. *Move.* Now her arms were tingling all over as feeling returned. She couldn't move. *Pick up the gun.* Her fingers cramped. She kneaded the muscles in her hands. *PICK UP THE DAMN GUN.* She reached for the gun. It was cold and heavy. She flexed her fingers around it. She'd shot a gun. She'd done it in an off-Broadway play. How did this one work? She wasted precious seconds fiddling with it, couldn't find a safety catch. She decided there wasn't one, put the gun down in her lap so she could free her legs.

With the pistol cold on her thighs, she leaned over to untie her feet. Everything hurt. Her body had been confined, the muscles shut down, for a long time. She hunched her shoulders up and down, easing the cramps. Arched her back. *Come on. Come on, body, warm up.*

The feet were easier. She could see what she was doing. This time only three knots held the rope around each ankle, but they were more complicated ones. She worked at them, her heart beating wildly. If he opened the door, she had only a few seconds to pick up the gun and blow him away.

After what seemed like an hour, the last knot was undone. Emma slid to the floor and crawled to the window. Shaking all over and numb with fear, she could no longer feel the tattoo burn on her stomach. All she thought of was the gun in her hand, the madman out there somewhere, and the smell of gas leaking slowly into the room.

Quietly, she lifted the shade an inch. Across the street she saw a guy tinkering with his car engine. Beside him another man seemed to be helping him. She raised the shade higher to get their attention, then heard footsteps. She ducked behind the bed. The door opened.

"There's somebody out there," Troland said softly. "We've got to move."

Emma fired the gun.

75

The sky was clouding over, the air was fragrant with cherry blossoms when Jason charged out of his building, turned right, and ran thirty yards to Riverside Drive.

"Damn." There wasn't a taxi in sight.

His forehead was beaded with sweat. From here at this hour, Queens was about forty-five minutes away. He hesitated, considering his options, then turned and sprinted across Eighty-fourth Street to West End Avenue. There, he caught sight of a battered taxi heading uptown. He hailed it.

"Hoyt Avenue, in Queens," he sputtered, getting in and slamming the door.

The taxi was so old there wasn't a handle on the inside. Its driver, a large black man with dreadlocks, silently made a U-turn and drove down West End.

"Go across at Eighty-first Street. It's fastest."

"You telling me how to do my job?"

"I'm in a hurry." Jason gulped at the air, trying to catch his breath. God, the taxi smelled terrible.

"Don't tell me how to do my job, mon." The driver turned across Eighty-first Street, anyway, and headed into the park.

On Second Avenue, the Fifty-ninth Street Bridge traffic was backed up to Sixty-eighth Street. With six or seven body-jolting jerks, the ancient taxi inched forward, advancing only a half a block with every light. Jason checked the driver's license. Shit. He was a trainee.

Jerk-stop, jerk-stop, jerk-stop. It was crazy-making. Jason looked frantically around for another taxi. He didn't see one in the sea of cars and vans on the five-lane avenue, all trying to merge left into the two-lane bridge entrance at Fifty-ninth Street.

The driver put a Rasta tape in his boom box and punched the play button. "Get Up, Stand Up." Bob Marley sang out from beyond the grave.

Jason clenched and unclenched his fists in fury as he watched the minute hand on the clock in the dashboard, clicking up the minutes in rhythm with the music and the rapidly mounting charge on the meter.

76

April went into the garage and climbed the stairs. Her ears were still red from Sanchez's ordering her around. Hell, no, she wasn't covering anybody. Not this time. It was dark in the back of the garage. At the top of the stairs, she saw a light switch, but didn't want to try it in case it was wired for a light inside the apartment. She put her ear to the door.

Outside it was quiet again. Maybe backup had arrived and Sanchez was filling them in. But inside, April could hear some movements now. Someone was definitely in there. She could hear footsteps crossing the room away from her. Then there was silence, but only for a second. The crack of a gunshot electrified her.

Without thinking, April raised her gun, stood back, and shot the lock off the door. Oh, God, she was without backup. Couldn't afford to wait. She kicked the door open. Crouched in the ready position with her arms forward and both hands steadying the gun, she moved in a semicircle, covering the room. Nobody there.

Then suddenly she gasped and lowered the gun.

Emma Chapman staggered through the bedroom door. She was naked and painted all over. A gun dangled in her hand.

Green-and-black patterned snakes with red eyes, and teeth instead of fangs, entwined with eagle's wings, were wrapped around two doctor's staffs that spiked the woman's sides. Red and orange flames rose from her ankles and raced down her arms. On her right cheek, red clown tears ran down her chin to water a burning black rose growing up a vine on her neck. Her stomach was enflamed and swollen, her eyes were wide with terror.

April pushed her shock at the sight away.

"Police," she said gently. "Give me the gun."

The woman tottered across the room towards her, nearly falling over the couch. "I shot him," she cried. The gun fell out of her hand.

"Watch out!" April screamed.

Grebs plunged through the door, the butane torch aimed at them, spitting fire. The blue torch flame roared casting a blinding light. It ignited the upholstered chair. Behind Grebs, the furniture in the bedroom was already ablaze.

April raised her gun but couldn't shoot.

"Get out of the way!" she screamed at Emma. Emma had come to a halt three quarters of the way across the room, blocking her line of fire.

"Crazy bitch, crazy gook bitch. Burn in hell."

Grebs lowered the torch to fire the chair by April's side. A blue flash shot at the fabric.

Crazy bitch! April wasn't taking that again. She reached out. "Emma, come on. Three steps and you're out of here."

Her face burned from the searing heat as Grebs torched the brown curtains at the window. Flames ate up the roller shade and licked at the ceiling. Grebs was at the window facing the garden.

A shot sounded from outside. The fire spread to the cheap rug on the floor.

"Emma, come on." April had her covered. She reached out one hand. "Come on."

Outside, April heard the shouts of Sanchez. "Get the hell out of there!"

"Come on, Emma," April coaxed.

Emma couldn't seem to move. Blinding light flashed at her five feet away, too far to burn her but close enough to smart.

"Hurry."

Animal sounds joined the roar of the torch.

"Fucking witch shot me. Fucking *bitch—*"

Grebs screamed obscenities. For an instant, April had a clear sight of him through the thickening smoke. She could see that he was bleeding, looking for a way out. There was no way out. The flare died. He smashed the window with the heavy cylinder. Another shot came from outside. It hit the window frame with a little *thuck*.

"Fucking shit—"

He swung around and torched the sofa. Choking black smoke billowed up.

Emma screamed. The rug was burning near her bare feet. April stepped forward and grabbed her hand. It was slippery. She hung on.

"Move." April pulled her toward the door. Her face burned, and now she was coughing, too. But April didn't want to leave without nailing the bastard who killed Ellen Roane. The torch spat at her again, forcing her farther back as Grebs moved to the kitchen where the stove was.

"He's going to blow up the house!" Emma cried.

"What?"

"He did something to the gas line. There's a leak."

April pushed Emma behind her as Sanchez charged into the room and grabbed her. April only had a second. The hot gray cloud surged around her, blowing out the broken window. She didn't want him to blow up the place, and didn't want him to get away. She held her breath against the suffocating fumes, raised her two hands together, and fired her gun in the line of duty for the second time ever. Grebs screamed. She saw him go down, his jeans and hair on fire. She raised her gun to fire a second time, but Sanchez had come back for her. He grabbed her and shoved her out the door, using himself as a shield as the fire inside roared and spread.

The last thing April saw was Grebs on fire, writhing on the floor when the explosion hit. The blast was enormous. It shook the earth and shattered windows all up and down the block. The roof collapsed above them, and the raging fire shot up into the sky.

77

Boom. Shock waves jolted the street, setting an overhead street light swinging wildly in the intersection in front of Jason's taxi. The car in front of them swerved to avoid a kid on a bike, skidding out of control.

"What the—"

The taxi driver slammed on the breaks, smashing Jason into the plastic divider that separated them.

"What are you doing?" Jason cried. "Go ahead."

The taxi spun out and stopped sideways in the intersection. Above, the light, still showing green, swung back and forth.

"You blind, mon?" the driver shouted over his rasta music. He pointed to the dense black smoke that was already beginning to spew up into the sky, several blocks ahead of them.

Horns started honking around them. They were blocking the traffic flow into the intersection.

"Go on," Jason said wildly. They had about six blocks to go. "Go on."

"No, mon, I don't want to get near no fire."

Fire. Oh, shit it was a big fire. Grebs set fires. Jason could see the flames now, shooting up over the tops of the two-story houses. Oh, God. Too late.

"Go on," he cried. "We're not there. Go on."

"Not going no farther, mon. We'll get stuck in there."

"It's only a few blocks. Hurry up." Jason dug in his pocket and pulled out the wad of bills he had left from his California trip. "I'll give you five hundred dollars to take me six fucking blocks. Come on. It'll only take you a few minutes."

The light turned red. The horns blared. The driver eyed the thick wad of bills. He shrugged.

"Okay, mon. It's your money."

Jerk, jerk, jerk. They lurched forward as the taxi accelerated into traffic moving the other way, causing a gridlock. Shrieking fire engines raced into the mess, adding to the chaos of a dozen furious horns honking all around them. Above them, the sky turned black. Jason got out on the side of the car that had a door handle and started to run.

78

The blast blew out the front wall of the garage apartment, causing the collapse of half the roof. Fire raged out of the jagged opening. A large piece of crumpled aluminum siding fell on the driveway in front of the garage door. Shattered glass littered front lawns and sidewalks all up and down the block.

The stakeout cop who had been tinkering with the car had seen Mike and April go into the garage. He'd followed to provide backup. He hadn't had time to make it up the stairs. The house shook with a deafening bang. April, Sanchez, and the woman hostage were blown out the door and propelled down the stairs, knocking the stakeout cop over.

Choking on smoke and plaster dust, all four struggled for air. Three of them had landed in a tangled heap on the cement floor. Emma lay curled motionless on her side. April sprawled over her legs. Sanchez's full weight came to rest on April's twisted ankle. The stakeout cop smashed against the wall, where two lawn chairs crashed on top of him. From upstairs came the powerful smell of charcoal, burning electric wires, and charred flesh.

Better get out of here. April was the first to move. Her ankle throbbed. Her eyes stung with smoke and dust. She couldn't see anything. She put her hand out to Emma. "You all right?" Of course she wasn't all right. April had crashed down on her hard. The woman had no clothes on. April could feel the black soot and plaster dust that clung to her sticky skin. Emma's fingers touched hers. She groaned, but didn't say anything.

Sanchez was a dead weight.

"Mike?" April cried. "Mike—"

"Uh." He grabbed the back of the blackened car, struggled to his feet. The heat in there was intense. He held out his hand to April, jerked her up. "We got to get out."

The stakeout cop untangled himself from the lawn chairs, cursing. "Come on," he said. He stepped forward and fell on his face. "Shit," he muttered. "Shit."

"Mrs. Frank." April leaned over her. "Mrs. Frank, can you stand up?"

"I don't know." Emma's voice was hoarse and panicked.

"It's okay, we'll get you out." She put her arm around Emma and helped her up, though she could hardly stand herself. Her jacket and pants were peppered with cuts and burns. Her hands and face, too. Her whole body felt scorched and bruised. She ignored it. She figured Emma felt a lot worse. Sanchez supported her other side.

April nodded at him to start moving, and saw that the fire had singed off his mustache and eyebrows. His upper lip was red.

Emma looked from one to the other. "He was going to—" Her blue eyes filled with tears.

"Yeah, but he didn't get to."

Soot covered the drawings on Emma Chapman's face. April could hardly see her through the stinging smoke. It looked like Emma had a clay mask on. That was all right, the woman probably had mud packs all the time. It looked as if her features were still perfect. They hadn't been damaged. April put a hand to Emma's hair. It was matted and dirty, but at least she still had it.

"I shot him," she told April. She was in shock.

April nodded. "Probably saved your life. Come on."

The stakeout cop was on his feet. The four of them slowly started moving. Only minutes had passed since the explosion. Three firemen in hats and rubber coats came into the garage to help them out. Outside, people were already gawking at the devastation, and the ferocity of the fire. Fire engines and police sirens wailed.

Fire equipment, police cars, three ambulances with their lights flashing were already on the scene. With the help of a fireman twice her size, April hobbled out into the chaos. The first thing she saw was a kitchen sink and part of its cabinet crashed onto the hood of a car in the street. The unmarked car from the Two-O was rubble.

It was dusk. In the fading light, people drawn out of their houses by the blast were complaining, pointing at the fire, shaking their heads. One woman with her hair in curlers rushed toward them shrieking, "Help me. Oh, God. He had a heart attack. He's in the house. He won't get up—" A black female fire fighter went to help her.

"Oh, God," April muttered. It was a mess. What would her mother say about her job now? Never mind the cuts and burns on her hands and feet, or the sprained ankle—if she was lucky. Sai Woo would look on dark side. She wouldn't say her daughter big hero for saving Noblewoman Trapped in Cave. She would say her daughter strong enough to blow up whole neighborhood. And still not married. Pah.

"I'm fine," she protested to the fireman, who wanted to deposit her in an ambulance. She wasn't getting into any ambulance. She turned back to Emma.

Emma's fireman had put his coat on her and carried her out because she had no shoes.

Sanchez touched her arm. "You okay?"

April nodded. "What about you?"

"Fine." He nodded, too.

She knew he wasn't fine. She could see the blood from many small cuts through the holes in his clothes. His face looked burned and one of his ears was the color of raw hamburger. Well, her ankle hurt like hell and was beginning to swell. It was his fault for falling on top of her, but she didn't want to mention it now. Maybe some day she'd tell him he wasn't good in close.

"Thanks," was what she said now.

"Yeah, what for?"

"Everything." She saw a car from the Two-O and turned away to help clear the street for the ambulance that was coming in for Emma.

The fireman stood there holding onto her. "Could you put me down? I need to call my husband." Emma still looked stunned.

"No, you'll cut your feet." The fireman cocked his head at the ambulance driver, a guy with a ponytail and a thick gold hoop in one ear.

The ambulance stopped and a white-jacketed medic jumped out of the front seat. "Who's first?"

"She is," April indicated Emma.

"Can she stand?"

"Not without any shoes, she can't. Hurry it up, will you. I got things to do." The fireman looked back at the fire.

The medic opened the back doors and held out some white cotton blankets to wrap Emma in so he could give the fireman back his coat.

"My husband's a doctor. I can't go to a hospital. Call him. I want to go home." Emma resisted being put in the ambulance.

"Got to get in, lady. It's the rules."

"Don't worry," April said quickly. "I know where he is."

Emma stared at her.

"I called him. He's on his way. He's the one who helped us locate you. He's a great guy."

Emma started to cry again.

"Come on, it's okay. In you go, and then I'll find him for you."

April helped the two paramedics put Emma into the ambulance. When they exchanged the coat for the cotton blankets, no one commented on the artwork on the woman's body.

April could hear the shouts of police and fire fighters, yelling at curious people not to cross the lines, not to try to go back to their houses yet. April got out of the ambulance.

Sanchez stood with Sergeants Joyce and Aspiranti, describing what happened, by the look of it. Down the block near the diner, Jason Frank was trying to argue his way past a roadblock.

April hobbled down the street toward him. "She's over here," she shouted to Jason. "He's a doctor, let him through," she ordered, flashing her ID.

Jason pushed through the uniforms, his face white with fear. "Where is she?"

"She's in that ambulance." April pointed at it. She tried to reach out and stop him, so she could tell him what to expect, what happened to Emma and what she looked like. But he didn't stop. He wanted to get to his wife and didn't hesitate, not for a second. April stood there on one foot, staring after him until Sanchez came to get her.